PRAISE FOR *THE AENEID*

"The *Aeneid* is a poem that, ever since it was written, has been continuously read, reinterpreted, reworked. . . . To translate it, then, is to contribute to a 2,000-year-old tradition. The best translations are true simultaneously to both Virgil's age and to the translator's own; they echo Virgil himself by fashioning a dialogue between past and present. Shadi Bartsch's new version of the poem is a demonstration of just how brilliantly this can be done. She is alert to the alien in Virgil's text as only a scholar in the twenty-first century could be. Her gaze is that of a feminist, a postmodernist, a student of postcolonialism. At the same time, however, her translation is free of any hint of condescension. . . . The compact quality of Roman poetry is almost impossible to replicate in English, but this would be hard to guess from Bartsch's translation. Consistently, she tracks Virgil's lines with a quite astonishing degree of precision."

—TOM HOLLAND, *The New Statesman*

"Close focus on a single word gets to the heart of what is always challenging about translation, especially in the case of a poet whose every word (and I mean that almost literally) is freighted with meaning. A translator has to make choices; any word they choose will carry its own nuance, a particular set of interpretations, implications and associations. Shadi Bartsch is alive to such difficulties. Her introduction notes the need to render the same Latin word differently in different contexts. She also highlights the interpretational difficulty that attaches to certain words which are central to the *Aeneid* and need to be rendered consistently in English: readers should note their reappearances."

—*The London Review of Books*

"Bartsch walks the tightrope between maintaining the grandeur of the original and making the poem accessible to modern readers. *The Aeneid* is the great refugee narrative of its own time, and it should be for our time too."

—NATHALIE HAYNES, *The Guardian*

"Bartsch gives us something special ... a vigorous, deeply felt and genuinely exciting version of the whole story. And so both books [Bartsch and Heaney] are here on my shelf to stay."

—*The Brazen Head*

"An excellent new translation ... The translation is so good that you forget you are reading 'a classic,' and can enjoy the book for its plot and characters."

—*The Free Lance–Star*

"Blending solid scholarship with poetic sensibility, classicist Bartsch delivers a new version of the foundational poem of Imperial Rome. . . . A translation that gives some sense of the Latin and the tautness of its lines; most other English versions are fully 30 percent or more longer than the original, but not hers. . . . Through seductions, treacheries, murders, deicides, and other episodes, Bartsch—her scholarly notes as vigorous as her verse—produces an excellent companion for students of the poem and of Roman history. A robust, readable, reliable translation of a hallmark of world literature."

—*Kirkus Reviews* (starred review)

"Pure Vergil ... alive, fast-paced, and at its best in the drumbeat of blood and fire that builds to the final stroke of the steadfast Aeneas."

—AMY RICHLIN, Distinguished Professor of Latin, UCLA

"A tight, readable translation with a welcome feminist outlook and savvy engagement with the poem's political and imperial themes and imperialist legacy. Its natural iambic voice, clear language, and faithfulness to the tight, fast-moving pace of Virgil's original make it a refreshing way for modern audiences to access the *Aeneid*'s power."

—ADA PALMER, award-winning author of
Reading Lucretius in the Renaissance and the Terra Ignota series

"The best version of the *Aeneid* in modern English: concise, readable, and beautiful, but also as accurate and faithful to Vergil's Latin as possible. And the 'Vergil's Latin' that she aims to stick close to reflects modern scholars' realization that Vergil's Latin is often difficult and strange; here it helps that she is one of the most accomplished Latinists to translate the poem, knows all the latest research, and is willing to wrestle with the most difficult passages. But this is not a translation just for scholars: Bartsch writes clear, vivid, concise lines that read well and read rapidly as she aims for 'a kind of parallel to the experience of reading Vergil in Latin.' The introduction and notes are concise, helpful, informative, provocative, and interesting. Readers, teachers, and students will find the kind of translation they need for private reading or a classroom encounter with the poem, and scholars may find that Bartsch has noticed new things in the Latin."

—JAMES J. O'HARA, George L. Paddison Professor of Latin,
University of North Carolina at Chapel Hill

THE AENEID

THE AENEID

VERGIL

Translated by
SHADI BARTSCH

THE MODERN LIBRARY

NEW YORK

CONTENTS

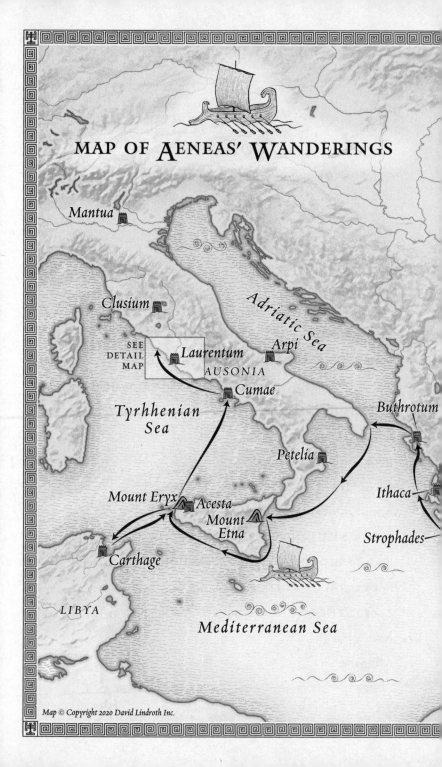

MAP OF ÆNEAS' WANDERINGS

Mantua

Clusium

Adriatic Sea

Arpi

SEE
DETAIL
MAP

Laurentum

AUSONIA

Cumae

Buthrotum

Tyrhhenian
Sea

Petelia

Mount Eryx

Acesta

Mount
Etna

Ithaca

Carthage

Strophades

LIBYA

Mediterranean Sea

Map © Copyright 2020 David Lindroth Inc.

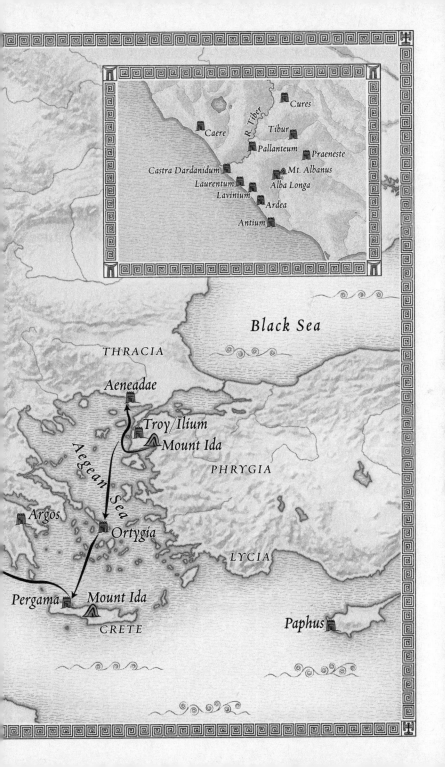

ACKNOWLEDGMENTS

A LONG THIS LENGTHY JOURNEY—whose goal, like Aeneas'
Italy, seemed to be constantly receding from me—I have had
the good fortune of receiving assistance from several senior schol-
ars of the *Aeneid* and well-known translators of Latin poetry. In
particular, I thank Susanna Braund for her generous feedback on
the first drafts of this translation, and Jim O'Hara for his likewise
generous feedback on the last drafts. Jim often shared his thoughts
on deciphering particularly taxing passages in the original. He also
shared with me his then unpublished commentary on Book 8 and
inflicted my translation on his students to gauge its readability. In
turn, both Jim and I often referenced the late Nicholas Horsfall,
whose commentaries on Books 2, 3, 6, 7, and 11 were invaluable to
me as I worked. Amy Richlin's kind suggestions were much appre-
ciated. I must also thank all the other editors and commentators
on the poem—too many, unfortunately, to mention here.

For their feedback on my interpretation of the *Aeneid* on differ-
ent occasions, I offer warm thanks to Benjamin Acosta-Hughes,
Clifford Ando, Yelena Baraz, Alessandro Barchiesi, Janet Downie,
Dennis Feeney, Bettina Joy de Guzman, Brooke Holmes, Anthony
Kaldellis, Leah Kronenberg, Sarah Nooter, Lee T. Pearcy, James
Rives, David Wray, and Froma Zeitlin. And I shouldn't omit the
many audiences for my talks about the *Aeneid* and/or its translation
who influenced and challenged me. They include undergraduates,
graduate students, and faculty at the University of California,
Berkeley; Brigham Young University; Bryn Mawr; Ohio State Uni-
versity; Princeton University; the University of North Carolina;
Boston University; and my home at the University of Chicago. I

apologize to others whom my memory (not nearly as tenacious as Juno's) has elided from this list.

A veritable crowd of undergraduate research assistants and interns contributed to the notes and drew up the glossary, as well as commented on the translation. In alphabetical order, I'd like to single out Isaac Easton, Donald Harmon, Julia Mearsheimer, Claudia Oei, and, last but not least, Alex Platt. You were my companions as I journeyed from Troy to Italy's Lavinian shores, and I feel I made the trip with friends worth their weight in gold. *Portantur opes pelago; dux femina facti.*

Heartfelt gratitude is due to the American Academy at Rome and to the University of Chicago, two institutions whose generosity made it possible for me to work on this translation for several years. I spent a delightful fall at the AAR as a senior resident, dishing out unsolicited advice and consuming superior fare. A flexible teaching schedule at the University of Chicago freed me to revise the manuscript constantly, usually while muttering aghast comments at my own prior versions.

The support of two influential women let this translation see the light of day. They are my agent, Wendy Strothman at the Strothman Agency, and Hilary Redmon, vice president and executive editor at Random House. They listened when I argued that a new translation was needed; they understood the rationale for this claim; and they found value in having a woman and a scholar of Latin translate a major work in the cultural history of the West. In more material terms, Wendy engineered an advance, and Hilary paid it—great teamwork. I hope I have not betrayed their trust. Both Hilary and my UK editor, Andrew Franklin, also offered wise suggestions for the introduction. It is much better, I know, for their intervention. Thanks are also due to Emily de Huff, the excellent copy editor retained by Random House to work on the manuscript, and Random House production editor Nancy Delia.

Along the same vein, it should go without saying that without the corrections and suggestions of all the kind people I mention, this would be a lesser work, and it would be still further from the impossible ideal that haunts every translator's mind. There is no endpoint to translating this poem: one could revise one's revision *ad aeternum,* and probably go mad in the process. Certainly I would not wish on anyone the torment that the poem's first eleven lines caused me. I rewrote them at least a hundred times, and probably shouted them in my sleep.

My most faithful reader and supporter has been my spouse, Robert Zimmer, who brought to the project a fine poetic ear, an endless amount of patience, and unwavering support. Together we read through my efforts bad and good. Even before the project, when we spent several weeks driving around Sicily on vacation, he claimed that all the entertainment he wanted was to hear my interpretation of the *Aeneid* (yes, this is hard to believe). One of the main reasons I undertook this translation was that Bob was so enthusiastic about the segment of Book I that I had rendered into English just for myself. This translation is dedicated to him.

SHADI BARTSCH
Narni, Umbria, September 2019

INTRODUCTION TO THE POEM

CAN VERGIL'S *Aeneid,* a two-thousand-year-old epic about the legendary ancestor of a Roman emperor, speak to us in the twenty-first century? The vast passage of time and the values of a different culture might suggest not. Yet in the West (and to some degree in the Byzantine East) we have never *not* been in conversation with the *Aeneid,* and the questions it asks have "no boundaries of time or space" (as Jupiter predicts of the Roman Empire itself at the epic's start). Through the ages it has served as an illuminating work to think *with* that reveals much about those who encounter its complex story. As successive centuries of scholars, teachers, and students interpreted the *Aeneid,* they exposed their own assumptions and beliefs about gender, politics, religion, morality, love, truth, nationalism, and destiny. For this reason, the history of the poem's reception has always had much to tell us about the values that those generations brought with them to the encounter. And it also invites us to look at ourselves, whether we count it as a classic in our own intellectual heritage or we come to it from outside the system of meanings and associations that undergird Western culture. In an age of refugees seeking to escape their war-torn homelands, an age of rising nationalism across the globe, an age in which many in Europe and the United States are suspicious of "the East" and its religious differences—in *our* age, that is—the *Aeneid* has more to say to us than ever, especially about the costs (and, to be fair, benefits) of national ideologies and the way that myths of origins and heroes are created. Make of this epic what we will, it insists on being a relevant conversational partner. And this is part of its genius. The *Aeneid,* a deeply thoughtful poem by a man who'd lived through the horrors of war and the compromises of peace, has proven to be timeless.

A BRIEF HISTORY OF THE POEM'S RECEPTION

Some great works of art are only accepted as canonical with the passage of time. But Vergil's *Aeneid* was an essential part of the canon right from the start. It was praised by other Roman poets as a great national epic, taken as such by the imperial family, and adopted in the Roman school curriculum. Early commentators took it to be praising the emperor Augustus by depicting his putative ancestor Aeneas as a hero. In the fourth or early fifth century, M. Honoratus Servius claimed in the introductory note to his *In Vergilii Aeneidem commentarii* that "Virgil's intention is to imitate Homer and to praise Augustus by means of his ancestors." Likewise, Tiberius Claudius Donatus at the start of his *Interpretationes Vergilianae* opined that the poet "had to depict Aeneas as a worthy first ancestor of Augustus, in whose honor the poem was written." It seemed incontrovertible to them that a poem about a pious man who came, saw, and conquered could not be read otherwise, and there are still readers today who take the same meaning from it. This is not without reason: Vergil was part of the inner circle of Maecenas, a friend of Augustus and a patron of the arts. He had even read parts of the poem to the emperor himself.*

In the early Christian community, however, there were many who felt that pagan poetry should not be read at all. They argued that such poetry contained false values and baseless myths, and portrayed the gods (plural) as schemers and rapists. In the fourth century, figures such as the Church father Jerome argued that

---

* For the evidence that Vergil sent parts of the poem to Augustus as he composed, and even recited, Books 2, 4, and 6 in front of the royal family, see Donatus' *Life of Vergil* 32; Servius' Commentary on *Aeneid* 4.323, 6.861. Neither of these sources suggests that Augustus found anything questionable in the narrative.

Roman literature was deleterious to the Christian's relationship to God, and Augustine famously revealed in the first book of his *Confessions* that he wept over the suicide of the Carthaginian queen Dido in the *Aeneid* instead of his own benighted soul. But later Christian medievalists such as Fulgentius (sixth century CE) and Bernard Silvestris (twelfth century CE) swept aside such problems by reading the poem allegorically as a kind of bildungsroman of the good Christian everyman.* According to this interpretation, the storm off Carthage in Book 1 represented the moment of a man's birth into the "shore of light," while Aeneas' love affair with Dido (Book 4) stood for the lusty and tumultuous teenage years. (Unsurprisingly, the Christian allegorizers were at a loss for what to do with most of the second half, especially the rather unchristian denouement in which the Christian everyman slaughters his prostrate enemy.) Another Christian allegorizer, Dante Alighieri, famously made Vergil his guide through Hell in the *Inferno*. Even if he jettisoned Vergil soon after the tour, Dante was influenced by the widely shared belief that Vergil had sensed the coming of Christ ahead of his time, mostly because Vergil in his Fourth *Eclogue* hailed a mysterious child as the bringer of a new golden age. As late as 1957, T. S. Eliot, abandoning allegory, described Aeneas as the prototype of a "Christian hero" in his essay "Virgil and the Christian World," claiming that the Vergilian world was "approximate to a Christian world in the choice, order, and relationship of its values" and that "Virgil, among classical Latin poets or prose writers, is uniquely near to Christianity" because uniquely "civilized."†

The *Aeneid* was also pressed into political service when convenient, which was often. Until the last century, most readers accepted its explicit pro-imperial program as a praiseworthy one, and adapted it to different political situations and different mores.‡ As Philip Hardie has remarked in *The Last Trojan Hero*, the

---

* Naturally, such a reading involves ignoring many aspects of the poem as we have it.
† Eliot (1957), 147.
‡ On the earlier part of the reception tradition, see especially Ziolkowski and Putnam (2008).

many moments in which the *Aeneid* shows one regime yielding to another rendered it "a natural text for successive installments of the *translatio imperii* [the transfer of power] . . . and the *translatio studii,* the transfer of education and culture from Greece to Rome, and thence to other countries and other languages."* From the conqueror Charlemagne, crowned "King of the Romans" by Pope Leo III in the year 800, to the "Holy Roman Empire" that followed, from the French and British monarchies to the rise of Mussolini, the *Aeneid*'s vision of a triumphant and endless Roman Empire has underpinned any number of imperial visions. Benito Mussolini's twentieth-century appropriation of the epic was particularly straightforward, inasmuch as he portrayed himself as the inheritor of Augustus' rule and a destined leader. The 1937–38 exhibit *Mostra Augustea della Romanità* (The Augustan Demonstration of Romanness) celebrated the two thousandth birthday of the emperor Augustus by analogizing Mussolini's military ambitions to those of Augustus and to the content of the *Aeneid* itself. Maps of Aeneas' voyage and memorials to "Pater Aeneas" featured prominently in the first part of the exhibit, helping Mussolini to create a legendary past for his divinely ordained empire. Earlier, the New England settlers had invoked the Trojan conquest of native Italians to justify the events of King Philip's War (1675–78),† while in nineteenth-century America, the story of a Trojan's westward voyage and his fulfillment of divine command resonated (for some) with the dubious concept of manifest destiny.‡ Over the centuries, the *Aeneid* buoyed the belief of Western nations in their right to expand, pacify, and in some cases colonize the "uncivilized other"; in their schools, it was a canonical text for the same (male) readers who, as adults, would populate new generations of the elite.

Today, however, Classics has lost its status as the *sine qua non* edu-

---

* Hardie (2014), 103.

† See Shields (2001).

‡ The Founding Fathers had been a little more wary, admiring the Roman republic but not so much the empire that Julius Caesar was pivotal in bringing into existence.

cational matter of a liberal education and an ideal training for a life in politics. At the same time, and perhaps uncoincidentally, the *Aeneid* is now rarely treated as a positive endorsement of empire-mongering, or of autocracy. Instead, we modern readers often feel the epic invites us to reflect on the negative costs of empire, the way history belongs to the victors, and the discredited voices that fall out of memory. I have mentioned refugees, too, and they populate the epic, but not in any simple way. It is a fugitive's false claims that lead to Troy's fall; it is sympathy for an exile that brings down Carthage; Aeneas himself is a refugee smiled on (eventually) by fate, and his switch from victim to conqueror gives us a perspective from which to view his new victims.* Among these many, ongoing undulations in what the *Aeneid* seems to mean, the only thing that has not changed in all this time is the plot of the epic itself.

THE PLOT OF THE *AENEID*

The *Aeneid* is an account of how a refugee from Asia—Aeneas, a member of the royal family of Troy—led his followers west to establish a new empire in Italy. After his city is destroyed by the Greeks in the Trojan War, Aeneas sets sail with other survivors in the hope of finding a new land to settle. It's not an easy voyage, for although he is fated—so Jupiter reveals in Book 1—to found the Roman Empire in Italy, Jupiter's wife, Juno, cannot forget the wrongs done her by the Trojans, and she will persecute the refugee until the very end of the poem. The first time we see Aeneas, his ship battered by a storm sent by Juno, he is wishing that he had died on the fields of Troy at the hands of his enemy Diomedes. A

---

* David Quint (1993) suggests that Vergil intends the Odyssean wanderings of Books 1 through 6 to be superseded by the Iliadic war of the second half of the epic, thus mirroring a thematic and political transition: "The process by which the Trojans go from being losers to winners thus matches the movement in the poem from one narrative form to another, from romance to epic" (50).

startling sentiment for an epic hero, and certainly a hint that we are not dealing here with an Achilles or an Odysseus. At this point, Aeneas resembles neither a great warrior nor a wily liar; the adjective Vergil has chosen for him is "pious," a piety that entails loyalty to his father, his family, and his gods. It is this piety especially (it is announced to us already in line 10 of Book 1) that drives him onward in the search for a new homeland, one that he eventually understands will be on the far western coast of Italy.

The epic starts *in medias res*. Though we don't know the details of his past yet, Aeneas has already had many adventures since he left Troy, and there are many yet to come. Landing on the shores of North Africa, Aeneas meets his mother, Venus, who directs him to Queen Dido's city, Carthage. We learn that Dido, too, has suffered: she fled from her native Tyre after her brother, King Pygmalion, killed her wealthy husband, Sychaeus. Like Aeneas, she has been storm-tossed, and she, too, has sought—and founded—a new city for her followers. She is the perfect audience for his tale.

In the gripping account of tragedy, deceit, and suffering that makes up Books 2 and 3, Aeneas tells Dido and their dining companions his story from the moment Troy fell. Believing the account of a lying Greek named Sinon who claimed that the Greeks had left and that the Trojan Horse would bring the Trojans luck, the Trojans eagerly wheeled it up to the Acropolis. That night Sinon let the Greek soldiers out of its belly. They opened the gates of the city to their army and destroyed Troy, murdering its men, enslaving its women and children, and burning its buildings to the ground. After a valiant effort to defend the city, Aeneas says, he escaped with his father Anchises, his son, and his household gods.

Because the Trojans misinterpreted prophecies along their voyage, Aeneas' group had to abandon the colonies they started in Thrace, Crete, and the Strophades Islands, all of which met with misfortune or bad omens. Finally, in Buthrotum (a Greek city in Epirus), Aeneas learned his destiny from the seer Helenus: he must seek out Italy, from which base his descendants would rule the entire world. But first he would have to consult the Sibyl in Cumae (on the western coast of Italy) for further guidance. On his way there, he and his crew were blown off course to Africa. Here Aeneas ends the story he tells the queen.

Thanks to the conniving of Venus and her son Amor, Dido has fallen desperately in love with the eloquent Trojan stranger by the time he finishes his speech. Juno is pleased: she wants Dido and Aeneas married so that he'll forget his mission to found a city in Italy. This city, fate has decreed, will defeat her beloved Carthage one day—better it should not exist! Aeneas and Dido consummate their relationship on a hunting trip, and Dido, we know, considers it marriage (as does Juno, the goddess of marriage). Aeneas contentedly helps Dido build up Carthage until Jupiter warns him it is time to leave. In response to his abandonment, Dido kills herself.

Book 5 describes the "Trojan Games" in Sicily, a series of athletic competitions set up by Aeneas in honor of his father. Next, in Book 6, Aeneas visits the Sibyl at Cumae. She prepares him for the famous *katabasis* (descent to the Underworld), where he will meet his recently deceased father. They find Anchises in the blessed fields of Elysium, where he describes the reincarnation or "metempsychosis" of the souls in the Underworld as Aeneas and his father watch a parade of future Roman heroes. Anchises warns Aeneas: as the Romans conquer the world, they must remember to "rule / the world with law, impose [their] ways on peace / grant the conquered clemency, and crush the proud in war" (6.851–53). Then the Sibyl leads Aeneas out of the Underworld through the ivory gates of false dreams rather than the alternative, the gate of horn through which true visions pass.

At this point, the "Odyssean" half of the poem is over, and Aeneas will be almost constantly at war from Book 7 through Book 12 of the epic. The Trojan ships voyage up the river Tiber to Latium, their final destination, where Aeneas persuades Latinus, king of the Latins, to give him his daughter Lavinia in marriage. Lavinia has already been promised to a local king, the Rutulian Turnus, and Juno steps in again, sending the Fury Allecto to madden both Lavinia's mother, Amata, and Turnus. Meanwhile, Aeneas' son Ascanius wounds a deer beloved to the Italians, and a local fight breaks out. Latin casualties incite the rest of the Latins to battle as events rapidly deteriorate out of Latinus' control.

Tiber's river god, Tiberinus, tells Aeneas to seek out a different ally: King Evander of Pallanteum, whose people are hostile to the Rutulians. As Aeneas puts together an army in Tuscany, the Trojans stay inside their camp. During the night, however, two of them, Nisus and Euryalus, leave on a mission to fetch him back, and meet violent deaths. On the next day Turnus manages to get himself shut inside the Trojan camp. He kills many before he jumps into the Tiber, blood-smeared and exhausted, to be carried away from the camp and back to his men. Meanwhile, Venus has seduced her husband, Vulcan, into forging special armor for her son (but not Vulcan's son!) Aeneas. The weaponry includes a shield on which Rome's future history is carved, but we are told Aeneas hoists it without understanding it.

Now Jupiter holds a council of the gods. He hears passionate speeches from the rivals Venus and Juno, but orders all the gods to hold back and let the Trojans and Italians battle it out without interference (this agreement is soon broken). On Earth, Aeneas sails back to the besieged Trojan camp with his new allies. Turnus and Pallas face off in a duel, and Turnus kills the boy and takes his sword-belt from his corpse as Aeneas rages through the battlefield, killing without mercy. The next dawn rises over the blood-soaked battlefield, when Aeneas' grief over the loss of Pallas leads him to sacrifice twelve living Italians over Pallas' fiery pyre. During a cease-fire in which both sides burn their dead, there is conflict in the Latin camp: Latinus calls for peace, the Latin Drances urges Turnus to engage in single combat with Aeneas, and Turnus angrily insults him. No matter—as they argue, the Trojan forces arrive unexpectedly. Fighting on the Italian side, the virgin warrior-queen Camilla is killed by the cowardly Arruns. Arruns in turn is struck dead by Diana's sentinel, Opis.

Both sides broker an agreement that Turnus and Aeneas should fight in single combat, but the pact is broken almost immediately when Aeneas is wounded by an anonymous arrow. When he returns to battle, he attacks Laurentum, King Latinus' city. In despair, Latinus' wife Amata kills herself. Turnus hears of the city's trouble and resolves to confront Aeneas once and for all. In Olympus, Jupiter at last persuades Juno to give up her rage and let Aeneas kill Turnus, which she agrees to allow on the condition that the victorious Trojans lose their culture, their language, and their name when they merge with the Italians. In the epic's final duel, Turnus' strength suddenly deserts him. He hurls a boulder at Aeneas but misses. Aeneas is more successful: his spear strikes Turnus in the thigh. On his knees, Turnus begs for his life, reminding Aeneas of their fathers' love for each of them.* Aeneas is about to grant his prayer when he sees on Turnus the sword-belt that the Rutulian had stripped from Pallas. In a fit of rage, he drives his sword through his supplicant and Turnus collapses in death. With this the epic ends, an ending so bleak and startling that many have wondered whether Vergil intended to write more before his sudden death in 19 BCE.

A NATIONAL EPIC?

At the beginning of the *Aeneid,* Jupiter assures his daughter Venus that the race of Romans who will rise from Aeneas' blood will rule the world: he, Jupiter, has granted them "empire without end." The reader thus knows that Aeneas will reach Italy and establish a great city for his people, and in addition, the narrative is regularly interspersed with otherworldly revelations (through prophecy, art, and what Anchises reveals in the Underworld) of the great Roman nation that will rise from Aeneas' blood and conquer the world. The *Aeneid* might then seem in every way to have given its readers a

---

* This is a scene both present in and absent from the *Iliad.* Hector is killed cleanly by Achilles, and so does not beg for his life; but his father Priam begs for his body from Achilles, reminding Achilles of his own father, and Achilles is moved and gives up the dead Hector for burial.

great national epic: a work that identifies mythical ancestors for its people, provides them with shared history, gives meaning to their struggles through the centuries, and, often, sets the stamp of divine approval on imperial expansion.

Obviously, the creation of such a useful national myth must involve alterations to aspects of the lived history that preceded it. Though these alterations gain value and credibility as time passes and become canonical, when first introduced they are still vulnerable to questioning. Surprisingly for a national epic, the *Aeneid* does not shy away from pointing out problems in its own credibility as "the new reality" of how Rome came to be. As we shall see, it is almost impossible to read the poem without being alerted to its status as fiction. As a result, rather than being simple propaganda, the *Aeneid* is in many ways a story *about* stories (or national myths), and how they work. It is an epic that tells a story of foundation but puts on display the fault lines at the base of its own edifice, revealing the mechanisms at work in wholesome origin-stories and justifications of imperial aggression.

A useful analogy is the Roman practice of *damnatio memoriae*. When unpopular emperors died or were murdered, the Senate might "damn their memory" as a sign that they were to be erased from history. As part of this *damnatio,* statues of that emperor were generally replaced or refurbished with the head of the new emperor. But replacing these heads was not always done in a subtle way. Rather than smoothing over the cracks where the new parts met, the Romans might leave a line at the neck where the new head had been added, or a new hairstyle that segued awkwardly into the remainder of a previous hairstyle. In such instances, the condemned emperor could not be said to have really been erased from history. Instead, his damnation to oblivion consisted of a visible reminder that he had been intentionally "forgotten." In Vergil's brilliant hands, the narrative of the *Aeneid* does a similar thing. It offers a vision of a stable and moral present but also reveals that underneath it lies another story.

And yet the *Aeneid* has rarely been understood as specifically reflecting on its own claims to tell a Roman origin-story. Even interpretations that are skeptical of its propagandistic slant merely suggest that it is in fact critical of Augustus, or critical of the cost of empire—thus reversing, but not jettisoning, the question of its ideological position in favor of or against autocratic power at home and the acquisition of empire abroad. As Alessandro Barchiesi remarks, this conventional binary of "pro-Augustan" and "anti-Augustan" does not serve Augustan literature well. It flattens the texture of the epic and transforms all its complications into judgments on Augustus.* Nevertheless, these arguments were the stuff of many debates in the second half of the twentieth century, when (to generalize a bit unfairly) European scholars interpreted the epic as a positive statement in favor of Augustus, and the Americans (often referred to as the Harvard School) emphasized the ways in which the epic is bleak and negative.† (Most work now tends to find many voices [or lenses] in the poem, providing a sort of polyvalence of values, with each point of view laying claim to its own truth about the world.)‡

In this introduction, then, the goal will not be to marshal the evidence for readings of the poem that praise or condemn the emperor Augustus, under whom it was written. Instead, we will look at what the poem has to say about itself—following the ancient scholar Aristarchus' famous dictum that "we should interpret Homer from Homer." And to do this, we must not ignore or discount moments of confusion or self-contradiction in the main narrative, but instead respect them and use them as clues to places where Vergil wants us to *think*, to see several simultaneous stories in operation rather than one. We should also be careful in accept-

* Barchiesi (1997), 253.

† Other binary approaches existed as well, such as the contrast between the epic's public, celebratory voice and the private, lamenting voice described by Adam Parry's "The Two Voices of Vergil's *Aeneid*" in *Arion* 2 (1963): 66–80.

‡ Conte (1986), 157, is eloquent on this multiplicity of voices.

ing authoritative statements, for even Jupiter can, and does, contradict himself. Fate cannot be escaped, but the path to the future is full of detours, confusion, and struggle.

OCTAVIAN AND AUGUSTUS

Vergil was born in 70 BCE during the late Roman republic, a period racked by civil wars. When he was just shy of thirty-nine, the general Octavian (later the emperor renamed Augustus, 63 BCE–14 CE) won a decisive battle at Actium against his opponents Marc Antony and Cleopatra, and Rome effectively became a monarchy under his sole control. Octavian dominated the Senate, quelled opposition, and established the Augustan Peace, the Pax Augusta. Vergil was completing his second great work at this time, the agricultural poem known as the *Georgics,* in which he not only referred honorifically to Octavian's victory at Actium in 3.28–39, but even promised to write a political epic about Octavian's triumphs (3.46–48). He presented a mini-version of the future epic in his description of a marble temple to be dedicated to Octavian: in the middle of this imaginary temple stands a statue of the emperor along with images of Octavian's Trojan ancestors. In front, triumphal processions pass by the temple's golden doors, festooned with pictures of Octavian's victories in the East.

In the end, though, this was not the epic Vergil wrote. He wrote the *Aeneid* instead. Perhaps Vergil realized an epic in praise of Octavian would be problematic, all the more so if (as may be possible) he was writing it at Octavian's specific request. For despite his triumphant emergence as a ruler, Octavian had a violent history. Reports prior to his final victory were of a vicious leader: the biographer Suetonius (c. 69–after 122 CE) and the historian Dio Cassius (writing a century after Suetonius) report rumors that he sacrificed as many as three hundred senators and equestrians at the altar of the Divine Julius (his adoptive father, Julius Caesar) after the defeat of Perusia (modern-day Perugia) in 40 BCE. Dio Cassius and the author of the play *Octavia* (probably written shortly after Nero's death) both suggest that his nickname at the time had been "the butcher." Seneca, in his essay *On Mercy* (*De clementia*), suggests that Octavian cruelly "buried his dagger in the chest of his friends" until he became Augustus and took up the practice of forgiveness (1.9.1–11.1). Octavian would not have seemed particularly laudable as an avatar of justice and clemency to a contemporary audience.

After he came to power, Octavian naturally tried to overwrite this checkered history, and, in large measure, he succeeded. He is mainly remembered for his forty years as an effective ruler of Rome. He spared many who had fought on behalf of his enemies (a policy of *clementia*). With the Senate's connivance, he had his name changed to Augustus ("revered," with positive moral connotations) in 27 BCE. He did not take the title of dictator or king, but only that of *princeps*, or first among the senators. And in the autobiography of his achievements that he left to posterity, the *Res Gestae*,* he announced a whole slew of positive deeds: he had avenged his adoptive father, Julius Caesar, against "a faction" (Antony and Cleopatra), dispensed money to the people, restored the republican government, donated to the public treasury, rebuilt parts of Rome, gotten rid of pirates, colonized Egypt, restored eighty-two temples of the gods, and much else. By the time he died in 14 CE, he had been in power for forty-five years, and this self-portrayal must have had powerful force as an evaluation of his reign. Although no one could have foreseen such longevity, this span of time gave credibility to his claim to have brought a lasting peace. History has mostly remembered him as Augustus, bringer of peace, and there are few ancient sources critical of his rule. Vergil had a shorter perspective than we do, however. He died in 19 BCE, not knowing how the Augustan era would turn out. It was definitely safer—at

---

* "Matters Accomplished." The whole text was inscribed on two columns near the Mausoleum of Augustus in Rome. It survives as an inscription in the Temple of Roma and Augustus in modern Ankara. A modern copy can be viewed outside the Mausoleum in Rome today.

least for his posthumous reputation—to write about Octavian's ancestor, Aeneas.

That Aeneas *was* their ancestor was an account endorsed by Octavian's family, the Julii (Octavian's grandmother was Julius Caesar's sister): they said their descent from Venus was specifically through her son, Aeneas, who brought the Trojans to Italy. Julius Caesar even minted coins in his own name that had the figure of Aeneas on one side and Venus on the other. Vergil emphasized the link between Aeneas and the Julians by bringing in a little-known "Iülus" as a son of Aeneas—the similarity between the names Iülus, Ilium (Troy), and Julius being no accident.* In the *Aeneid*, we have a nice line of succession: Aeneas founds Lavinium; Lavinium gives way to Alba Longa, under Iülus' rule; and Alba Longa gives way in turn to Rome, which is founded by and named for Aeneas' (and Iülus') descendant Romulus. With Aeneas as his hero, Vergil could avoid dealing with contemporary politics and still address Augustus' declared values. He refers to Augustus' regime only in the future tense, not only in divine proclamations, but also in Book 6, when Aeneas' dead father shows him the history and heroes of the future Roman Empire, and in Book 8, in which scenes from Rome's (future) history are carved on his shield.†

So, one might say, the poem can still be read as pro-Augustan propaganda. It celebrates Augustus and his father in its prophecies, explicitly calls Rome's founder and their ancestor Aeneas "pious," and glorifies major events in Rome's (future) history, including the ones that led to the ascendancy of the Augustan regime.

As I've said, early in the twentieth century, and especially in Europe, the *Aeneid* tended to be read "positively" in this way: "a classic vindication of the European world-order," as Stephen Harrison has

---

* A better-known name for Aeneas' son was Ascanius, which Vergil also uses.

† W. H. Auden was unimpressed. In his poem "Secondary Epic," he criticizes Vergil's technique of looking forward from Aeneas' time and mocks the poem's suggestion of an eternal Rome by suggesting that Vergil could have looked further, to Alaric's sack of Rome in 410 CE and beyond.

characterized it.* But the "negative" school that has developed since then has focused more on the suffering and loss invariably caused by the rise of great empires, of which there are many instances in the epic. In particular, many twentieth-century critics have turned to the violent ending of the epic, in which Aeneas kills his pleading victim. They suggest that Aeneas, prefiguring Augustus' days as Octavian, was violent when there was no need to be, and much evidence has been amassed on either side, depending on whether readers concentrate on references to order, civilization, and similes evoking the defeat of the old pre-Olympian dark forces, or to suffering, death, and the other legacies of war. So, is the poem really a poem about pious Aeneas, or does it demonstrate the cost of the peace that Aeneas (like Octavian) procures, namely, the many acts of violence required to establish it? As the scholarship argues on and on, each side using parts of the poem that support its claim, it seems clear that no definitive answer can be had. Perhaps other questions will supply us with richer insights into the poem.

AENEAS

What kind of character is Aeneas? Vergil calls him pious, a complicated term that means he does his duty by his fatherland, gods, and family (rather than just being God-fearing in a monotheistic sense). In addition, he embodies the main traits of the two great Homeric heroes: both Odysseus' questing nature and Achilles' lack of mercy in battle. Finally, he is a character who lives by the mandate of destiny. Aeneas is fated to marry King Latinus' daughter in Italy and establish a dynasty that will fuse two different races—Trojans and Italians—to produce, eventually, the glorious and triumphant Romans. Here, then, was a Roman poem which tried to rival the cultural authority of the Homeric classics that had been

* Harrison (1990), 4.

written at the dawn of Greek culture. While the epic wasn't written at the beginning of Rome's rise, it engaged with and challenged the Homeric epics by explicitly referring to them and evoking their heroes. It also did something more: it told a story of a nation as much as of an individual.

But Aeneas is, nevertheless, a problematic hero, and not just because to some he seems a bit bland. It is because the *legend* of Aeneas is problematic. On black-figure Greek vase paintings from the second half of the sixth century BCE, Aeneas can been seen fleeing Troy with his son, his father, and sometimes his wife: authority for his escape from Troy thus exists. But the literary tradition that Aeneas brought with him was not complimentary. In the *Iliad* he fought against the Greeks but, on several occasions, needed to be rescued—by his mother, Venus, by Apollo, and by Poseidon—from greater warriors than himself. Worse, there exist pre-Vergilian sources for the Aeneas legend in which Aeneas *betrayed* Troy to the Greeks in exchange for payment or safe passage. In other words, several of the best-known versions of Aeneas' escape from Troy implicated him in its fall after ten years of resisting the Greeks, a grave handicap for a proto-Roman hero.* Yet Vergil not only depicted Aeneas as a hero, not a traitor, he also established the Aeneas of the *Aeneid* as the principal figure for posterity. From the time of its publication, the epic became so influential that not many traces of the earlier Aeneas remain. Few modern students of the epic have heard of Aeneas' past as the pre-Vergilian traitor or the medieval traitor (another negative tradition, influenced by two post-Vergilian accounts that falsely claimed to be written by eyewitnesses at Troy!).† But since Vergil certainly knew the negative

---

* On the alternative Aeneas legends, see especially Casali (2014) and Chiappinelli (2007).

† Dictys of Crete was the companion of Idomeneus during the Trojan War. A certain Q. Septimius published Dictys' purported diary of the Trojan War in the fourth century CE. Medieval readers took his story literally, along with Dares' similarly late "Fall of Troy." Guido delle Colonne's prose narrative of the Trojan War, *Historia destructionis Troiae,* is based on Dares and Dictys.

tradition about Aeneas—and was reacting to it in his own epic—if we ignore this history, we will miss the extent of Vergil's genius and much of the poem's self-reflective quality.

At least at first glance, Vergil's pious Aeneas seems the antithesis of a traitor. As we have seen, the Latin term *pius* has a broader compass than the English word "pious" and refers to at least three simultaneous kinds of piety: piety toward the Olympian and household gods, as manifested in prayer, obedience, and offerings; piety toward one's family and ancestors, in particular the male line; and piety toward one's country, which demands a willingness to die fighting for it. Aeneas is characterized as pious in over twenty places in the epic. He even seems to know his own reputation: when he meets his mother, Venus, disguised as a mortal, later in Book 1, the first words out of his mouth are "I'm pious Aeneas" (1.377–78). So he would seem to stand in sharp contrast to that wily Homeric hero Odysseus, the man of many tales, who knows well how to lie when it suits his benefit and who introduces himself by saying "I am known to all for my tricks," and also to the proud and selfish Achilles, who withdrew from battle and let his allies die because his honor had been slighted. The *Aeneid*'s hero models many of the Romans' own beliefs about themselves—piety, self-sacrifice, endurance. In the episodes in which Aeneas seems less heroic and more confused than his Homeric predecessors, the critics credit precisely his piety, maintaining that it is a difficult quality in an epic warrior.

This "official" label of piety ties Aeneas directly to Octavian/Augustus, who was likewise dubbed "pious" by the Roman Senate. Just eight years before Vergil's death, Octavian's largely symbolic "restitution of the republic" resulted in a Senate decree honorifically renaming him Augustus (at his suggestion) and arranging for "the placement of a gold shield in the Julian senate-house, which the senate and Roman people gave to me in recognition of my virtue, mercy, justice, and piety" (*Res Gestae* 34). Copies of the shield preserved from antiquity trumpet these four qualities, thus stamping Augustus with *pietas* as surely as his adoptive father before him had laid claim to *clementia* (mercy). It is possible that the surviving members of the Roman senatorial class suppressed an involuntary twitch even as they voted Augustus this honor. (Cicero, one of the victims of Augustus' rise to power, was not around to suppress a twitch.) Or perhaps, as the historian Tacitus claims, the senators were too relieved at the end of incessant warfare to care much.

Piety also appears as an Augustan quality in the autobiographical *Res Gestae,* which recasts many of the emperor's actions, including his brutality in the civil war following Caesar's assassination, in terms of Roman virtues. Augustus' piety manifests itself as filial piety, in the need to avenge his father; as religious piety, in his restoration of Rome's temples after his victory; and even as piety toward republican Rome, in that he claimed to have restored its traditional government (never mind if he pulled all the strings). As such, the *Res Gestae* themselves are a sort of palimpsest of the past. Set up in stone across the Roman Empire, these accounts became the Roman people's official memory of Augustus' battles and good works, and as Augustus himself slipped into legend to be followed by a series of unquestionably bad emperors, he would have seemed to have increasingly filled his own shoes.

The appearance of pious Aeneas in the *Aeneid*, then, can be a reference to Augustus himself and his attempt to gloss over the memory of his former self, Octavian. It can also stand as an advance refutation of any suggestion that Aeneas could in fact be impious. Only Dido, the woman Aeneas lies to and abandons, dares to question that piety explicitly, though the Italians of the epic might have had unvoiced doubts as Aeneas cut their throats over Pallas' pyre. But before we can question Aeneas' piety on the basis of his acts, we need to explore it on the basis of his self-presentation. We must look at what he says about himself, especially in Books 2 and 3. It is here that we can discover whether Aeneas is an autobiographer or a spinner of yarns, a model hero or an unreliable one, an Octavian or an Augustus.

AENEAS' STORY

In Books 2 and 3, Aeneas narrates a mini-epic about how he got from Troy to Carthage.* Just as Odysseus tells his story to the king and queen of Phaeacia in *Odyssey* Books 9–12, Aeneas tells his story to Queen Dido. Although readers often forget that Aeneas is telling this story, it is worth remembering that Vergil does not interrupt in his own voice to support Aeneas' tale. Aeneas, then, could be treated as a storyteller much in the vein of Odysseus—and the poet often prompts us to do so by inserting contradictions or peculiarities in Aeneas' account and also by drawing attention to the fact that he is said to "sing" his story the way a poet would (4.14). Why has Aeneas been immune to this characterization? Perhaps the word "pious" has something to do with it. Pious men—certainly in the Christian sense of the word—don't lie. But like Odysseus, Aeneas is indubitably the bard of the *Aeneid*'s first section. Odysseus always told his stories to reflect well on himself and to encourage the hospitality of his new hosts, sometimes even in a way that concealed his true identity.† The story Aeneas tells the Carthaginian queen Dido—soon to be his lover—reflects well on him too, highlighting his bravery, his endurance, and above all his piety.

The story is riveting: the spellbound Dido asks to hear it again and again. And yet, Vergil repeatedly provokes us to wonder how much of it is actually true and how much adapted for the circumstances. For example: When Aeneas lands at Carthage and meets his mother, Venus, she gives him an outline of Dido's story of exile and flight from Tyre. Dido's husband, Sychaeus, was murdered by her brother, Pygmalion, at the family altar. Sychaeus appeared to Dido in a dream vision, showed her his wounds, and told her the truth, urging her to flee. Shocked and grieving, she gathered some companions and left her native land forever. After suffering at sea,

---

* See Horsfall (1979) and (1986) on how this tale differs from the older accounts of Aeneas' wanderings.

† However, Odysseus' craftiness brings pleasure to Athena (cf. *Odyssey* 13.287, 291–99), while it is a more questionable quality in a man noted for Roman *pietas*.

she made land, and now, despite hostile neighbors, she has founded a new city. All of these details are news to Aeneas—and valuable information. For when he tells Dido his own life story, Aeneas repeats, in many details, what he knows about her. He tells her of his dream vision of the dead Hector, who appears to him with bloody wounds and tells him to flee. He speaks of Priam's cruel slaughter at the altar. He lost his spouse, Creusa, and fled his homeland with items of precious value (the household gods rather than gold) and a group of companions. The sea voyage, the suffering, the attempt to found a city—all of these are in Aeneas' story. The possibility that Aeneas is imitating Dido's life story even explains a detail that has puzzled scholars of the poem: Aeneas claims to be astonished at Hector's wounds in his dream. But this makes no sense, since the dream comes well after Achilles has mauled Hector by the walls of Troy. But Aeneas' version mimics Dido's surprise at seeing Sychaeus' wounds in *her* dream.*

If these parallels suggest Aeneas knows how to spin a tale to win sympathy, another set of striking parallels suggests that Aeneas could be a liar, a question the epic does not let us ever resolve. The epic's most famous storyteller (and liar) is Sinon, the fake "Greek refugee" who Aeneas claims is responsible for the fall of Troy. Sinon's story of Greek persecution persuades the Trojan king, Priam, to offer him pity, protection, and Trojan citizenship. Aeneas wants the same things from Dido and echoes several of Sinon's circumstances and claims for sympathy: exile from one's homeland after escaping death; potential rejection by the country he has stumbled upon by chance; invocations of the gods; stories of one's own goodness and piety; and emphatic comments about hating the crafty Odysseus. Both Sinon and Aeneas tell such good stories that they

---

* The commentator Servius even says of another part of Aeneas' story that he said it because of the echoes to Dido's story! Biow (1994) notes all these parallels and points out repetitions in terminology as well: *in somnis, iactatus, traiectus,* and others. O'Hara (2007) provides an insightful study of inconsistencies in Latin epic in general; his remarks on the *Aeneid* are particularly important, and are reflected in my remarks above.

are embraced and welcomed. Ultimately, however, each storyteller causes the death of his kind host—in one case Priam, in the other Dido.

But if Sinon's story already existed in the tradition, how could Vergil be using it to set up parallels to Aeneas? In fact, *Sinon's story is absent in prior (extant) accounts of the Trojan War*. We know that Sophocles wrote a tragedy called *Sinon*, but we have no way of knowing what that Sinon did or said in it. In the other pre-Vergilian accounts in which Sinon is mentioned, he participates in the action (e.g. signaling the Greeks, or opening the Horse) but has nothing to say. It may be only in Vergil that a figure once believed to have betrayed Troy arrives on Carthaginian shores and tells the queen a long story in which the *real* traitor of Troy is a man named Sinon who tells a long story.... Did Vergil invent the story Sinon tells just to make us think twice about the story Aeneas tells?

Other hints at the narrative ingenuity of Aeneas' tale come out of his descriptions of events he could not have seen. He knows about the secret beacon to the Greek ships at Tenedos. He names the order in which the Greek leaders descend from the belly of the Trojan Horse on a rope (Odysseus/Ulysses is appropriately first). He sees the murderer Pyrrhus simultaneously from both outside and inside Priam's palace; he knows what Hecuba says to her husband; he describes Priam slaughtered by the altar but also lying dead on the beach. What are we to make of this? It seems any careful reader of Aeneas' story will have doubts about some of the details. As David Quint has remarked, "The poem invites us to read Aeneas' storytelling in this way and to indulge in the hermeneutics of suspicion."*

---

* Quint (2018), 34. Ahl (1989) makes an excellent argument for such suspicion vis-à-vis both Odysseus and Aeneas. Perhaps we should have been primed to that "hermeneutics of suspicion" by the *Odyssey*, not only because Odysseus likes to dissimulate his identity in his stories, but also because when he comes back from his travels, he tells Penelope about all his adventures—minus the philandering. (Emily Wilson, in the introduction to her translation of the *Odyssey*, has suggested we could even translate the first lines of the epic as "Sing to me of a straying man, Muse"!)

By doing this, Vergil invites us to reflect on the creation of seductive narratives per se—one of which, of course, is his own epic. As I have mentioned, it was *so* seductive that everyone promptly forgot about the main tradition about Aeneas before the *Aeneid*: that he was a traitor. In most of the relevant sources that predate the *Aeneid,* many of them conveniently gathered in Dionysius of Halicarnassus' *Roman Antiquities* 46, Aeneas neither fights to save Troy nor goes to Rome. Whether it's the version of Hellanicus of Mytilene, Sophocles' *Laocoön,* Hellanicus of Lesbos, or Menecrates of Xanthus, Aeneas betrays the city of Troy, or joins the Greek side, or never founds a new town in Italy, or founds Rome—with Odysseus! Menecrates' version is particularly interesting: Aeneas betrayed Troy to the Greeks because he hated Paris and his father, Priam, so much: "For Aeneas, being scorned by Alexander and excluded from his prerogatives, overthrew Priam; and having accomplished this, he became one of the Achaeans" (*Roman Antiquities* 1.48.3, translated by Ernest Cary).*

Once we know about the alternative Aeneas(es), many of the scenes in the books about Dido and Aeneas will remind us of the accounts *prior* to Vergil's poem—and this is part of what I mean when I say the *Aeneid* is a poem that meditates on its own status as a newly crafted national myth by (obliquely) pointing to other traditions.† A few examples: (1) When Aeneas is examining Dido's temple to Juno, one of the scenes on the temple wall is a depiction of Aeneas himself "mixed in with the Greeks" (1.488). Later, Aeneas repeats this language when he tells Dido that he and a small group put on Greek armor and proceeded "mixed in with the

---

* For discussion, see Ahl (1989), 27–28, and Horsfall (1986), 16, who confirms that the account of Aeneas as traitor was known in Republican Rome. On the tradition of Aeneas as traitor in general, see Ahl (1989), Chiappinelli (2007), Horsfall (1986), and Scafoglio (2012), who discusses the Homeric evidence for hostility between Aeneas and Priam (cf. *Iliad* 13.458–61). On the difficulties of Dionysius' testimony, see Horsfall (1979).

† Horsfall (1981), 145, remarks, "If we turn to the 'classic' inconsistencies of the poem, it is striking how often both versions are established and traditional."

Greeks" (2.396), believing they could thereby catch more Greeks off guard. Why include this phrase to start with, and then explain it away, if you want to *conceal* the alternative tradition in which Aeneas does abet the Greeks? In his account of how Aeneas betrayed Troy, Menecrates of Xanthus, as we've seen, says just this, though in Greek, not Latin: Aeneas "become one of the Greeks" (Dionysius of Halicarnassus, *Roman Antiquities* 1.48.3).* (2) Like Sinon, Aeneas claims to Dido that he and the Trojans are destitute of everything after their shipwrecks (1.599–600); yet he still has plenty of gifts for Dido, and then Latinus, from the royal treasures of Troy, including Helen's wedding regalia, various crowns, and even Priam's scepter. When did he get those? And how? Knowing that in another tradition he was given Trojan treasure by the Greeks in return for betraying the city should prompt us to engage in that "hermeneutics of suspicion."† (3) When Aeneas is telling his story to Dido, he says something very oddly phrased: that he not only saw Troy's terrible destruction, but was a great part of it.‡ This is a strange way to say he fought on the city's behalf; it suggests instead that he participated in Troy's fall.§ (4) There are even hints in the narrative that suggest Vergil wanted us to wonder whether Dido knew Aeneas was a traitor, but fell in love with him during his "story" because the gods made her do so. At the end, when she knows he is leaving, she asks herself, rather significantly: "Why should I pretend now? What could be worse than this?" (4.368). Was she, then, pretending before? Pretending what? And as Dido furiously watches the Trojans boarding their ships to sneak out of

* As Roger Macfarlane pointed out to me (communication of November 27, 2019), it's interesting in this regard that Horace, in his *Carmen Saeculare* of 17 BCE (a public hymn commissioned by Augustus), seems careful to point out that Aeneas founded Rome *sine fraude* (without deception).

† On this allegation, see the perceptive comments of Ahl (1989), 26, and Horsfall (1986).

‡ *"quaeque ipse miserrima vidi / et quorum pars magna fui,"* 2.5–6.

§ The only parallel language in the epic at 10.426 reinforces the idea that to be part of something is to work toward it.

Carthage, she not only compares them to looters, but also berates herself by saying,

> Poor Dido, do his impious actions touch you *now*?
> Better then, when you shared your rule. So much
> for his pledges, the man they say carried his gods
> and hauled his father, weak with age, upon his back!
> (4.596–99)

As Sergio Casali (1999) points out, the reference to impious actions (*impia facta*) suggests that she knew that the story Aeneas told her was a sanitized version, but she loved him nonetheless—and offered him half her kingdom.* It is also worth noting that the narrator himself characterizes Aeneas' actions here as a trick (*dolus*, 4.296), a word used six times in connection with Sinon and the Trojan Horse in Book 2—more than with any other topic. My point is not that Vergil is seditiously seeding the epic with the bad Aeneas, but rather that he lets us see that the revised Aeneas *is* a revision. As Roland Barthes has noted, what we must guard against is not so much ideology as the way in which ideology masks and conceals itself.† And Vergil's *Aeneid* refuses to mask itself. Vergil *shows* us how he rewrote the biography of the emperor's distant ancestor to make him enduring and above all pious, and how his revision serves an imperial purpose.

REMEMBERING TO FORGET

What does it mean to create one version of a story that points to other, suppressed versions? This is not a Vergilian fumble but a masterful way of showing that we are being *asked* to forget, itself an

---

* Whose impious actions are these? The text leaves it ambiguous, and many readers have automatically taken them to be Dido's—though she is not the one associated with piety or impiety.

† Barthes (1957), 109–59.

act that resurrects the forbidden memory, as with my analogy to the practice of *damnatio memoriae,* a move to "cancel" bad emperors by altering their statues. Just as the seams between the statues' bodies and their new heads actually reminded the viewer of what she was supposed to forget, so the *Aeneid* has seams through which we can see the previous Aeneas, condemned by the *Aeneid* to oblivion—but not quite. By including other traditions, the epic invites us to remember what we are being told to forget. One might even think of this gesture as demonstrating that the powers that be can rewrite history and can expect readers and writers to fall in line—unless the seams of an earlier history show through.

As if to confirm the fictionality of his own *and* Aeneas's story, Vergil deploys the term *vates,* a soothsayer-poet, throughout the epic, to refer both to himself and to the producers of false narratives in his own narrative: the prophet Calchas, and the soothsayers from whom Dido seeks counsel in Book 4. The *vates* Calchas (2.122) is an open liar and dissimulator, and he makes up a tale about the gods in order to condemn Sinon to death (so Aeneas tells us). The soothsayers (they too are *vates*) are ignorant and have no capacity to see into the future (4.65). We might find this curious, given Vergil's depiction of a glorious future for Rome in Books 6 and 8! And what, then, are we meant to think when Vergil asks the muse Erato to guide the poetry of Vergil, her *vates,* at 7.41? The implication is that Vergil is no different from the other dubious poet-bards in his own poem—and that he chose to cast himself in this way.

We can now ask *why* Vergil decided to draw our attention to different versions of the legend he rewrites. It's not surprising that Vergil chose to take the lesser-known Aeneas and make him the better-known Aeneas, a pious man rather than a traitor, given that he was writing his epic under Aeneas' ostensible heir and the current Roman emperor. Perhaps he wanted his poem to provide a cornerstone for the Pax Augusta. But Vergil was also invested in showing us precisely what he was doing and offering us other ways to read his poem. Above all, he was reminding us that stories are important. In every culture, political stories account for the way a culture's values and nature are defined in the current day. As Aaron Seider reminds us, collective memories are shaped by a community's coming together around *one* story and letting the other variants (at least, of that story) go. Such stories are often necessary, after all, to justify war, reinforce racial stereotypes, and seek monopolies on moral value. They also knit people together. It's complicated.*

MEMORY AND EMPIRE

Did Vergil write the *Aeneid* in response to the collective memory he saw forming under the emperor Augustus, a memory that would slowly override that of the pre-Augustan Octavian? Was he both helping to create that collective memory, but also warning us about his creation? If so, we can think of the *Res Gestae* as being like books of the *Aeneid* that never show the cracks in the ideological edifice of the newly constructed past. Mark Antony's name never appears in the *Res Gestae;* he is reduced to a nameless "faction." Acts of Octavian's cruelty vanish under claims to *clementia*. We are told that Octavian's goal was never to gain power but to avenge the death of Julius Caesar. And although, had Mark Antony won, it would have been Octavian who was cast as the traitor to Rome, in the *Res Gestae* he characterizes himself as the epitome of *pietas* to gods, man, and state. Like Aeneas, he claims to eschew rule over the conquered: he is simply the *princeps*. Vergil did with Aeneas what Augustus did with Octavian—that is, wrote a new version of a tainted figure.

---

* In the *Aeneid* we even see characters creating new memories, often by misremembering the past (Seider, 2013). We see this happen in *Aeneid* Book 7 when Aeneas "remembers" his *father's* prophecy about the Trojans eating their tables: this was actually a curse delivered by the terrifying and hostile Harpy Celaeno in Book 3, but she has vanished from the story, and presumably from future Trojan legend as well; meanwhile, instead of tables, they are really eating their "plates." In Book 3, after getting it wrong before, Anchises suddenly remembers, a bit tardily, that Italy, not Crete, is the ancient mother of the Trojans. And of course, throughout, it seems we are to re-remember our knowledge of who Aeneas once was.

The *Aeneid* is not a cipher with which to unlock Augustan propaganda—it is more than that—but it does make us reflect on which versions of history (or tradition) get passed down and which do not survive. It also makes us reflect on the role of memory in binding a people or a nation together.* Seider (2013) argues that "memory in the *Aeneid* acts as a social and narrative mechanism for integrating a traumatic past with an uncertain future" (4). Such memories are required in order to give a stranded people a sense of nationhood, a sense of meaning, a sense of origin and destination. Some memories fall out of favor and need to be appeased or erased and replaced with better and more palatable stories—as has already happened so many times in European history. And so, in the *Aeneid,* on both a small and a large scale, we see some memories being formed and others being let go. Aeneas chooses *not* to remember the night in the cave as marriage, even though Dido does.† Jupiter chooses to omit Remus' murder by Romulus in his prophecy at 1.292–93, and the forward-looking shield of Aeneas gets significant details wrong when it needs to. We see Jupiter telling Juno things that are inconsistent with what he has told Venus—overriding his own versions of what fate means. There is thus a sense in which Vergil, Aeneas, and Augustus are all doing the same thing: creating a collective memory by, in part, engaging in a collective forgetting.

More: an insistence on the importance of memory and forgetting undergirds the *Aeneid*'s whole narrative. From the poem's first lines, Juno's unwillingness to forget her grudges is the cause of the Trojans' suffering; and when that suffering ends, it's because Juno relents and agrees to support the Trojans—as long as their name and culture are forgotten (12.819–25, 834–37). This is Troy's final

---

* As Conte (1986) puts it, "The epic code is the medium through which society takes possession of its own past and gives that past the matrix value of a model" (124).

† If Hera's claim is not enough, Gordon Williams in *Tradition and Originality in Roman Poetry* (Oxford, 1968), 372, tells us that at the time of the poem, "marriage could exist without ceremony and formality, simply by consent of both parties."

status: although Aeneas has fought so hard to bring a "new Troy" to Italy, all markers of that identity, except religion, will disappear in its synthesis with the Italians. It takes this "forgetting" of Trojan identity to soothe Juno into forgetting her anger. It is surely not by accident that in Book 6, Vergil includes Plato's theory of the cycle of souls (metempsychosis), in which the dead have to forget their past in order to want to be reincarnated. Forgetting is essential if Octavian is to become Augustus, and if vengeance is to become *clementia* for his enemies. Aeneas casts his murder of Turnus at the end of the epic as an act of *pietas* on behalf of Pallas: and *perhaps* it is significant that Octavian would make the same claim on behalf of his father in the *Res Gestae*.* Yet Turnus' murder stands in contrast to all this other forgiveness and forgetting. In Book 6, Anchises tells Aeneas to remember to spare the defeated ("grant the conquered clemency," 6.853), but Aeneas has forgotten this in favor of another memory: one triggered by Pallas' sword-belt, now worn by Turnus. It is the memory of Pallas' death that then drives him to kill Turnus, to plant his sword in the man with the same verb that described him planting a city on the shores of Italy (*condo*; see translator's note). Had Aeneas not remembered Pallas' death, Turnus would have lived. Interestingly, the mechanism for awakening his memory is, in effect, a work of art: a sword-belt carved to tell a story.

Vergil's biographer Suetonius tells us an astonishing tale. In 19 BCE, when Vergil was on his deathbed, he summoned his friend Varius and asked him to burn the *Aeneid* before it was published (*Life of Vergil*, 39). We are not given a reason for this request, and in any case, the poem—Rome's great national epic—was made public immediately after Vergil's death at the direction of the emperor Augustus. But why would Vergil want his labor of more than ten years, his third and greatest work, to be destroyed? Two possible

---

* As James O'Hara has shown in *Death and the Optimistic Prophecy*, the accounts of the future given by the prophets in the epic generally leave out facts the immediate listener would not want to hear. Like the optimistic interpretations of the epic itself, they are only partial versions of a complicated story.

explanations have been advanced: first, that the poet was embarrassed by the epic's small number of unfinished lines (and the contradictions I have pointed out) and believed that it needed a finishing touch; second, that the violent conclusion to the story in Book 12 was not meant to be the actual ending, because how could our last sight of "pious Aeneas," the Trojan exile responsible for Rome's founding, be a man berserk with rage plunging his sword into the chest of his wounded and pleading enemy (so much for pardoning the defeated)? But I do not think these answers are persuasive. A writer does not destroy a ten-thousand-line masterpiece because it is marred by some half-lines, and the poem's violent end is not random, but picks up and resonates with its major themes, even reusing, in a different sense, the main verb of the opening lines—*condo,* meaning to plant (a city—or a sword).

One can only speculate, but it is curious that for so long, few scholars have acknowledged the way Vergil's narrative invites us to think about narratives, including itself. Vergil gives us so many clues to prompt us to think about stories, self-representation, and memory, but we continue to explain them away, including, in Book 6, Aeneas' departure from the Underworld through the gate of ivory, the gate of false dreams, after his father has predicted the future glories of Rome. We have even found it merely "puzzling" that the tracing of a Julian genealogy that goes back to Iülus/Ilus— presumably a raison d'être of the entire poem—runs into a competing tradition when Anchises identifies Silvius, Aeneas' posthumous son, a figure that has no relationship to the Julians, as the ancestor of the Romans (6.763). This disturbing claim lies at the center of the poem: Silvius, not Ascanius/Iülus, fathers the kings of Rome. It is a direct challenge to the role of Iülus as a tie between the Julians and Aeneas.*

The reading of the *Aeneid* as a piece of propaganda itself, I would argue, is precisely what its author worked so hard to avoid—which leads me to wonder if the dying Vergil realized, in a flash of lucid-

---

* See O'Hara (2007), 88–89.

ity, that this would be his poem's fate, right from the start, and therefore made his deathbed request.

DISCREDITED VOICES

The interpretation offered here is not the only way to read the poem, whose richness and complexity make it "good to think with" for so many other topics, from its elaborate metaphors to its complicated interaction with the Homeric epics, from its invocation of order over disorder to its polyphonic voices and multiple points of view. But precisely because the *Aeneid* (unlike the *Iliad* and the *Odyssey*) is an epic of foundation and has tacitly stood behind European quests for empire—quests disguised as bringing civilization to the benighted—it seems all the more important that we should be attentive to its "benighted" voices. David Quint, talking about the motif of the curse in epics before and after the *Aeneid*, points out that those who utter such curses are inevitably the losers, and that "the red man, the monster, the Eastern woman, the monster who is also a black man provide a catalog of types of the colonized 'other' into which the imperial epic turns the vanquished. . . . Nonetheless, these voices of resistance receive a hearing, as the epic poem acknowledges, intermittently, alternative accounts vying with its own official version of history: they are the bad conscience of the poem that simultaneously writes them in and out of its fiction" (99). We should consider, then, the unseductive narratives, the losing narratives, the ones that have not been granted legitimacy by scholars and readers, the ones that have gone nowhere, the ones that have tacitly been dismissed as hysterical and untruthful—or, as Gian Biagio Conte (1986) puts it, "the layers of suppressed cries and anguished, repressed memories" (154). Among these I do not count the stories of the Trojans or the Italians: the perspective of the former largely dominates the main narrative, while the latter end up triumphant in that the very name of Troy disappears after the Trojans join them.

Instead, let us turn to Dido's story. It has been easy to depreciate for so many reasons: she breaks the vow of chastity that sustains her identity, she is an "Eastern" foreigner (originally from Tyre) and belongs to a culture later opposed to the Romans, she loves too passionately (thanks to Venus and Amor), she gives up the task of building Carthage in order to spend time with Aeneas; she is over-come by rage and grief upon his departure; and of course she is a woman. Last but not least, for Vergil's readers she would have evoked Cleopatra, the dangerous Egyptian queen who was the lover of Augustus' rival Mark Antony. So Dido's remarks both be-fore and after she learns that Aeneas plans to leave have usually been dismissed as unworthy of serious consideration. It is now time to redress the balance.

Consider Dido's belief that she and Aeneas are married, often dismissed as wishful thinking. Here we are clearly presented with the incompatible intentions of two goddesses: Juno, who says they will be married (4.126: "I'll join them in a stable marriage; she'll be his," using words like *conubium* and *hymenaeus,* "marriage" and "wed-ding hymn"), and Venus, who only hopes for a temporary dalliance that will keep Aeneas safe in Carthage. Dido takes one point of view (Juno's), Aeneas the other (Venus'), and we are given no rea-son to privilege one over the other, except that Aeneas follows "fate." Or does he? Until Mercury's mission to prod Aeneas into reassuming his "destiny," Vergil makes it clear that Aeneas plans to stay in Carthage permanently as Dido's partner. As Jupiter says to Mercury,

> Go, my son:
> call the Zephyrs, glide down on your wings
> to meet the Dardan leader, who expects a future
> in Tyre's Carthage and ignores the towns chosen
> by fate. (4.222–26)

The lack of ambiguity here makes it all the more dubious when Aeneas assures Dido that he never intended to stay in Carthage; in his panic after Mercury's visit, he seems to have changed his whole story retroactively (again?). When he goes to speak to Dido, he tells her that not only were they never married, but if he could, he'd rebuild Troy rather than stay with her:

> I never held a husband's torch, or made that pact.
> If the fates would let me live the life I wanted
> and resolve my worries as I'd like,
> I'd first take care of Troy and my people's
> sweet remains. (4.339–43)

It is true that he never held a torch, and Aeneas, too, is entitled to his point of view. But it should not be given so much authority that it trumps statements by Juno and Jupiter as well as Dido.

Since she believes they are married, it's not surprising that Dido is shocked when she learns that Aeneas' men are preparing the ships for departure. Surprisingly, he has instructed his men to prepare their journey in secrecy and to "dissimulate" their departure to the queen (the narrator calls this "a trick," though Aeneas tells them he will speak to her later). But Aeneas claims to Dido that he *didn't* dissimulate and she should not claim he did (4.337–38: "I didn't try / to sneak away from here—don't pretend I did"). Dido's anger at Aeneas' abandonment is given textual justification that few of the epic's commentators seem to have absorbed, and the same for her charge that Aeneas is impious in his behavior toward her. After this, yes, Dido deteriorates rapidly into thoughts of revenge and suicide—death awaits her at the hands of her neighbors in Libya anyhow.* But her point of view is as justified as any other voice in the *Aeneid,* and it should not be disqualified as "female"—as it was already a century after Vergil, when the satirist Juvenal re-

---

* The critical reading that denies her language legitimacy has hinged largely upon the presence of a single word, *culpa,* "guilt": at 4.172, Dido hides/shields her guilt by calling their relationship marriage. Earlier (4.19), *culpa* is the word she uses for betraying her first husband, Sychaeus, to whom she'd sworn an oath of eternal fidelity following his tragic death.

marked on how sick he was of erudite women who defended Dido over dinner (*Satires* 6.434–35)! In corroboration of Dido's perspective, there are other episodes in the epic in which Aeneas' behavior is impious, such as his sacrifice of twelve living humans on Pallas' funeral pyre. Achilles descends to similar barbarism in the *Iliad*— and the narrator condemns it as an "evil deed" (*Iliad* 23.175–76) even if Achilles is not, like Aeneas, supposed to be "pious."

Rather than giving further examples of women whose comments contain valid information or perspectives, Creusa and Amata among them (Aeneas' bride, Lavinia, utters not one word), I want to turn to the goddess Juno, whose rage drives the epic. *Her* voice is certainly not silenced, but her enduring rage at the Trojans is made to seem unreasonable, both because it arises from sexual snubs and because Jupiter and Venus think it is irrational. However, Juno's precursor in rage is the heroic Achilles of the *Iliad,* and their relationship is made clear by a clever intertextual pun. The first word of the *Iliad* is "rage": *menin,* in Greek. The first words Juno speaks in the *Aeneid* elide to make the homophone *menin* as well: "*me ne incepto*" ("am *I* [to desist from] my plan," 1.37), spoken aloud, would be pronounced "*menin-cepto.*"* A goddess has taken on Achilles' sulking rage, but in her it is treated as both more deadly and more silly. The other angry women of the epic are likewise undermined, either by the characters or by the narrator: when Mercury warns Aeneas of Dido's rage, he adds, "Females are a fickle thing, / always prone to change" (4.569–70), and the crew who see her pyre from a distance know "what a woman's passion could unleash" (5.6). Amata, upset at the arrival of the Trojans, is "seething with a woman's angst and anger" (7.344), angst and anger being gendered female here. And of course it is the female Fury Allecto who has the capacity to cast rage into Amata and Turnus. But if rage (excluding battle-fury) is so female, what are we to think of Aeneas' rage at the end of the epic? Here Aeneas is described in the same terms as the angry Juno who has tried to destroy the Trojans. His

---

* As ingeniously pointed out by Levitan (1993).

rage is "savage," like Juno herself in 1.4; what triggers him is memory (also 1.4); he "burns" with fury (Juno in 1.29); and his question "Should I let you slip away?" likewise echoes (more closely in the Latin) Juno's first indignant question at 1.37: How could the Trojans be saved from her? In the epic's last image, Aeneas brings our minds to none other than the unforgetting and unforgiving Juno. The furious goddess has subsided, but the rabid Roman takes her place. And here this national epic ends.

TRANSLATOR'S NOTE

WHAT IS THE POINT of a new English translation of the *Aeneid* when so many already exist? There are many excellent translations of the poem in circulation, several of which have long been favorite choices in schools and colleges as well as among the general public. But all translators bring a certain worldview with them, and to date, this view has been mostly a male, European-American point of view. Perhaps, then, it is not insignificant that I grew up as a foreigner in other people's countries (including Indonesia, Iran, and the Fiji Islands as well as Europe)—not as a refugee, but as an outsider to the dominant culture, an observer rather than a participant. And I am a woman in a discipline that was still marked by gender imbalance when I was doing my studies; of the many teachers and professors I worked with, only one was female. Compounding all this, Latin literature was largely written by men for men and read by a comparatively small elite. But as I have argued, I don't think the *Aeneid* brings those biases with it: instead, it invites us to explore what they mean. In my translation, I have made a conscious effort not to automatically accept the poem's dominant perspectives. These might *seem* to be presented as a universal point of view, but—if we listen—they work to undermine their own authority. Since triumphal narratives often triumph by obscuring less authoritative ones, I have tried, in the introduction and notes, to help the first-time reader of the *Aeneid* see the muted threads in its tapestry.

I have also tried to create a radically different reading experience by being attentive to the *pace* of Vergil's epic. Latin, a dense, lapidate language without definite articles, can say much in a few words. This generally means that to translate any line of Latin verse, one must expand the line considerably to have it make sense in idiomatic English; often, too, one must spell out what can be simply alluded to in Latin. Take, for example, Neptune's statement to the winds at Book I, line 136: *"Post mihi non simili poena commissa luetis."* This means something like "Later, you will atone to me for the things you have done, but your punishment then will not be the same as your punishment now, which is only a rebuke in words." This translation increases the original seven words to thirty-one— and is hardly practicable.* And this difficulty in turn means that translators of the *Aeneid* to date have had three options: to produce a work that is much longer than the original; to keep line-to-line correspondence but end up with long, unwieldly verses that weigh down the speed of the original; or to reproduce the shorter lines and fast tempo of the poem by sacrificing some of the content or writing what critics sometimes call "a poem in its own right." I did not want to write a poem in its own right; I wanted to stay as close as possible to the language of the original *and* maintain its tempo. Allen Mandelbaum's 1961 translation, which I admire, is very close to the Latin but lengthens the original by a third, while the poetry of other translations moves away from Vergil's own language. Here I've tried to respect the Latin while matching the translation to the poem line by line (with variations as demanded by syntax) and not allowing any line of verse to take more time than Vergil's.

Time matters, because reading—at least in Greek and Latin poetry—is all about time. Roman poets wrote in a variety of meters depending on the genre of their work (epic, elegy, lyric), and those meters in turn were composed of a number of "feet" per line. Each foot contained a combination of long and short syllables; since Vergil wrote in dactylic hexameters, each line had six feet of three or two syllables each, a mixture of long and short. The total aural

---

* My translation reads: "Then / you'll get what you deserve, and it won't be in words!"

effect combined syllabic length, the ictus (the stress on the first syllable of the foot), and the naturally stressed syllable of each word used. The meter, imagery, and effects—such as alliteration—were what made the "poetry," since the Romans did not use end-rhymes. But because English meters work by stress rather than syllabic length, it is impossible to reproduce the effect of Latin meter in English.* Instead, one can use stress to correlate with the number of feet by using six "beats" per line, as I have mostly done. After some experimentation, I compromised between the familiarity of Shakespearean blank verse and Vergil's meter by allowing six, sometimes five, beats in my iambic lines. (Dryden's translation, dating to the seventeenth century, also uses iambs, along with end-rhyme.) These beats are the beating heart of the poem: they carry it forward in time and space and bind the aural experience together.

Along with trying to stay true to the original while reproducing some of the excitement and immediacy of the Latin poem, this problem of time and space posed my greatest technical challenge. One concession I made to the compact quality of Latin verse was to omit formulaic expressions that could be left out without affecting the meaning. For example, the Latin contains a lot of "Having said this, s/he then . . ." Latin in general also features a lot of hendiadys (two words for one idea), which I have sometimes short-

---

* Let's take the first line of Longfellow's *Evangeline* as an example. Like the *Aeneid,* it is written in dactylic hexameter, but even so English cannot reproduce the combined effect of ictus, stress, and syllable length. In the illustration from Longfellow below, I have capitalized the stressed syllables, which are also the syllables where the ictus falls. In the English, there is no complicated tug between different stress locations, and syllable length is not a consideration. In the following line of Latin dactylic hexameter, the first line of the *Aeneid,* I have capitalized the words' native stress, italicized the syllables on which the ictus falls, and underlined the long syllables. Since these effects do not fall in the same places, the result is much more complicated than the English line:

Longfellow: THIS is the FORest primEVal. The MURmuring PINES and the HEMlocks: six clear beats.

Vergil: <u>AR</u>ma VIR*um*-que CA*no*, <u>TROI</u>-*ae* qui <u>*PRIM*</u>-us ab <u>OR</u>-is: six beats (ictus); nine long syllables; six natural stresses, but only three in the same place as the ictus.

ened. I have very occasionally left out other low-content phrases ("While these events were taking place in Carthage . . .") and, when forced to, patronymics. I have not, however, written half-lines to match Vergil's unfinished half-lines—as a translator, I frankly welcomed the extra space to catch up if I was running over in length.

The third greatest challenge has been, of course, vocabulary. Latin words do not map cleanly onto English words, and this gives every translator a choice of which term brings the most appropriate nuances for the situation. At the same time, some words in the poem carry a particular semantic and ideological load that should not be concealed from the reader by a variety of ever-changing translations. Consider the verb *condo*. *Condo* basically has the sense of "to put x in y" or "to store / put away x" (including in one's memory). It also means to bury, to hide, to plunge a weapon into a body, to found or establish (as a city)—and to compose verse! Accordingly, there is no one translation of a given word that the translator can use consistently if the poem is to make good sense. But the translator *can* choose to signal the places where the poet's use of the verb delivers a striking message. In the case of *condo*, we are told at the beginning of Book 1 that Aeneas will "found" the high walls of Rome, and throughout that book, the verb often recurs in this sense. But at the end of Book 12, the meaning of *condo* as a foundational act is transformed into Turnus' murder, as Aeneas *sinks* his sword into Turnus' chest. It has been important to me to bring this across in the translation, so I have used the same English verb, "plant," in both the first and this last instance. Another important verb is *cano*, "to sing," which is the traditional word for writing or reciting epic poetry: "I sing of war and a man." When Dido exclaims of Aeneas' story that he *sang* of so many wars, I have retained the verb even though it is slightly jarring in the English because it is an important marker that connects the *Aeneid* as a poem to Aeneas' story.

Any translator confronting the *Aeneid* faces one obvious and immediate problem (as its early translator Dryden observed): what to do with the words *pius* and *pietas*. This adjective and noun pair (it is the adjective with which Aeneas himself is most often characterized) have no exact correlations in English: *pius* does not quite mean "pious" in the Christian sense but is characterized by devotion to family, gods, and country; loyal, faithful, responsible, dutiful, and patriotic—and the noun *pietas* includes the same meanings. I therefore had to face the question: Should I select the correct translation for *context* each time the word occurred (as in fact I often do with less charged terminology), or should I use the same word each time, showing the thread it weaves throughout the epic? Since the term is used so self-consciously by Vergil himself, the answer must be the latter, and likewise for *impius*, as in the *impius Furor* of Book 1. And since no English word will cover the ideological breadth we need (we can hardly talk of good Aeneas and ungood Furor), I have chosen the best path I could find, which is to keep "pious" and "piety" but to mark their first appearances in the poem with a note reminding readers of the cluster of meanings these words contain. It is up to the reader now to keep this in mind, and to remember that pious Aeneas is not lighting candles to a monotheistic entity.

Finally, there is the matter of sound. Vergil was a master of alliteration and used it to great effect, often matching the sound to the semantic content of the verse. One famous example is the noise of the winds enclosed in their mountain cave in Book 1, lines 54–56: *"Illi indignantes magno cum murmure montis / circum claustra fremunt."* Here, the repetition of the *m* sounds evokes the murmuring noise of the winds, and my translation tries to maintain this effect:

> They roared around the latches
> outraged. Over them, the mountain murmured
> mightily.

Another well-known example comes as the twin snakes approach the Trojan coast to murder Laocoön and his two sons. The

Latin there is full of sibilants, creating an onomatopoeic effect to evoke the serpents' hiss, and my English, I hope, is pretty hissy too (2.209–11).

> The sea foamed and splashed: then they were ashore.
> Their eyes were flaming, shot with blood and fire.
> As they hissed, they licked their jaws with flicking tongues

Like Vergil, then, I have relied on alliteration rather than self-consciously poetic language. This is true also in places of high drama, both in the original and in the translation. Euryalus' death offers an example (9.434ff):

> his neck slumped
> like a purple flower cut down by a plow,
> bending as it dies, like a poppy's drooping
> neck when heavy rain drags down its head.

(This alliteration, however, is not always correlated to the places where Vergil uses it, as my primary aim has been to maintain clarity and meter.)

Vergil also uses elision (the disappearance of the final syllable of a word before the initial vowel of another word) to create effects that unfortunately can't be replicated in English, like his famous description of the "misshapen mass" of the Cyclops (3.658): *"monstrum horrendum, informe, ingens."* In Latin this line would lose many of its syllables and run together in a misshapen mass itself: *"monstrorrendinforimngens."* My translation simply reads "a gross misshapen massive monster," using alliteration and a series of run-on adjectives as a substitute for Vergil's brilliant line. There is only so much one can do!

The principles and practices I have written of above are part of a conscious philosophy of translation that I adopted for this work. Another important part of that philosophy was to keep the intended audience in mind. I anticipated not only an audience of student readers and the general public who would like a readable version of the *Aeneid,* but also readers who could press the text and know that they could get a reliable idea of what Vergil actually said—for example, graduate students and teachers without Latin. This has been one reason for my attempt to stay close to the original and to avoid metaphors not in the source text, to resist extending a short line into a long line, compressing or expanding at random, and to avoid simply following my own poetic flights of fancy.

The classicist D. E. Hill wrote in 1978 that "none of the popular Vergilian translations" can provide what is required for teaching Vergil in translation. I believe that that is probably still true, and may always be.* After all, every translation imports something of the translator into the text. For all my efforts to be transparent, this is *my Aeneid.* So I have tried to alleviate that problem. Hill argued for the importance of rendering verse in verse; of not changing the alien features of a different culture so as to make them familiar to the modern reader; of not choosing unusual or highfalutin words where Vergil uses ordinary ones; of not eliminating place-names, genealogies, and customs. He stressed likewise the importance of a strong metrical beat and of line-to-line correlation. Finally, he pointed out that literal need not mean pedestrian, and that a translation "freed from the text and soaring into literary beauties" does us no good—if we want to read *Vergil.* With all of this I am in strong agreement, including around archaizing or sounding "old-fashioned." Although this may seem to confer dignity on a text, and dignity has value (one might think of the enduring popularity of the King James Bible), Vergil's contemporary readers did not experience him as an archaizer, nor should we. On the plus side, this means that this translation sheds any artificial claims to the weighty authority of a text too "classical" to be read, enjoyed, and even challenged. As Kate Kellaway wrote in *The Guard-*

* D. E. Hill, "What Sort of Translation of Virgil Do We Need?" In Ian McAuslan and Peter Walcot, eds., *Virgil* (Oxford, 1990).

ian of Seamus Heaney's translation of *Aeneid* Book 6, "Getting the diction right—so that the ancient is neither modern nor archaic—is the challenge. And Heaney shows that plain words are storm-proofed. It is about more than George Orwell's tired prescription: 'Never use a long word where a short one will do.' It is about how plain language, like plain speaking, has integrity." This translation, too, strives for such integrity.

There are, of course, differences of register in the poem: it is more dignified in some places than in others. While the narrative is generally simple and straightforward, some individual speakers have their own styles, which I have tried to communicate in the English. Juno's often obnoxious and colloquial voice is especially striking. Here she is in Book 10, pointing out that Aeneas deserves what he gets:

> Fine, he came to Italy guided by fate
> (or forced by mad Cassandra): did *I* urge
> him to leave his camp and trust his life to winds?
> To put his son in charge, rely on walls,
> rile up Tuscan loyalties and peaceful clans?
> Which god drove him to deceit? What harshness
> of mine? Where's Juno here, or Iris from the sky? (67–73)

Aeneas, however, is almost always serious—or despairing. His mission allows for little levity, and indeed, the first time we see him he is wishing he were dead. Here he is apostrophizing his old enemy Diomedes from the *Iliad*:

> "Three and four times fortunate, all you who died
> by Troy's high walls under your fathers' gaze!
> O Diomedes, bravest of the Greeks!
> I wish I'd fallen on Troy's fields, my blood spilled
> by your strong right hand, where fierce Hector perished
> on Achilles' spear, and huge Sarpedon too . . ." (1.94–99)

At times we have moments of almost slapstick humor in the narrative. They are particularly frequent in Book 5 during the Trojan Games, as when an impatient ship captain throws his helmsman overboard, or when Nisus slips in dung and trips someone else in turn. On the other hand, similes are often in a loftier register, as are temporal transitions—dawns and nightfalls—and as such we often get high epic lines such as "And now Dawn left Tithonus' saffron bed / to pour fresh light upon the land." I have tried to respect such shifts in tone, while avoiding what Emily Wilson has called in her recent translation of the *Odyssey* "the Charybdis of artifice and the Scylla of slang." I have also maintained Vergil's original metaphors, even if at times they seem strange to us: wings compared to oars, ships guided by reins, and natural phenomena personified. (His similes are also striking: a battle as a hailstorm, a crippled ship as a maimed snake.) I have not softened features of antiquity that are unpleasant to us today: female slaves are not "maids," and they are given away as prizes for games without further comment. Jupiter is a rapist, of both boys and young women. The hero Aeneas may be pious, but that doesn't stop Turnus from calling him a "half-man" (in fact, the charge of effeminacy was a common Roman view of "soft Asiatic types" in Vergil's own day).

Though the highest praise bestowed on a new translation is that "it reads like a work of poetry in its own right" (almost every translation I own sports such a blurb on its back cover), I have tried instead to create a parallel to the experience of reading Vergil in Latin. To that end, and to the best of my knowledge, this is the only translation that combines all the following features in a single version of the poem: the use of meter, line-to-line correspondence, verses that do not exceed Vergil's six beats, simplicity of language, a full glossary, fidelity to the original, the Vergilian effects of alliteration and assonance, notes on the text when modern readers might not be aware of the subtext, and of course an introduction. But all principles aside, translating the *Aeneid* has been a labor of love. My four years of being immersed in this poem at the level of individual lines that I have reshaped over and over again have brought me an even greater appreciation of the mind that crafted it. I hope that reading this version of Rome's foundational epic brings you some of the pleasure that reading it in Latin brings to me.

THE AENEID

THE AENEID.

BOOK I

LANDFALL AT CARTHAGE

My song is of war and a man: a refugee by fate,
the first from Troy to Italy's Lavinian shores,
battered much on land and sea by blows from gods
obliging brutal Juno's unforgetting rage;
he suffered much in war as well, all to plant
his town and gods in Latium. From here would rise
the Latin race, the Alban lords, and Rome's high walls.

Remember for me, Muse. Tell me the reasons. What pain,
what insult to her power, moved the queen of gods
to drive a man famous for piety* through misery   10
on misery? Can such anger grip gods' minds?

An ancient city built by colonists from Tyre
faced Italy and Tiber's mouth across the sea:
wealthy Carthage, fierce and fond of waging war.
They say that Juno loved her best; even Samos
came in second. Here the goddess kept her weapons
and her chariot; this land would rule the world
if fate allowed. This was her aim and hope.
But she'd heard that men of Trojan blood
would topple Carthage and her heights one day.   20
They'd be a people proud in war, an empire
fatal for her Libya. This was what the Fates had
spun, this was Juno's fear. She remembered
how she'd fought at Troy to help her cherished Greeks.

Still other reasons for her rage and bile
remained deep-rooted in her heart: Paris' scornful
verdict on her beauty, the honors paid by Jove
to kidnapped Ganymede, her hatred for that race.*
Enflamed by this, she barred from Latium
the sea-tossed Trojans, the few left by the Greeks   30
and cruel Achilles. They roamed for many years,
over many oceans, forced on by the Fates.
To found the Roman race required such great effort.

Sicily had slipped from sight. The Trojans gladly
sailed for open sea, their bronze prows churning foam.
But Juno, nursing her eternal wound, thought
to herself: "Am *I* to leave off from my plan
and fail to turn the Trojan king from Italy?
It seems that Fate forbids it. Then how could Pallas
burn the Argive fleet and drown its crew, just to   40
punish the mad crime of Ajax, son of Oïleus?*
On her own, she hurled Jove's* lightning from the clouds,
wrecked the ships, and whipped up waves with wind;
she grabbed up Ajax in a gust and spiked him on sharp
reefs—the man puffed fire from his punctured chest!
But *me,* the queen of all the gods, Jove's wife
and sister too, for years I've had to fight
against a single race! *Now* who'll worship me
or put gifts on my altars as a supplicant?"

Her hot heart fixed on these thoughts, Queen Juno reached   50
Aeolia, a land that teemed with storms and clouds.
In his colossal cave, King Aeolus
ruled the warring winds and howling gales
and locked them up inside. They roared around the latches
outraged. Over them, the mountain murmured
mightily. Aeolus, sitting in his stronghold,

scepter in his hand, soothed their angry spirits.
Otherwise, they'd seize the oceans, lands,
and deepest sky, and blast them all away.
It was this fear that made the mighty Father   60
hide them in a lightless cave and heap mountains
on top. He chose a king who swore he'd curb
the winds or free their reins as he was told.
Now Juno came to wheedle him: "Aeolus,
the father of the gods and king of men
chose you to calm the waves or whip them up with wind.
A race I hate travels the Tuscan sea:
they bring the beaten gods of Troy to Italy.
Rouse the winds to gale-force, sink the ships,
or scatter them and fling the crew into the sea.   70
In my retinue are fourteen gorgeous nymphs;
Deiopea is the loveliest of all. She's yours—
just do me this favor. I'll join you both
in lasting marriage, so she'll spend her years
with you and make you father to fair children."

Aeolus said: "Your task, O Queen, is to know
your wish and will; mine, to make it happen.
Thanks to you, I have this little kingdom
and Jupiter's goodwill, I dine with gods,
I'm master of the storms and wild weather."   80

Saying this, he struck the hollow mountain
with the butt-end of his spear. A battle-line
of winds rushed out the rift and swept over the lands.
Notus, Eurus, and Africus, full of storms,*
settled on the sea as one and churned it
from its bed; they rolled huge waves to shore.
Next came the shouts of men, the shriek of ropes.
At once, storm-clouds snatched the sky from sight.

Black night brooded on the sea. The heavens
thundered, frequent flashes tore the dark.   90
All signs warned the men that death had come.

At once Aeneas' knees buckled with chill.
He groaned and held up both hands to the stars:
"Three and four times fortunate, all you who died
by Troy's high walls under your fathers' gaze!
O Diomedes, bravest of the Greeks!
I wish I'd fallen on Troy's fields, my blood spilled
by your strong right hand, where fierce Hector perished
on Achilles' spear, and huge Sarpedon too;
where Simoïs rolls in its stream so many shields   100
and helmets, so many bodies of the brave."

As he spoke, the howling north wind hit the sails
head-on and pushed the sea up to the stars.
The oars snapped and the ship swung broadside
to the waves; a wall of water crashed on deck.
Some sailors hung on crests, some saw seabed
as each wave loomed up. The sea boiled with sand.
Notus snatched three ships and hurled them onto reefs
that lurked mid-sea, the ones Italians call Altars,
huge spines near the surface. Eurus drove   110
three boats into the shoals, a sorry sight, and smashed
them on the rocks. Sand built up around them.
Before Aeneas' eyes, a giant wave broke on
the ship of good Orontes and his Lycians.
It threw the helmsman off the deck headfirst into
wild waters. Eddies spun the ship around
three times, then the raging undertow engulfed it.
A few men surfaced in the vast abyss. Weapons,*
planks, and Trojan treasure floated in the waves.
The storm seized Ilioneus' sturdy ship,   120
brave Achates' ship, Abas' ship, and old

Aletes' ship. They all let in fatal water
through the hulls' loose seams and gaping cracks.

Now Neptune sensed the sea's chaos and clamor,
the storm Aeolus sent. He felt the churning
of the sluggish waters of the deep. Perplexed,
he raised his peaceful face and scanned the sea.
He saw Aeneas' wave-tossed ships, the Trojans
swamped by swells and the ruin of the sky.
Juno's angry treachery was clear to him.   130
He called Eurus and Zephyrus,* and said to them:

"Is it your noble birth that makes you bold?
You winds now dare to mingle sky and earth
and stir up waves without permission? Why,
I should—But first I'll soothe the wild sea.
Then you'll get what you deserve, and not in words!
Get out of here, now, and tell your king:
rule over the sea and savage trident's *mine*
by lot, not his. *His* kingdom is the cave
where you live, Eurus. Let him strut in that court   140
and rule there—once his winds are jailed."

Faster than his words, Neptune soothed the swells,
routed huddled clouds, brought back the sun.
Cymothoe and Triton pried the ships off crags;
Neptune helped them with his trident. He cleared
pathways through long shoals and calmed the sea,
skimming wave-crests lightly in his chariot.
Just as riots often fester in great crowds
when the common mob goes mad; rocks and
firebrands fly, their fury provides weapons;*   150
but if they see a man of weight in piety
and service, they hush and wait to hear him;
he guides their minds and soothes their hearts with words—

just so, all the tumult of the sea died down
once Neptune scanned the waters. He turned his team
and let them run free under cloudless skies.*

Aeneas' tired crew fights to reach the nearest
shore; they bend toward the Libyan coast.
There, an island's deep bay forms a harbor
with its sides. Every wave from the high sea   160
is broken here and fans out to the curving coves.
On both sides sheer cliffs and matching crags
menace the sky, but underneath, safe pools
lie wide and still. Above, a rustling forest
sets the scene, dark with trembling shade.
A cave with rocky overhangs faces the front.
It has freshwater pools and stones for seats,
the home of nymphs. Here no cables tie
the weary boats, no anchor bites the sand.
Aeneas enters with his ships, seven left   170
from all the fleet. With great love of land,
the Trojans reach the shore they craved, disembark,
and rest their sodden limbs on sand. Achates
is the first to strike a spark from flint.
He kindles fire with leaves and sets dry fodder
on the flames, then feeds the blaze with twigs.
Weary from their wandering, they fetch the pots
and spoiled grain they rescued from the waves, then dry
the food with fire and crush it under stone.

Meanwhile Aeneas scales a cliff, and scans   180
the spread of ocean, wondering if he'd perhaps see
some Trojan ships, sea-tossed Antheus, Capys,
or Caicus' shield attached to a high stern.
There's no ship in sight, but three stags stray
along the shore. Behind them come whole herds
of deer, the long line grazing through the gorge.

He stops and grabs his bow and flying shafts,
the weapons loyal Achates holds for him.
First he drops the leading stags, whose antlers
branch on heads held high. Then he drives   190
the panicked herd all through the leafy woods.
He only stops after he's vanquished seven
massive beasts, the number of his ships.
Back at port, he splits the meat among his crew
and shares the wine which kind Acestes poured
in heavy jars when they left Sicily—
a hero's gift—and comforts their sad hearts.

"My friends: we're no strangers to misfortune.
You've suffered worse; some god will end this too.
You slipped past savage Scylla and her crags that rang   200
with barks, you saw the Cyclops' rocks. Be brave,
let go your fear and despair. Perhaps someday
even memory of this will bring you pleasure.
Through good times and bad, through many trials,
we make for Latium.* There the fates
promise us rest; there Troy must rise again.
Hold on. Save your strength for better days to come."

So he says. Though he's sick with crushing cares,
he feigns hope on his face* and clamps down his deep pain.
They prepare the game, their future feast,   210
hacking hide from ribs, laying bare the guts.
Some slice the quivering meat to thread on spits,
some set cauldrons on the shore and tend the fires.
Sprawling on the grass, they restore their strength
with food, gorging on old wine and fatty game.
Once their hunger's sated and the dishes cleared,
they ask after lost friends, talking at length,
wavering between hope and fear—are they alive,
or have they met their end, now deaf to any calls?

Pious Aeneas* grieves the most, but secretly: 220
for keen Orontes' fate, for Amycus, for Lycus'
cruel death, for brave Gyas, brave Cloanthus.

Now their grief was done. Jupiter looked down
from heaven's height onto the sail-swept sea,
the lands and shores and far-flung folk. From his
lofty seat, he fixed his gaze on Libya.
And as he dwelled on his concerns, sad Venus,
her eyes wet with shiny tears, came to him.
"You who rule the lives of gods and men,
a terror with your thunderbolts, what did   230
my Aeneas and the Trojans—so many
dead already—ever do to you? All lands
are closed to them on Italy's account.
You promised once that they'd give rise to Romans,
that in the circling years leaders would rise
from Teucer's blood to rule the land and sea.
Father, what made you change your mind? This was
my consolation for Troy's fall and tragic ruin
when I weighed one fate against the other.
Now the same curse hounds them, after all   240
their suffering! Great king, has their pain no end?
Antenor could dodge the Greeks at Troy, reach
Adriatic shores in safety, and travel deep
into Liburnia. He saw Timavus' source,
where the sea comes inland through nine paths
and bursts out noisily, engulfing fields with surf.
He founded Padua, a home for Teucrians,
gave his citizens a name and put away
his Trojan armor. Now he lives in peace, retired.
But we, your blood! You promised us the heights of heaven,   250
then betrayed us to a single female's rage.
Our ships are lost and we're kept far from Italy.
This is our prize for piety? This, our triumph?"

. . .

Smiling at her with the look that calms the sky
and storms, the forefather of gods and men
gently kissed his daughter and replied:
"Let go your fear, Cytherea. Your people's fate
remains unchanged: you'll see Lavinium and
its promised walls, you'll raise great-souled Aeneas
to the stars. I haven't changed my mind.   260
Since this worry gnaws at you, I'll tell you more,
and unroll the secrets of the fates. Your son
will wage wide war in Italy, subdue
ferocious tribes, and give them walls and customs.*
After the Latins lose, Aeneas will be king
in Latium three summers and three winters.
His son Ascanius, now called Iülus
(he was Ilus during Ilium's reign)
will rule for thirty cycling years of cycling months.
He will move Lavinium's seat of power   270
and strengthen Alba Longa with high walls.*
Here, when Hector's line has ruled three hundred
years, the priestess Ilia, pregnant by Mars,
will have his twins.* Romulus, clad in his foster
mother's tawny wolf-pelt, will gladly lead
his people. With Mars' help, he'll build Rome's
walls and name the Romans for himself.
On them I set no boundaries of time or space:
I've granted empire without end. Even cruel
Juno, terror of the land and sea and sky,   280
will change her plans and (like me) favor Romans:
people of the toga, rulers of the world.
So I've decreed. As years slip by, an age
will come when Assaracus' house will conquer
Argos and crush Phthia and famed Mycenae.*
Trojan Caesar* will be born, of lovely Venus' line,
whose rule will reach all shores, his fame the stars

—Julius, a name passed down from great Iülus.
Freed from worry, you'll greet him in the skies.
He'll come laden with Eastern spoils, and men will pray   *290*
to him; harsh centuries of war will cease.
Ancient Trust and Vesta, Remus and Quirinus
will set down laws; the awful iron Gates of War
will close. Inside, impious Rage, crouched on
brutal weapons, tied up with a hundred knots
of bronze, will roar from blood-stained jaws."

Now Jupiter sent Mercury, the son of Maia,
to make sure the lands and citadel of Carthage
would greet the Trojans kindly, and so Dido,
blind to fate, would not drive them off. He flew   *300*
across the width of sky, sweeping wings like oars,
and soon reached Libya. He did his task: the people
quelled their fierce hearts; the queen especially
took up a calm and kindly view of Trojans.

Pious Aeneas worried greatly through the night.
When gentle dawn appeared, he decided to explore
this unknown land, to find out where he'd sailed
and learn who lived there, animals or men—
what he saw looked wild. Then he'd bring back news.
He hid the fleet inside an inlet hemmed   *310*
by woods, close to overhanging cliffs,
among the quivering shade of trees. Then he left
with two broad-bladed spears, Achates at his side.

His mother met him in mid-forest, with a young girl's
face and dress. She had weapons that a Spartan
girl might carry, or Harpalyce of Thrace,
who tires horses and outruns the rushing river
Hebrus. Huntress-like,* she'd slung a handy bow
across her back. Her hair streamed on the wind,

her knees were bare, a knot held up her dress's folds.   320
Meeting them, she asked: "Young men, did you
chance on any of my sisters roaming here
in a lynx's dappled hide, holding a quiver,
or shouting on the heels of a foaming boar?"

Venus' son replied to her as follows:
"I haven't seen or heard a trace of them.
But how should I address you? Your face and voice
do not seem mortal. Goddess—as you must be—
are you Apollo's sister? Does nymph-blood run in you?
I hope that seeing you will ease our hardship.   330
What skies are these, where on earth have we washed up?
Tell us. We don't know this place or people.
We're wanderers, and driven by the winds and tides.
My hand will offer many victims at your altars."

But Venus said: "I don't deserve such honor.
We Tyrian girls all sport a quiver, we all tie
the laces of our purple boots high on our shins.
You see a Punic colony, Agenor's men.
But Libya, unsubdued in battle, borders us.
Dido of Tyre is our queen: she left her home   340
fleeing her own brother. It's a long and complex
tale of wrong, but here's the gist of it:*

Sychaeus, Dido's husband, had more land
than any Tyrian. Poor Dido loved him greatly.
Her father married them when she was still a virgin.
But Pygmalion, her brother—a prodigy
of evil!—was the king. Some mad feud estranged
the men, and her impious brother, blind with lust
for gold, caught and killed Sychaeus at the altar,
indifferent to his sister's love. For long that swine   350
concealed his crime. He tricked the heartsick wife

with empty hope and spun her many tales.
But in her dreams, her husband's ghost appeared to her
unburied, raising his pale and eerie face.
He showed her the cruel altar, his pierced chest,
and described the evil hidden in their home.
He urged her to leave their land at once,
and revealed a treasure buried long ago—
an unknown weight of gold and silver—for the trip.
Shaken, Dido planned escape, selected friends.   360
Those who loathed or feared the tyrant gathered.
They seized whatever ships were ready, loading them
with gold. The riches that the greedy man had craved
voyaged the sea, and a woman led the act!
They reached this place where you now see great walls
and the growing stronghold of new Carthage,
a region they call Byrsa from their purchase—
as much land as a bull's-hide cut in strips could circle.*
But who are you, what country are you from,
where do you head?" Aeneas answered with a sigh,   370
and drew his words from deep inside his heart:

"Goddess, if I traced my story from the start
and you had time to hear the history of our pain,
the Evening Star would close the day and heaven's gates.
We come from what was Troy—perhaps its name has reached
your ears? But as we traveled many seas, a storm
drove us to Libya's coast. I'm pious Aeneas.
On my fleet, I carry the Penates, gods snatched
from the enemy; my fame reaches the sky,
my blood is Jove's. I head for Italy, our home.   380
I launched twenty ships upon the Phrygian sea,
following fate, and my mother showed the way.
Just seven ships survive, lashed by wind and waves.
And I—I roam the Libyan desert, unknown, beggared,

spurned by East and West." Venus was annoyed
by these complaints, and she cut his laments short.

"I doubt the gods despise you, whoever you may be.
You breathe the air, you're near a Tyrian town.
Continue, and you'll reach the palace of the queen.
I have some news: your friends are safe,* your fleet   390
is here, blown by shifting winds—unless
my parents taught me augury in vain.
See those twelve swans gladly flying in formation?
Jove's great eagle plunged from open skies
and scattered them. Now, regrouped, they land
in a long line, or gaze at those who've landed.
Just as they've returned, flapping their wings
in play, wheeling round the sky with honks,
so too your ships and men have entered port
or now approach the harbor with full sail.   400
Keep on, and follow where the trail leads."

As she turned away, her neck gleamed rosily,
her ambrosial hair gave off a divine scent
and her robes grew longer, flowing to her feet.
Her gait too revealed the goddess. But Aeneas,
when he recognized his mother, called to her:
"Why trick your son so often with disguises?*
You're as cruel as the other gods. Why can't I
ever hold your hand in mine, or speak frankly?"

Grumbling so, he turned his steps to town.   410
As they went, Venus veiled them in dark mist
and draped them with a heavy cloak of cloud,
so no one could see or stumble on them,
or cause delay or ask why they were there.
She herself went up to Paphos, happy to

go home, where her temple's hundred altars
were fragrant with fresh wreaths and warm with incense.

Meanwhile they hurried on along the path.
They climbed a hill that steeply overhung
the town, and looked down on the citadel.   420
Aeneas admired its size (once it had mere huts),
its gates, the hubbub and the cobbled streets.
One group worked to raise the walls and fortify
the citadel; they rolled up rocks by hand.
Some shaped homesteads, circling them with trenches,
or chose a sacred senate, laws and offices.
Here men hollowed out a harbor; there they laid down
bedrock for a theater, and hacked tall columns
out of cliffs to ornament a future stage.
They were like busy bees in fields of flowers   430
in the early summer, when they lead out
their grown young or cram the combs with honey
and swell them with sweet nectar, or unload
returning bees, or join in ranks to drive
the idle throng of drones off from their hives.
The work hums along, the honey smells of thyme.
"Lucky you, whose walls are rising now,"
cried Aeneas as he stared up at the rooftops.
Fenced around by mist, he walked the crowded streets.
Amazingly, he mixed with them and no one saw.   440

The city center held a thickly shaded grove
where the Tyrians, tossed by storms at sea,
had first dug up the omen Juno spoke of,
a stallion's head—meaning they'd be a race
unmatched in war and prosperous through the ages.
Here, Dido of Tyre was building Juno a huge
temple, rich in gifts, rich in her godly presence.
At the entry rose bronze stairs, the doorposts too

were bronze, the door creaked on bronze hinges.
In this grove first, a sight appeared that eased   450
Aeneas' fear and let him dare to dream
of safety, to have more hope in troubled times.*
As he scanned each detail of the giant temple,
waiting for the queen, and admired the city's
fortune and its craftsmen's skill and work, he saw
the stages of the Trojan War, the battles blazoned
by their fame across the world, Atreus's
sons, King Priam, and Achilles cruel to both.
He stopped in tears: "Achates, what place on earth,
what land isn't steeped in what we've suffered? Look: 460
it's Priam. Here too, glory has rewards;
the world weeps, and mortal matters move the heart.
Let go your fear. This fame will bring some safety."
He spoke, and fed his soul on empty images,
sighing heavily. Tears streamed down his face.

He saw the men who fought by Pergamum.
Here, Greeks fled as Trojan youths pursued.
There, the Phrygians ran, and plumed Achilles chased them
in his chariot. He recognized in tears
Rhesus' snowy tents. Bloody Diomedes   470
had killed these men, whose deep sleep was their downfall,
and taken Rhesus' high-strung horses to his camp
before they tasted Trojan grass or Xanthus' stream.*
Here Troilus tried to get away, his armor lost—
poor boy, no equal to Achilles in a fight.
His horses dragged him on his back; tangled with
the chariot, he still held the reins. His neck
and hair trailed on the ground, his spear-butt scored the dust.
Meanwhile Trojan women, hair unbound, headed
with a robe to the temple of Athena.   480
Sad supplicants, they beat their breasts, but
the hostile goddess kept her eyes fixed on the ground.

Achilles had dragged Hector round the walls of Troy
three times, and now he hawked his corpse for gold.
Aeneas groaned deep in his heart, when he saw
the spoils, the chariot, the very body of his
friend,* and Priam stretching out defenseless hands.
He saw himself as well, mixed in with the Greeks,*
and the Eastern army, and black Memnon's spears.
Penthesilea led the crescent-shielded   490
Amazons, a fighter-queen afire and ardent
in the crush. A golden sword-belt crossed below
her naked breast, a virgin dared to fight with men.

While these wonders held Aeneas' gaze,
while he stared at each sight riveted,
beautiful Queen Dido came into the temple,
a retinue of soldiers packed around her.
Like Diana leading dances on Eurotas'
banks or Cynthus' peaks, surrounded by
a thousand mountain nymphs, a quiver on her back   500
—she's the tallest of the goddesses around her,
and Latona's heart is pierced with silent joy—
so Dido gladly went among her people,
tending to the building of her future kingdom.
Under the temple's vaulted roof, facing the doors,
she sat on her high throne, fenced in with spears,
giving laws and statutes to the men, assigning
the work fairly or setting tasks by lot.
Suddenly Aeneas saw, as they pushed through
a great mob, Antheas, brave Cloanthus and   510
Segestus, with the other Trojans whom black storms
had flung apart at sea and driven to far shores.
Aeneas was stunned; Achates, struck by joy
and fear. They were keen to greet their friends,
but these events unnerved them. They stayed concealed,
veiled in hollow mist, to hear the men's news.

Where were their crews moored? Why were they here?
—since in the clamor, envoys picked from all the ships
were coming to the shrine to ask for help.

When they'd entered and had leave to speak,   520
the eldest, Ilioneus, calmly began:
"Queen, whom Jupiter allowed to build a city
and to curb proud tribes with laws, we wretched
Trojans, tossed by storms on every sea,
plead with you to save our ships from hungry flames.
See what state we're in and spare a pious race.
We don't come to plunder Libyan homes
with swords or divert stolen booty to the shore:
such brutal arrogance is not in beaten hearts!
There's a place the Greeks have named Hesperia,   530
an ancient land, strong in war and rich in soil.
The Oenotri settled it. Rumor says
their children call themselves 'Italian' from
their leader's name. This was our heading when Orion's
storms and sudden tides drove us onto lurking
shoals and swamped us. The insolent south wind
scattered us through waves and hidden rocks.
Now a few of us have drifted to your shores.
What race is this? What land's so barbaric that it
sanctions this behavior? We're kept away from shore   540
by threats of war. We can't set foot on land.
If you scorn humans and their weapons, at least
assume the gods know justice and injustice!

We had a king, Aeneas. No one was more just
or pious, nor more powerful in battle.
If fate preserves him and he breathes the air,
not yet sleeping with the cruel shades below,
we're not afraid. You'd be proud to match
his kindness. Sicily too has towns and fields

for us. Our kinsman lives there, famed Acestes.　　　　　550
Let us haul ashore our wind-lashed vessels,
saw planks out of trees and bind together oars.
If we can sail for Italy with king and crew,
then we'll gladly make for Latium there.
If there's no hope, and Libyan waters hold Aeneas,
best of Trojans, and Iülus too is gone,
we'll return to the Sicilian straits, the homes
we built and left behind, and king Acestes."

This was Ilioneus' speech. All the
Dardans roared assent to it as one.　　　　　560

Dido answered briefly, her eyes downcast:
"Trojans, let go your fear and your worries.
Harsh necessity and my new kingdom force me
to be careful and to post guards on the borders.
Who doesn't know Aeneas' race, or Troy,
Trojan courage, and the flames of that great war?
We Punics don't have minds so dull; when the Sun-god
yokes his team, he doesn't shun our city.
If you hope for broad Hesperia and Saturn's
fields, or king Acestes and the land of Eryx,　　　　　570
I'll provide safe passage and help you with supplies.
If you wish to settle here alongside me,
the city that I'm building's yours. Beach your ships.
Both Tyrians and Trojans will be the same to me.
How I wish your king Aeneas were here, driven
by the same south wind! I'll send out trusty scouts
along the shores and have them scour all Libya,
in case he's shipwrecked near our woods and towns."

Brave Achates and father Aeneas, encouraged
by these words, had long been keen to breach　　　　　580

the mist around them. Achates urged Aeneas first:
"Goddess-born, what thoughts surge in you now?
You see that all is safe, the fleet and crew are here.
One man's absent, whom we ourselves saw drowning
in the sea. The rest is as your mother said."

He'd hardly spoken, when at once the cloud
around them parted, melting into open air.
There stood Aeneas, gleaming in the clear light,
godlike in his face and shoulders: the goddess
Venus had graced her son with flowing hair,   590
the glowing skin of youth, and shining eyes:
the way skill transforms ivory to art, the way
a golden bezel sets off marble or plain silver.

His appearance startled everyone. At once
he spoke to Dido: "I'm here—the one you asked about,
Aeneas of Troy, plucked from Libyan waters.
O Queen, only you have ached for Troy's ordeal
and shared with us your town and home—we few
left by the Greeks, worn out on land and sea
by every blow, bereft.* We don't have means   600
to offer fitting thanks, nor do the remnants
of the Trojans scattered through the world.
May the gods—if they honor pious men,
if there's justice anywhere, and conscience,
—reward you in kind. What lucky ages
bore you? What parents had a child like you?
While rivers flow to seas and shadows cross
the mountain slopes, while sky pastures the stars,
your honor and your name and praise will last
for me, whatever country calls." He grasped the hands   610
of Ilioneus and Serestus, right and left,
then others, brave Cloanthus and brave Gyas.

. . .

Dido was left speechless at the sight of him
and all his suffering. She asked, "What ill luck
drives you through such danger, goddess-born?
What force brings you to these arid coasts?
Are you *that* Aeneas, the son of kindly Venus
and Anchises, born next to Simoïs at Troy?
I do remember Teucer* came to Sidon once,
exiled from his country, looking for new lands   620
with Belus' help. My father then was sacking
wealthy Cyprus—he'd just conquered it.
Since then I've known about the fall of Troy,
your name, and the Pelasgian kings. Teucer himself,
though your enemy, praised the Trojans highly.
He claimed he came from ancient Trojan stock.
So come, young men, enter my home. Fortune once
harassed me with hardship like your own. At last,
the fates let me settle in this land. Knowing
pain, I can learn to help the pain of others."   630

As she led Aeneas to her royal halls,
she called for sacrifice in honor of the gods.
Just as thoughtfully, she sent the sailors
on the shore twenty bulls and one hundred
giant boars with bristling backs, a hundred fatty
lambs and ewes. The gods rejoiced at the gifts.*

Inside, the palace was prepared with regal splendor
and the feast was set out in the center. There were
cloths embroidered skillfully in purple,
silver vessels on the tables, and, engraved   640
in gold, her ancestors' brave deeds, a lengthy list
of countless heroes' exploits since her people's start.

. . .

Paternal love did not allow Aeneas to rest.
He sent Achates quickly to the ships to tell
Ascanius the news and bring him to the city.
As a father, all his care was for his cherished
son. He also told Achates to bring presents
saved from ruined Troy: a cloak stiff with golden
thread, a veil edged with saffron-dyed acanthus—
Argive Helen's finery, taken from Mycenae   650
when she left for Troy and her illicit marriage,
her mother Leda's gorgeous gifts. Also,
a scepter that once belonged to Priam's
eldest daughter, Ilione, a necklace set
with pearls, a crown ringed twice with gold and gems.
Achates headed for the ships, wasting no time.

But Venus was reflecting on new plans and plots:
how Amor could change his looks and take the place
of sweet Ascanius, sparking the queen to madness
with his gifts, folding flames into her marrow.   660
She feared a dual house and fork-tongued Tyrians,
and Juno's cruelty chafed at her. With night, her cares
returned. So she addressed her son, winged Amor:
"My son, my strength, my refuge, the one source
of my power, who scorns the giant-slaying bolts
of Jupiter, I beg you as a supplicant.
You're aware of how Aeneas, your half-brother,
is harassed on land and sea by jealous Juno's
rage, and you've often grieved over my grief.
Now Phoenician Dido has him; she delays him   670
with her flattery. I fear how Juno's welcome
will turn out—she won't be slow to seize her chance.
My plan is to outwit her. I'll circle Dido
with a blaze beyond the reach of any god.

She'll be mine, bound by deep love for Aeneas.
Hear my thoughts on how to do this. The prince,
my greatest care, now leaves for Sidon's colony
at his loving father's call, with gifts
the sea and Trojan flames did not destroy.
I'll put the boy to sleep and hide him high   680
on Cythera, or in my holy shrine in Cyprus,
so he won't know the scheme or stumble on it.
Take his shape for just one night. Boy for boy,
craftily put on his well-known face, so that
when delighted Dido takes you on her lap
while wine flows at the royal feast, while she holds you,
planting her sweet kisses on you, you'll breathe
hidden flames and secret poison into her."

Amor listened to his dear mother, took off
his wings, and gladly tried out Iülus' gait.   690
Venus poured calm sleep into Ascanius
and took him, warm in her embrace, up to
her shrine's high groves, where gentle marjoram
surrounded him with flowers and sweet shade.

Now Amor left as told, gladly taking regal
presents to the Tyrians. Achates led him.
He found Dido sitting in the central hall
on a golden couch with splendid rugs.
And now Aeneas and the Trojan men arrived.
They reclined on purple coverings.   700
Slaves fetched water for their hands, set out
bread in baskets, and offered silky napkins.
Fifty female house-slaves were in back, to keep
the larder stocked and orderly, and tend
the fires. Two hundred other men and women,
matched in age, brought out the food and goblets.
Tyrians came too, crowding through the festive

threshold, invited to recline on ornate couches.
They admired Aeneas' gifts and they admired
"Iülus," the god's bright face and lying words.*   710
Poor Dido above all, marked for future ruin,
couldn't sate her soul; the sight set her on fire.
The boy, the presents, charmed her equally.
Iülus hugged Aeneas and clung to him, filling
his false father's heart with love. Then he sought out
the queen. Her eyes, her heart were fixed on him,
she stroked him on her lap—unhappy Dido,
not knowing the trap the great god laid. Mindful
of his mother, Amor bit by bit erased   720
Sychaeus, trying to revive new love
in a heart so long asleep, so long unused.

At the first lull in the feast, tables were cleared,
great wine-jars set up and ringed with wreaths.
The house was filled with noise; voices ricocheted
around the vaulted halls. Lighted lamps hung from
gold chains; the tapers' flames routed the night.
The queen called for a bowl heavy with gems and gold,
which Belus and his heirs had always used.
She poured in unmixed wine. A hush fell as she prayed.   730
"Jupiter, they say you set the laws for hosts.
May this day be glad for those from Troy
and for the Tyrians; let our children mind it.
May Bacchus who brings joy attend, and good Juno.
Tyrians, honor and support our union."
Dido poured a gift of wine upon the altar,
the first to touch the goblet to her lips,
then challenged Bitias. No slouch, he drank
the foaming cup, swilling from the gold.
Next, the other princes. Long-haired Iöpas,   740
great Atlas' pupil, plucked his gilded lyre.
He sang of lunar cycles, eclipses of the sun,

the origins of man and beast and rain and fire,
the star Arcturus, the wet Hyades and twin
Bears, why winter suns are quick to dip
into the Ocean, what makes cold nights linger.
The Tyrians doubled their applause, the Trojans too.
Doomed Dido too was drawing out the night
with varied talk, but the cup she drained was love.
She had many questions: about Hector, Priam,   750
the armor Memnon had when he arrived,
Diomedes' horses* and Achilles' strength.
"Better yet: tell us from the start, my guest,
the story of Greek treachery, your people's ruin,
and your travels: it's the seventh summer now
that you've roamed through all the lands and seas."

BOOK 2

AENEAS' STORY:
THE FALL OF TROY

———————

They all fell silent, fixing their eyes on Aeneas.
From his seat of honor, he began: "Queen,
you ask me to relive an anguish beyond words:
how the Greeks destroyed Troy's kingdom and her wealth.
I saw the piteous events myself—I played
no minor part. Which of cruel Ulysses' men,
what Dolopian or Myrmidon could speak
of it dry-eyed? Meanwhile damp night hurries
from the sky, the setting stars urge us to sleep.
But if you long so much to learn of our ordeal,   10
to hear in brief the tale of Troy's last throes,
though I shudder at this memory of grief,
I'll begin.

                      Broken by war, snubbed by fate,
the Greek leaders had seen many years slip by.
They built a giant horse with the help of Pallas'
skill, interweaving ribs with planks of pine.
They claimed it was an offering for their safe return;
that rumor spread. But they filled the horse's hidden
flanks with soldiers picked by lot: the massive
womb was packed with warriors and weapons.*   20

There's an island, Tenedos, in sight of Troy—
famed and wealthy once, while Priam's Troy still stood.

Now it's just a bay with treacherous mooring.
The Greeks sail there and hide on a deserted beach.
We think they've left, sailing for Mycenae
on the wind. All Troy shakes off her lengthy grief.
The gates are opened and we go with joy to see
the empty Doric camps, the deserted shore.
Here Dolopians had camped, and cruel Achilles!
The fleet moored here, and here the front lines fought!   30
Some gape at the gift (our ruin!) to unwed
Athena, amazed at its size. Thymoetes
urges us to bring it in and set it on
the citadel. Perhaps this is treason, perhaps
our destiny. Capys, and anyone with sense,
says to hurl this trap, this suspect gift of Greeks,
into the sea, or set a fire under it,
or bore into its hollow womb to probe inside.
The crowd is undecided; we split into two camps.

Then Laocoön, a huge mob in his wake,   40
runs down in a hurry from the city heights.
Still far, he shouts: 'Poor Trojans, are you mad?
You think the enemy has sailed away? Are Greek
gifts free of guile? Is that Ulysses' nature?
Either enemies are hidden in the wood,
or else this thing was built to breach our walls,
to watch our homes and city from above.
Some trick lurks here. Citizens, don't trust the horse—
I fear Greeks, even bringing offerings.'
With all his force, he flung a giant spear   50
at the jointed curving belly of the beast.
It stuck there quivering; the hollow space
inside the womb responded with a groan.
And if the gods and fate had not been hostile,
we'd have breached the Argive lair with swords.
Troy and Priam's citadel would still be standing.

. . .

Now a group of Dardan shepherds in an uproar
dragged a man to Priam, hands bound behind his back.
They didn't know he'd let them stumble onto him,
that he planned to throw Troy open to the Greeks.   60
He was poised and ready for two outcomes:
to ply his tricks or meet a certain death.
Trojans rushed from everywhere, crowding round
the captive, keen to see and jeer the loudest.
Now hear how the Greeks baited their trap, and from
one act of treachery, understand them all!
Jostled and unarmed, facing all our stares,
he stood and gazed round at the Phrygian ranks
and groaned: 'What land, what sea, can save me now?
What fate's in store after my suffering?   70
I have no place among the Greeks, and worse,
the hostile Trojans want my blood.' With this lament
he changed our minds and checked our impetus.
We prompted him to tell us who he was, what news
he had, why he might hope for pity though a captive.
Finally, he set aside his fear and spoke.
'King, I'll tell you everything, all the truth,
come what may. I won't deny I'm Greek.
I'll say this first: if wicked Fortune's ruined
Sinon, she won't make him an empty liar too.*   80
Has some news of glorious Palamedes,
Belus' son, yet reached your ears? He spoke out
against the Trojan War, so the Argives killed him
on false charges, though he was innocent.
Now they mourn the man they robbed of light.
He was our relative, and when I was a boy,
my pauper father sent me as his page.
While power lent him safety and he prospered
in the royal council, I too had some fame
and honor. But when he left the shores of life   90

thanks to sly Ulysses' malice (you know it well)
I wore out my life in grief and shadows,
livid at the murder of my blameless friend.
Madman that I was, I didn't hold my tongue:
I swore vengeance, if we won the war
and I got home to Greece. My words roused hate—
my first slip on ruin's path. From then on,
Ulysses terrified me with his accusations
and spread rumors to the army to get allies
for his plot. He didn't rest till Calchas helped—   100
but why tell a tale that no one wants to hear?
Why play for time? If all Greeks are the same, and you
know I'm Greek, kill me now. The Ithacan
would love it, the Atridae would pay handsomely.'

Now we burned still more to hear what happened,
blind to this great evil, to Greek skill in lies.
He went on, shaking with contrived emotion:

'The weary Argives often wanted to break camp,
to leave the endless fighting and abandon Troy.
How I wish they had! But harsh weather kept them   110
from the sea, and the south wind scared them
every time they launched. Once this horse of maple
planks* was built, storms thundered across the sky.
Worried, we dispatched Eurypylus to quiz
Apollo's oracle. He brought us back grim news.
"Greeks: when you first came to Trojan shores,
you pacified the breezes with a virgin's blood.*
Only blood will get you back to Greece: offer
a Greek life." When the army heard this news,
we were stunned. Our blood ran chill with fear.   120
Who had the fates selected? Who did Apollo want?
Then the Ithacan dragged out the prophet Calchas
and told him to reveal the gods' intent. Many

warned me even then about the cruel crime
Ulysses planned. But though they saw it coming,
they kept quiet. Ten days the seer sat silent
in his tent; he would not pick a man to die.
At last, driven by Ulysses' threats, he spoke
and marked me for the altar—as they'd planned!
All agreed: the death each feared for himself   130
was bearable when shunted onto one poor wretch.
The awful day arrived. The rites were readied,
grain was salted, bands were tied around my temples.
I broke free, I confess it! I cheated chains and death
and spent the night concealed in swampy rushes,
lurking till they'd left—if by chance they would.
Now I've no hope to see my former homeland,
my darling children, or my longed-for father,
whom the Greeks may punish for my flight,
avenging my offense by killing those I love.   140
I beg you by the gods above, by the powers
that know truth, by whatever trust still stands
unsullied among humans, pity my ordeal
and a soul that suffers so unfairly.'

These tears won him life, and even pity.
Priam himself had the chains that bound
his hands and feet removed, and spoke kind words:
'Whoever you may be, forget the Greeks you've lost:
you'll be one of us. Just tell me the truth:
Why did they build this giant horse? Who made it,   150
and what for, an offering or a siege?'
Sinon, schooled in falsehood and Greek guile,
raised his hands, now free of chains, up to the sky,
and cried: 'I call to witness the eternal flames
and sacred powers, the altar and the cruel
sword I fled, the holy bands I wore as victim!
It's right to break my sworn oath to the Greeks,

it's right to hate those men and bring to light
all that they hide. No homeland, no laws hold me.
Troy, if I speak truth, if I repay you richly,   160
then keep your pledge, save me as I save you.
From the start, the Argives' every hope, their trust
in victory, depended on Athena. But when
godless Diomedes and that architect
of crime, Ulysses, crept into her shrine to steal
Pallas' fateful likeness,* killed the guards,
seized the sacred statue, and dared defile
the goddess' headbands with their bloody hands,
Greek hopes waned, receded, ebbed away.
Their strength is crushed, the goddess is estranged.   170
Pallas gave signs of this with clear omens.
Hardly was the statue set in camp when flames
shot blazing from its staring eyes, its wood
poured sweat, and incredibly, Pallas herself
sprang up three times, brandishing her sword
and quivering spear. At once Calchas told us
that we had to leave and brave the seas; our swords
would not raze Troy without new signs from Greece.
We had to pacify the gods we'd traveled with
in our curved keels. So they're sailing to Mycenae   180
to rearm and get good omens; they'll be back
just when you don't expect them. This was Calchas' reading.
They built the horse on his advice, to atone
for the Palladium and the offended goddess.
He ordered them to raise a towering mass
of woven planks that reached up to the sky,
so big it couldn't pass your gates into the city
and save you now that the Palladium is gone.
If your hands pollute Athena's offering,
then utter ruin will bring down Priam's empire   190
(may the gods turn back the omen on the seer!),
but if you help the horse climb to the citadel,

Asia will bring great war to Pelops' walls,
and ruin will fall on *our* children instead.'

Through this trap, this skillful lying, Sinon's story
won us over. We were captured by forced tears
and falsehoods—we, whom Diomedes and Achilles,
ten years, a thousand ships, had failed to conquer.

Now another crisis, still more terrifying,
struck our suffering people, panicked our blind hearts.   200
Laocoön, chosen by lot as Neptune's priest,
was slaughtering a huge bull at the altar.
Suddenly, twin snakes from Tenedos—
I shudder at the telling—headed for the shore,
their giant coils cutting through calm waters,
their chests and blood-red crests raised high over
the surface. Behind, their tails skimmed the sea,
giant slinky corkscrews leaving a huge wake.
The sea foamed and splashed: then they were ashore.
Their eyes were flaming, shot with blood and fire.   210
As they hissed, they licked their jaws with flicking tongues.

Our blood drained and we scattered from the sight.
They made a beeline for Laocoön. First
they twisted round his two sons' tiny bodies,
feeding on their helpless flesh with fangs.
Then they snared the father as he ran to help
bringing his spear. They bound him with huge loops,
twice circling his waist and throat with scaly trunks
as their heads and necks towered above.
As he tried to break their knots with both his hands,   220
his headbands slimed with venom and black gore,
his awful shrieks rose to the sky—like the bellows
of a wounded bull when he's escaped the altar
and dislodged the ax half-buried in his neck.

Then the two snakes glided to the shrine of Triton's
daughter and her Trojan citadel, and hid
under her statue's feet and rounded shield.
And now a new fear crept into our shaken hearts.
We said Laocoön deserved to pay this price,
since his spear-tip wounded sacred wood,   230
since he flung his profane weapon at the horse.
We resolved to take it to Athena's temple
and appease the goddess with our prayers.
We breached our walls—our own!—and laid the city open.
Then we set to work. We laid down gliding wheels
under the hooves and hemp ropes round the neck.
The deadly mechanism climbed our city, weapons
in its womb. Boys and unwed girls thronged round it
singing hymns, glad to touch the cable. The thing
slid ominously to the citadel. O Troy!   240
My land, home of gods! Dardan walls
famous in war! Four times the horse balked at the gates,
four times its womb clattered with swords.
But we pressed on, careless, blind with passion: we set
the fatal monster on our sacred citadel.
Then Cassandra told our future, but no Trojan
would believe her—this was Apollo's will.
And we, poor things, on our final day of life,
decked the holy shrines with wreaths throughout the town.

The heavens wheeled and night arrived from Ocean,   250
veiling earth and sky—and the Greek treachery—
with far-flung shadow. Scattered through the city,
the Trojans were silent. Sleep held their weary bodies.
Meanwhile the Greek fleet left Tenedos under
the moon's complicit quiet, heading for familiar
shores. The king's ship lit a beacon, and Sinon,
saved by gods and cruel fate, secretly freed
the soldiers from their prison in the pinewood womb.

The unlatched horse returned them to fresh air. Cruel
Ulysses, Sthenelus, Thessandrus gladly   260
left the hollow belly on a lowered rope:
next, Acamas and Thoas; then Achilles' son
Neoptolemus; Machaon and
Menelaus; then the horse's builder
Epeus. Marauding through a city sunk
in wine and sleep, they killed the guards. Opening
the gates, they met their friends and joined up as planned.

It was the time when sleep first comes to weary mortals,
creeping over us, the sweetest gift of gods.
But in my dreams, grieving Hector came to me,   270
weeping floods of tears, looking as he did
when dragged behind Achilles' chariot:
black with bloody dust, his swollen ankles pierced
by thongs. How pitiable, how altered from the man
who took Achilles' armor as his spoils,
who lobbed Trojan flares onto Greek prows!
His beard and hair were matted with dry blood
and he had the many wounds received in fighting
for his city's walls. Weeping myself,
I spoke to him in grief: 'Light of our land,   280
Troy's most trusted hope, why have you come
so late? What shores sent you, longed-for Hector?
We're exhausted from the slaughter of our people,
the great sufferings of our men, our city.
But who so vilely mangled your kind face?*
What's the meaning of these wounds?' No reply
to this, no time for useless questions. He heaved
a groan from deep inside and said: 'Get out,
goddess-born, save yourself from flames.
Greeks control the city: Troy falls from her heights.   290
Enough's been done for Priam and our country:
if Pergamum could be defended, I'd have done it.

Troy entrusts her holy rites and gods to you.
Take these partners of your fate, and once you've crossed
the sea, build them great walls.' From the shrine,
he fetched the holy headbands and the ever-living
flame of Vesta, goddess of the hearth.

From the city there rose mingled screams of anguish.
More and more—although my father's home
was set apart and blocked by trees—the noise   300
grew louder, war's full horror closed on us.
Shaken from my sleep, I scaled the highest point
of the roof, and stood straining to hear.
The sound was like a fire fanned by raging wind
that devastates the wheat; like rivers pouring down
a mountain-slope to flatten farmlands and ripe crops
(the oxen's work) and drag trees headlong. A shepherd hears
the noise from his rocky crag, and listens, baffled.
Then truly how the Greeks keep faith was clear to see.
Deiphobus' great palace fell, devoured by fire.   310
Ucalegon's next door was bright with flame.
Sigeum's broad straits mirrored the inferno.
The shouts of men, the blare of horns, rose to the sky.
Crazed, I grabbed my sword. I had no plan, and yet
I burned to band a group for war, to storm
the citadel with friends. Rage and fury drove me.
I felt it was a lovely thing to die in battle.

But now Panthus, Othrys' son, the priest of Phoebus,
slipped past the Greek spears to sprint in panic
to my door, holding our defeated gods,   320
dragging his small grandson by the hand. I asked:
'Panthus, where's the heart of battle? Where's our stand?'
At my words he groaned and said; 'The final day
has come for Troy, the hour of no escape. We were
Trojans, this was Ilium, our fame was great.

Cruel Jupiter has given everything
to Argos. Greeks rule in our burning city.
The horse stands on the citadel disgorging soldiers,
the victor Sinon revels as he feeds the flames.
Greeks in thousands gather at the open gates,   330
the most who've ever come from great Mycenae.
Still others man the check-points, swords unsheathed:
a glinting line of blades prepared to kill.
Our guards at the entrance have no room
to fight, but still resist and battle blindly.' Panthus'
words and the gods' will propelled me into armor
and to the city's flames, where grim Fury
and the clamor called me, where shouts rose to the sky.
Riphaeus and Epytus, a mighty fighter,
joined us, appearing in the moonlight. Dymas   340
and Hypanis blended with our band, and young
Coroebus, Mygdon's son, who'd just arrived
in Troy, on fire with passion for Cassandra.
He was fighting for his in-law Priam
and the Phrygians—unhappy man, who didn't follow
his bride's warnings when the god inspired her.

When I saw them gathered, on fire for the fight,
I spoke to rouse them further: 'My friends, so brave
for a lost cause: if you're set on joining me
in certain death, you see the way things stand.   350
All the gods whose strength supported Troy
have left their shrines and altars. The city you defend
already burns. Let's die by plunging into war.
Our only refuge is to have no hope of refuge.'
This fired their frenzy. We became like wolves,
prowling in night fog, mere bellies driven by
harsh hunger, our pups with parched throats waiting
in their dens. We went past hostile spears to meet
our end, making our way to the city's heart.

Black night swept round us, dark and void.   360
Who could describe the death and devastation
of that night, what tears could match our anguish?
Our ancient city fell, so long a seat of power.
There were bodies everywhere. They lay unmoving
in the streets and houses, in the temples
of the gods. But we are not the only ones
to pay with blood. Bravery returned to beaten
hearts as well; Greek victors fell. All around
were bitter grief and fear, and different scenes of death.

The first Greek to meet us with a band of men,   370
Androgeos, wrongly took us to be allies
and addressed us affably: 'Hurry, men!
What's the reason for this slowness? Others
search for booty and grab spoils from burning Troy.
Are you just now coming from the ships?'
Our answers strained his trust: he saw at once
he'd stumbled on the enemy. He stepped back
stunned and falling silent—as if he'd just
trampled on a hidden snake in prickly brambles,*
then recoiled in fear as the adder reared   380
in rage, puffing out its sky-blue hood.
Like this, he fell back, horrified to see us.
We charged the group and fenced them in with swords.
On unfamiliar ground, they panicked—and we
slaughtered them. Fortune favored our first clash.
Buoyed by this success, Coroebus yelled
exultantly: 'My friends, this is Fortune's path.
Let's take the way to safety that she's shown,
swapping shields and helmets with the Greeks.
Is it deceit or bravery? Who cares in war?   390
They'll give us their armor.' He took Androgeos's
blazoned shield and crested helmet as his own.
Then he strapped a Greek sword to his side.

Dymas, Rhipeus, and all the men did too,
delighted. They armed themselves with these new spoils.
We moved on, mixed in with the Greeks,* under their gods.
We fought many scuffles in the murky dark,
we dispatched many Danaäns to Hades.
Others scattered to the ships and the safety
of the shore. Some scaled the massive horse   400
in shameful fear to hide inside the well-known womb.

How wrong it is to trust the gods against their will!
Cassandra, Priam's daughter, was being dragged
by her long hair from Pallas' inner shrine.
In vain she turned her burning eyes to heaven
—her eyes, since her gentle hands were bound with rope.
Coroebus could not bear the sight. Mad with rage
he plunged into the fray, ready to die.
We followed, all of us, closing ranks and rushing.
But we were overwhelmed by friendly spears   410
thrown by Trojans from the temple roof.
Our Greek crests and armor caused this wretched carnage.
Then the Greeks, groaning angrily at our
attempted rescue, rallied from all sides and charged:
Dolopians, fierce Ajax, the Atridae—
like a breaking storm, when all the winds collide,
west with south and east, driven by Dawn's horses,
and the forests shriek; Nereus whips the sea-foam
with his trident, churning up the depths.
Those we'd routed by our trick and driven   420
through the city in the dark of night, return.
They're the first to recognize our shields
and lying armor, to note our different dialect.
It's over. Their numbers crush us. Coroebus
is first to fall. He's killed by Peneleus
at the warrior goddess' altar. Rhipeus
dies too, Troy's most just and righteous man

(the gods didn't care). Dymas and Hypanis
perish, speared by their friends. Your piety
does nothing, Panthus, nor Apollo's ribbons.   430
O Troy's ashes, death pyre of my people,
I swear by you that as you fell I didn't run
from risk or Argive spears. If my fate were death,
I'd have earned it like a warrior. Our group
splits up. I have Pelias and Iphitus
(one slowed by age, the other by Ulysses' wound).
Shouts near Priam's palace summon us at once.
And here the scale of war eclipses every battle
and the city full of death; here the God
of War has truly gone berserk. We see the Greeks   440
storming the palace doors, their shields providing shelter.
Next ladders hug the walls and men inch up the rungs,
holding shields in their left hands against missiles
and grasping ramparts with their right. When the Trojans
see the end, on the very brink of death
they break off pieces of the roof and battlements
to use in their defense, throwing down the gilded
beams so prized by our ancestors. Others
draw their blades to guard the palace doors below,
crowding round them in dense ranks. Our courage   450
wakes again, and we run to help the royal
home, relieve the men, and reinforce the beaten.

There was a hidden rear entrance to the palace
to a passage running between Priam's halls.
While the kingdom lasted, poor Andromache
often took this path to see her royal in-laws,
unattended, taking small Astyanax
to his grandfather. Through this I reach the roof,
where doomed Trojans hurl their spears in vain.
At the roof's sheer edge a tower rises skyward.   460
From this, you could see all Troy, the Greek ships

and their camp. We strike this tower with our swords
where its joints are most stressed by the many floors
and pry it from its perch. Shoved over the edge,
it plunges with a crash, bringing ruin with it,
crushing the Greek soldiers far and wide.
But others take their place; the barrage
of rocks and varied missiles never ceases.

Here's Pyrrhus, flashing in bronze armor,
exulting with his weapons at the entryway, like   470
a snake fed by toxic plants, whose bloated length
chill winter shields under the soil. Come spring,
he sheds his skin, emerging new and shiny,
coiling his sleek length upward to the sun;
his three-forked tongue darts in and out.
Great Periphas and Achilles' armor-bearer
and charioteer, Automedon, storm the palace
with the Scyrians and throw up torches
on the roof. In front, Pyrrhus makes short work
of heavy doors. He snatches up a double ax   480
and tears the bronze jambs from their hinges, hacks
the panels, smashes solid oak. A window opens
to the palace; long halls and courts appear.
He sees Priam's sanctuary, used by kings
of old, and armed men guarding at the entrance.
Inside, moans mix with sobbing and confusion,
the vaulted halls resound with women's weeping.
The clamor rises to the golden stars.
Terror-stricken mothers roam the spacious rooms
or cling to doorposts, kissing them. Pyrrhus   490
presses forward with his father's strength. No lock,
no sentries slow him down. The doors collapse
before his battering ram and fall off damaged hinges.
Brute force has made a path, and the Greeks break in,
butcher the front guard and fill the place with troops.

They swoop in faster than a churning stream
that's burst its banks and smashes through the dikes:
a wall of water floods the fields, dragging
herds and stalls across the land. I saw blood-crazed
Pyrrhus charge in with the two Atridae.   500
By the altar I saw Hecuba, her sons'
one hundred wives, and Priam, polluting with his blood
the altar-fires he'd blessed. The fifty marriage beds
that promised many children, the doors that flaunted
foreign gold and spoils—all of it destroyed.
The Greeks owned everything the fire spared.

Perhaps you wonder about Priam's fate.
When he saw Troy fallen, his palace blasted open,
the enemy squarely inside, the old man strapped
his long-neglected armor to his shaking frame,   510
a futile act, and took his useless sword.
He ran to die among the mass of Greeks.
In the palace center, beneath the open sky,
there was a giant altar. An ancient laurel tree
leaned over it and cast shade on the house-gods.
Hecuba was huddled here with her daughters,
like doves driven earthward by dark storms. They sat
clinging to the gods' statues in worthless hope.
When she noticed Priam taking up the armor
of his youth, she cried, 'What deadly thoughts, poor husband, 520
make you arm yourself? Where are you rushing?
This is no time for such help, even if
my Hector were here himself. Come: this altar
will save us all, or we'll die together.' She drew
the old man close and sat him in that sacred place.

Now Priam's son Polites rushes in,
fleeing Pyrrhus' butchery, past Greek spears,
through long halls and empty courtyards, wounded,

with Pyrrhus in fierce pursuit, so close
to catching him and pushing in the spear.   530
In his parents' sight at last, their son
goes down. His life and blood gush out together.
At this, Priam, himself at death's door,
cannot hold back. He shouts in fury: 'Pyrrhus!
For this murder, for all your outrages
I hope the gods pay you as you deserve,
if there's any piety in heaven
that cares about such things—forcing me to see
the slaughter of my son, fouling a father's eyes!
Achilles, whom you claim as father in your lies,   540
was no such enemy to Priam. He had respect
for the rights of supplicants, for their trust
in him! He gave me Hector's pallid corpse
for burial, and let me go back to my throne.'
The old man threw his feeble spear. The clanging bronze
of Pyrrhus' shield blocked it easily; it dangled,
useless, from the central boss. Pyrrhus replied:
'Then be my messenger—go tell my father
of the evil deeds of his degenerate son.
Now die.' The old man was dragged trembling to the altar,   550
slipping in his dead son's blood. Pyrrhus grabbed
his hair, and with his other hand unsheathed
his flashing sword. He sank it in the king's side
to the hilt. This was Priam's end,
the death that fate had given him: to watch
Troy fall in flames. Once proud ruler over Asia's
countless lands and people, he lies now on the shore,
a giant trunk without a head, a nameless corpse.*

Then a ghastly dread came over me.
When I saw the old king gasping out his life   560
from that brutal wound, I froze, thinking of
my dear father and Creusa all alone—

our household sacked, small Iülus maybe
dead already. I turned to see which men were left.
They'd all abandoned me:* exhausted and despairing,
they'd fallen off the roof, or stumbled into flames.
I was the only one of them alive.

As I roamed through Troy, staring at a city
lit by fire everywhere, I saw Helen*
inside Vesta's shrine, lurking in a corner.   570
She feared the Trojans' hatred for her role
in our defeat, but also the Greeks' vengeance,
and the anger of her cuckold spouse. A curse
to Troy and Greece, the hateful thing clung to the altar.
Flames of rage rose in my heart—I wanted vengeance
for my country. She had to die for what she did.
'Why should she go safely back to Sparta
and her home, Mycenae, a triumphant queen?
Why should she see her husband and her family,
tended by a throng of captive Trojan boys   580
and girls? Priam perished by the sword, Troy burned,
the Dardan shore so often oozed with blood—for this?
No! Punishing a woman brings no glory,
but *this* would win me praise—rubbing out
this foulness with the punishment that she
deserves. I'll drink my fill of flames of vengeance
and appease the ashes of my people.'
But as I raved and blustered in my rage,
my gentle mother showed herself to me
never before so clear, shining purely   590
in the dark, showing her divinity,
as she appears to other gods. She took my hand
to stop me. These words came from her rosy lips:
'My son, what great sorrow spurs this reckless rage?
Why so angry? Where's your love for us?
Won't you go see if Anchises, aged and weary,

is where you left him, and if your wife, Creusa,
and your son Ascanius are still alive?
Greek ranks mill all around them. If not for my care,
flames would have them, swords would spill their blood.   600
Don't blame Paris, or Helen's hateful beauty.
It's the cruelty of the gods that's overturned
our wealth and hurls Troy from her heights. Look:
I'll tear away the swirling mist that dulls
your human vision with its damp embrace.
For your part, don't fear to carry out
your mother's orders: obey her advice.
Here, where you see a heap of ruins, boulders
torn apart, and dusty smoke that billows high,
Neptune's prying up the walls and bedrock with his   610
giant trident, shaking and uprooting the whole
city. Here, savage Juno's first to seize
the Scaean Gates. She furiously calls the allied
army from the ships, her sword strapped at her side.
There, Tritonian Pallas holds the heights.
Her aura and her savage Gorgon-shield gleam bright.
Jupiter himself infuses them with strength
and spirit, himself goads on the gods against Troy's army.
Escape, my son, and give up on your efforts.
I'll stay and set you safely at your father's door.'   620
She spoke, then vanished in the night's thick shadow.
Awful shapes appeared, and the power
of the gods that hated Troy. Now I clearly
saw all Ilium collapsing in the flames,
and Troy, once Neptune's city, toppled from her roots—
like an ancient ash that mountain woodsmen
hurry to uproot. They strike the wounded trunk
with axes many times. As each blow shakes
the leafy crown, the tree seems just about to fall.
Bit by bit, it's overwhelmed. It groans   630
and topples, leaving ruin in its wake.

The gods guide my descent, and I slip through
hostile fire. Spears and flames retreat before me.

When I reached the entrance to my parents'
ancient home, my father—whom I was so keen
to carry to the mountain heights, the one
I looked for first of all—refused to live
or suffer exile now that Troy was lost.
'*You* should go,' he said, 'your lifeblood is still
fresh and you have your strength. Escape!   640
If the gods had wanted me to live, they'd have
saved my home. It's enough—too much—to have
survived the sacking of the city once already.*
Say goodbye, and leave my body lying here.
On my own, I'll find a Greek to kill me; he'll take
my spoils out of pity. Burial's no matter.
I've delayed the end too long, hated by
the gods, useless since the king of gods and men
struck me with his thunderbolt's hot breath.'*

So he said, unmoved, and would not stir.   650
All of us broke down in tears: my wife, our son,
the slaves. We begged him not to drag us down
with him or help the Fate pursuing us.
He refused, sticking to his plan and place.
Again I rushed to arm myself, choosing death—
unhappily, but were there other options now?
'Did you think I'd run off, father, leaving you?
Did a parent's lips utter this sacrilege?
If the gods want Troy annihilated,
if you've resolved to add yourself and yours   660
to her collapse, the door is open. Soon Pyrrhus will
come from Priam's pools of blood, Pyrrhus, who
butchers sons in front of fathers, fathers at
the altar. Kind mother, you saved me from the swords

and flames for this? So I could see the enemy
invade our house, see my father, son,
and wife slaughtered in each other's blood?
Fetch my armor, men! The last light calls the conquered.
Lead me to the Greeks! I'll fight this war again.
Not all of us will die today without revenge!'   670

Again I fastened on my sword, lifted my shield
by its strap, and went to leave. But at the door,
my wife fell to my feet, and held up little Iülus.
'If you're going to your death,' she said,
'take us to die with you. But if the past has shown
that you can trust your weapons, guard this house first.
You're deserting your small son, your father
and your future widow—just think to whom!'

She was filling all the house with her lament,
when suddenly, amazingly, there came an omen.   680
As we held our son in both our arms and grieved,
a soft light seemed to pour out from the top
of Iülus' head, and a harmless fire
licked his tender curls and flickered round his face.
Shaking and afraid, we rushed to knock the flames
out of his hair and douse the sacred fire with water.
But my father looked up at the stars with joy,
stretching out his hands to heaven. He prayed:
'Almighty Jupiter, if any prayers move you,
look at us, that's all: and if our piety   690
is worthy, help us and confirm your omen.'

At the old man's words, a sudden thunder
rumbled on our left, and a shooting star
fell from the sky and flew across the dark,
trailing flame and blinding light. We watched it
glide over the rooftops and then bury

its bright path in Ida's forests. Just a glowing
wake remained. Sulfur smoked from all the land.
Now my father was defeated. He rose, prayed to
the gods, and hailed the sacred star. 'No more delay!   700
Gods of Troy, I follow you. I'll go where
you lead us. Save my household and my grandson.
This sign is yours, Troy is in your power.
I give in, my son. I won't refuse to leave.'
Already the inferno grew louder through the city.
We could feel the rolling waves of heat.
'Come, then, dear father, hold my neck,' I said.
'I'll take you on my back, you won't weigh me
down. Come what may, we'll share one danger,
or one escape. Let small Iülus stay with me.   710
My wife will trail our passage at a distance.
House-slaves, pay attention. As you leave the city,
there's an ancient shrine of Ceres on a hill;
it's abandoned. Near it grows an ancient cypress
tended by our fathers' reverence for many
years. Take different paths—we'll meet right there.
Father, take the holy vessels and our gods.
I've come from lengthy battle and fresh slaughter.
I can't touch them till I clean myself in flowing
water.' I issued these commands, threw a tawny   720
lion pelt over my brawny shoulders, then bent
to lift my burden.* Small Iülus held
my hand, keeping up with childish steps.
My wife followed us; we stayed in the shadows.
And though I was so recently indifferent
to spears and crowds of hostile Greeks, I was anxious
now, set on edge by every breeze and sound—
fearful for my burden and companion.
Just as we approached the city gates
and I thought we'd made it safely to the end,   730
suddenly the sound of swiftly marching feet

seemed to come our way, and my father, peering
through the dark, shouted 'Run, my boy, they're close!
I can see their flashing shields and gleaming bronze!'
Here some spiteful power robbed me of my wits.
I panicked, and as I bolted off the path,
running from the route I knew, my wife,
Creusa, was sadly ripped from me by fate.
Did she stop? Get lost? Sink down in exhaustion?
I don't know. I never saw my wife again.   740
I hadn't turned to find her gone or thought
of her until I reached the knoll with Ceres' shrine.*
Here, when we gathered finally, one soul
was missing, gone from husband, friends, and son.
I lost my mind, accusing every man and god.
Was there a crueler blow to me in fallen Troy?
I left my son, Anchises, and the Trojan gods
with the others, concealed in a valley's bend.
Then I strapped my sword on, turned back to
the city. I was set on risking everything,   750
retracing all of Troy, exposed to death again.
First I went back to the walls and the dark gate
through which I'd left. I looked for my former
footsteps, and traced them backward through the night.
Horror filled me everywhere; the very silence
scared me. Next I went home just in case
she'd backtracked to the house. The Greeks had taken it.
Wind fanned the hungry fire to the roof, flames rose
over everything, and heat-waves warped the air.
I left. Then I returned to Priam's palace and   760
our citadel. There, in the vestibule
of Juno's empty shrine, cruel Ulysses guarded
spoils with Phoenix. All around was Trojan treasure
torn from plundered temples: altars of the gods,
golden bowls, giant heaps of looted garments.
Rounded up, trembling mothers with their children

stood all around in lengthy lines. I even
dared to shout into the night, filling
the streets with my unhappy cries, calling
'Creusa' many times. It was in vain.   *770*
But as I ran through all the city's homes,
searching endlessly, sad Creusa's ghost
appeared to me, larger than I knew her.
I was aghast. My hair stood up, my voice
stuck in my throat. She reassured me, saying:
'Dear husband, don't give in to this mad grief.
None of this takes place without the gods' consent.
It's not right for you to take Creusa with you
as your wife. Olympus' ruler won't allow it.
Your fate's a long exile. You'll plow the endless ocean   *780*
and make it to Hesperia, where the Lydian
Tiber* gently flows through fertile fields. There,
good fortune and a kingdom with a royal bride
are yours. Don't cry for your beloved Creusa.
I won't see the haughty homes of Myrmidons
or Dolopians, slave to a Greek woman.
I'm a Trojan, Venus' daughter-in-law.
The great mother of the gods keeps me here,
on these shores. . . . And now goodbye . . . Love our son.'
She dissolved into thin air, leaving me   *790*
in tears, wanting to say so much. Three times
I tried to throw my arms around her neck,
three times the ghost I tried to hold flowed through
my hands—like a light breeze or a fleeting dream.
At last, the night was over, and I joined my group.

Here, I was surprised to find a giant crowd
of new companions who'd poured in: women, men,
and soldiers, a grieving throng escaping Troy.
They came from all around with what they had,

prepared to cross the sea to any land I chose.   800
By now, the morning star was rising over
Ida's heights, bringing in the day. The Greeks
maintained their blockade at the gates. No hope of help.
I gave up, lifted Father, and struck out for the hills."

BOOK 3

AENEAS' STORY:
MEDITERRANEAN WANDERINGS

"After the gods saw fit to shatter Asia's power
and Priam's guiltless people—proud Ilium in ruins,
Neptune's Troy still smoking from the ground—
omens drove us to seek exile far away
in empty lands. By Phrygian Ida's foothills, near
Antandros, we toiled to build a fleet, unsure where
the Fates would take us, where we'd settle. Others joined us.
Summer had just started when we spread our sails
to Fortune at my father's order. Tearfully
I left the shores and harbors of my land, the fields   10
of former Troy, sailing for deep seas: an exile,
with my people, son, and gods of sky and hearth.

Far off lies a land Mars loves, with wide plains
tilled by Thracians. Fierce Lycurgus ruled there
long ago; his gods and he were once Troy's allies
when our luck still stood. I sailed there, setting
our first town along the curving shore. It was
called Aeneadae, for me. But the fates
were hostile. I was making offerings to my mother
and the gods who help new ventures. On the shore   20
I sacrificed a glossy bull for Jupiter.
There was a mound nearby with cornel shrubs
on top, and bristly myrtles with sharp spikes.

I went to tear green branches from the soil
so I could spread fresh sprigs upon the altar.
But then I saw an awful omen, beggaring
belief. When I pulled the first plant from the ground,
breaking off its roots, beads of black blood
stained the soil with gore. An icy fear
set me shaking—my terror froze my blood.   30
I tried again. I pulled a grudging shoot
from a new plant, trying to solve the mystery.
This shrub oozed dark blood too. My thoughts confused,
I prayed to the woodland nymphs and father Mars,
guardian of the Thracian fields, to make
the vision harmless and remove the omen.
But when I grabbed a third clump, pulling
harder, bracing my knees on the sand, I heard
(can I speak of this?) tearful groans come from
beneath the mound. A cry rose up: 'Aeneas,   40
must I bear your mangling too? Spare my corpse
and don't pollute your pious hands. I'm no stranger,
but a Trojan, and this blood is not from wood.
Oh, escape this cruel and grasping shore!
I'm Polydorus. Here a crop of iron spears
covered my torn flesh and grew into sharp branches.'
I stopped then, overcome by fear and doubt.
My hair stood on end, I couldn't make a sound.

Poor Priam sent this Polydorus, his own son,
to the king of Thrace to raise in secret, sending   50
much gold too. He'd lost trust in Trojan weapons
when he saw the siege around the city.
But the king, once Troy's might was crushed, her fortunes
in decline, joined in Agamemnon's triumph.
He broke every sacred law, slaughtered the boy,
and seized the loot. (Unholy lust for gold! Is there
nothing men won't do for you?)

. . .

                    When my terror
left me, I described the omens to our leaders,
above all my father, and asked for their opinion.
All felt we should leave that evil land   60
where guest-rights were defiled, and sail with the south wind.
We gave Polydorus a fresh funeral,
heaping up a mound of earth, and built him a high
altar, somber with dark ribbons* and black cypress.
The women circled it, their hair loose in our custom.
We fetched saucers foaming with warm milk
and bowls of sacrificial blood to lay his shade
to rest. For one last time, we called his name.

As soon as we could trust the tide, when the wind
had calmed and soft sighs called us to the sea,   70
we hauled the ships to shore, filling the beach,
and sailed from port. Towns and lands receded.
There's a sacred island in the deep, dear to
the Nereïds' mother and Aegean Neptune.
It roamed untethered till the pious Archer*
fastened it to Myconos and high Gyaros.
A stable home for humans now, it scorns the winds.
We sailed here; its peaceful harbor safely welcomed
my spent crew, and we revered Apollo's town.
King Anius met us—king of men and Phoebus'   80
priest, crowned with holy laurel leaves
and sacred ribbons. He knew his longtime friend Anchises.
We clasped hands in friendship and entered his home.

I was praying in a shrine of ancient stone:
'Apollo, give my weary people walls, a home,
a lineage and lasting town. Save this new Troy,
and the remnants left by cruel Achilles and
the Greeks. Who will lead us? Where to settle?

Inspire us, Father, and provide us with a sign.'
At once the surroundings seemed to shake—   90
the doors, the divine laurels, the whole hill.
The tripod boomed, the inner sanctum opened.
As we sank to earth a voice came to our ears:
'Sturdy sons of Dardanus! The land that first
produced your ancestors will gladly welcome you
when you return to her rich soil. Find your
ancient mother. There, Aeneas' line, the sons
born from his sons, will come to rule all lands.'
At Apollo's words, there was a roar of joy, but
confusion too. We wondered what this place was   100
where Phoebus told the strayers to return.
My father, thinking through the tales of old,
said 'Listen, leaders, here's what we can hope for.
Crete, the birthplace of great Jove, is home to
a Mount Ida, the cradle of our race.* Men live
in its hundred spacious cities and rich kingdoms.
From here (if the story's right) great father Teucer
left for Trojan shores and picked a place
to rule. Our city with her citadel had not
yet risen, and we lived in lowland valleys.   110
Crete's home to the Great Mother—and
the Corybantes' bronze cymbals, Ida's grove,
the silent rites, the harnessed lions that pull
her chariot. Let's take the path the gods commend.
We'll placate the winds and sail for Crete.
It's not a lengthy trip: with Jupiter's goodwill,
three days will see our fleet on Cretan shores.'
Anchises made due sacrifices at the altar:
a bull to Neptune, one to fair Apollo, a black
lamb to Storm, a white lamb to helpful Zephyr.   120

Rumor had it that Idomeneus, prince
of Crete, was exiled from his kingdom. Its coast was clear—

an island free of enemies, with empty homes!
We left Delos' port and swept the sea, skirting
Naxos' hilltop Bacchants, green Donusa,
Olearos, snow-white Paros, the scattered
Cyclades: islands parted by rough straits.
The sailors roared and gave it all they had. We urged
them on: 'Let's get to Crete! Our ancestors!'
A fair wind rose up at the stern behind us.   130
At last we beached on the Curetes' ancient shores.
I eagerly built walls around our longed-for
'Pergamum,' a name that pleased my people.
I urged them, 'Love your homes, build us a citadel.'

And then, when our boats were drawn up on dry sand,
when the men were busy with new brides and farms,
and I with giving laws and homes, suddenly
from some foul tract of sky a plague arrived
to rot our flesh, our trees, our crops: a time of dying.
Men left sweet life behind or staggered down   140
death's path. The Dog Star burned the barren fields
and parched the grass; the sick plants bore no fruit.
Father wanted us to cross the sea again,
to beg Apollo's favor at his oracle
and ask: Would the tired Trojans ever reach
their goal? Where could we find help for hardship?

It was night. Sleep held the birds and beasts of earth.
The sacred statues of the Phrygian gods
that I'd rescued from the flames of Troy
stood before my eyes as I lay sleeping,   150
revealed in the shining light the full moon cast
as it flooded through the windows. They spoke
and eased my worry: 'Of his own accord,
Apollo sends us to your home, to tell you here

the things he'd prophesy for you at Delos.
When Troy was burned, we took you as our leader;
we crossed the swollen ocean in your fleet.
We'll raise your children to the stars and give
an empire to your city. *You* must build great walls
for a great race and bear your long ordeal.   160
Your town cannot stay here. Apollo didn't
want these coasts to be your home, not Crete!
There's a place (the Greeks call it Hesperia),
an ancient land, strong in war and rich of soil.
The Oenetri settled it. We hear their heirs
now call it Italy after their leader's name.
Here's our proper home, where Dardanus
and Iäsius were born, the founders of our people.
Rise, and gladly tell your father news that can't
confuse him. Let him look for Corythus   170
and Italy. Jove forbids the Cretan fields.'
I was dumbstruck by the sight and sound of gods.
It was no dream. I saw them openly—their hair
with holy bands, their faces right before me—
and I dripped with icy sweat. Leaping from
my bed, I raised my pleading hands to heaven,
praying. Then I offered unmixed wine upon
the hearth. After this ritual, I gladly told
Anchises what had happened, all in order.
He saw we had two parents and a double line.   180
He'd made a fresh mistake about our ancient home.
'My son, so troubled by Troy's fate,' he said,
'Cassandra was the only one who saw this.
I remember now she said this was the fate
foretold for us, and often spoke of our Italian
kingdom in the west. But who'd believe in Trojans
coming to Hesperia? And whom could she
convince back then? Let's yield to Apollo and

the better path.' We all obeyed him happily,
leaving this home too—only a few stayed.   190
We spread our sails and skimmed across the endless sea.

Once our boats reached open water, with no land
in sight, just sky and ocean all around,
a black cloud lodged over us, bringing night
and storm; the ocean bristled with dark shadows.
Wind whipped the water into looming waves.
We were tossed and scattered in the vast abyss.
Clouds rolled in to hide the sky. Damp night
stole our daylight, lightning split the clouds.
Thrown off course, we wandered the waves blindly.   200
Even Palinurus couldn't tell the dark
from day, or get our bearing in mid-sea.
For three uncertain days, three starless nights
we wandered in dark fog over the water.
On the fourth, at last, we saw a land rise up.
We made out distant hills and curling smoke.
We furled the sails and strained against our oars,
churning up foam at once, sweeping across the waves.
The Strophades islands took me in—I was
safely on dry land. Their name is Greek; they're in   210
the great Ionian sea. Vile Celaeno
and her Harpies had been living there
since Phineus' home was closed to them*
and they fled their former feasts. Nothing fouler,
nothing worse has ever risen from the Styx
to show the anger of the gods. They're birds
with young girls' faces, but their belly-droppings stink,
their hands are hooked, their faces always pale
with hunger. When we sailed into this port, we saw
lush herds of cattle in the fields, a flock of goats   220
grazing the grass, and no shepherds anywhere.
We fell on them with swords, and called the gods

and Jupiter to share our spoils. Then we made some
seats along the curving coast and ate rich meat.
Suddenly, the Harpies were there from the hills:
a ghastly swoop of beating, clattering wings.
They tore our food and fouled it all with filth.
Besides their horrid shrieks, the stench was awful.
We tried again. At the far back of a cave
screened by trees and skittering shadows all around   230
we prepared our meal and lit the altars
once again. And again from some new place
or secret lair the screeching throng flew round our food,
sliming it with crooked claws and filthy beaks.
I told my men to grab their swords: to war
with this vile flock! They obeyed, and hid their shields
and weapons in the grass. This time, when
the Harpies swooped down screaming to the curving
shore, Misenus blared his horn to signal
from his lookout. My men charged in for the strange fight.   240
They gashed the stinking sea-birds with their swords.
But the Harpies' plumes and backs received no wounds.
They glided off in rapid flight and left behind
their half-eaten booty and their reeking waste.
By herself, Celaeno perched upon a rock,
a prophetess of grief. This shriek burst from her chest.
'So it's war you want, sons of Laomedon?
As thanks for our butchered cows and bulls,
you drive the faultless Harpies from their homeland?
Then hear my words and fix them deep inside your heart.   250
The mighty Father told Apollo this, and *he*
told me, and I, the greatest Fury, now tell you.
You sail for Italy, summoning the winds:
you'll reach her and her ports will open to you.
But you won't set walls around your fated city
until wrenching hunger and your harm to us
will have your jaws gnawing your very tables.'*

She spoke and winged her path back to the woods.
But my men's blood froze with sudden fear;
courage gone, they called on me to plead for peace,   *260*
not with swords, but vows and prayers, no matter
if the things were goddesses or grotesque birds.
On the shore, Anchises called on the great gods,
his palms stretched out, promising them sacrifice:
'Gods, ward off these threats and this disaster.
Be kind and protect the pious.' He ordered us
to rip the mooring from the shore and free the rigging.
South winds filled the sails: we fled through foamy waves
along the path our helmsman and the winds dictated.
Zacynthus' woods appeared in mid-sea,   *270*
then Dulichium, Samê, and the sheer cliffs
of Neritos. We rushed past rocky Ithaca,
Laertes' land, and cursed the soil that nurtured cruel
Ulysses. Soon the cloudy peaks of Mount Leucata
could be seen, and Apollo's headland, feared
by sailors. Weary, we approached the little town,
anchored, and moored our ships along the shore.

Against all hope, we'd finally reached land.
We cleansed ourselves for Jupiter, burned altar
offerings, and filled the shores of Actium   *280*
for Trojan games. My naked comrades wrestled
slick with oil, as in Troy, glad to have
evaded countless cities of the enemy.
The sun circled a full year, and icy winter
scuffed the waves with northern winds. I fixed a shield
of curving bronze that great Abas once carried
to the temple doorpost with this dedication:
'Aeneas gives these spoils from the Greek victors.'
Then I had the sailors take their seats and leave
the port. Eagerly, they swept the sea with oars.   *290*
Soon Phaeacia's peaks vanished behind us.

We skirted Epirus and reached Chaonia's
harbor, then climbed on foot to steep Buthrotum.
Here we heard astounding news: Helenus, son
of Priam, ruled over Greek cities. He'd won Pyrrhus'
wife and scepter—*that* Pyrrhus, Achilles' son!
Andromache was once more married to a Trojan.
I was stunned, and burned with great desire
to speak to him and understand what happened.
I set out from port, leaving ships and shore,   300
and saw Andromache outside the city,
in the woods beside a second Simoïs,*
giving Hector's ashes their sad yearly gift,
calling on his spirit by his empty grave's
green sod. She'd raised two altars in his honor—
a place for tears.* When she saw me with my Trojan
troops, she panicked at this ghostly sight and froze.
Then warmth fled her body and she fainted.
When she finally revived, she asked:
'Is this really your face, do you really bring news,   310
goddess-born? Are you alive? Or, if life's light
has left you, where is Hector?' As she wept,
her laments filled land and sky. In this frenzy
I could barely get in a few words. Distressed,
I stammered awkwardly: 'I do live—a life
of constant danger. Don't doubt what you see.
But what has happened since you lost the best
of husbands? Have you met with better fortune,
Hector's Andromache? Or are you Pyrrhus'
concubine?' Her face cast down, she whispered: 320
'Polyxena was the luckiest, forced to die
by Troy's high ramparts at Achilles' grave.
She wasn't given to some man, a lottery prize.
She never warmed the victor's bed in slavery!
When Troy was burned, they took me overseas.
I bore the scornful sneers of Achilles' son

and gave birth as a slave. Then he married Leda's
child, Spartan Hermione, and gave me
to Helenus, one slave to another.
But Orestes, love-mad for his stolen bride,   330
driven mad by Furies for his matricide,
killed Pyrrhus when he caught him at Achilles' altar.
At his death, part of Pyrrhus' kingdom
went to Helenus, who named the fields
and all Chaonia for Trojan Chaon, then built
a Pergamum, this fortress on the heights.
But what winds or fates gave you your course?
Which god let you stumble on our shore?
What of the boy Ascanius? Does he live
and breathe the air? The son that your Trojan wife—*   340
Does he love the mother that he lost?
Do his father and his uncle Hector rouse
the bravery and manhood he inherited?'
She poured this out in sobs, stirring up grief
in vain, when Priam's son, the hero Helenus,
arrived from the city walls with many men.
He knew his fellow Trojans, and he gladly led us
to his home, shedding floods of tears
as he spoke. I saw a little Troy, a tower
like the great one, and a parched stream they called Xanthus.   350
I embraced a 'Scaean Gate,' and my Trojans
shared my pleasure in this kindred city.
The king received us in his spacious hall.
In the central court we poured libations.
The food was served on gold, bowls were raised for toasts.

And now one day, then another, passed. Breezes
called the sails; they billowed with the south wind's swell.
I approached Helenus and asked:
'Son of Troy and spokesman of the gods, you know
Apollo's will, his tripods and his laurels,   360

the stars, the speech of birds, the omens of
their flight. All the holy signs favor
our voyage, all the gods urge me to sail
to Italy and try for distant lands.
But the Harpy Celaeno has prophesied
strange horrors, warning us of dreadful anger
and vile famine. Tell me the first dangers
to avoid, and how to conquer future hardship.'
Helenus offered heifers in due order
and asked the gods for peace. He untied the bands   370
around his holy head, and took me by the hand
up to your shrine, Apollo. Awe pervaded me
as the seer chanted words from the god's mouth:

'Goddess-born, it's clear you sail the seas
with divine favor. The king of gods assigns
men's fates; he turns the tides of fortune and
the world. I can tell you some small part of this,
so you'll safely cross calm seas and dock
in an Italian port. Fate forbids my knowing
everything, and Juno stops my telling it.   380
First Italy. In your ignorance you plan
to sail into her ports, thinking she's nearby.
But there's no direct heading, no way around
long coasts. Before you build your city on safe
land, you must pull your oars in the Sicilian
sea. Then Italy's salt waters, Avernus' lake,
and Aeaea, Circe's island, must be crossed.
So store these signs deep in your memory.
When a huge sow meets your worried eyes
by a lonely stream with oak-lined banks,   390
lying on the ground with thirty in her litter,
the piglets at her teats all white, herself white too:
that place will be your city, and an end to hardship.
Don't fear you'll eat your tables in the future.

Follow fate. Apollo will come when you call.
But the lands and coasts of Italy that neighbor
us and that our own seas wash: avoid them!
All the towns are held by evil Greeks.
The Locri of Naryca built their walls
close by; Idomeneus' army holds Salento's   400
plains; Meliboean Philoctetes rules
little Petelia, safe in her walls.
When your ships have reached the other coast,
once they're moored and you've put altars on the shore
to pay your vows, veil your head under
your purple cloak: to see a hostile visage
as the sacred fire burns will ruin the omens.
Observe this custom in your rites, you and your men.
Let your sons of sons keep it with purity.
But when the breezes blow your boats along   410
Sicilian shores, and Pelorus' straits grow wide,
take a lengthy detour, tack left by land and sea.
Avoid the coast to starboard. They say these lands
were once a single mass. Later, convulsed
by violence, they leapt apart. The lengthy course
of time can cause such massive change. The sea
flooded in and severed Italy
from Sicily. It rushed between the fields and cities
parted by new shores and narrow foaming straits.
Scylla guards the right side, ruthless Charybdis   420
the left. Three times a day it gulps a mass of water
to the lowest spiral in its depths,
then spurts it to the sky, lashing stars with spray.
Scylla's lair is a dark cave. From here,
her mouths emerge to drag ships onto rocks.
What you see at first is human: to the waist,
a girl with lovely breasts. Below this, there's
a sea-monster with wolves around its belly;

finally, a fish-tail. Bend around Pachynus'
headland, though a long and circling journey, rather   430
than confront vile Scylla in her stinking cave
and the crags that echo barks of sea-blue dogs.
Also: if I'm a seer of any wisdom,
if Apollo fills my mind with truth,
I'll tell you one more thing that's worth it all,
goddess-born, and I'll repeat it many times:
Worship mighty Juno's power first and foremost
with your prayers; offer vows and pleasing gifts
to win her favor. This way you'll leave Sicily
at last, and sail in triumph to Italy.   440
Once you've reached the town of Cumae, near
Avernus' whispering woods and sacred lakes,
you'll see Sibyl raving deep inside her cavern.
There she sings the fates and stores her words
on leaves. She puts in order what she wrote
and locks it in the cave, where the leaves stay still
and keep their place. But when the door swings open
and a gentle breeze disturbs them, buffeting
the weightless fronds, she never thinks to catch them
as they fly around the cave, nor to put them   450
back in place, fitting verse to verse. So men
depart no wiser, and they hate the Sibyl's home.
Don't fear that this delay will be too costly, even
if your men complain and the voyage calls
the canvas to the deep as fair winds fill the sails.
Meet the Sibyl, plead with her to chant
her oracles herself and to set free her voice.
She'll describe the tribes of Italy, the wars
to come, how to bear or bypass each ordeal.
If you honor her, she'll bless you with fine sailing.   460
So much I can say in my own voice. Now go,
and raise great Troy to heaven by your acts.'

. . .

When the seer had spoken these kind words,
he sent gifts of gold and chiseled ivory
to the ships. He filled the hulls with silver,
copper basins from Dodona, a triple-
layered breastplate of gold chain mail
and a striking cone-shaped helmet with
a horsehair crest—Neoptolemus's armor.
My father got gifts too, along with horses,   470
guides, and rowers, and weapons for my men.

Meanwhile Anchises had us rig the sails:
not a minute of delay if fair winds blew!
Apollo's prophet hailed him with great honor:
'Anchises, fit to share proud Venus' bed,
loved by gods, twice saved from Trojan ruins,
here's Italy: seize her at full sail.
But avoid her coastline on this side;
the part Apollo offers you is further.
It's your luck to have a pious son.   480
Now go. I waste the surging winds by speaking.'
Andromache was also sad at this last parting.
She brought out garments sewn with gold embroidery,
and a Trojan cloak for Iülus, just as lovely.
Heaping him with gifts of cloth, she said, 'Take these
too, my boy: they're testimony to my craft
and the lasting love of Hector's wife,
Andromache. Accept these last gifts of your people,
you, my sole surviving image of Astyanax.
His eyes, his hands and mouth were just the same,   490
and now he'd be a young man of your age.'
I wept as I spoke my parting words:
'Live well, you whose fate has been fulfilled
while we are called from destiny to destiny.
You've won your relief. There's no sea to plow,

no fields of Italy to seek as they recede.*
I pray that you have better fortune in your
second Xanthus and the Troy built by your hands.
May the Greeks never encounter them!
If I ever reach the Tiber and its fields,   500
and see the ramparts granted to my race,
one day we'll make a single Troy in spirit
from our sister cities, joining Italy
to Epirus. We share our founder, Dardanus,
and our sad past. This can be our children's task.'

Back at sea, we skimmed Ceraunia's cliffs,
the shortest path to Italy by ship. The sun
was setting and the hills darkened with shadow.
That night we sprawled along the shore, cradled by
the longed-for land, and drew lots for the next day's oars.   510
Scattered on the beach, we ate and bathed;
sleep soothed our tired limbs. Night's chariot,
driven by the Hours, was not yet near her apex
when zealous Palinurus rose to check the winds
and listen to the breezes, noting every star
that crossed the silent night: the rainy Hyades,
Arcturus, the Twin Bears, Orion armed in gold.
Seeing all was well across the clear sky,
he blared his bugle from the stern. We broke up camp,
took to sea and spread our sails' wide wings.   520

Blushing Dawn had set the stars to flight
when far away we saw some hazy hills—
Italy's low profile! 'Italy,' Achates
cried out first; 'Italy!' the crew shouted
in joy. Anchises filled a giant bowl with wine
and crowned it with a garland. He took a stand
on the high stern and called upon the gods:
'O gods who rule the land and sea and storms,

grant us an easy passage, send fair breezes.'
The winds picked up, and soon we saw a harbor   530
with a temple of Minerva on the heights.
We trimmed the sails and turned the prows to land.
Eastern tides had carved the bay into an arc;
it projected rocky walls that foamed with salty
spray. The temple, set back from the shore, was not
in sight, but two cliffs sent out bluffs like open arms.
Here I saw four horses, our first omen.
Snowy white, they grazed across the fields.
Anchises cried: 'New land, you bring us war.
Horses wear war's gear; this herd threatens war.   540
Yet horses can be trained to pull a chariot
and wear a harness. There's a hope of peace.'
Now we invoked Pallas' sacred power,
goddess of the battle-clash, the first to greet us
in our joy. Then we veiled our heads with Trojan
robes and burned due gifts at Argive Juno's altar,
the honor Helenus had ordered us to pay.

Our prayers duly said, at once we turned
the yardarms and their sails to the wind,
and left these risky lands settled by Greeks.   550
We saw the gulf of Tarentum (Hercules' city,
if the story's true). Then Juno's shrine loomed up,
and Caulon's fort and Scylaceum, wrecker
of ships. From far we saw Sicilian Etna.
We heard the ocean roaring loudly, and waves
breaking on rocks and crashing on the shore.
The shallows boiled around us, the tide swirled with sand.
My father shouted: 'This must be Charybdis!
Helenus told us of those cliffs and jagged rocks.
Save yourselves, my friends, pull hard on the oars!'   560
They did as told, and quickly. Palinurus
was the first to twist his groaning prow to sea:

the fleet tacked leftward using oars and wind.
A curved wave thrust us to the sky, then sank.
As it fell, we plunged down to the depths of Hades.
Three times the cliffs and rocky caves boomed out,
three times the spray erupted, splattering the stars.
Now both wind and day abandoned us. Lost,
worn out, we drifted to the Cyclopes' shore.

The harbor there is vast and still, sheltered   570
from the wind, but Etna roars with terrible
eruptions nearby. At times she spews black fog
that smokes with tar and red-hot ash, and hurls up
fiery spheres that lick the stars; at times
she belches boulders, the mountain's mangled entrails,
or throws great hissing globs of molten lava
up to the sky. Her plunging crater seethes and bubbles.
The story's that Enceladus's body, scorched by
lightning, stretches crushed under this mass. Over him,
huge Etna exhales fire from the fissures   580
in her cauldron. When he shifts his weary side,
all Sicily spasms and creaks; smoke blocks out
the sky. That night, hidden in the woods,
we rode out monstrous terrors. We couldn't see
what made the sounds—there were no stars,
nothing luminous, just clouds in pitch-black sky.
The witching hour engulfed the moon in fog.

Day broke and the sun's first rays appeared.
Dawn dispelled damp shadows from the sky.
Suddenly a stranger staggered from the forest.   590
He was ragged and emaciated, barely
human. He approached us on the shore,
extending pleading arms. We stared at the reeking
man, the matted beard, the clothes fastened by thorns.
And yet he was a Greek, once sent to Troy to fight us.

When he saw our Trojan clothes and armor
from afar, he froze in terror for a moment,
then rushed madly for the beach, sobbing
and imploring us: 'I beg you by the gods
and stars, by the bright air that we breathe: *600*
take me with you, Trojans! Anywhere is fine,
I'll be content. I know I sailed in the Greek fleet,
I confess I fought against Troy's gods.
If this was such an awful crime, scatter my body
in the waves, drown me in the endless sea.
If I die, at least I die by human hands.'
He grabbed my knees and clung there, cringing at my feet.
We urged the man to tell us who he was,
his lineage, the story of his suffering.
Anchises himself didn't wait, but gave the man   *610*
his hand, cheering him with this clear pledge.
Finally, he set aside his fear and spoke.
'I'm Ithacan, unfortunate Ulysses' friend:
Achaemenides, the pauper Adamastus'
son. I wish I'd stayed poor—but Troy called to me.
The crew forgot me here, in a Cyclops' dismal
cave, when they fled this grisly place.
Inside it's dark and vast, all gore and bloody
meat. The man himself's a giant—his head bumps
the stars! Gods, keep this monster from our lands.   *620*
He's too ugly to be seen, not great at talk.
He lives off his victims' entrails and black blood.
With these eyes, I saw him grab two of our men
as he lounged inside his cave. He broke
their bodies on the rocks; the entrance swam
with sprays of blood. I saw him chew the corpses
as they oozed black gore—the still-warm bodies twitched!
But he paid. Ulysses wouldn't stand for it.
He kept a cool head even in this crisis.
When the Cyclops, stuffed with food and sunk in wine,   *630*

laid down his lolling head and sprawled his bulk
across the cave to sleep, belching gobs of gore
and bloody wine, we prayed to the great gods,
then drew lots, surrounded him as one,
and pierced his giant eye with a sharpened stake,
that eye which lurked alone under his scowling brow
like a Greek shield or Apollo's sun. We were
happy to avenge our comrades' ghosts at last.
But you must get away from here, poor fools! Run,
rip your mooring from the shore! A hundred other   640
grim Cyclopes (just like Polyphemus,
they pen their woolly sheep inside their caves
and milk their udders; they're just his size and shape)
live above this curving shore in the high hills.
Three times the full moon's risen while I've dragged
my life out in the forests and the hidden lairs
of beasts. I watch them from a cliff, and shudder
at their voices and their stomping feet.
I get a meager living from the trees—berries
and hard nuts—or I rip out grass to eat.   650
I scan my surroundings: yours is the first fleet
I've seen approach these shores. Do what you want with me;
I'm yours if I can just escape this evil tribe.
You cut short my life instead, I don't care how.'

Right then we saw the shepherd Polyphemus
himself on a hilltop, moving his vast bulk
among his flock and heading for the shores he knew,
a gross misshapen massive monster with no eye.
He used a pine trunk as a staff to guide his steps.
With him were his woolly sheep, his only joy,   660
the only consolation for his fate. He plunged
into the deeper water, past the waves, and washed
the blood that dribbled from his empty socket,
grinding his teeth, groaning. Then he walked out

deeper. Still the water didn't reach his hips.
We were anxious to escape at once, and take
our worthy supplicant. Quietly, we cut
the ropes and bent to oars, churning up the water.
The Cyclops heard, and turned toward the sound
But he had no way to capture us, no strength   670
to match the pull of the Ionian sea.
He roared so loudly that the ocean's waves all
trembled. Italy was frightened far inland
and Etna's curving caves boomed in response.
The Cyclopes heard him. They rushed to the harbor
from the high hilltops and woods, and packed the shore.
We saw the brotherhood of Etna stand there
helplessly, each with one grim eye, an awful
gathering. Their heads struck clouds, like oaks whose crowns
reach to the sky, or cone-clad cypresses   680
in Jupiter's deep forests and Diana's grove.
Sharp fear drove us headlong. We set the ropes
for any tack that filled the sails with favoring wind.
Helenus had advised me not to steer through
Scylla and Charybdis, where the slightest slip
on either side meant death. We wanted to reverse,
but just then a north wind rose from narrow Cape
Pelorus. We passed Pantagias' rocky delta, the bay
of Megara, low-lying Thapsus. These were the shores
that Achaemenides, luckless Ulysses' friend,   690
showed to us as we retraced his trip.

An island once known as Ortygia spans the bay
of Syracuse, facing wave-washed Plemyrium.
They say the stream Alpheus started here and flowed
below the sea unseen. Now it mixes
with Sicilian waves at Arethusa's delta.
We worshipped the local deities, as ordered,
then passed the fertile soil of Helorus' marsh.

Next, we scraped by Pachynus' high cliffs
and jutting rocks. Camerina's there (Fate   700
wouldn't let her move away), and the fields
and town of Gela, named after its rushing river.
Steep Acragas displayed massive walls from far,
a place that raises stallions of great spirit.
As the winds picked up, I passed Selinus' palms;
we skirted Lilybaeum's shoals and hidden reefs.
Drepanum's port and shore of sorrow took us in.
Here, after so many storms at sea, I lost
my father Anchises—my help in every care
and crisis. Best of parents, rescued in vain from great   710
jeopardy, you abandoned your tired son.
Helenus, though he warned of many horrors, did not
predict this grief for me, nor did grim Celaeno.*
This was my last hardship, the end of my long travels.
When I left, the god sent me to your shore."

Such was the god-sent fate Aeneas told
his spellbound audience, such his voyage.
Ending it at last like this, he fell silent.

BOOK 4

DIDO'S SUICIDE

———

But love's pain had already pierced the queen.
She fed it with her life-blood; the hidden flame
consumed her. Aeneas' courage and his noble
birth haunted her thoughts. His face and words
lodged in her heart. Love let her find no rest in sleep.

As Dawn lit up the land with Phoebus' torch
and drove damp shadows from the sky, Dido
turned in anguish to her second self, her sister.
"Anna," she said, "such nightmares torment me.
Who *is* this stranger sheltered in our home?   10
How proud and brave he is, and what a warrior!
I think, and with good cause, that he's the child of gods:
fear shows up lesser men. How cruelly fate
has treated him! What wars he fought and sang of!
If I hadn't sworn, firmly and forever,
not to give myself to anyone in marriage
when my first love died and stole our future,
if weddings didn't sicken me, perhaps I'd yield
to this one fault.* Anna, since the death of poor
Sychaeus, when my brother drenched our altar   20
with his blood, this man alone has moved
my heart and made me waver. I recognize
the traces of that flame I felt before.
But I'd sooner have the depths of earth gape open,
and almighty Father hurl me down to Hades

with his bolt, to the pallid shades and inky
night, before I disobey my conscience
or its laws. The man who first married me
still has my love. Let him guard it in his grave."
As she spoke, she soaked her chest with tears.   30
Anna answered: "Sister, dearer than life itself,
will you waste away in grief and loneliness
and never know sweet children, Venus's rewards?
Do you suppose his ghost cares, or his ashes?
It's true no suitors moved you in your grief,
not in Libya, nor in Tyre. You scorned Iärbas
and the other chieftains whom rich Africa
has fed on triumphs. Will you even fight a love
that pleases? Do you forget where you live? The towns
of invincible Gaetulians sit on one side,   40
wild Numidians and cruel reefs hem us in;
opposite are arid lands where Barcans
rampage far and wide. Should I mention wars
brewing with Tyre, or your brother's threats?
I think the Trojan ships followed this heading
with divine support and Juno's favor.
What a city you'll see rise, what a kingdom,
with this husband and his Trojan soldiers.
How Punic glory will soar with such wealth!
Beg for the gods' favor, and if you get good omens,   50
be lavish with your guest. Find reasons to delay him
while Orion's wintry storms rage on the sea,
while the boats are damaged and the weather harsh."

Her words fed the fire of a burning heart,
gave hope to hesitation, weakened shame.
At first they went to shrines and asked for blessings
at the altars. They offered chosen sheep to Phoebus,
Father Bacchus, and to Ceres Lawgiver,
but most of all to Juno, who minds the marriage bond.

Lovely Dido held the cup in her right hand   60
and poured the wine between a snowy heifer's horns.
She paced along the bloody altars and gods' statues,
doubled the day's offerings, and read with care
the throbbing guts of animals laid open.
But what can prophets know?* What use are vows
and shrines to the obsessed? The flame devoured
her soft marrow; the silent wound throbbed in her heart.
Unhappy Dido burned. Mad with love, she wandered
through the city—like a careless doe pierced by
a shepherd's arrow from afar as he roams   70
the Cretan forest with his bow. Unknowing,
he leaves the shaft behind; she bolts through Dicte's
groves, the fatal arrow in her flank.
Now Dido led Aeneas through the fortress
and showed him Sidon's riches and her rising city,
faltering mid-sentence as she spoke to him;
now she hosted the same banquet when night fell,
and madly begged to hear his hardships once again;
once again she hung on every word he said.
When all were gone, as the moon's dim light died out   80
and the setting stars urged her to sleep, she grieved
alone inside her empty home, and threw herself
onto his couch. She saw and heard him in his absence,
or pulled his son onto her lap, captured by
the likeness, hoping she could cheat her shameful love.
The towers stayed half-built, the soldiers did no drills,
no workers fortified the port and ramparts
for a war. Projects were put off: the walls'
menacing mass, the cranes that reached the sky.

As soon as Juno, Jupiter's dear wife, saw Dido   90
in the fever's grip, saw her reputation
would be no block to passion, she accosted Venus:*

"Quite the prize you've won, a splendid catch,
you and your boy (that great divinity!):
a single woman trapped by two gods' tricks.
I know quite well you fear my town and hold
the houses of high Carthage in suspicion.
But what will be the end of this? What will we
achieve? Let's aim instead at lasting peace
and a pact of marriage. You have what you wanted   100
all this while: Dido burns with love, frenzy
courses through her bones. You and I can rule
this land with equal power. Let her serve a Trojan
husband; her Tyrians will be his dowry."

Venus realized Juno's words were insincere—
designed to shift Italian might to Libyan shores.
So she countered: "Who'd be mad enough
to turn this down or pick a fight with you,
so long as Fortune likes this plan of yours?
But I don't know Fate's will. Would Jupiter   110
approve a single city filled with Tyrians
and Trojans, mingled peoples joined by a pact?
You're his wife—you try your prayers on him,
and I'll take your lead." Royal Juno answered:
"Leave that task to me. Now I'll tell you briefly
(listen!) how to make our plan succeed.
Aeneas and doomed Dido plan to hunt together
in the forest when tomorrow's Titan brings
the dawn and bares the lands with light.
As the huntsmen run to ring the woods with nets,   120
I'll send down a deluge, dark with rain and hail,
and shake the sky with thunder. The group
will scatter, swallowed by black night, but Dido
and the Trojan prince will come to the same cave.
I'll be there, and if you're sure you want this,

I'll join them in a stable marriage;* she'll be his.
This will be their wedding." Venus, smiling at
the trick's transparency, agreed to this request.

Dawn rises over ocean's rim, and as day breaks,
a chosen band goes from the city gates to hunt.   130
They have broad-bladed spears for game, cordons and nets.
Massylian riders and keen-scented hounds rush out.
The Phoenician chiefs wait at the entrance
for the queen, who lingers in her bedroom.
Her splendid stallion, decked in gold and purple,
champs fiercely on the foaming bit. At last she comes
in a Sidonian cloak with an embroidered edge,
her retinue around her. Her quiver's gold,
gold binds her hair, a gold brooch pins her purple robe.
Her Trojan friends approach, as does glad Iülus.   140
Aeneas himself, handsome past all others,
partners her and joins his band with hers.
He's like Apollo as he leaves the Lycian winter
and the river Xanthus, going to his mother's Delos
to renew the dance. At his altars, Cretans and
Dryopians and tattooed Agathyrsi roar.
The god strides over Cynthus' slopes. On his flowing
hair, young laurel leaves are bound with gold;
arrows jangle on his shoulder. With such grace
Aeneas goes, godlike beauty on his face.   150
When they reach the hills and pathless haunts,
wild goats disturbed from rocky heights
go bounding down the slopes. Elsewhere deer
speed across the open fields in dusty,
huddled herds, and leave the heights behind.
In the valley, young Ascanius enjoys
his fiery horse, passing others at a gallop,
hoping to see a frothing boar among
the docile herds, or a tawny mountain lion.

. . .

Meanwhile the sky begins to change. Loud rumblings   160
bring on a sudden storm of rain and hail.
They scatter through the fields—the Trojan men,
the band of Tyrians, and Venus' Dardan grandson,
cowed and seeking cover; torrents run down the hills.
Dido and the Trojan prince reach the same cave.
Ancient Earth and Juno, goddess over marriage,
give the signal.* Lightning flashes, nymphs howl
from the hills, the sky is witness to the wedding.
This was the first day of death, the first cause
of ruin. She's unmoved by rumor or appearance   170
and no longer plans to hide her love: she says
they're wed. With this word she masks her fault.

At once Rumor races through Libya's great
cities, Rumor, swiftest of all evils; she thrives
on speed and gains strength as she goes. At first
she's small and scared, but soon she rears to the skies,
her feet still on the ground, her head hidden in clouds.
They say that Earth, riled to anger at the gods,
bore her last: Coeus' and Enceladus's
sister. She's fast of foot and fleet of wing, a huge   180
horrific monster. Under all her feathers lurk
(amazingly) as many watching eyes and tongues,
as many talking mouths and pricked-up ears.
She flies by night, between the sky and earth, screeching
through the dark. Her eyes don't close in welcome sleep.
By day she perches as a lookout on high roofs
or towers and alarms great cities. She's as fond
of fiction and perversity as truth. And now
she gladly fills the people's ears with varied
stories, giving equal time to false and true: 190
Aeneas, born of Trojan blood, is here.
Lovely Dido deigns to sleep with him;

they pass the winter's length in luxury,
unmindful of their kingdoms, slaves to shameful lust.
The foul goddess spreads this gossip on men's tongues,
then quickly turns her path to King Iärbas.
What she says enflames him and builds up his rage.

This man was born to Hammon and a Libyan nymph
he'd raped. On his sweeping land, he built a hundred
shrines to Jupiter; a hundred altars burned   200
eternally as watchmen for the gods. The ground
oozed sacrificial gore, the doors were bright with garlands.
They say he prayed at length before the divine
images and altars, maddened, set afire
by the bitter rumor. He raised pleading hands:
"Almighty Jupiter, we Moors worship you
with wine when we feast on ornate couches.
Do you see this outrage? When you hurl your bolts,
is our terror pointless? Does lightning from the clouds
land randomly, despite our fear? Are its rumblings   210
empty? A woman wandered to my land. She paid
to build a paltry town. I gave her shores to till
and local laws. She scorned my marriage offer
and took Aeneas in her kingdom as her lord.
And now! That Paris, with his retinue of half-men,*
a Lydian scarf tied on his oily hair, enjoys
what he stole, while *we* bring presents to your
so-called shrines, and revere an empty name."

The Almighty heard him as he clutched the altars
praying. Jove turned his gaze to Dido's city   220
and the lovers who'd forgotten their good name.
Then he ordered Mercury: "Go, my son:
call the Zephyrs, glide down on your wings
to meet the Dardan leader, who expects a future
in Tyre's Carthage and ignores the towns chosen

by fate. Fly through the rapid breezes with my words.
This isn't what his lovely mother promised me
he'd be, nor why she saved him twice from battle
with the Greeks. He was to rule an Italy
of war-cries, pregnant with an empire; to start a race   230
from Teucer's ancient blood, and control the world.
If this great venture and its glory leaves him cold,
if he won't labor for his own fame, does he
grudge Ascanius the citadels of Rome?
What's his plan? Why this Libyan loitering?
What of Italy's new race and the Lavinian
fields? He must sail! That's my message—tell him."

Mercury prepared to carry out his mighty
father's order. First he bound gold sandals
on his feet, winged to carry him high over   240
land and sea, as fast as whirlwinds. He took
the wand with which he calls pale souls from Orcus
and takes others to grim Tartarus, gives sleep
or denies it, and opens dead men's eyes.
Using this, he drove the winds and skimmed
the stormy clouds. And now, in flight, he saw
strong Atlas' summit and his sheer slopes.
His peak supports the sky; dark clouds hug the piney
crest and lash it constantly with wind and rain.
Snow blankets his shoulders, rivers tumble down   250
his wrinkled chin. His beard bristles with ice.
Here Mercury first landed, hovering
on balanced wings. Then he dove down to the ocean,
hurling his body headlong like a gull that skims
the shores and reefs where fish abound. Just so,
between sky and earth, the god from Cyllene
flew to Libya's sandy shore, parting the winds,
leaving behind Atlas, the father of his mother.
As his winged feet lit down by the city outskirts,

he saw Aeneas building forts and homes.   260
The sword he wore was starred with tawny jasper,
the cloak clasped on his shoulders gleamed with purple dye,
a gift rich Dido wove for him, working the cloth
with golden thread.* Mercury accosted him.
"So, you lay foundations for high Carthage?
Building a fine city, acting the good husband?
You forget your kingdom and your fate!
The ruler of the gods himself, whose power moves
the earth and sky, sent me down from bright
Olympus through the rapid breezes to say this: 270
What's your plan? Why this Libyan loitering?
If this great venture and its glory leaves you cold,
if you won't labor for your own fame, think of
Ascanius's future, the hope of your heir Iülus:
he's owed the rule of Italy, and the soil
of Rome." When Mercury had said this much,
he left the sight of mortals with his final words
and vanished into thin air, gone from view.

The vision stunned Aeneas and struck him senseless.
His hair stood up, his voice stuck in his throat.   280
Aghast at such a warning and the gods' command,
he burned to get away, to leave that land of pleasure.
But what should he do? With what words approach
the queen, who would be furious? How begin?
He thought quickly, weighing all his options,
trying different angles, turning it all over.
As he reflected, this decision seemed the best.
He called Mnestheus and Sergestus and sturdy
Serestus, and told them to prepare the fleet without
a word—to fetch the men to shore, rig the ships, and   290
hide the change of plans.* Meanwhile, since good Dido
would never think their deep love could be severed,
he'd try to speak to her. He'd pick the sweetest

moment and the right tone for his words. Swiftly,
gladly, they obeyed and set to work.

But Dido sensed the trick (who can deceive
a lover?) and the launch they planned. Now everything
seemed suspect, even if it wasn't. That same impious
Rumor told the desperate queen the fleet prepared
to sail. On fire, she raved in frenzy through the city   *300*
like a Maenad roused by shaken rattles
and the shouts of "Bacchus!" every other year,
when revels spur her on and Cithaeron's clamor
calls by night. At last Dido confronted him:
"Traitor! Were you hoping you could hide
this outrage, and sail away without a word?
Our love doesn't hold you back, nor the pledge
you made me, nor the painful death I'll die?
Why so quick to rig the fleet, when the skies
are wintry? Why cross the deep when north winds blow?   *310*
How cruel! If you didn't make for foreign fields
and unknown homes, and ancient Troy still stood,
would you head for Troy across these waves?
Is it me you run from? By my tears and by your
promise (nothing else is left me in my grief),
by our wedding, by the marriage we've begun,
if I deserve anything from you, if you
found me at all pleasing, pity my poor home,
put off your plan, I beg, if there's still time to beg.
Because of you, the Libyan tribes and Nomad kings   *320*
detest me, and my Tyrians are hostile. Because
you're leaving me, my honor's ruined, and my one path
to the stars—my reputation. My guest (this word's
the sad remnant of 'husband'), to whom do you
abandon me—to what sort of death? Should I
await Pygmalion, my brother, who'll raze my city?
Iärbas, who'll enslave me? If at least I'd made

a child with you, if a small Aeneas played
inside my home, who looked like you despite it all,
I wouldn't feel so lonely and betrayed."   330

She begged. But warned by Jupiter, he kept
his face unmoved and, with effort, curbed his feelings.
At last he answered briefly: "Queen, I'll never
fault your kindness, nor any act you care to list.
I'll never regret the memory of you,
while I draw breath, or remember my own self.
A few points in response. I didn't try
to sneak away from here—don't pretend I did.
I never held a husband's torch, or made that pact.
If the fates would let me live the life I wanted   340
and resolve my worries as I'd like,
I'd first take care of Troy and my people's
sweet remains; Priam's high walls would stand,
I'd build a second Pergamum for the defeated.
But as it is, Apollo and the oracles
of Lycia have made great Italy my goal,
my love, my land. If the citadels of Carthage
and the vision of your Libyan city hold you,
a Phoenician, why begrudge Trojans their land
in Italy? We too may seek a foreign kingdom.   350
Whenever nighttime covers Earth with its damp shadows
and shining constellations rise, my father's troubled
ghost alarms me in my dreams. He says
I've harmed my dear son Ascanius by robbing
him of western rule and fated fields. And now,
the gods' own go-between, from Jupiter himself
(I swear on both our lives), has brought an order
through the rapid breezes. I saw him in full
daylight, in the city, I heard him with these ears.
Stop enflaming both of us with your complaints.   360
I make for Italy, but not of my free will."

. . .

She'd already turned away, watching him
askance, her eyes roaming restlessly. Now she
scanned him coldly up and down, and burst out
angrily: "Traitor, no goddess was your mother!
You're no Dardanian! The Caucasus' sharp peaks
gave birth to you and Caspian tigers suckled you.
Why should I pretend now?* What could be worse than this?
Did he suffer as I wept, or look at me,
or yield to tears and feel pity for his lover?   370
Where should I start? Now neither mighty Juno
nor the Father, Saturn's son, takes care of justice.
No trust is safe. I took him in, a beggar cast up
on my shore, I gave him half my kingdom—madness!
I saved his men from death, I saved his missing fleet!
How this rage rips through me! First Apollo, then it's
Lycian prophecies, then, sent by Jove himself,
the gods' own messenger brings grim news through the breezes!
As if the gods lose sleep, or worry over this!
I won't stop you or refute you. Go, follow   380
the winds to Italy, chase your kingdom through
the waves. If the gods of justice can do anything,
I hope reefs bring you your reward! You'll cry
'Dido' often as you drown. I'll haunt you with black
flames, and when cold death divides my soul and body,
my ghost will stalk you everywhere. Wicked man,
you'll pay. I'll know, the news will come to me in Hell."
Heartsick, she broke off her speech and rushed
out of his sight, gone from the light of day.
She left him hesitating fearfully, planning   390
to say more. Slave-women took her fainting body
to her marble chamber, and set her on her bed.

Pious Aeneas wanted to console her pain
and soothe her grief with words. Yet—though his great love

shook him to his soul—he groaned and followed
the gods' orders, going to see the fleet.
Now the Trojans fell to work in earnest.
Eager to escape, they pulled the ships to shore,
set afloat the pitch-smeared keels, and brought in
leafy branches from the woods for making oars.   400
You could see them swarming all over the city:
like ants, when they pillage a huge heap of grain,
mindful of the winter, and store it in their home:
a long black stream hauls plunder through a narrow
pathway in the grass. Some roll giant grains,
pushing with their shoulders; others mind the line
and chastise stragglers. The pathway teems with work.
What did you feel then, Dido, as you watched?
How did you grieve, seeing from your citadel
the bustle on the shore before your eyes,   410
seeing the bay alive with so much shouting?
Cursed love, you make us stoop to anything.
Again Dido's forced to plead with him and weep,
to submit her pride to love, and beg.
She can't leave any stone unturned; her life's at stake.

"Anna, you see the haste along the shore.
They come from everywhere! The canvas calls
the winds, glad sailors wreathe the sterns. Because
I knew this suffering was possible, I'll be
able to endure it. Just do me one favor   420
in my grief, since that liar was your friend
and used to trust you with his private thoughts.
Only you could catch him in an easy mood.*
Go talk to my proud enemy and plead with him.
I took no oath at Aulis with the Greeks, to ruin
the Trojan race, I sent no fleet to Pergamum,
I didn't exhume Anchises' ghost and ashes.*
Why does he ignore my words? What's his rush?

As a last gift for his grieving lover, let him
wait for easy sailing and fair winds.   430
I'm not begging for the marriage he betrayed,
or that he lose his precious empire, Latium.
I just need time, some peace and space for passion,
until Fortune teaches me to bear my loss.
I ask this final favor (have pity for your sister).
If he agrees, my death will pay him back with interest."

Her unhappy sister takes these words and tears
to Aeneas many times. But no sobs
can move him, and he's closed to any plea: the fates
oppose it, and the god stops up his kindly ears.   440
He's like an oak, its wood stronger with age,
which Alpine winds try to uproot, blasting it
from every side. As it creaks, leaves from its shaken
trunk lie thick over the ground, but the tree sticks
to its crag, pushing its crest up to heaven
and its roots as far into deep Tartarus.
Though the hero's buffeted on every side
by endless pleas, and his great heart grieves,
his mind remains unmoved, the tears are spilled in vain.

Then unhappy Dido prays for death in earnest,   450
distraught at her fate. It sickens her to see
the sky, and strange omens fortify her plans.
When she sets gifts on the incense-burning altars
the holy water blackens (horrible to speak of);
the wine she pours turns into filthy gore.
She tells no one these sights, not even Anna.
And besides: her home held a marble temple
to her former husband, which she honored greatly,
decking it with festive wreaths and snowy fleeces.
From this she seemed to hear her husband's voice,   460
calling her when dark night held the earth.

On the roof, a lonely owl often cried its
gloomy hoot, dragging long notes into sobs.
Many other prophecies of seers gone by
scared her with grim warnings. In her dreams,
fierce Aeneas chased her. She always found herself
alone on a long road, in a frenzy,
looking for her Tyrians in desert lands,
like mad Pentheus, when he sees a throng
of Furies, two Suns and two Thebes, or like Orestes   470
in a play, when he's chased across the stage—
his mother's in pursuit, armed with torches
and black snakes; vengeful Furies block the exit.

So, in madness' grip, she decides on death.
Her grief has won. She secretly mulls over
the right means and moment. Then she calls her worried
sister, hiding her intent, her face serene
with hope: "Sister, wish me joy: I've found a way
to bring him back or be released from love.
In distant Ethiopia, where mighty Atlas   480
whirls the starry sky upon his shoulder,
by the bounds of Ocean and the setting sun,
I've found a priestess from Massylia, a guardian
of the zone of the Hesperides, feeder
of the serpent there who guards the sacred branches.
She sprinkles viscous honey and the sleep of poppies
on its food. She claims her spells can ease the cares
of those she chooses, and cause deep pain in others.
She stops the flow of streams, turns back the orbit
of the stars, and wakes the dead at night. You'll see   490
the earth quake underfoot and ash trees walk down mountains.
Dear sister, I call the gods and your sweet self
to witness: I'm forced to arm myself with magic.
Go raise a pyre in the inner court, under
the open air. Add the clothes and weapons he left

in our room, impious man,* and the marriage
bed that was my ruin. I must wipe out every
memory of that devil, as the priestess says."
She falls silent, pallor sweeps her face.
Anna can't imagine that these unknown rites   500
conceal her sister's death—she can't conceive
of such insanity. She fears nothing worse
than when Sychaeus died. So she follows orders.

The pyre stands in the inner court under the sky,
piled high with pine and oak. The queen adds wreaths
and crowns it with dark foliage. On their bed,
she puts his clothes, his picture, and the sword he left.
She knows what's next. Altars stand around the pyre.
The priestess, with loose hair, shrieks the titles
of three hundred gods, Erebus and Chaos   510
and triform Hecate, Diana's triple faces.
She scatters drops to symbolize Avernus' water,
and herbs cut down at moonlight with bronze sickles,
bursting with the milk of inky poison,
and the warty love charm from the forehead
of a foal, torn off before its mother took it.*
Dido, holding holy grain in pious hands,
stands by the altar in one sandal, her robes loosened.
She calls upon the gods and stars that know her fate.
Then she prays to any divine power who's just   520
and mindful, and cares for unrequited love.

Darkness falls. Through the land, weary creatures
wallow in sweet slumber; a hush is on the woods
and restless seas. The stars have circled halfway
through their path and every field is still. The beasts
and bright-hued birds who live among the clear lakes
or nest in thorny shrubs sleep in the silent night.*
But not heartbroken Dido, who can't ease into rest,

who can't let night into her eyes or heart.   530
The pain only grows worse. Her love surges again,
her great anger ebbs and flows. She broods over
her worries, turns them over in her heart.
"What now? Should I go back to my old suitors,
like a fool, and beg to be a Nomad wife,
though I rejected them so many times before?
Should I board the Trojan fleet, and fill
their every wish? As if they were grateful
for my help, or remembered my warm welcome!
And if I asked, they wouldn't let a hated woman   540
on their haughty ships. Poor thing, don't you
know or feel the treachery of Trojans yet?*
I could leave alone and join the swaggering
sailors, or take my Tyrians and my household
with me, ordering the group I barely
tore from Sidon to set sail again. No.
Die as you deserve; kill grief by the sword.
Sister, you did this: you yielded to my tears,
added ruin to my folly and betrayed me.
I could have lived in innocence, unwed   550
and free of grief, like a creature in the wild.
I broke the vow I made Sychaeus' ashes."

These cries burst from Dido's broken heart
while Aeneas slept on his high stern,
set on going, all the preparations made.
As he dreamed, the same god came to him
and seemed to warn him once again. He was
like Mercury in every way, his voice,
his color and blond hair, a handsome youth.
"Goddess-born, can you sleep in such a crisis?   560
Are you crazy? Don't you see the dangers all
around you, or hear the helpful west wind blowing?

She's plotting treachery and terror, she's set
on death and feeds the surges of her rage.
Won't you get out while you can? All too soon
you'll see the water churning with her ships,
torches burning, and the shore seething with flames,
if Dawn finds you lingering in these lands. Come!
No more waiting! Females are a fickle thing,
always prone to change." He blended with black night.   570

Aeneas was aghast at the sudden vision.
He rose from sleep and roused his crew to action.
"Wake up, men, and man the benches! Hoist
the sails at once! A god sent from the upper air
urges us—again!—to slash the braided hawsers
and depart at once. We follow, sacred god,
whichever one you are; we gladly obey.
Stay with us, assist us: show us helpful
star-signs in the sky." He seized his flashing sword
and struck the ropes with its bare blade. The same   580
fever gripped them all. They rushed to rig the sails
and leave the shore. The fleet covered the sea;
rowing hard, they swept the waves and churned up foam.

And now Dawn left Tithonus' saffron bed
to pour fresh light upon the land. But when
Dido from her tower saw the first rays shining,
the fleet leaving with hoisted sails, and the shore
and harbor empty, the crew gone, she beat
her lovely chest three and four times, and tore
her golden hair. "O Jupiter! Will he go, then,   590
the foreigner who jeered at my kingdom?
Shouldn't we grab every weapon in the city
and give chase? Hurry, drag ships from the docks,
take up torches, give out swords, pull on your oars!—

What words are these? Where am I? What's this madness?
Poor Dido, do his impious actions touch you *now?**
Better then, when you shared your rule. So much
for his pledges, the man they say carried his gods
and hauled his father, weak with age, upon his back!
I could have seized him, hacked him up, and thrown his body   600
in the sea! I could have killed his men, or
Ascanius himself, and served him to his father!
I might have failed, but I was dying anyhow:
Who was there to fear? I should've torched his camp
and fleet, snuffed out father, son, and all
their race, then thrown myself onto the pyre!
O Sun, who lights the world with flame, and Juno,
witness to my pain, enabler of our love,
and Hecate, howled to by night on city crossroads,
and vengeful Furies, gods of dying Dido: 610
direct your might at his deserving treachery
and hear my prayers. If that cursed man must reach
port and make it to the shore, if the fates
of Jupiter demand it and this end is fixed,
let him suffer war with daring tribes, banished
from his land, torn from Iülus' embrace.
Let him beg for help and see the unjust deaths
of friends. And when he's yielded to an unfair peace,
don't let him enjoy his kingdom or sweet life.
Let him die too young, unburied on the sand.   620
I pour out this final prayer with my lifeblood.
Tyrians, you must torment his sons and all
his future race. Make this offering to my ashes.
Let there be no love or treaties between us.
Rise up from my bones, unknown avenger,
hunt the Dardan colonists with flames and swords,
now or any times there's strength to strike!
My curse is this: our lands, our seas, our swords will clash.
The Trojans will fight wars for generations."*

. . .

Now Dido's thoughts went skidding here and there: 630
How soon could she end her hated life?
She spoke briefly to Barce,* Sychaeus' nurse
(since her own was black ash in her former land):
"Nurse dear, fetch my sister Anna. Tell her
to sprinkle herself with spring water, and quickly
bring beasts and offerings for sacrifice.
That's her task. You, put on a holy headband.
My plan's to complete the rituals I started
for the Stygian god, and end my grief
by setting fire to the hateful Trojan's pyre."   640
The nurse dashed off with creaky zeal. But Dido,
wild and trembling at her awful plan,
her bloodshot eyes darting around, her cheeks
ashen and splotchy at her coming death,*
burst into the inner court and climbed the pyre,
beside herself. She unsheathed the Dardan's sword,
a gift not meant for such a use. When she
saw the Trojan clothes and well-known bed,
she lingered for a bit with thoughts and tears,
then lay down and spoke her final words: 650
"Sweet remnants of love—sweet while god and fate
allowed—take this soul, free me from this grief.
I'm done with life; I've run the course Fate gave me.
Now my noble ghost goes to the Underworld.
I built a shining city, gazed upon its walls,
avenged my husband on my evil brother:
happy, all too happy, if only Trojan keels
had never touched my shores." She buried her face
in the bed and cried, "I'll die, though unavenged:
I choose to join the shades like this. Let the cruel   660
Trojan's eyes drink in this fire from the sea,
and take with him the evil omen of my death."
As she spoke, her servants saw her falling

on the sword. The blade bubbled with blood
and stained her hands. A cry went up in the high hall.
Rumors reeled around the shaken city.
Houses groaned with grief and women's wails,
and the sky echoed the clamor, as if Carthage
or ancient Tyre were falling, and the enemy
were in the city—raging fires rolling through   670
the homes of men and temples of the gods.*
Her sister heard the noise and ran, half dead with fear.
She cut through the crowd, raking her face with nails,
pummeling her breast, and cried to dying Dido:
"This was your plan, my sister? You wanted to trick *me*?
The pyre, the flames and altar, were for *this*?
You left me with so much to grieve for! Did you
scorn my company? I'd have shared your fate:
one pain, one sword, one instant should have taken us.
Did I build the pyre and call upon our gods   680
just to be absent, heartlessly, as you lay here?
You've destroyed us both, sister, and our people
and the elders and your city. Let me wash
your wounds with water, let me touch my lips
to your last breath." She climbed the steps and held
her dying sister, stroking her and sobbing,
staunching the dark blood with her own dress.
Dido tried to lift her heavy eyes again—
she couldn't. The deep wound hissed inside her chest.
Three times she tried to rise, leaning on her elbow;   690
three times she fell back on the bed. With dimming eyes
she sought the light of sky, found it, and groaned.

Then almighty Juno, pitying her long
and painful death, sent Iris from Olympus
to free the trapped soul from its mortal bonds.
Because her death, poor thing, was not deserved
or fated, but premature and in the heat of passion,

Proserpina hadn't plucked one of her golden
hairs yet, nor condemned her soul to Stygian Orcus.
So dewy Iris flew down on her saffron wings,   *700*
trailing a thousand colors through the sunlight.
She stopped over her head: "I take this offering
down to Dis, as told, and free you from your body."
She cut a strand of hair. At once all warmth
slipped away; Dido's life ebbed to the winds.

BOOK 5

TROJAN GAMES

———————

Aeneas and his crew sailed out to sea.
Resolute, he cut through waters dark with wind,
gazing back at city walls lit up by flames—
poor Dido's pyre. No one knew what caused the blaze,
but they knew the great grief of a love betrayed
and what a woman's passion could unleash.
Their hearts were somber with foreboding.
When deep sea held the ships, and no land could
be seen—just sky and sea on every side—
dark rain-clouds settled overhead, bringing night   10
and storm; the waves bristled with shadow.
The pilot, Palinurus, cried from his high stern:
"Why so many cloud-banks closing on the sky?
What awaits us, father Neptune?" He told the crew
to trim the sails and bend to the strong oars,
bearing down out of the wind, and said: "Brave
Aeneas, not even if Jupiter would promise,
could I hope for Italy under these skies.
The winds have changed and roar across our path
from the dark west, the air thickens to mist.   20
We can't resist or hold our course. Fortune
has defeated us: let's follow where she calls.
The friendly shores and harbor of Sicilian Eryx
are close, if I remember rightly and can trace
our journey back by the same stars I charted here."
Pious Aeneas replied: "That's what these winds call for.

I've watched you struggle vainly for some time.
Change your route. No country has a greater
call on me, there's no place I'd rather dock
our tired ships more than Acestes' homeland,   *30*
whose soil cradles the bones of my father."
They made for port. The west winds, now welcome,
filled the sails; the ships rode swiftly on the swells.
At last, with joy, they landed on familiar shores.

From a far hill, Acestes marveled at their coming
and went to meet the allied ships—a rough sight
with his spears and Libyan she-bear's pelt.
Crinisus, a river-god, had sired him on
a Trojan mother. Mindful of his parents,
he rejoiced at their return, glad to help   *40*
the weary men with pleasing rustic riches.

When East's bright dawn had driven out the stars,
Aeneas called the sailors to him from across
the shore, standing on a knoll to speak.
"Great Dardans, noble race of divine blood,
a year has passed, the months have turned full circle,
since we put my godlike father's bones in earth
and offered sacrifice on his sad altars. Unless
I'm wrong, that day is here. I'll always count it bitter,
but I'll always honor it (as the gods wished).   *50*
On this day—whether I roamed the Libyan shoals
in exile, or were caught at sea or prisoned
in Mycenae—I'd observe my vow to offer
annual rites, and heap the altar with due gifts.
We stand before my father's very bones and ash.
It was the will and power of the gods, I think,
that let us travel to a friendly port. So come:
let's conduct this ceremony gladly.
We'll ask for winds, and when our city's built,

I hope to honor him in his own temple yearly.   60
Trojan-born Acestes offers you two bulls
for every ship. Summon our native gods
to feast, and those our host worships as well.
If the ninth day's dawn brings gentle weather
and the sun's rays light our mortal earth,
I'll hold Trojan contests—first for the quick ships;
then the fastest runner; then for someone strong
and skilled with spears or flying arrows, or
brave at landing blows with rawhide boxing-gloves.*
All of you, come try to win a palm as prize.   70
And now hush: wreathe your heads with leaves."

Aeneas bound his brow with Venus' myrtle.
So did old Acestes, Helymus, and young
Ascanius. The others followed suit. Then he
left the gathering, going to the grave mound,
many thousands crowding all around him.
Now he duly poured onto the soil two bowls
each of unmixed wine, fresh milk, and holy blood.
He scattered purple flowers and prayed: "Sacred
father, once again I greet your ashes, shade,   80
and spirit, you whom I saved from Troy—but why,
since I was not allowed to look for Italy
with you, or those fated fields, or the unknown
Tiber?" At his words, a glistening snake slid out
from the tomb's base, drawing seven giant coils.
It calmly circled round the mound and altars.
Its back was mottled with blue spots, its scales
gleamed bright with gold—like clouds behind a rainbow,
colored by the sun's rays with a thousand hues.
Aeneas was stupefied to see it. The snake's   90
long body glided through the polished cups
and bowls. It tried the feast, and harmlessly
went back inside the tomb, leaving the altars.

Aeneas renewed his father's rites with still more zeal,
uncertain if the serpent was the place's spirit
or Anchises'. He duly killed two sheep, two sows,
two heifers with black hides, and poured the wine
from bowls, calling on the soul of great
Anchises, the shade he wished to come from Acheron.
His men gladly offered gifts from what they had.   *100*
They heaped the altars high and killed the bulls.
Others, spread out through the grass, lined up
cauldrons, or roasted spitted meat on coals.

The day they'd waited for arrived: Phaëthon's horses
brought the ninth dawn and a cloudless sky.
Acestes' fame, his noble name, had roused
the local people. They thronged along the shore,
glad to see Aeneas' men—and to compete.
First, trophies were put out for all to see:
sacred tripods, palms and leafy crowns,   *110*
prizes for the winners, as well as weapons,
robes dyed purple, gold and silver bars.
The bugle rang out from a mound: the games were on!

Four matching ships with heavy oars were chosen
from the fleet to enter the first race.
Mnestheus led the *Kraken*'s eager crew—he'd be
Italy's Mnestheus of the Memmi clan.
Gyas led the giant ship *Chimaera,* its bulk
huge as a city. A Dardan crew propelled
its triple rows of oars and triple decks.   *120*
Sergestus, founder of the Sergian clan, captained
the massive *Centaur*. On the sea-green *Scylla*
rode Cloanthus—your ancestor, Cluentius.

Far out to sea, a boulder faced the foaming shore.
At times, when swollen waters pounded it and

winter winds concealed the stars, it was submerged.
In calmer skies, its level crown rose peacefully
above the sea, a pleasant stop for sunning gulls.
Here Aeneas propped a leafy oak-branch, a living
marker: it was the sailors' sign to turn around   130
and circle back on their long course. Starting spots
were set by lot. Far off, on the sterns,
the captains stood out in their gold and purple.
The crews were crowned with poplar leaves; their bare backs
glistened, rubbed with oil. They took up seats
along the benches, arms taut on the oars, and waited, intent
on the signal. Their hearts pounded fiercely,
tense and desperate with desire for glory.
When the piercing bugle sang, the ships sprang
forward from their berths. The sailors' cries struck   140
the high skies; taut arms strained to churn the sea,
plowing paths in parallel, tearing furrows
in the sea with oars and three-pronged beaks.
Not even speeding chariots, springing
from their stalls, devour racetracks with such speed,
when the drivers strike their team with rippling reins
and lean forward to snap the horses with the lash.
All the grove was roaring with the shouts
and cheers of fans. The sheltered shores echoed their cries.
The din pounded the hills and set them ringing.   150

As the crowd erupted, Gyas left the rest behind
and took the lead. Cloanthus was in second place.
His crew was better, but his boat was sluggish
from its weight. Behind them, neck to neck,
Centaur vied with *Kraken,* trying to seize the lead.
First *Kraken,* then huge *Centaur* ran ahead.
Then both raced together, prows aligned.
They split the salt sea with long keels. As they

neared the reefs, closing on the turning-post,
Gyas, leading at the midpoint of the race,   160
rebuked his pilot, Menoetes: "Why so far
to starboard? Steer this way! Hug the reef,
have the port oars graze it! Let the other boats stay
farther out!" But Menoetes feared the lurking
rocks and pulled the prow back out to sea.
Gyas cried again, "You're off the course!
Steer for the rocks!"—and now he saw Cloanthus
on his tail, steering a tighter tack, cutting
to the left between the roaring rocks and
Gyas' ship—and he glided to the front,   170
getting to safe water, leaving the post behind.
That was the last straw. Gyas flared up in
a fury, tears wetting his cheeks. Forgetting
dignity and the safety of his crew, he shoved
slow Menoetes from the stern into the sea
and took the rudder himself, urging on his team,
turning the tiller shoreward. When Menoetes,
heavy, surfaced from the depths at last,
an old man dripping in drenched clothes, he struggled
to the level rock and sat on its dry crown.   180
As he fell, as he swam, the Trojans laughed.
They laughed to see him vomit floods of sea.

Sergestus and Mnestheus, in last place,
rejoiced at the chance to overtake slow Gyas.
Near the rocks, Sergestus took the lead.
He was ahead, but not yet by a boat-length.
His rival *Kraken*'s prow was closing on him.
Mnestheus strode midships among his oarsmen
urging them: "Now's the time to bend to oars,
men of Hector, whom I picked as comrades   190
in Troy's final hour. Use the strength and spirit

you had in Libya's shallows, the Ionian sea,
and the greedy waves of Cape Malea.
I don't aim for victory and first place now
(and yet—but only *you* pick victors, Neptune);
but being last means disgrace! Fight it, men,
avoid this ignominy!" All bent to oars
in fierce rivalry. The bronze stern shuddered
with great strokes and the sea flew by. Gasps shook
their bodies and dry mouths, their sweat ran in streams.   200
And now chance brought the glory they desired:
Sergestus succumbed to lunacy and drove
his boat still closer to the rocks and into danger.
Unhappy man—his boat rammed onto jutting reefs.
The rocks shook and the oars snapped on sharp edges.
The damaged prow was wedged in place. With a shout
the crew leapt up to deal with the delay
and pulled the shattered oars in from the sea
with iron-plated poles and sharp-tipped hooks.
Mnestheus' good luck here made him even keener.   210
A swift pull of oars, with the winds he prayed for,
put him near the shore as he returned—
like a dove abruptly startled from her nest,
where she and her sweet chicks hide in the rocks.
Flushed out, she darts in fear to the fields,
beating her wings loudly; but soon she glides
along the steady air and skims a sky-blue path.
So Mnestheus' *Kraken,* heading homeward,
cut the waves, gliding after her first spurt.
He left Sergestus struggling in the spiky reefs   220
and shallows, calling out for help in vain,
learning how to race with broken oars.
Next, Mnestheus chased *Chimaera*'s giant bulk.
The boat had no pilot, and Gyas fell behind.
Now only Cloanthus led, already near
the goal. Mnestheus made a massive effort.

. . .

At this the shouting doubled. They all cheered
the ship in second place; the sky echoed the din.
One crew would hate to lose the glory of an honor
all but won. They'd trade their lives for victory.   230
The others were encouraged by success. Belief in
victory spurred them on. And perhaps they'd have
pulled ahead and won, but Cloanthus stretched
both hands to the waves and poured out prayers:
"Rulers of the sea, whose waters I now sail,
on shore I'll gladly kill a white bull at your altars—
I'll pay this vow, then throw the entrails in your
briny waves and pour you unmixed wine."
Beneath the sea, Phorcus' choir, the Nereïds,
and the virgin Panopea heard him.   240
Father Portunus himself propelled the boat
ahead. Quicker than south winds or flying arrows,
the vessel sped to land and settled in the harbor.
Then Anchises' son, summoning them all,
had the herald loudly proclaim Cloanthus
as the victor, and veiled his brow with living laurel.
The crews picked prizes for their ships: for each,
wine, three bulls, and a large silver ingot.
Special gifts went to the captains: for the winner,
a gold-stitched cloak, richly worked along the edge   250
with Meliboean purple in a double wave.
A boy was woven on it, the prince of leafy Ida,
chasing swift stags with his spear—you could almost
hear him gasp. An eagle, bearer of Jove's bolt,
plummeted to grab him with hooked claws.
The aged guardians vainly raised their hands
to heaven, and dogs barked madly at the sky.
The man in second place received a breastplate
made of golden chain mail, three layers thick,
which Aeneas himself had ripped from Demoleos   260

when he beat him near high Troy's Simoïs: both
a thing of beauty and protection in a battle.
His slaves Phegeus and Sagaris could barely
hold it on their shoulders, but when Demoleos
wore it, he chased straggling Trojans at a run.
Third place was a matched pair of bronze cauldrons
and cups of silver that were rough with carved reliefs.
As they were proudly leaving with their prizes,
all with purple ribbons round their temples,
Sergestus, who for all his skill had barely wrenched   270
his ship off the sharp reefs, now pulled into harbor,
mocked, pride lost, oars gone, one tier disabled.
Just like a snake a bronze wheel crushes on the road,
or one smashed by a traveler's cruel stone:
mangled and half-dead, it's desperate
to glide away, but can't. It keeps coiling
its long body, fiercely rearing up its neck,
hissing, eyes like fire; but the maimed part drags it
down, and the snake weaves knots and falls back
on itself—so the ship limped under oars.   280
Still, it spread full sails and reached the port.
Aeneas gave Sergestus the gift he'd pledged, happy
that the ship was safe, the crew on land.
The prize was a Cretan slave girl handy in
Minerva's work, Pholoë; she nursed twin sons.

The contest over, pious Aeneas headed
to a grassy field hemmed in by woods
and curving hills. The middle of this valley
formed a natural racetrack. The hero arrived,
many thousands with him, and sat on a raised seat.   290
He offered gifts to lure any brave souls
eager to compete in running, and displayed
the prizes. Trojans and Sicilians gathered
from all sides. First Nisus and Euryalus,

the latter marked by beauty and green youth,
Nisus by his pious love for him. Next,
prince Diores, of Priam's royal line,
then Salius and Patron, the first Acarnian,
the other a Tegean of Arcadian blood.
Next were two Sicilians, the woodsmen Helymus   300
and Panopes, followers of old Acestes;
and many others, lost since to tradition.
Among them all, Aeneas said: "Listen to
my words: you'll be glad to hear them. Not one
of you will leave without a prize from me.
Each man will get two Cretan arrows bright
with polished iron, and a double-headed ax
embossed in silver, same for all. The first three
will get extra gifts, and olive wreaths to wear.
First place wins a horse with gorgeous trappings.   310
Second place, an Amazonian quiver
full of Thracian arrows, with a broad gold strap
tied with a shining gemstone clasp. The man
who's third will leave happy with this Argive helmet."

They took their spots. At the signal, suddenly
they sprang out from the gates and sped over
the distance, rushing on like storm-clouds. When they
saw the finish line, Nisus flashed into
first place, faster than winged lightning and
the wind. Next, but next by a long interval,   320
came Salius. Further back, Euryalus
was third, Helymus right behind him. Diores
was on Helymus's heels in turn,
looming at his shoulder—and if the track
were longer, he'd have edged in front of him
or left in doubt who won third place. And now,
almost at the very end, they were closing
on the goal, exhausted, when unlucky

Nisus skidded in a pool of slippery blood
where bulls slaughtered for a sacrifice   330
had soaked the ground and lush green grass with gore.
He was already relishing his victory
when he fell, going down face-first.
He lay there in the filthy dung and sacred gore.
Even so, he remembered his love for
Euryalus. Rising from the slime, he tripped
Salius, who went tumbling to the earth.
To applause and friendly cheers, Euryalus
raced on to the triumph Nisus had granted.
Next was Helymus; Diores took third.   340
But Salius deafened the giant stadium
and the elders in front with loud cries: his prize
was stolen from him by a trick! Euryalus'
popularity and graceful tears protected
him—and his purity, so lovely in a
lovely boy. Diores loudly backed him up:
he'd lose third prize, if Salius won first.
Father Aeneas said, "Your gifts are safely yours.
No one will change the list of winners. But I
can pity the misfortune of my blameless friend."   350
He gave Salius the huge pelt of a Libyan
lion, a load of shaggy fur and gilded claws.
Then Nisus said: "If the losers get such prizes
because you pity stumblers, what gift do I deserve?
I'd have won the crown of victory,
if not for the same bad luck that Salius had."
He showed his face and body, slimed with filthy dung.
Aeneas, best of leaders, laughed and had
a shield fetched, Didymaön's work, torn
by Trojans from the temple door of Neptune.   360
He gave the fine young man this gorgeous gift.

. . .

The race was over and the gifts distributed.
Now he said: "If there's a man of ready heart
and courage, come, wrap your hands in hide, put up
your fists!" He set out double prizes for the boxing,
a bull with gilded horns and garlands for the victor,
a sword and handsome helmet to console the loser.
At once, the strongman Dares lifted up his head
and stood. A murmur rippled through the crowd.
He was the only one who'd boxed with Paris.   370
He'd knocked out the champion Butes, a giant
who claimed his lineage from Bebrycian
Amycus, and laid him dying on the yellow
sand, near the mound that held great Hector.
Such was the towering man who stood to fight.
He showed his muscled shoulders, stretching out
his arms in turn, throwing punches in the air.
He needed a rival: but who from that huge crowd
would dare to face the man and bind their hands with leather?
Thinking everyone had yielded him the prize,   380
Dares stepped up at once to where Aeneas sat,
grabbed the prize bull by the horn, and said:
"Goddess-born, if no one dares to fight with me,
how long must I stand? I shouldn't have to wait.
Let me take the prize." All the Trojans roared
in favor: he should be given what was promised!

But Acestes raked Entellus with harsh words
as they sat together on their grassy bench.
"Entellus, what's the point of your great past
if you meekly let this great prize go without   390
a fight? What happened to your idol, the trainer
Eryx? Was he famous for no reason? What of
your glory throughout Sicily, the prizes hanging

in your house?" He answered: "Fear hasn't dulled
my love of glory, but my blood is sluggish
with the slowness of old age. My strength is gone.
If I were in my youth, the same age that scoundrel
trusts in as he preens, if I were like that,
it wouldn't take a prize for me to fight, or some
fancy steer. I don't care about the gifts."   400
He flung into the ring immensely heavy boxing
gloves that fierce Eryx had worn in his matches
when he'd bound his hands with the hard hide.
The crowd gasped at the huge gloves made of pelts
from seven giant bulls, stiff with lead and iron.
Dares himself gaped the most, and backed away.
Great-souled Aeneas handled the gloves' weight,
the great mass of twisted bands of leather.
The old boxer said with spirit: "Imagine if
you'd seen the gloves of Hercules himself,   410
the grim struggle on this very shore!
Your brother Eryx* wore these gloves (look,
they're smeared with blood and splattered brains)
to face great Hercules, and I wore them
while I still had strength and younger blood,
before old age sprinkled white hairs on my head.
But if my gloves scare Trojan Dares, and
pious Aeneas and Acestes are agreed,
let's fight on equal terms. I'll give up Eryx'
gloves, fear not, and you take off your Trojan ones."   420
He threw the lined cloak from his shoulders, baring
his huge frame, his giant limbs and muscles,
and stood hulking in the center of the sand.
Father Aeneas brought out matching gloves,
and bound the hands of both with equal weight.
They stood on tiptoes, holding their arms high up
to the sky. Then they bobbed around,
keeping their heads out of range, feinting

with their hands, sparring for an opening.
Dares' youth made him better on his feet.   430
Entellus' strength was in his arms and bulk,
but his stiff knees shook, gasps racked his huge frame.
The men threw many useless punches, but landed
many too, hitting hollow flanks, thumping
each other's chests. Often their hands strayed
to ears and heads. Their jaws rattled with the impact.
Entellus, solid and unmoving, stayed in place,
dodging blows by watching carefully and twisting.
Dares looked like he was laying siege and placing
catapults around a mountain fort or town.   440
He tried this route and that, probing everywhere
with skill, pressing him with varied jabs—no luck.
Entellus rose and raised his right arm high,
but Dares saw the blow aimed from above
and nimbly dodged it. The man squandered his strength
on the air, and worse still, himself heavy, tumbled
heavily, his vast bulk landing on the ground—
like a pine hollowed with age and torn up by
the roots on Mount Erymanthus or great Ida.
Excited, Trojans and Sicilians leapt up;   450
their shouts rose to the sky. Acestes, feeling pity,
quickly ran to lift his old friend from the ground.
But the hero wasn't slowed or scared by falling.
He came back fiercer: his anger brought him strength.
Shame kindled him, and trust in his own skill.
He chased Dares round the ring in fury, landing
endless blows with both his fists. There was no pause,
no chance to rest. He was like a hailstorm
rattling roofs—so dense were the punches that
the hero rained on Dares, pounding him all over.   460

Father Aeneas didn't let this fury last—
Entellus was berserk with bitter rage.

He stopped the match, pulling out exhausted
Dares, and soothed him with these words. "Poor man,
have you lost your mind? Don't you see
his strength is not his own, but backed by gods?
Give in to their power." So the contest ended.
Dares' faithful friends hauled him to the ships.
His knees couldn't support him and his head flopped
side to side. He was vomiting thick clots   470
of blood and teeth. His helpers were called back
to fetch the sword and helmet, but the palm and bull
were for Entellus. He was in high spirits,
puffed up by his prize. "Goddess-born Aeneas,
and you Trojans, see what strength I had
when young, see the death from which you've rescued
Dares." Then he stood before the bullock,
his prize for victory, pulled back his right fist,
and slammed the heavy glove between its horns.
The skull caved in, spilling out the brains,   480
and the bull collapsed to earth and twitched in death.
Over it he poured these heartfelt words: "Eryx,
I offer you this life for Dares'; better so.
I won. Now I'll retire my gloves and talent."

Aeneas next invited anyone who wanted
to compete in archery, and named the prizes.
A large band helped him raise the boat-mast of the ship
Sergestus steered. Feeding a rope through the top,
he attached a fluttering dove: their arrows' goal.
The contestants came and threw their lots   490
in a bronze helmet. To loud cheers, first place
went to Hippocoön, Hyrtacus' son. Next,
Mnestheus, who'd placed in the ship race, still wreathed
with the olive leaves around his brow.
Eurytion was third—famed Pandarus' brother,
who was told to break the treaty back at Troy

and aimed his bow into the mass of Greeks.
Last from the deep helmet came Acestes' name.
He too dared to try the task of younger men.
Each man bent his pliant bow, putting muscle   500
into it, pulling arrows from his quiver.
From the twanging bow of young Hippocoön
the first vibrating shaft sliced through the air.
It flew straight to the wooden mast and stuck.
As the mast shuddered, the dove fluttered
in fear. The whole place rang with loud applause.
Next keen Mnestheus stood and drew his bow.
He pointed high, aiming both eye and arrow
at the mark. He didn't manage to impale
the bird—bad luck—but he broke the knotted rope   510
around her foot that tied her to the mast.
The dove, released, flew southward to dark clouds.
Eurytion had long since held his arrow taut
and his bow drawn. Praying to his brother,
he peered for the dove as she beat her wings
in joy in the empty sky, rising to the night,
and shot her. She fell lifeless, leaving her soul
in the stars, returning the lodged arrow.

Acestes was still there, but the prize was gone.
He shot his arrow to the heavens anyhow   520
to show his veteran skill and ringing bow.
And then, a sudden miracle took place, important
in the future*—as its fulfillment showed,
when stern prophets at last knew its meaning.
Soaring through the empty sky, the arrow
blazed a flaming path, then vanished in the breeze,
like a shooting star falling from the heavens
that draws its shining trail across the sky.
The Trojans and Sicilians were amazed
and called upon the gods. Great Aeneas did not   530

reject the omen. He hugged happy Acestes,
heaping him with lavish gifts, and said:
"Take these, father. The great king of Olympus
shows by such signs you'll win honors like no
other. This prize belonged to aged Anchises,
a bowl embossed with figures. Thracian Cisseus
gave it him long ago, a handsome gift,
a token of himself and a pledge of love."
He ringed Acestes' brows with living laurel
and named him winner, first among them all.   540
Good Eurytion readily gave up his place
though he alone shot down the soaring bird.
The man who broke the rope was next in gifts,
last, the one whose arrow was wedged in the mast.

Before the contest ended, Aeneas summoned Iülus'
friend and guardian, Epytides, and told
those loyal ears: "Go and tell Ascanius,
if his boy troops are prepared, and their horses
marshaled in straight rows, to lead them in
and show himself in armor, in honor of his   550
grandfather." He told the crowd packed in the lengthy
circuit to clear out, leaving the fields empty.
The boys advanced before their parents' eyes,
shining on their bridled horses. Trojans and
Sicilians roared in admiration as they passed.
Their hair was bound with cropped wreaths in the old way.
Each held double iron-tipped cornel lances,
some slung polished quivers on their back.
Soft coils of twisted gold sat on their collarbones.
Three squadrons with three captains galloped in.   560
Twelve boys were in each group. The separate ranks
gleamed brightly, following their leaders. One glad
troop of boys was led by little Priam,
his grandfather's namesake—Politus' child, future

father of Italians. He rode a Thracian horse,
a tall prancing piebald with white brow and
pasterns. Next came Atys. The Latin Atii
trace their clan and ancestry to him—
little Atys, a boy loved by the boy Iülus.
Last, and handsome past the rest, Iülus   570
steered a Sidonian horse that lovely Dido
gave him to remember her, a pledge of love.
The others rode on old Acestes' native steeds.
The Dardans clapped to welcome them, as they watched
the anxious boys, feeling joy at the sight:
young faces that recalled passed generations.
Happy on their horses, the boys circled the field
before their parents' eyes. From a distance,
Epytides yelled and cracked his whip: the sign.
Each troop split in equal halves who rode apart.   580
At the call, they wheeled back to meet again
and charged with spears—a military tactic.
One side wove a pattern, the other mirrored it.
They formed intersecting circles riding left
and right. Their play looked like armed battle.
At times they risked their backs in flight, at times attacked
with swords, at times rode in peaceful pairings.
Just so the Labyrinth in high Crete, they say,
was woven of blind walls, its paths an enigma
of a thousand forking ways that foiled all clues,   590
each slip uncaught and irrevocable.
The sons of Troy tangled their horses' paths,
weaving battles and retreats in play,
like dolphins cutting Libyan and Carpathian waters
as they skim the seas and breach the waves.
Ascanius renewed this custom and this contest
for his horsemen when he circled Alba Longa
with her walls. He taught the native Latins
to observe it as he did with the young Trojans.

The Albans taught their own children; great Rome   600
inherited and kept the ancient ritual.
The boys now stand for "Troy," the troops are "Trojan."
These were the games observed in honor of Anchises.

And now Fortune changed and showed her perfidy.
As they performed games for the annual rites, Juno
hurried Iris earthward to the Trojan fleet,
backing her with wind, scheming, not yet
satiated in her ancient grudge.
Iris flew along the rainbow's thousand hues.
Her quick descent was seen by none. She sighted   610
the giant gathering, and, on the shore,
the deserted harbor, the abandoned fleet.
On the empty beach, the Trojan women
wept for lost Anchises, looking at the ocean
through their tears. They deplored the many reefs
and voyages that faced their weary people still.
Sick of sea and hardship, they longed to settle.
Iris mixed among them, no novice in the art
of harm. She shed her goddess's clothes and face
and became Beroë, Doryclus' old wife,   620
who'd once had a family and famous sons.
She pushed through the Trojan women, saying:
"Unlucky us, that Greek hands didn't haul us off
to die in war beneath our country's walls!
Unhappy race, what does Fortune have in store?
This is the seventh summer since Troy's fall, and still
we bear this journey through the lands and seas,
the hostile reefs and skies, chasing receding
Italy through endless seas. We're on land
owned by our kinsman Eryx and our host Acestes.   630
Who'll stop us from laying walls for our own town?
O fatherland, and gods saved from the Greeks in vain,

will no city be called Troy? Will we never
see Simoïs and Xanthus, Hector's rivers?
Come, help me set these cursed ships on fire.
In my sleep, I saw the prophetess Cassandra
handing me lit torches: 'Seek Troy here,' she said.
'This is your home.' Now's the time for action:
such omens call for no delay. I see right here
four altars raised to Neptune. He'll give us fire—and daring."   640
She was the first to seize a deadly torch.
With effort, she held it high, swung it, and threw.
The women were shocked and stupefied.
Now the oldest woman in the crowd,
Pyrgo, royal nurse to many sons of Priam,
said: "Women, this is not Doryclus' wife,
Beroë. Note the signs of divine beauty,
her burning eyes, her bravery. Look at
her face, how she sounds and how she walks.
I myself just left Beroë. She was sick,   650
and sad that she alone would miss the rites
and could not pay Anchises his due honors."
At first the women were divided: they stared
at the ships with angry looks, torn between
fierce longing for their present spot
and the lands to which Fate called. Iris rose up
through the sky on level wings, and as she left,
she drew a massive rainbow in the clouds.
Now they shouted louder, maddened by
the omen. Some snatched fire from nearby hearths,   660
others robbed the altars. They hurled branches, leaves,
and burning torches at the ships. Fire raged
amok over the seats and oars and painted sterns.

Eumelus brought the message to the gathering
around Anchises' tomb: the ships were burning!

Looking back, they saw a rising billow of black ash.
Ascanius, just now happily leading
his troops, galloped fiercely to the chaos
at the ships. His breathless guardians couldn't catch him.
"What's this new madness, my poor citizens?" he cried.   670
"What are you doing? It's not hostile camps of Greeks
you set on fire, it's hope itself! Look, I'm your
Ascanius!" He threw his helmet at his feet,
the one he wore to play at battle. Aeneas
and a band of Trojans rushed up too.
But the women scattered fearfully along
the shore to hide in any rocky nook or wood.
They shunned daylight and their deed. Sane again,
Juno driven from their hearts, they knew the men.

But this didn't stop the flames, or sap their wild   680
strength. Beneath the sodden wood, the pitch
was live, spewing smoke and smoldering,
eating at the hulls, wrecking the ships' frames.
Heroic strength and streams of water were no use.
Pious Aeneas tore his clothing from his chest,
stretched out his hands, and begged the gods for help:
"Almighty Jupiter, if you don't hate the Trojans
one and all, if your former piety
still cares for human suffering, let our ships
survive, save our fragile hopes from death.   690
Or if we merit it, kill what's left of us
with your deadly bolt, drown us by your hand."
He'd hardly finished when a dark storm broke out
with a violent downpour. The fields and steep hills
shook with thunder. Black rain poured in sheets
across the sky, driven by the strong south wind.
The ships filled up with water. It soaked their half-burned
timbers until all the smoke and flames were out.
The hulls, except for four, were saved from ruin.

· · ·

Aeneas was shattered by this bitter loss.   700
His grave concerns pulled him this way and that:
Should they forget their destiny and stay
in Sicily, or aim for the Italian coast?
Then old Nautes, Athena's only student,
who'd been famous for his foresight (the goddess
always told him what the gods' great rage
would bring, and what the chain of fate required),
this Nautes comforted Aeneas. "Goddess-born,
let's follow where fate draws us, even if we backtrack.
Come what may, we'll win out by endurance.   710
Dardanian Acestes comes from divine stock.
Entrust this willing partner with your plans
and set him over those who've lost their ships
or are sick of your great project and your fate.
Pick old men and women wearied by the sea,
all the weak, all who fear the risks,
and let these tired people have their city here:
if you permit, they'll call the place Acesta."

His old friend's advice disturbed Aeneas,
and now his worries tore at him still more.   720
As black Night in her chariot drove across
the heavens, suddenly the image of Anchises,
his father, came to him, descending from the skies:
"Son, dearer than my life while I had life,
so troubled by Troy's fate: I visit you
at Jupiter's command. *He* drove the fire
from your ships, at last showing pity.
Follow the fine counsel that old Nautes gives:
take only chosen men, the bravest hearts,
to Italy. In Latium there'll be a harsh   730
and rustic race for you to crush. But first,
come to Dis's hellish home. I'll be by deep

Avernus. Impious Tartarus's sullen shades
don't keep me; Elysium's my home, and the lovely
gatherings of the good. Chaste Sibyl will bring you
once you've offered pools of blood from black-skinned sheep.
You'll learn about your people and your city.
Now goodbye: damp Night wheels in her mid-course,
I can feel the breath of cruel Dawn's horses."
He dissolved like smoke into thin air.   740
Aeneas cried: "Now where are you rushing,
and from whom? Who stops us from embracing?"
Then he woke the sleeping fire's embers
and humbly worshiped Trojan Lar and white-haired
Vesta's shrine with sacred grain and incense.

Next Aeneas called his friends, Acestes first,
to tell them Jupiter's command, his dear
father's guidance, and what he had decided.
Their debate was short: Acestes said yes.
They formed a colony of women and the willing,   750
people with no need for boundless glory.
The rest repaired the rowers' benches and the timbers
eaten by the fire, adding new oars and ropes.
They were few, but spirited in war.
Aeneas sketched out city limits with a plow,
assigning homes. He called the districts Ilium
and Troy. Trojan Acestes loved his kingdom.
He formed a court and gave laws to new senators.
On Eryx' summit, near the stars, they built a shrine
to Venus of Idalia. A priest and sacred   760
grove were granted to Anchises' tomb.

Now nine days of feasting passed. The altars
had been honored and calm winds smoothed the seas.
The south wind called them to the deep again.
A gale of lament went up along the curving

shore: they embraced, delayed a day and night.
The very men and mothers who'd found the sea
too harsh, the gods' power unbearable,
now wanted to endure the pain of exile.
In tears himself, good Aeneas offered comfort   770
with kind words and left them with Acestes.
He ordered three calves killed for Eryx, a lamb
for the Storms. Then he had the mooring loosened.
He stood high on the prow holding a bowl,
his head ringed with olive leaves, and poured
clear wine and entrails on the briny sea.
Eagerly, the sailors swept the sea with oars.
As they sailed, a fair wind rose behind them.

But meanwhile Venus, distraught, went to speak
to Neptune. She poured out passionate complaints.   780
"Neptune, Juno's fierce rage and stubborn heart
force me to stoop to every kind of plea.
Time's passage doesn't soften her, nor piety.
She's unbowed by Jupiter's commands and Fate.
Her malice has devoured a Phrygian city,
dragged the scraps of Troy through every torture.
But that's not enough—she persecutes dead bones
and ashes! Her rage makes sense to her alone.
You saw yourself the trouble she caused recently
on the Libyan waves, mingling sea and sky,   790
unwisely betting on Aeolus' storms.
She dared this in *your* realm. She even set
the Trojan women on a path of crime:
they burned the ships, sank the fleet, and forced
the men to leave their friends on unknown shores.
I beg of you, let the rest sail safely,
let them reach Laurentian Tiber—if this is right,
if the goddesses of Fate give them this city."
Then Saturn's son, tamer of the deep seas, said:

. . .

"You've every right to trust my kingdom, Venus: 800
you were born in it. And I've earned this trust:
I've often stopped the sky and sea's great frenzy.
On land no less, I helped Aeneas; Simoïs
and Xanthus can attest to it. When Achilles
pinned the panicked Trojans to the walls,
sending thousands to their deaths, stopping up
the groaning streams so Xanthus couldn't reach
the sea, I rescued Aeneas in a cloud
as he fought brave Achilles, a greater man
in strength and dearer to the gods, even though   810
I wanted to uproot Troy's lying walls—the walls
I built!* I haven't changed my mind; let go your fear.
He'll reach Avernus' harbor safely, as you wish.
There'll only be one man to mourn for, lost at sea.
One life will pay for many." So Neptune soothed
and cheered the goddess's heart. Then he yoked
his wild horses with their golden harness
damp with foam, and fed out rein. He sped across
the ocean's surface in his sea-blue chariot.
Under the thundering axles, waves sank down,   820
swells subsided, and the clouds dissolved.
Up came his many-shaped companions, giant whales,
Glaucus' old troop, Palaemon, Ino's son,
speedy Tritons, all of Phorcus' army, Thetis,
Panopea and Melite at his left,
Thalia, Nesaea, Cymodoce, Spio.

At this a calm joy lulled Aeneas' anxious mind.
He ordered that the masts be raised at once
and the sails be stretched out on the yardarms.
As one, the crew hauled on the ropes, letting out   830
the canvas to the left and right. As one

they turned the high yards; fair winds moved the fleet.
Palinurus, in the front, led the dense
armada. The rest were told to tack his course.
Damp Night was near the midpoint of the sky,
and the sailors, sprawling by their oars
on rigid benches, were resting peacefully,
when Sleep, gliding from the stars above,
breached the dark and chased away the shadows,
looking for you, Palinurus, bringing fatal   840
slumber to a guiltless man.* In Phorbas' shape,
the god sat on the ship's high stern and made his pitch:
"Palinurus, Iäsus' son, the seas themselves
propel us, the winds blow evenly—there's time to rest.
Lay down your head, steal your tired eyes from work.
I'll take on your duties for a while."
Palinurus barely glanced at him: "You ask
me of all men to trust the sea's calm face
and quiet waves, to have faith in this monster?
As if I'd leave Aeneas to the lying breezes!   850
The clear skies' treachery has fooled me many times."
He held the tiller tight, not letting go,
and fixed his eyes upon the stars above.
Then the god shook over him a branch that dripped
with Lethe's dew and drugs of Stygian strength.
It shut his swimming eyes against his will.
He'd hardly slumped in unexpected rest
when Sleep bent over him and pitched him in the sea.
As he fell, he ripped the rudder from the stern,
calling often on his friends, but unheard.   860
Sleep rose on his wings into the sheer air
and the fleet sailed on as safely as before,
unperturbed, as father Neptune had assured.
As Aeneas' ship approached the Sirens' crags
(once treacherous and white with many bones)

where boulders battered by the surf roared endlessly,
he realized he was drifting with no pilot.
Groaning deeply, he himself took up the helm across
the midnight sea, sick at heart for his friend's fate:
"Ah, Palinurus, rashly trusting in calm winds   870
and sky, you'll lie unburied on an unknown shore."

BOOK 6

A VISIT TO HADES

So he said, in tears, and gave the fleet free rein.
At last they glided into Cumae's bay
and turned the prows to face the sea. The anchor's
bite secured the ships; the shore was fringed
with curving keels. Young men sprang out eagerly
onto the sand of Italy. Some tried to strike out
sparks from flint's deep veins, others scoured the forest,
home to many beasts, or noted streams they'd found.
Pious Aeneas made for great Apollo's temple
and the vast cave nearby, the sanctuary   10
of dread Sibyl, into whom the Delian seer
breathes his mind and mission, unveiling the future.
They neared the gold-roofed temple in Diana's grove.

It's said that Daedalus, fleeing Minos' kingdom,
trusted himself to the sky on sweeping wings,
taking this unusual passage to the frosty
North. At last he floated down on Chalcis' peak.
Back on land, he pledged Phoebus his wings—
his oars for flight—and built a lofty shrine.
On its doors he carved Androgeos' death   20
and the Athenians who paid an awful price,*
seven sons each year: an urn holds the lots.
Facing this, the land of Crete soars from the sea.
Here's Pasiphae's ruinous passion for a bull,
their stealthy coupling, and their son, the hybrid

Minotaur, a monument to awful lust.
Here's his lair, the labyrinth of no return.
But its builder Daedalus took pity on
a princess' love,* and solved the tangled turns,
guiding Theseus' blind footsteps with a thread.   30
Icarus, you'd be here too, if grief allowed.
Twice your father tried to carve your fall in gold,
twice his hands fell from his work. Aeneas wanted
to scan every detail, but Achates, sent
ahead, returned with Glaucus' child Deiphobe,
priestess of Diana and Apollo. She said:
"This is no time to be gaping at the sights.
Kill seven bulls who've never felt the yoke
and just as many sheep." His men were quick
to carry out the sacred task. Then the priestess   40
called the Trojans into her high temple.

There's a cliff at Cumae whose vast flank is cut
into a cave with openings to a hundred shafts.
Through them rush the Sibyl's answers, hundredfold.
As they reached the cave, she cried: "We must consult
the oracle at once: look, the god is present!"
At the door, her complexion changed, her hair
sprang loose, she began to pant: her heart was full
of frenzy. She seemed taller, and her voice
was not a human's, for Apollo was approaching   50
and she felt his breath. "Trojan Aeneas!" she cried.
"You hesitate to offer vows? Yet only then
will the mighty jaws that shake this cavern open
wide and awe us." Silence. A chill shiver swept
the Trojans' hardy bones. Their king prayed from his heart:
"Phoebus, you who always pitied Troy's great pain,
who directed Paris' arrow to pierce Achilles,
you've led my voyage through the many seas
that flow around the continents—to far

Massilian tribes, to fields that fringe the Syrtes.   60
At last we've come to Italy's receding shores.
Don't let Ilium's fate still hound us. All you gods
and goddesses: if Troy and her great fame were once
an aggravation, now with justice you may
spare the race of Pergamum. Holy priestess,
you who see the future, let the Trojans live
in Latium (I only claim land owed to me
by Fate) with their straying, storm-tossed gods.
I'll raise a shrine of solid marble to Phoebus*
and Diana, and choose feast days for Apollo.   70
Once I rule, I'll build a great shrine for you too,
kind Sibyl. I'll include the secret prophecies
you told my people, and consecrate your priests.
But don't entrust your oracles to leaves, or they'll
end up muddled, playthings spun by whirling
breezes. Chant them yourself, I beg." He stopped.

The Sibyl still could not accept Apollo.
She spiraled through the cave, trying to force
the great god from her mind. But he wore her out
still more, and forced the seer to his will.   80
On their own, the hundred huge shafts of the cave
swung open, wafting out her answers. "Trojans:
you've left behind the sea's great risks at last,
but graver ones remain on land. The Dardans
will attain Lavinian land (let go this worry),
but they'll wish they hadn't. I see brutal wars
and bloody torrents frothing in the Tiber.
There too you'll find a Simoïs, a Xanthus, and
Greek camps. In Latium you'll find a new Achilles,
he too a goddess's son. And worse, there's Juno   90
everywhere. A poor supplicant, how many
towns and tribes of Italy you'll beg for help!
The cause of so much trouble for the Trojans?

Again a foreign bride, a foreign wedding.
Don't give up at these misfortunes. Be as brave
as Fortune lets you. The first path to safety
will surprise you: it'll appear in a Greek city."

The Sibyl sang these fearsome riddles
in her shrine, wrapping truth in darkness
as her cave echoed round her, as Apollo   100
flicked her reins and sank his spurs in deeper.
When her seizure ended and her ravings stopped,
the hero Aeneas spoke. "No aspect of these
labors is unknown to me. I've foreseen
them all, and thought about each one of them. I ask
one thing. It's said this spot's a doorway to Hell's
ruler and the murky swamp of Acheron.
Let me see my dear father face to face:
teach me how, open the sacred portal.
He was the one my shoulders saved from flames   110
and a thousand hostile spears all around us.
He shared my journey. At my side he took on
all the oceans, all the threats of sky and sea,
a feeble man bearing a fate beyond old age.
He even begged me to approach your doors
and seek you as a supplicant. I pray,
be kind, pity a father and his son. You can:
Hecate granted you Avernus' groves to rule.
If Orpheus could summon his wife's shade
with his Thracian lyre's melody,   120
if Pollux shared his brother's death, and often
took his place in Hell—and what of Theseus
and Hercules? My blood too is that of Jove."

He grasped the altar, praying, and the Sibyl spoke.
"Anchises' Trojan son, born of divine blood,
it's easy to descend into Avernus.

Night and day the door of dusky Dis lies open.
To trace your steps and see the light again:
here's the toil and effort. A few, justly loved
by Jove, whom blazing courage carried to the sky,   130
succeeded—sons of gods. Forest fills the center;
the dark embrace of Cocytus surrounds it.
But if this urge compels you, if you must indulge
this folly, twice crossing the Stygian swamp,
twice seeing black Tartarus, hear then
your first task. A golden branch with golden
leaves and stubborn golden stems hides in the murky
foliage of Proserpina's sacred tree,
concealed by forest and the valley's gloom. None
may penetrate the hidden alcoves under earth   140
until they've plucked its golden growth: lovely
Proserpina ruled that it must be a gift
for her. If one branch is plucked, a new one
takes its place, and grows gold leaves as well.
Scour the deep woods. Once you've spotted it,
pluck it off by hand. If you're the one fate calls,
it'll break off easily. If not, no force,
no blade, will help you tear it off. Also:
I have sad news. A friend's corpse lies along
the shore and pollutes the fleet with death   150
while you seek advice and loiter at my door.
First take him to his resting-place and bury him.
Then offer black cattle—the first expiation.
This way you'll see the Stygian groves at last,
the lands barred to the living." Her mouth snapped shut.

Aeneas left the cave, walked on. He stared
sadly at the ground as he considered
this blind turn of events. Loyal Achates
kept him company and shared his worries.
They covered many topics as they talked: 160

What friend did the Sibyl mean, what body
needed burial? And then they saw Misenus
on the sandy shore, his life cut short unfairly,
Aeolus' son Misenus, most skilled of men
to fire up hearts for battle with his bugle's blare.
Marked out by his spear and trumpet, he used
to fight against his friend, great Hector. But when
victorious Achilles robbed Hector of life,
this bravest of heroes joined Aeneas
as companion, following no lesser leader.   170
But when he seized his hollow horn to make the seas
resound, challenging the gods in song (the fool!),
jealous Triton grabbed him up, if the tale
is true, and drowned him in the rocky surf.
They all raised loud laments around the body,
pious Aeneas the most, then carried out
the Sibyl's orders. In tears, they heaped logs on
the pyre and strove to raise it to the sky.
They entered ancient woods and wild lairs.
Pine trees fell, holm-oaks rang to axes' strikes,   180
oaks and ash trees fissured as the axmen drove in
wedges. They rolled huge rowans down the hills.

Aeneas led the work and spurred the men.
His tools were theirs. But in his somber heart
he thought of what he'd learned, and gazed over
the far-flung forest. Just then by chance he prayed:
"I wish the golden branch would show itself
in this vast wood right now—since what the Sibyl said
of you, Misenus, turned out all too true."
At his words, twin doves flew down from the sky,   190
landing on the grassy sod before him.
The great hero knew his mother's birds
and gladly prayed: "Be my guides, if there's a path,

and wing your way into the woods, wherever
that lush branch casts shade on loamy soil.
And you, my goddess mother, help me in my
hour of need." He spoke, and stopped to see
what signs the doves gave, where they went.
As they fed, the birds flitted from spot to spot,
always staying in his line of sight.   200
When they reached Avernus' jaws and reeking gorge,
they quickly rose, gliding through the crystal air,
and perched right where he'd hoped, on the dappled tree.
The gold's shining aura shimmered through the branches.
It looked like mistletoe in winter's cold, when
its green leaves ring around a foster-tree's
smooth trunk, the yellow flowers blooming. This was
how the shining gold appeared, growing
on the shadowed oak, rustling in the breeze.
At once Aeneas grabbed it. He snapped it eagerly   210
as it held on,* and took it to the priestess' shrine.

On the shore, the Trojans mourned Misenus,
offering last rites for his thankless embers.
They raised a massive pyre, fragrant with pine
and planks of oak, then wove dark foliage
along its sides and set up gloomy cypresses
in front. His gleaming armor crowned the top.
Some prepared hot water, boiling it in cauldrons.
They washed and anointed the cold corpse
and set the man they wept for on a bier, groaning,   220
giving him the purple robes owed to the dead.
Others raised the massive litter, an unhappy
duty, and set a torch below, eyes averted
for the rite. A pile of gifts went up in flames:
frankincense and foodstuff, olive oil in bowls.
When the blaze collapsed into gray cinders,

they washed the thirsty ashes, his remains, with wine.
Corynaeus laid the bones in a bronze urn
and walked around the men three times with sacred
water—the dew of a fertile olive branch—   230
sprinkling it to cleanse them, saying the last words.
Pious Aeneas built the tomb, a giant barrow
topped off with Misenus' armor, oar, and trumpet
below a looming bluff now called Misenus
after him. The name will last through all the ages.

Next he quickly carried out the Sibyl's orders.
There is a deep and yawning cave, its mouth
a giant jagged gape. A black lake and a forest's
shadow shield it. No bird can wing its way
across it with impunity: so putrid is   240
the breath its black jaws pour out to the upper air.
For this the Greeks called it Avernus, birdless.
The priestess set four steers with pitch-black hides
before the altar. She poured wine on their heads
and plucked the tall bristles between their horns
to throw into the sacred flames as offerings.
Next she called on Hecate, who moves Heaven
and Hell. They cut the steers' throats and caught
warm blood in bowls. Aeneas' sword struck down
a black lamb for the Furies' mother, Night, and her   250
sister, Earth; a barren cow for Proserpina.
He lit night altars to the Stygian king,
setting whole bulls on the flames, pouring
fatty oil over the burning entrails.
At the rising sun's first rays, the ground rumbled
and forest ridges shook. As Hecate approached,
dogs seemed to howl through the half-light.
"Get out, get out, unholy ones," the Sibyl cried.
"Leave all the grove behind! And you, Aeneas,

quickly grab your weapon from its sheath.   260
Now you must be brave and resolute."
Raving, she flung herself into her open cave.
Aeneas kept pace, and not with timid steps.

O gods who govern souls, O silent shades, Chaos,
Phlegethon, and mute expanses of the night,
let it be right to tell what I have heard, let me
show what's buried deep in earth and darkness.

They went, faded figures in the lonely night,
through the lifeless, empty realm of Dis,
as if through a wood under a clouded moon's   270
thin light, when Jove has plunged the sky in shadow
and black night leaches color from the world.
At the entrance, in Orcus' very jaws,
Grief and vengeful Sorrow made their beds,
and Pale Diseases, sad Old Age, and Fear
and ill-advising Hunger and shameful Poverty,
forms horrible to see, and Death and Suffering,
then Death's brother Slumber, and the Joys
of evil men. Facing them were murderous War
and the Furies' iron chambers and mad Discord,   280
her serpent hair bound up with bloody ribbons.
There a giant dark-leafed elm spread out
its ancient branches. They say false Dreams
live on it, clinging under every leaf.
Many other ghastly forms of freaks
were stabled by the doors: Centaurs, biform Scylla,
Briareus' hundred arms, the beast of Lerna
hissing horribly, Chimaera breathing fire,
Gorgons, Harpies, and the ghost of three-trunked
Geryon. Aeneas shook with sudden fear.   290
He grabbed his sword and held its naked edge to them.

If his wise guide hadn't chided him that these
were insubstantial wraiths and flitting images,
he'd have rushed to slash the shadows pointlessly.

From here began the path to hellish Acheron's
violent whirls of water. It seethed and swirled,
belching sand into the river Cocytus.
Filthy Charon, wearing stinking rags,
ferried ghosts across the stream. His lengthy
beard was matted stiff, his eyes stared fixed   300
and fierce. A dirty wrap was tied around his neck.
He poled the boat himself, tending to the sails,
toting bodies in the dingy raft. He was old,
but it was the green and raw old age of gods.
All the crowd came streaming to this shore:
mothers, men, the lifeless bodies of brave
heroes, boys and unwed girls, sons placed
on the pyre before their parents' eyes—
as many as the forest leaves that fall
in autumn's early chill, as many as the birds   310
who flock to land from sea, when the winter
drives them south to sunny lands. There
they stood, pleading to be first to cross,
stretching longing hands toward the farther bank.
The surly boatman took now some, now others.
The rest he shoved far from the sandy shore.
Aeneas was surprised and moved to see the tumult.
He asked: "Why are they rushing to the stream?
What do these souls want? Why are some left behind
while others sweep black water with the oars?"   320
The ancient priestess answered in few words:
"Anchises' son, the gods' true child, you see
the sluggish depths of Cocytus and Styx,
by which gods fear to swear false oaths. All this
crowd you see lacks burial—or any recourse.

The ferryman is Charon; his passengers have graves.
He can't carry anyone across the awful
roaring waters till their bones find rest.
They flit around these shores one hundred years.
At last they board and reach the bank they've craved."   330
Anchises' son stopped still and stood, mulling over
many things. He pitied these souls' unfair fate.
He saw Leucaspis and Orontes, leader of
the Lycian fleet, both sad without funerals.
The south wind had submerged the men and ships
as they sailed on storm-swept seas from Troy.

Now the helmsman Palinurus passed by him.
Lately, on the course from Libya, as he read
the stars, he'd toppled from the stern into deep sea.
Aeneas, barely making out his sad form   340
in the gloom, cried out his name. "What god stole you
from us, and threw you in the sea? Tell me.
I've never found Apollo false, but when
he spoke of you he lied: he prophesied
that you'd stay safe across the sea to Italy.
Is this how he keeps his word?" But the helmsman
said, "Apollo's cauldron didn't lie to you,
my lord, Anchises' son. No god drowned me at sea.*
The helm, my posting, violently swung from me
as I held it tight and planned our course. I fell   350
and dragged it with me. I swear by the harsh seas:
I feared less for me than for your ship.
Her tiller gone, her helmsman overboard,
would she founder in the rising waves?
For three winter nights the fierce south wind drove me
through the endless sea. On the fourth dawn,
I could just sight Italy from a high crest.
I was closing on the shore, almost safe,
but as I grabbed at rough rock-holds, weighed down

by wet clothes, a cruel tribe set on me   360
with knives, thinking me a prize, the fools.
Winds and waves now roll me by the shore.
I beg you by the lovely light of sky, the air,
by your father, and your hopes for young Iülus,
save me from this hell, since you've overcome it,
and throw soil on my corpse if you reach Velia.
Or if *you* have a way, if your goddess mother
shows you one (you couldn't ford this stream
and Styx's swamp without divine assistance),
take my poor hand, take me on board with you,   370
so that at least in death I'll find a place of rest."
So he begged, but the priestess countered:
"Palinurus, why this dread desire to see
the Stygian waters and the Furies' cruel streams,
to approach the bank unburied and uncalled?
As if the gods' fates could be bent by prayer.
But take my words as comfort for your pain:
moved by divine omens, nearby folk
from cities far and wide will appease your shade.
They'll raise a tomb for you and pay due offerings.   380
That spot will always be called Palinurus."
His cares were lifted at these words, his sorrow
banished for a while. The name brought him joy.

And so they went on, heading for the river.
But from his stream the boatman saw them coming
from the silent grove and turning to the bank.
He was quick to shout out a rebuke.
"You two, armed and making for my river:
stop right there and tell me why you're here.
This is a place of shadows, of Sleep and sleepy Night.   390
Living bodies may not ride my Stygian boat.
I wasn't pleased to transport Hercules

over the lake, nor Theseus and Pirithoüs—
and *they* were sons of gods, never defeated.
One wanted to chain Tartarus's guard-dog.
He dragged him trembling from the king's own throne!
The other planned to steal our queen from Dis's bed."
Apollo's seer answered in few words:
"We have no such scheme; you needn't be upset.
Our weapons don't bring violence. Your guard can scare   400
the bloodless shades with barks for all eternity,
the bride can chastely stay inside her uncle's home.
Aeneas of Troy, famed for piety and warfare,
visits his father in the depths of Hell.
If this model of great piety means nothing,
at least you know this branch." She took it
from her robe, and his swollen heart let go
its rage. No more was said. He marveled at
the sacred gift, the fateful branch displayed
after so long, and swung his dark stern to the shore.   410
Expelling all the souls that sat along the transoms,
he cleared the gangway. Then he boarded huge
Aeneas in his stitched-skin boat. It groaned
under the weight; marsh-water flooded in.
At last he set them safe across the river, man and
seer, onto the slimy mud and gray-green reeds.

There sprawled giant Cerberus, in a cave
along the bank. He snarled at them from all three throats.
When the priestess saw his snaky hackles rise,
she tossed him a gob of honey and drugged grain   420
to make him sleep. Three starving throats sprang open,
greedy to snatch the morsel. Then his massive bulk
slumped to the ground, spanning the whole cave.
Now that the guard was sunk in sleep, Aeneas entered,
quick to leave the stream no man could ford again.

. . .

At once he could hear voices: the loud wails
and weeping souls of babies cheated of sweet life.
At the start, a black day tore them from their
mothers' milk and buried them in bitter death.
Next were those wrongly condemned to die.   430
Jurors drawn by lot decided where they'd go.
Minos was the magistrate. He shook the urn
and called a council of the dead to judge the crimes.
Next were the despondent suicides.
Though innocent, they threw their lives away,
sick of the light of day. How gladly now they'd welcome
pain and poverty, just to breathe the air!
But divine law forbids it. The gloomy waves and
hateful swamp confine them, and the nine coils of
the Styx. Close by, he was shown the Fields of Mourning, 440
as they're called. They stretched in all directions.
Here were those whom heartless love consumed
with cruel pining. Secret paths and myrtle trees
concealed them and their passion lived past death.
He saw Phaedra, Procris, and Eriphyle,
sadly showing stabs her cruel son inflicted,
Pasiphae, Laodamia, and Evadne.
With them was Caeneus, once transformed into a man,
then given back her former shape by fate.
In this great wood, Phoenician Dido, her wound   450
still fresh, wandered with them. When the Trojan
hero neared and saw her misty shape among the ghosts
—as when one sees, or thinks one sees, a new moon
climbing through the clouds when the month is young
—he spoke to her in tears with tender love:
"Unhappy Dido, so the news I heard was true?
You're dead, a suicide by the sword? But—
did I cause your death?* I call the stars and gods
to witness: if the Underworld allows the truth,

I left your shores against my will, O Queen.*   460
The orders of the gods, which force me now
to walk through shades and squalor in deep night,
forced me those days too. How could I think
I'd cause you so much pain by my departure?
Stop, don't rush from my sight. Who is it
you run from? Fate gives us a final chance to speak."
With these words he tried to soothe the raging soul
that looked at him so fiercely. His tears fell.
But Dido turned away, her eyes fixed on the ground,
her face just as unaltered by his speech   470
as hard flint or a rocky crag of marble.
At last she broke away hate-filled, and hurried
to the shaded forest where Sychaeus, her first
husband, shared her pain and matched her love.
Aeneas was shaken by her unjust death. His eyes
followed her with tears and pity as she left.*

He struggled on his given path. And now they reached
the farthest fields, set aside for heroes in war.
Tydeus met them with Parthenopaeus,
great in battle, and the shade of pale Adrastus.   480
Also Trojans who fell fighting, lamented
to the skies. He groaned to see the crowded ranks:
Thersilochus, Glaucus, Medon, Antenor's
three sons, Polyboetes, priest of Ceres,
and Idaeus with his chariot and armor.
The souls thronged round him to the left and right.
To see him was too little: they wanted to linger,
to walk with him and learn why he had come.
But the Greek chiefs and Agamemnon's army
shook in fear when they saw the hero's weapons   490
gleaming in the gloom. Some turned round to run,
just as they once scuttled to their ships. Others
raised a weak war-cry that mocked their gaping jaws.

. . .

And now he saw Deiphobus, Priam's son,
his whole body mangled, his face and both his hands
with cruel gashes, ears ripped from his ruined head,
his nose slashed to the nostrils—a shameful injury.
Aeneas hardly knew the trembling shade that tried
to hide its ghastly wounds, and questioned his old friend:
"Great warrior of Teucer's noble blood,   500
who chose to punish you so viciously? Who took
such liberties? On that final night, I heard,
you fell onto a heap of mingled corpses,
exhausted from your massacre of Greeks.
I raised your empty tomb on Rhoeteum's shore,
and loudly called your shade three times. Your name
and armor mark the place, but I never found you,
friend, to bury you before I left our country."
"Friend, you left nothing undone," said Priam's son.
"You paid the honors due Deiphobus's ghost.   510
My fate and Spartan Helen's heinous crime threw me
in this hell; *she* left me these souvenirs.
You know we filled that final night with foolish
revelry. You must recall it all too well.
When the deadly horse pregnant with infantry
entered our citadel, Helen faked a Bacchic
frenzy and launched the shrieking Trojan women
into dance. Then she raised a giant torch
to signal to the Greeks from our acropolis.
I was in my luckless marriage-bed, worn out   520
with worry, lost in sleep. A deep, sweet rest
was pressing on me like the peace of death.
My darling wife removed the weapons from our house
and stole the trusted sword under my head.
She flung the entrance open and called in Menelaus,
no doubt hoping this great favor to her lover
would erase the infamy of her old sins.

What's left to say? He burst in with Ulysses,
the father of all crime. O gods, pay back the Greeks
in kind, if I ask for vengeance justly!   530
But tell me now what brought you here alive.
Did you steer off course as you were sailing?
Is this some god's command? What fate hounds you so,
that you'd approach this place of murk and misery?"

Meanwhile, Aurora in her rosy chariot
had crossed the summit of the sky, and perhaps
they'd have used up all their time in talk,
but the Sibyl, his companion, warned him curtly:
"Night falls fast, Aeneas. We waste our hours weeping.
Here the path splits into two. On the right,   540
the route leads past the walls of mighty Dis, our way
to Elysium. The left path sends the wicked
to their punishment in godless Tartarus."
Deiphobus replied: "Don't rage at me, great priestess.
I'll return and take my place among the dead.
Go on, glory of our land. Be luckier
than me." So he spoke, turning away.

Aeneas stole a quick glance back. To the left,
under a cliff, was a massive fortress ringed with
triple walls and a raging moat of fire: 550
Phlegethon, hurling thunderous rocks.
In front, a giant gate and adamantine pillars.
No human force, not even warring gods,
could rip them out. An iron tower reached the sky.
There Tisiphone crouched wakefully, her bloody cloak
hitched high. She watched the entrance day and night.
You could hear groans and savage lash-strokes,
irons clanking, chains being dragged. Terrified,
Aeneas stopped to listen to the clamor.
"Virgin, what were their crimes? What tortures are   560

inflicted here? Why does this wailing fill the air?"
The seer began: "Famed leader of the Trojans,
no good souls may cross this evil threshold.
When Hecate assigned Avernus' woods to me,
she taught me all the ways gods punish men.
Cretan Rhadamanthus rules these cruel realms.
He hears and rebukes deceit, making men
confess the secret crimes they relished when alive,
the guilt they pointlessly delayed till death's late hour.
Vengeful Tisiphone, carrying her whip,   570
at once leaps down to flay the guilty. She thrusts
her vicious snakes at them, calling on her cruel
sisters. Finally the awful gate swings open
with the screech of grating hinges. Do you see
her awful lurking shape guarding the entrance?
More savage still is what's inside: massive Hydra,
her fifty black mouths gaping. Then Tartarus itself
plunges to a sheer abyss, a fall to darkness
twice as far as when we gaze at high Olympus.
The Titans are there, an ancient race of Earth   580
struck down by lightning. They grovel in the dregs of Hell.
I also saw Aloeus' twins, giant bulks
who tried to tear down heaven with their hands
and dislodge Jupiter from his high realm.
I saw Salmoneus paying a cruel price
for mimicking Jove's lightning and Olympian thunder.
He rode in triumph through Greek cities and
his home town, Elis, brandishing a torch, taking
for himself the honor due the gods, the fool,
faking the impossible—storms and lightning—   590
with bronze cymbals and the beat of hooves.
The mighty father flung his fire-bolt through
the heavy clouds—*he* didn't need the smoky light
of sputtering torches—and hurled him straight to Hell.
Tityus was here, foster-son of Earth,

his body sprawling through nine acres. A filthy
vulture digs into his deathless liver (always
ripe for torture) with its curving beak,
foraging for dinner, at home deep in
his guts. The reborn organ gets no rest.   600
Should I mention Lapiths, Pirithoüs, and
Ixion? A black cliff looms over them,
on the verge of falling. Golden legs gleam on
their couches and a feast of royal opulence
is spread: but the leader of the Furies sits
right there, forbidding them to reach for food,
always leaping up, raising her torch, and shrieking.
All those who loathed their brothers during life,
who beat their parents or caught clients in a web
of fraud, or sat on gold they'd just acquired, putting   610
no part aside for family (the biggest group),
or were murdered in adultery, or fought
in civil wars, or broke faith with their masters—
locked up, they wait for punishment. Don't ask
what punishment. There's no one form or fate.
Some heave along huge boulders, or lie outspread
on wheel-spokes. Doomed Theseus will sit forever
in a chair, and Phlegyas, who suffers most,
chides all of them and cries among the shades:
'Be warned, learn justice, do not scorn the gods.'   620
This one sold his country and let a tyrant
rule it. This one made and remade laws for money.
Incest drove one to his daughter's bed.
All dared monstrous crimes—successfully.
A hundred tongues and mouths, an iron voice,
wouldn't let me cover the varieties
of evil, nor all the names for punishments."

This said, Phoebus' aged priestess told him: "Come,
return now to the road; end the task you started.

We must hurry. I can see the ramparts built   630
by Cyclopian forges and the arching gateway.
Our orders were to set the gift down here."
They went along the dark path side by side,
crossed the open ground, and reached the doors.
Aeneas entered first. He sprinkled himself with fresh
water, then set the branch at Proserpina's threshold.

They were done, the goddess' gift delivered.
The fields of joy were next, the sweet green groves
held by the fortunate, homes of the blessed.
The fields were bathed in dazzling light by skies   640
wider than ours, and a different sun and stars.
Some exercised in grassy rings, or fought
mock battles, grappling on the golden sand.
Others stamped their feet in dance, singing songs.
The Thracian seer was there in his trailing robe.
He played his lyre's seven strings in rhythm,
plucking notes with fingers or an ivory pick.
Teucer's ancient race was there, his handsome sons,
great-souled heroes born in better years: Ilus,
Assaracus, and Troy's founder, Dardanus.   650
Aeneas marveled at their phantom chariots
and armor, the spears fixed in the earth, the horses
freely grazing far and wide. The men's love
of chariots and armor, of feeding their sleek
stallions, lasted after death. He saw
others to the right and left, feasting
in the meadows, singing glad odes in groves
fragrant with laurel, where the great stream Eridanus
surfaces to flow among the trees.
Here were legions wounded fighting for their   660
country, priests who'd led pure lives, pious
poets with songs worthy of Apollo,
men who bettered life by new inventions,

and those whose merit set them down in memory.
All their brows were bound with snow-white ribbons.
As they thronged around, the Sibyl spoke to them,
Musaeus first (he was in the center
of the crowd, tallest by a head). She asked:
"Tell me, happy souls, and you, best among poets,
what land, what place holds Anchises? It's for   670
his sake we've come, fording mighty Erebus."
The hero answered briefly: "No one's home
is set. We live in shady groves, or by
the river-banks' soft bends or meadows sweet
with streams. But if this is what you want, you must
climb this ridge. I'll show you an easy path."
He walked ahead, pointing out the shining fields
below. The other two descended from the heights.

Deep in that lush valley, Father Anchises
made a careful count of gathered souls   680
as they waited for the light above. He happened
to be tallying his family, his dear
grandsons' fates and fortunes, natures and great deeds.
When he saw Aeneas coming to him through
the meadow, he stretched out both arms eagerly.
Tears ran down his face and he exclaimed:
"You've come at last? I knew your piety
would overcome the dangers of the trip. Do I
see your face, my child, and hear that voice I know?
I expected this would happen, I counted   690
down the days. My worry's been rewarded.
You've come so far by land and sea to visit me,
dear son, and you've suffered so much hardship.
How I feared that you'd be harmed in Libya!"
He answered: "Father, your sad ghost, visiting
so often, made me cross this boundary.
Our fleet waits on the Tuscan sea. Let me clasp

your hand, don't pull back from my embrace."
Tears soaked Aeneas' face. Three times he tried
to wrap his arms around his father's neck; three times   700
his hands passed through the insubstantial shade, as if
it were the merest breeze, a fleeting dream.

And now Aeneas saw, at the valley's end,
a sheltered wood with rustling branches, and
the river Lethe flowing through this peaceful place.
The souls of countless peoples flitted here,
the way bees haunt a meadow's many-colored flowers
in the still of summer, circling round bright
lilies as the whole field buzzes with their hum.
This sudden sight startled Aeneas. He asked   710
for explanation: "What is that far-off river?
Who are the many men who throng its banks?"
Anchises said: "These are the souls to whom
fate owes new bodies. They drink from Lethe's stream:
it offers peace and long oblivion. I've yearned
so long to show and tell you of them face to
face, this gathering of my family, so that
you'd be still happier at finding Italy."
"But father, must we think that some souls pass from here
to life above, taking up the weight of flesh   720
again? Why this awful longing for the light?"
"I'll tell you, son," Anchises said. "You won't remain
confused." And he explained each thing in order.

"First: the sky and land and liquid fields of sea,
the silvery sphere of moon, and Titan the sun—
Spirit nurtures them within, and Mind's infused
throughout, animating mass and mixing with it.
From here comes the race of men and beasts, the lives
of birds, the monsters under Ocean's marble surface.
These seeds have a fiery vigor, and their source   730

is heavenly. But harmful matter slows them down,
and they're blunted by our bodies, which must die.
So men fear and want, grieve and feel glad.
Locked in this dark dungeon, they can't perceive the sky.
Poor things, even when life leaves them on the day
of death, not every sin or canker of the flesh
fully recedes. Many habits harden
over time, and in this way become ingrained.
So they pay for former crimes by torment:
exposed to hollow winds by crucifixion,   740
washed clean of infection in a whirling flood,
or cauterized by fire—we all suffer our soul's
cure. Then we're sent to wide Elysium.
A few of us stay in this happy place
until long years have purged the final taint of matter
and time's great wheel has come full circle: only
ether's spirit, the fire of pure air, remains.
When the rest have cycled through a thousand years,
the god calls them in clusters to the river Lethe:*
These forgetful spirits hope for resurrection   750
into bodies. They start to want to see the sky."

Falling quiet, Anchises drew his son and Sibyl
to the center of the bustling crowd.
From a hill, he studied the men marching by
and knew their faces in the long procession.

"Come," he said, "I'll reveal the future glory
of our Trojan lineage, and the Italians
who wait for us, splendid souls who'll take our name.*
I'll teach you your destiny. Do you see
the young man leaning on the headless spear?   760
By lot, he'll be the next to reach the light
above, his blood mingled with Italy's:
Silvius, an Alban name, your last-born son.

Lavinia, your wife, will bear him in a forest
when you're elderly: a king, to other kings
a father. Through him our race will rule in Alba Longa.*
Next is famous Procas, glory of the Trojan
race. Then Capys, Numitor, and your namesake
Silvius Aeneas, your match in piety
and weapons—if he can take up Alba's throne.   770
What young men!—see the great strength that they show,
the civic crowns of oak leaves on their heads!
They'll found Nomentum, Gabiï, Fidena;
they'll set Collatia's fortress on the hills.
Pometiï, Castrum Inuï, Bola, and
Cora will be names, now just nameless lands.
Mars' son Romulus will join his grandfather
on earth, Trojan through his mother, Ilia.
Do you see his helmet's double crests?
His father honored him with his own emblem.   780
Under his rule, shining Rome will spread
her empire through the world, her spirit to Olympus,
and set a single wall around her seven hills.
She'll be rich in sons—like tower-crowned Cybele,
riding in her chariot through Phrygian towns,
happy in the gods she bore, a hundred grandsons
in her arms, all divine, all heaven-dwellers.
Now turn your eyes, look at this race, your Romans.
Here is Caesar, with all of Iülus' children
who'll come under the sky's great axis. And here: 790
the man you hear so often promised to you,
Augustus Caesar, born of gods, who'll bring
a golden age to Latium,* where Saturn lived,
and push his empire past the Garamants
and Indians to lands beyond our stars,
beyond Sun's yearly path, where Atlas hoists the sky,
turning the star-studded sphere on his shoulder.
Even Caspian lands and the Black Sea dread his

approach; they already fear the prophecies.
The seven deltas of the Nile tremble in terror.   800
Hercules himself did not cross so much land,
although he shot the bronze-hoofed deer, brought peace
to Erymanthus' woods, and scared the Lerna with
his bow; nor triumphant Bacchus, using vines
to steer his team of tigers as he drives down Nysa's
summit. Will we hesitate to put our courage
to the test? Does fear keep us from our home
in Italy? Who's that far off, distinct with his
olive crown and offerings? I see the gray beard
of King Numa, called from humble Cures   810
and its pauper fields to power. He'll impose
the rule of law. Next is Tullus, who will
shatter the land's peace and push into armed
ranks slow men long since unused to triumph.
The boaster Ancus follows him, even now
too taken with the masses' favor. Do you wish
to see the Tarquin kings, and the proud soul
of Brutus the avenger, who won back the fasces?
He'll be the first to hold a consul's power and
the cruel axes. For lovely liberty, he'll kill   820
his own sons when they stir up revolution,
unhappy man, however later ages tell it.
His love of country won—and his great greed for glory.
Far off you see the Drusi and the Decii,
Torquatus (brutal axman) and Camillus, savior
of the standards. That shining pair in matching armor,
in concord now while darkness presses them:
if they ever reach the light of life, ah,
the wars, the slaughter they'll stir up! The father-in-law
swoops down from his Alpine ramparts and   830
Monoecus' heights while his son-in law masses
the Eastern enemy! My sons, don't warm to war,
don't turn your sword against your country's heart.

You who trace your blood back to Olympus, stop first,
drop your weapon from your hand, my kin!
This one's* fame comes from the Greeks he killed at Corinth:
he'll ride in victory to the lofty Capitol.
That one will destroy Argos, Agamemnon's
Mycene and Perseus (great Achilles'
heir), avenging Troy and Minerva's looted   840
temple. Who'd omit great Cato, or you, Cossus?
Or the Gracchi and two Scipios, Libya's
ruin, thunderbolts of war; Fabricius,
powerful though poor, Serranus sowing furrows?
You Fabii, why hurry? Maximus,
you'll be the only one to save our land by lagging.
Others, I believe, will beat out bronze* that seems
to breathe and chisel living faces out of marble.
They'll excel in pleading lawsuits, and they'll trace
the heavens' paths and chart the rising stars.   850
You, Roman, remember your own arts:* to rule
the world with law, impose your ways on peace,
grant the conquered clemency, and crush the proud in war."

They were struck with awe. Anchises added:
"See Claudius Marcellus, marked by splendid spoils?
Victorious, he strides along, the tallest there.
This horseman will steady Roman power
in a time of chaos, trample rebel Gaul and
Carthage, and for the third time offer captured arms
to Romulus." Aeneas saw a handsome young man   860
near Marcellus, in bright armor, but his face
showed little joy, and his eyes were downcast.
He asked Anchises: "Who is that who goes with him?
A son? A son's son from this noble stock?
How his comrades cheer! What a fine impression!
But black night flaps around his head with her grim shadow."
Then tears welled in Anchises' eyes. "My child,

don't ask about the great grief of your people.
The fates will offer us the merest glimpse of him;
they won't let him live long. Would the Romans seem   870
too powerful to you, O gods, if he were ours?
What mighty groans of men the Field of Mars
will send to our great city! What a funeral
you'll see, Tiber, as you pass his tomb's fresh soil!
No other Trojan boy will so exalt the hopes
of his Latin forefathers, nor will the land
of Romulus ever boast his like again—
his piety, old-time honor, and unconquered
strength. He'd have had no equal in a fight,
no matter if he met the enemy on foot   880
or horse, spurring on his stallion's sweaty flanks.
Unhappy boy, if you can change your cruel fate,
you'll be a true Marcellus. Fill my arms with lilies;
I'll scatter these bright flowers for your soul,
my kin—just poor offerings and an empty
rite." So they passed through the whole region
in the misty air, and surveyed it all.
Anchises led his son through every sight
and fired his spirit with a love of future glory.
Then he told him of the wars he'd have to fight   890
and spoke of the Laurentians and Latinus'
town, the hardships to avoid, those to endure.

There are twin Gates of Sleep.* One, they say, is made
of horn, and lets true visions pass through easily.
The other gleams with complex work in ivory,
but through it shades send lying visions to the light.
Anchises and the Sibyl brought Aeneas
to this gate and sent him through. He hurried
to the ships and joined his crew. They sailed
along the coastline to Caieta's harbor   900
and cast anchor. The sterns rested on the shore.

BOOK 7

ITALY—AND WAR

Caieta, once Aeneas' nurse, you died here too.*
The city named for you now has eternal fame.
This honor marks your bones and resting place
in great Hesperia—if that is any glory.

After her burial rites, when the grave-mound had been
raised, pious Aeneas waited for calm seas,
then made his way from port under full sail.
The breezes blew past sundown and the shining moon
lit up their path; the ocean gleamed with shivery light.
First they grazed the shores of Circe, the Sun's   10
wealthy daughter. Around her, dangerous groves
resounded with her singing. In her lofty halls
she kindled cedar to dispel the dark, and wove
a whirring shuttle through her loom's fine warp.
From here they faintly heard the angry growls
of lions yanking at their chains and roaring late at night,
and bristly boars and bears raging in pens, and huge
howling shapes of wolves—human once, but
altered from their form by the cruel goddess's
magic herbs. They wore the face and fur of beasts.   20
To spare the pious Trojans from the horrors
of this port and hateful shore, Neptune
filled their sails with helping winds and pushed
their ships to safety past the foaming shoals.

. . .

The sea began to blush with sun, and saffron Dawn
high in her rosy chariot shone bright.
Suddenly the winds died down and every gust
was still. The oars pulled slowly in the marble sea.
Then Aeneas, on his ship, saw a lengthy
stretch of woodland. At that spot, the lovely Tiber,   30
yellow with thick sand and churning eddies,
burst into the sea. All around, the varied
birds for whom the banks and stream were home
caressed the sky with song and flew among the trees.
He told his crew to point the prows to land.
Happily, they sailed into the shaded stream.

Come, Erato!* I'll unfold the kings, the times,
the state of ancient Latium when foreign troops
first landed on Italian shores; I'll call
to memory the incidents that started war.   40
Goddess, guide your poet. I'll tell of brutal clashes,
battle lines, courage that sent kings to death,
Etruscan warriors, and all of Italy
in arms. A greater series of events begins,
a greater task for me.

                         Elderly King Latinus
ruled these fields and quiet cities in long peace.*
They say that Faunus fathered him on Marica,
a Laurentian nymph. Faunus' father, Picus,
traced his blood to Saturn, founder of the race.
By the gods' decree, Latinus had no sons;   50
one was lost to him in childhood. A single
daughter tended that great house—now of age
and ready for a husband. Many from wide
Latium and Italy were wooing her.

Turnus was the handsomest of all, and
of noble ancestry. The royal queen was keen
to make him son-in-law (her love for him was striking).
But sacred omens blocked this with a string of horrors.
A laurel tree with holy leaves stood in the royal
home's inner court, revered for many years.   60
They say father Latinus found this tree
when he built the citadel. He made it sacred
to Apollo, and named his folk Laurentians.
Now a swarm of bees (amazing!) occupied
its crown, sailing through the clear air
with a mighty buzz. They wove their feet and formed
an instant beehive hanging from a leafy branch.
At once the seer pronounced: "I see a foreign man
arriving with an army—his path, his goal
are like the bees'; he plans to take our heights!"   70
Then, when chaste Lavinia lit the altar
with a sacred torch, standing by her father,
they saw her long hair catch on fire—horrible!
Her headdress crackled as flames scorched it;
the tiara, bright with many gems, blazed up.
She herself, engulfed in smoke and orange
light, scattered sparks through all the house.
This was felt to be miraculous and awful:
seers foresaw that she'd be famed in life
and legend, but bring great conflict to her people.   80

The king, worried by these omens, visited
the oracle of Faunus, his prophetic father,
in great Albunea's grove, which echoes
with a sacred spring; the air is foul
and dark. Here the Italians and all
Oenotria seek guidance when in doubt. Once a
seer has given gifts, he lies in the silent night
on pelts of sheep he's killed, waiting for dreams,

and sees an eerie host of phantoms flit around
with varied voices. He has the right to speak 90
with gods; he talks to Acheron in deep Avernus.
Here Latinus, likewise seeking answers,
sacrificed a hundred woolly sheep.
He spread their pelts and lay on them to rest.
A sudden voice spoke out from the deep grove:
"Don't wed your daughter to the Latins, son,
don't trust the marriage that's already planned.
Foreigners will come to be your sons-in-law.
They'll raise our name up to the stars by blood.*
Their sons will see the world under their feet. 100
They'll rule as far as both the seas seen by the circling
sun." Latinus didn't hide what Faunus said,
the warning given in the silent night.
When the men from Troy tied fast their fleet
to the river's grassy bank, flitting Rumor
had already spread it through Italian towns.

Aeneas, handsome Iülus and the leading princes
sprawled under a tree's high branches to prepare
their meal. They set flatbreads on the grass
as plates for food (so Jupiter himself advised) 110
and added woodland fruits to these spelt disks.
By chance, when everything was eaten, hunger
made them gnaw the thin round crusts, and break
with daring hands and mouths the disks of fateful
bread, quartered sections one and all.
"See, we eat our tables, too!" said Iülus—
only that, a joke. But this comment
marked the end of hardship. Stunned, Aeneas
seized on Iülus' words and hushed his son.
He spoke at once: "I greet you, country owed to me 120
by fate, and you, the faithful gods of Trojan hearths.
This is our home, your native land. My father

(I remember!) left me with this fateful secret:*
'When you come to unknown shores, my son,
and hunger makes you eat your tables, then,
despite exhaustion, know you're home. Set your buildings
here first, and heap ramparts around them.'
This was that same hunger, this was the last
trial we had to face, an end to exile.
At sun's first light let's happily explore   130
this land, and learn who lives in it, and where
they've set their towns. We'll branch out from the port.
Now honor Jove with offerings, pray to Father
Anchises, and refresh the altars' wine."

He wound a leafy sprig around his head,
calling on the local guardian spirit, Earth,
the first of gods, nymphs and unknown streams,
then Night, its rising constellations, Ida's Jove,
and the Phrygian Mother, all in order,
then his parents, one in heaven, one in Hades.   140
The mighty Father thundered three times loudly
in the clear sky, and flourished in his hand
a cloud that blazed with golden rays from high above.
At once rumor swept the Trojan ranks:
the time had come to build the fated walls!
Quickly they renewed the feast, setting up
and garlanding the wine, glad at the great omen.

At the start of day, when Titan's torch lit up
the land, they scattered to spy out the towns,
the coast and country. Here was Numicus' lake,   150
here the river Tiber, here lived strong Latins.
Aeneas picked a hundred envoys of all ranks
and sent them to Latinus' lordly home,
decked with branches from Athena's olive tree
and taking presents for the king, to ask for peace.

No delay: they rushed off at a rapid pace.
Meanwhile he traced future walls with shallow trenches
on the shore, building his first town, circling it
with parapets and ramparts, like a camp.
When the envoys came, they saw the Latins' towers   160
and high homes, and passed under the city gate.
Outside the walls, boys and young men in their prime
trained horses in the dust, tamed teams for chariots,
pulled bows taut or hurled vibrating lances,
challenging each other to boxing or a race.
One rode ahead to tell the aged king: imposing
men in foreign clothes had come to Latium.
Latinus had them called inside the palace
and took his seat on his ancestral throne.

On the city peak, Laurentian Picus' palace   170
rose up huge and hallowed on a hundred columns,
a site eerie with woods and ancient rituals.
Auspicious kings received their scepters and the rods
of office here. Their senate-house and sacred feasts
were here, and here, at lengthy tables, the elders
sat to eat after they'd sacrificed a ram.
Statues of the ancestors stood in a row
inside the vestibule, hewn of ancient cedar:
Italus, the vine-grower Sabinus
with his curving scythe, ancient Saturn   180
and the bust of two-faced Janus, other early
kings, and those wounded fighting for their country.
Many weapons too hung on the sacred doorposts:
captured chariots and curving ax-blades, crests of
helmets, giant bolts from city gates, spears and
shields, bronze prows torn from ships. Picus himself,
the horse-tamer, sat there with an augur's staff,
his tunic edged in purple, a sacred shield
in his left hand. His lover Circe, lost to lust,

used her golden wand and drugs to change him   190
to a bird, and sprinkled colors on his wings.*

In this holy temple, on his ancestral throne,
Latinus called the Teucrians inside.
When they came, he said to them serenely:
"Speak, Dardanians. We know your city
and your race, we'd heard that you were sailing here.
Why? What cause, what need carried your ships
to Italy through spans of dark blue sea?
Perhaps you lost your way or storms blew you
off course—sailors often meet with such bad luck.   200
You've traveled up our stream, you dock at our harbor.
Don't reject our welcome. The Latins are the race
of Saturn; no chains or laws compel us to be just,
only free will—we keep our old god's ways.
I recall (the story dims with passing years)
how old Auruncans claimed that Dardanus, born
in these fields, later left for Phrygian Ida's
towns and Thracian Samos—now it's Samothrace.
He sailed from here, his Tuscan home of Corythus.
These days his throne is in the starry sky's gold   210
court. His altars add to the gods' numbers."

Ilioneus answered him: "My king,
distinguished son of Faunus, no dark storms
or torrents forced us to your land, nor did
stars and coastlines lead us off our course.
We came on purpose to this city, willingly,
driven from our kingdom—once the greatest
the sun saw as he came from high Olympus.
Our race goes back to Jupiter: we men
rejoice in this. Our king has Jove's great blood: 220
Aeneas of Troy, who sent us to your shores.
The fierce storm the vicious Greeks unleashed on Ida's

fields, how Fortune made the worlds of Asia
and Europe clash in war—this everyone has heard,
even those who hold the farthest lands cut off
by Ocean's tides, even those beyond the zone
of scorching sun, the middle of the earth's five tracts.
We sailed from that deluge across endless seas.
We beg a small home for our native gods,
a harmless stretch of shore, with air and water.   230
We won't disgrace your kingdom. Your fame and our
gratitude for such a gift will never fade.
Italy will not regret she welcomed Trojans.
I swear this on Aeneas' life and strong right hand,
by which pacts were made and battles fought:
many tribes and nations sought us for themselves*
and hoped to make us allies. Don't scorn us if we come
with olive sprigs and words of supplication.
The gods' fate made us seek your land. Dardanus
began here, and here Dardanians return.   240
Apollo sends us urgent orders: 'Come back
to Tuscan Tiber and Numicus' sacred pools.'
Our leader also brings small tokens of our former
glory, relics saved from burning Troy. With this
gold cup, Anchises poured libations at the altar,
and this was Priam's finery when he judged
the nations: a sacred scepter and a diadem,*
and robes that Trojan women toiled to weave."
Latinus fixed his gaze upon the ground.
His face was still, but his eyes moved in thought.   250
The clothing stitched in purple didn't move him,
nor did Priam's scepter. His daughter's marriage
was a far greater concern. He reflected
on the oracle of ancient Faunus.
Was this the man foretold by fate, who'd come
from foreign lands to be his son-in-law, to share
his power equally? Would this race excel

in bravery and overcome the world by force?
He spoke at last with joy: "May the gods support
our plan and their prophecy! You'll get your wish, 260
Trojan. I don't spurn your gifts. While I rule,
you won't lack for fertile land or miss Troy's wealth.
Just let Aeneas come himself, if he so much
wants to be my guest-friend and my ally:
he shouldn't fear kindly faces. My condition
for this pact will be to clasp his hand in mine.
You then take this message to your king.
I have a daughter, but my father's shrine
and many omens warn me not to marry her
to one of us. It's said my son-in-law will come 270
from overseas to Latium, that our blood
will lift our name up to the stars. I think
the fates demand your king—and if I'm right,
I'm ready." Latinus picked out horses from his
stables, whose high stalls held three hundred. He sent them
to the Trojans right away: stallions
with saddlecloths of purple thread. Golden
neck-chains dangled from their chests, their coverings
were gold, and their teeth champed on gold bridles.
He sent a chariot for absent Aeneas 280
and a horse-team of celestial stock, their nostrils
snorting fire. They came from crossbreeds bred by clever
Circe, who'd mated stallions stolen from her father
with mortal mares. Aeneas' men returned on them
with Latinus' gifts and words, and news of peace.

Cruel Juno was just coming back from Argos,
Inachus' town, in her airborne chariot.
Far off, from the skies of Sicily, she saw
glad Aeneas and the Trojan fleet. She saw
their houses rising, sailors trusting to the land, 290
the ships unmanned. Stopping short, pierced with pain,

she shook her head and poured out heartfelt words:
"Oh no! That hated race, those Phrygian fates opposed
to mine! Why didn't they perish on Sigeum's fields?
Why won't these losers lose? Why didn't they burn
in burning Troy? So they've found a way
through war and conflagration? Is my power spent,
or my loathing satisfied? These fugitives—
I hated them and dared to hunt them through the waves,
I fought these exiles across every ocean.   300
The strength of sea and sky was used up on these men!
What use was Scylla, or the Syrtes, or awful
Charybdis? Now the Trojans settle by the longed-for
Tiber, safe from sea—and me. Mars could
kill off all the giant Lapiths; the gods' father
gave up ancient Calydon to soothe
Diana's rage; undeserving victims both.*
But I, Jove's mighty wife, who dared everything
I could, who turned to every tactic: *I'm* losing
to Aeneas. If my powers aren't enough,   310
why not stoop to begging anyone? If I
can't move the gods above, then I'll move Acheron.*
Granted: I can't keep him from his Latin kingdom,
I can't change Lavinia's destined marriage.
But I *can* delay crucial events! I *can*
destroy their nations! Let son-in-law and father
join: the price will be their people. My girl,
your dowry will be blood, Rutulian and Latin.
Bellona waits to be your bridesmaid. Hecuba
won't be the only woman to give birth   320
to wedding flames. Venus' son will be the same,
a second Paris, a fatal torch for this new Troy!"

She's done. The dreadful goddess makes for land.
She rousts the grief-bringer Allecto from the Furies'
lair in Hell's dark murk, she who relishes

grim wars and rage and treachery and evil crimes.
Even her father, Pluto, and her hellish sisters
hate this monster—so many are her awful forms
and faces, so many black snakes swarm on her.
Juno goads her with these words: "Virgin   330
born of Night: take on this task, a favor just for
me. Save my name and honor from disgrace
and ruin. Don't allow Aeneas' men to sway
Latinus with a marriage, and seize Italy.
You cause loving brothers to seize swords, you wreck
families with feuds, and visit whips and death
on homes. You have a thousand names and ways of harm.
Look into your box of tricks, undo the pact
of peace, and sow the crimes of war. Let men
want swords, seek them, seize them, instantly!"   340

Allecto, steeped in serpent venom, swooped at once
to the Laurentian ruler's halls in Latium
and stalked Amata's silent door. The queen
was seething with a woman's angst and anger:
Trojans had arrived—was Turnus' marriage safe?
Now Allecto flung a snake from her black hair.
It pierced Amata, then plunged deep into her heart
to derange her into ruining her own home.
With viperish breath it slid between her clothing and
smooth breasts, too subtle to be felt in her mad state.   350
The giant snake became a golden chain
around her throat, then melded with her headband.
Unobserved, it wove into her hair and slunk
across her frame. At first, while the poison just
attacked her senses, winding fire round her bones,
before she felt the full flame in her heart,
she still spoke gently, like a mother, shedding
tears for her daughter and the Phrygian wedding:
"Will you give Lavinia to these Trojan exiles?

Don't you pity her, or yourself, her father?   360
Or me? Whom that lying pirate will abandon
at first breeze, departing with his stolen bride!
This is how that Trojan shepherd came to Sparta
and stole Leda's daughter Helen off to Troy!
What about your oath, your old love for your people,
the pledge you gave so often to my nephew Turnus?
If her husband must be foreign to the Latins,
and father Faunus' orders bind you, I say
every land is 'outside' if our kingdom doesn't
rule it: that's what the gods meant. Turnus too,   370
if you trace his people's origin, is from
Acrisius and Inachus: a Mycenean."

But when she saw that he opposed her and
her words were wasted, and when the Fury's poison
penetrated to her bones, pervading her,
then poor Amata, goaded by the monster,
rampaged in a shameless frenzy through the city.
Like a spinning top that whirls under the whip,
when little boys, intent on play, lash it round
an empty yard in circles; the childish band   380
is captivated by its curving path,
and wonders at the spinning boxwood toy
given life by blows: just so, Amata whirled
across the city and its warlike people.
She faked a Bacchic trance and flew into the forest.
Committing worse crimes as her madness
grew, she hid her daughter in the leafy hills
to rob the Trojans of their torch-lit wedding,
shrieking "Bacchus, only you deserve her!
She holds the pine-topped stalk for you; she honors   390
you in dance; for you, she tends long hair."
Rumor flew. Right away the same strong urge
to find new homes drove all the raving mothers.

They left home wearing fawn-skins, their heads bared
to wind,* or filled the air with warbling howls,
holding vine-branches as spears. The queen herself
stood in the center with a burning torch, fevered,
singing wedding hymns for Turnus and her daughter,
her bloodshot eyes darting around. She shouted
fiercely: "Latin mothers, hear me, all of you: 400
if your pious hearts still care for sad Amata,
if you feel anguish for a mother's rights,
untie your hair and join my Bacchic revelry!"
With Bacchus' goads Allecto whirled the mad queen
everywhere, through the woods and dens of beasts.

Once she saw she'd honed Amata's fury well
and ruined Latinus' plans and family,
at once her dark wings took the awful goddess
to daring Turnus' town. They say that Danaë
built it with Greek settlers when the swift South Wind   410
carried her there. In old times it was called
Ardea, and the name's still famous, but her peak
is past. Here Turnus was sleeping soundly
under his high roof in dark of night.
Allecto shed her fierce face and Fury's body,
taking on the look of an old woman.
She lined her ugly brow with wrinkles, added
headbands and white hair, and wove in olive sprigs,
becoming ancient Calybe, priestess of Juno.
She stood in front of him and said: "Turnus,   420
will you let so much effort go to waste
and yield your scepter to the Dardan settlers?
The king denies you marriage and the dowry won
by blood. A foreign heir is chosen for the throne.
Go then, fool, face thankless danger, mow down
Tuscan soldiers, keep the Latins safe.
Almighty Juno ordered me to say this to you

as you rested in the calm of night. Get up,
gladly arm your men and march them out
to battle from the gates. Set afire the Phrygian   430
chiefs and painted ships camped by our lovely stream.
The gods' great power calls for it. If King Latinus
won't perform the wedding that he swore to, let him
pay the price and learn what Turnus is in war!"

Scoffing at the priestess, the young man said:
"The news that ships have sailed the Tiber's stream
has not escaped my ears, as you think:
don't exaggerate the danger. Nor has Juno
lost her love for me. But as for you: old age
and cobwebs have the better of you, auntie.   440
They cause you false concern, tricking a seer
with silly fears and the fights of kings. Your job's
to guard the statues and the temples of the gods.
Men will manage war and peace. This is their work."

Hearing this, Allecto blazed up in a rage,
and even as he spoke, a sudden seizure took him.
His eyes bulged in terror: so many serpents hissed
around the awful form he saw. He struggled to say
more, but she turned wild burning eyes on him
and shoved him back. Two snakes rose from her hair.   450
She cracked her whip and said from rabid lips:
"Look! Here I am, bested by old age
and cobwebs, tricked by silly fears and the fights
of kings. I've come from my deadly sisters' home,
and in my hand I bring you war and death."
She hurled a firebrand at the man. Smoking
with dark light, it sank deep into his chest.
A dreadful fear cut off his drowsiness at once.
Sweat poured down and soaked him to the bone.
Crazed, he roared for weapons, looked for them in bed   460

and in the house. Battle-frenzy boiled in him,
and lust for war, but anger most—like a seething
cauldron sitting over flaming twigs; they crackle
and the liquid dances with the heat, then the froth
rises and the boiling water bubbles over
and spills out; thick vapor rises in the air.
The peace was ruined. Turnus told his chiefs to march
on King Latinus: they should arm themselves,
save Italy, expel the enemy: he could
handle both the Trojans and the Latins.   470
He called the gods as witness to his vows.
The Rutulians urged each other on:
Turnus' handsome youth and strength moved some,
some his royal blood, some his fame in fighting.

While Turnus filled Rutulian hearts with courage,
Allecto's Stygian wings propelled her to the Trojans
with a new idea. She checked the riverbank
and saw bright Iülus flushing game into his snares.
The Fury cast a sudden frenzy on his dogs.
She daubed the well-known scent of deer onto their snouts,   480
so they'd be hot to hunt. This was the first
cause of conflict, this roused country folk for war.
There was a gorgeous stag with giant antlers
which Tyrrhus and his sons had taken from
its mother's teats and reared—Tyrrhus, keeper
of the royal herds and the king's wide fields.
Silvia, their sister, groomed this docile deer
with love. She twined soft garlands around his antlers,
combed his coat and washed him in the clear springs.
He let her pat him and ate from the master's table.   490
He'd wander through the forest and willingly return,
however late at night, to the door he knew.
This stag was far from home, following the river
down the grassy banks, where the heat was less.

Iülus' frothing dogs, on the chase, surprised him.
Ascanius himself, on fire to win high praise,
aimed an arrow from his curving bow. Some god
firmed his wobbling hand, and the shaft
flew hissing through the deer's flank and belly.
He fled wounded to the safety of his home   500
and made it to his stall, moaning, bloody,
filling the house with cries as if begging for help.
Sylvia's the first to beat her arms in grief.
She calls her hardy countrymen to help.
They're there suddenly (dread Allecto still hid
in those silent woods), one with a charred stake,
one a heavy knotted club. What each man gropes for,
his rage makes a weapon. Tyrrhus by chance
was splitting oaks in four, pounding in the wedges.
He calls his troops and grabs his ax, breathing fury.   510

The cruel goddess sees her chance for sabotage.
She rushes from her lookout to the stable roof
and sounds the shepherd's signal from on high.
Her bugle blares a hellish sound. At once
the deep woods shudder, echoing the sound.
Diana's distant lake hears it, and Nar's river
white with sulfur, and Velinus' springs.
Scared mothers press their children to their breast.
Rough farmers, quick to answer, seize their swords
and run from everywhere toward the frightful   520
sound. The Trojans likewise break up camp,
pouring out to bring Ascanius support.
Battle lines are drawn. This is not some rustic
brawl with heavy clubs and fire-charred stakes.
They fight with two-edged swords; a black crop
of iron bristles far and wide. Bronze armor
flashes in the sun, its light reflected by
the clouds—like wave-crests whitening when the wind

picks up; the ocean rises slowly, the swells build;
at last waves tower from the seabed to the sky.   530
Now a whistling arrow drops a young man
out in front—Almo, Tyrrhus' oldest son.
The wound lodges in his throat; blood wells up
to choke his breath and bubbling tries at speech.
Many corpses fall around him: old Galaesus
too, as he comes up to plead for peace, most just
of men, richest in Italian pastures; five flocks
of bleating sheep, five herds of cows grazed on
his grounds, a hundred plowshares tilled his land.

With both sides matched, the battle rages on the plain.   540
So Allecto—her promise fulfilled, the war
now steeped in blood, and men already killed
—leaves Italy and whirls airborne to Juno.
She reports, in the proud tone of a victor:
"See my acts: discord and the grief of war.
Now let them be friends or join in treaties!
I've splashed the Trojans with Italian blood.
I'll add this too, if you say you want it:
I'll spread the war to nearby towns with rumors,
and fire their souls with insane lust for war   550
so they'll run to help from all around. I'll sow
the fields with swords." But Juno says, "Enough
of terror and deceit. The causes of the war
are set. They fight hand to hand, fresh blood wets
the weapons chance provided. Let Venus' peerless son
and King Latinus celebrate such wedding rites.
The lord of high Olympus does not want you
wandering at will through the breezes of the sky.
Leave this place. If there's further need
for action, I'll take care of it myself."   560
Allecto raises wings that hiss with snakes
and leaves the heavens for her home in Cocytus.

In central Italy, at the foot of mountains,
there's a famous place, spoken of by many:
the valley of Amsanctus. All around, dark forest
rings it with dense leaves. At the center,
a loud torrent spins and tumbles boulders.
There's an eerie cave with holes for cruel Dis's
breath to rise; from a massive crater's reeking
jaws, Acheron erupts. Here the Fury   570
hides her hated power, relieving earth and sky.

Meanwhile Saturn's daughter adds her final flourish
to the war. All the shepherds from the front
rush into town, bringing back the dead boy
Almo and Galaesus with his mangled face.
They implore the gods and call upon Latinus.
Hearing cries of "Murder!" in the heated crowd,
Turnus feeds their fear: "Trojans are called to rule,
our blood will mix with Phrygian, I'll be banished!"
Those whose mothers gamboled in a Bacchic trance   580
among the pathless groves, drawn by Amata's name,
come together from all sides and call for battle.
Through some malign influence, now everyone
demands war's horrors—against omens, against fate.
They crowd and push around Latinus' house.
He stands like a rock steadfast against the sea
when crashing breakers come its way, a mass
that doesn't move as waves smash all around it.
The cliffs and foamy reefs roar uselessly;
seaweed slams its side and slurps back out to sea.   590
But the king can't stop the reckless plan—
it goes as savage Juno wills it, even though
he calls so often on the gods and empty breezes.
"Fate has broken us, a storm sweeps us away,"
he cries. "My poor people, you'll pay the price
for blood you spill unjustly. Turnus, your crime

will reap harsh punishment; you'll beg the gods
too late. Now I retire—robbed of a good
death in my old age." He fences himself
in his house and drops the reins of state.   600

There was a custom in Italian Latium
which Alban towns have since held sacred. Great Rome
observes it when she's roused to fight and wreak
war's sorrows on the Getae or Hyrcani
or the Arabs, to march eastward to India
and claim our standards from the Parthians.*
There are twin Gates of War by name, feared
and revered in the cult of cruel Mars.
A hundred brazen bolts and iron's eternal strength
bind them. Their watchman Janus never leaves his post.   610
When the elders have resolved on war, the consul,
marked out by his Gabine belt and Quirine toga,
unlocks the creaking gates and calls for war.
The men muster; bronze horns blare with hoarse
assent. This is the custom that Latinus
should have observed in raising war against
Aeneas' men: to open the grim gates.
But the father of his people will not touch them.
Rejecting that foul task, he hides himself in shadows.
So Juno herself, queen of gods, glides down   620
and strikes the sluggish portal with her hand.
The hinges turn, the iron Gates of War burst open.
Italy, so calm and steadfast once, is blazing.
Some leave on foot across the fields, some wildly stir up
dust on rearing stallions. All want weapons.
Men rub down their shields and spears with grease,
polish them, and whet axes on grindstones. They're glad
to hoist the standards, to hear the trumpets blast.
Five great cities set up anvils to forge arms:
strong Atina and proud Tibur, Ardea,   630

Crustumerium, and towered Antemnae.
They hammer hollow helmets and bend willow-stalks
for shields. Some forge breastplates out of bronze
and shining greaves from pliant silver. The honor due to
plow and sickle, all their love of farming—gone.
They recast their fathers' swords. The trumpets give
the sign, the watchword's shared. In a rush, one grabs
a helmet from his house, another drives his trembling
horses to the yoke, grabbing his shield and
golden three-plied chain mail, his trusty sword.   640

O Muses, open Helicon's gates of song for me.
Which kings were roused to war? Which chiefs and armies
filled the fields? What men were raised on Italy's
rich soil back then, what weapons fed her fire?
You remember, goddesses, and you can tell it.
Only the faintest breath of legend wafts to us.

The first to enter war is harsh Mezentius
from Tuscan shores, a despiser of the gods,
and his troops. Lausus, his son, is near, breaker
of horses, hunter of beasts. No man is more   650
handsome, except Laurentian Turnus. Lausus
brings a thousand soldiers with him from Caere—
but in vain. He deserves more than his father's
orders, and a father not Mezentius.

Next Aventinus, handsome son of handsome
Hercules, parades his palm-decked chariot
and winning team. His shield sports his father's emblem:
Hydra circled by a hundred snakes. The priestess
Rhea bore him secretly into the realm
of light within the woods of Aventine.   660
She slept with the god Hercules—he'd just
murdered Geryon and reached Laurentian fields,

where he washed his Spanish cows in Tuscan waters.
His men bring spears and savage pikes to war.
They fight with tapered swords and Samnite bayonets.
A giant cape sweeps round their leader, a matted
lion-skin that once was Hercules's cloak.
The awful mane and ivory teeth rest on his head.
Like this, a horrid sight, he walks into the palace.

Next, twin brothers from the town of Tibur   670
(named for Tiburtus, their other brother):
Catillus and keen Coras, men of Argive origin.
They rush to the front through a sea of weapons,
like two cloud-born Centaurs hurtling down
a mountain peak, leaving Homole and snowy
Othrys at a breakneck pace: the huge forest
yields to them, branches buckle and snap loudly.

Praeneste's founder, Caeculus, is there as well.
Every age has thought him born to Vulcan
in a herd of cows, a king discovered   680
at the hearth. He comes with a rustic legion
drawn from far and wide: men from high Praeneste,
the fields of Juno's Gabiï, cold Anio, and
Hernican crags dewy with streams; men you nourish,
rich Anagnia, and you too, Amasenus.
Not all have weapons, clanging shields, or chariots.
Most sling pellets of black lead, others hold two
spears in their hands. On their heads they wear
gray wolf-skin caps. Their custom is to march
with bare left feet; rawhide boots cover the right.   690

Messapus the horse-breaker, son of Neptune,
protected by the gods from death by sword or fire,
at once calls to arms his soldiers so long idle,
his troops unused to war, and grips his sword again.

They're from Fescennia and Aequi Falisci,
Soracte's heights, Flavinia's fields, Ciminus'
mountain lake, and Capena's woods.
They march in ranks and hymn their king,
like snowy swans among the drifting clouds   700
coming back from feeding, when they call
in rhythm from long throats; the river Cayster
and its Asian marshlands echo far and wide.
No one would think armored ranks of a huge force
were mingling here, rather that an airy cloud
of raucous birds was blown from open seas to shore.

Here's Clausus, of ancient Sabine blood. He brings
a great army—himself a match for it. His tribe
of Claudians has now fanned out through Latium,
ever since the Sabines joined with Rome. With him,
a huge corps from Amiternum, old Quirites,   710
a band from Eretum, soldiers from Mutusca's
groves, Nomentum and Velina's fields,
Tetrica's rough crags, Mount Severus,
Casperia, Foruli, and the stream Himella;
men who drink the Tiber or the Fabaris,
men from freezing Nursia, the Ortine ranks,
the Latins and men watered by unlucky
Allia: as many as the waves that cross
the Libyan sea when harsh Orion dips in winter
waters, as dense as corn-ears parched by eastern sun   720
on Hermus' plains or the tawny fields of Lycia.
Shields clang, Earth trembles at the tramp of feet.

Halaesus, Agamemnon's son, hater of Troy,
yokes horses to his chariot. He sweeps along
a thousand fierce tribes for Turnus: men who plow
Massica's vine-rich soil, men sent by Auruncan
elders from their hills, those from Cales and

Sidicinum's plain, men from the banks of
shallow Volturnus, rough types from Saticula,
and a throng of Oscans carrying smooth spears   730
that come with leather throwing-straps. They battle
hand to hand with sabers, and hold left-handed shields.

Oebalus, my poem won't pass over you.
They say that Telon sired you with the nymph Sebethis
late in life, when he ruled the Teleboeans
in Capreae. His father's holdings didn't sate
the son. Now he lords it over broader land—
the Sarrastian tribes, plains watered by the Sarnus,
Rufrae, Batulum, the fields of Celemna,
and men within the walls of apple-rich Abella.   740
They throw boomerangs, like German tribes,
and strip the bark of cork-trees for the helmets
on their heads. Their bronze weapons shimmer.

Ufens, you were sent to war from hilly Nersae.
You have great fame for luck in battle. Your men
are unkempt Aequiculans, who feed themselves
by hunting in the forests. Their soil is hard.
They work the earth while armed, and love to seize
new spoils, and to live off what they steal.

Next, priest Umbro of the Marruvïï,   750
bravest of men, sent by King Archippus,
his helmet decked with fronds of fertile olive.
He has the skill to sprinkle sleep on venom-breathing
snakes and vipers by his spells and touch.
With his art, he charms their anger, heals their bites.
But he can't cure a wound from Trojan iron;
his mesmerizing chants, the herbs he picked
on Marsian hills, will not help his wounds.

Umbro, how Angitia's forest and Fucinus'
glassy waters and clear lakes will weep for you.*   760

Virbius goes to war as well, Hippolytus's
handsome son, sent by his mother Aricia.
He grew up in Egeria's grove, near the
marshy shores and laden altars of kindly
Diana. They say his crafty stepmother murdered
Hippolytus, who paid his father's curse in blood,
torn to pieces by his bolting horses. Yet he
was restored to starry skies and breezes, reborn
through the Healer's herbs and Diana's love.
Then the mighty Father, outraged that a human   770
should rise from Hell's shades to the light of life,
plunged the finder of this healing art
into Styx's waters with his lightning bolt.
But kind Diana hid Hippolytus and sent
him to the forest of the nymph Egeria,
so he could live a humble life in the Italian
woods, his name changed to Virbius. Horses
are forbidden from her temple and her sacred
groves, since they broke both man and chariot
in their terror at the monster from the sea.   780
On the plains, his son trains high-strung horses as his
father did, and drives a chariot to war.

Turnus, the most handsome, gallops back and forth
before the line, armed and tallest by a head.
His helmet sports a triple plume. The Chimaera's
on its crown; her jaws breathe Etna's fire.
The more the fight flows raw with blood,
the more she roars, dark-flamed and feral.
His smooth shield sports a giant emblem: golden
Io, raising horns, a cow already clad   790

in hide, and Argus, the girl's guardian. Her father,
Inachus, pours water from the embossed urn.

Next a cloud of infantry, shields crowded
on the field: Argive men, Aurucan bands,
Rutulians, Sicanian veterans,
a Sacranian column, Labici with painted
shields, those who farm the woods of Tiber
and Numicus' sacred springs, who till with rakes
Rutulian hills and Circe's headland (fields that Jove
guards with Feronia, who loves green groves); those who   800
hold Satura's pitchy marsh, and the lowlands
where the icy Ufens plunges in the sea.

To crown the men, Camilla from the Volscians,
a warrior-queen. She leads a female cavalry
like blooms in bronze. Not for her a woman's tasks,
Minerva's spindle or a basket of wool skeins.
She's steeled for battle and outruns the winds on foot.
She'd fly above the topmost tips of uncut stalks
and not hurt the tender ears when she did,
or run across the sea, skimming the high swells,   810
and not splash her quick feet with the water.
All the young men and a crowd of mothers
flood from homes and fields in wonder as she goes,
gaping in amazement at the royal purple
cloaking her smooth shoulders, the brooch clasping
her hair with gold, the Lycian quiver that she carries,
and the shepherd's staff of iron-tipped myrtle.

BOOK 8

AN EMBASSY TO EVANDER

_____

As bugles blared their strident notes, Turnus waved
the standard on Laurentum's citadel, spurred
his eager horse, and clanged his sword and shield.
At once, all hearts were troubled. In the anxious tumult,
Latium swore loyalty; the young men
raged for war. Messapus, Mezentius
(the mocker of the gods), and Ufens led. They called in
conscripts far and wide and stripped the fields of farmers.
Venulus was sent to noble Diomedes
to ask for help. He told him Trojans camped   10
in Latium—Aeneas' fleet had docked with his
defeated gods; he claimed he was the fated king.
Many tribes had allied with the Dardan chief;
his name was heard through Latium. What he
meant by these first steps, what he wanted out of
war if Fortune favored him, was perhaps clearer
to Diomedes than to Turnus or Latinus.

This was the scene in Latium. The Trojan hero
knew it all; he tossed on a great tide of worry.
His mind flew quickly here and there, shifting   20
sides, weighing all the options—as quick
as water shimmers back a trembling light
when rays of sunshine or the radiant moon
land on the bronze bowl, the beam flutters far
and wide, then angles up and roams the ceiling.

. . .

It was night. Deep sleep held the weary animals
of all the lands, the birds and beasts. Father
Aeneas, heartsick at the threat of war,
lay down on the bank beneath the sky's cold
canopy, and finally let himself sleep.   30
A local god, old Tiberinus, came to him,
rising from his lovely stream among the poplar
branches. He wore flowing gray-green linen;
a crown of reeds shaded his hair. He spoke
and eased Aeneas' worries with these words:

"Goddess-born, you restore our city, Troy,
and save her heights from enemies forever.
Laurentian lands and Latin fields have longed
for you. Here's your certain home, your household gods.
Don't give up, or fear the threats of war: 40
the gods' swollen anger is all over.*

Soon—in case you think this dream's a lie—
you'll find a giant sow by my bank's oaks,
lying there with thirty newborn in her litter:
a white sow resting, with white piglets suckling.*
By this sign, you'll know Ascanius will found
famed Alba after thirty years roll by.
I foretell the truth. Now (take note) here's how
to bring about what's needed for your victory.
Pallas' Arcadians, who followed King   50
Evander in his war, chose to settle here.
They placed their city, named Pallanteum
after their ancestor, among the hills.
They wage an endless war against the Latins.
Bring them to your camp and make a treaty.
I myself will guide you there along my banks;
you'll outpace the current with your oars.

Up then, goddess-born: when the stars first set,
give Juno her due prayers and calm her angry threats   *60*
with humble vows. Honor me after you've won:
you'll see me grazing my banks in full flood,
cutting through the loamy fields, sky-blue
Tiber, the river heaven loves the most. My great
home is here; high Etruria's my source."

He sank in the deep river, plunging to its bed.
Night and slumber left Aeneas. He rose
and faced the sun's glow in the eastern sky,
then ritually cupped river-water in his hands
and poured this prayer to the air: "Nymphs,   *70*
Laurentian nymphs, source of all the rivers, and you,
father Tiberinus, with your sacred stream,
accept Aeneas and protect him now at last.
Pity my ordeals, wherever your springs
rise, whatever soil you well from in your glory.
I'll always honor you with gifts and worship,
hornéd river, ruler of Hesperia's streams.
Just stay close and make your omen true."
Now he chose two galleys from his fleet,
fitting them with rowers and armed men.   *80*

But see! a sudden marvel met their eyes.
In the woods, they saw a snowy sow
and her white litter, lying on the grassy bank.
Pious Aeneas killed the sow and piglets
for great Juno, and set up an altar.
All that night's full length, Tiber calmed
his swell and kept his currents still. His surface
was as level as a pond or placid swamp—
no struggle for the oars going upstream.
As cheers rose, they hurried on their journey;   *90*
the pitch-glazed pine boats smoothly slipped along.

The woods and waters by the banks were dazed to see
far-flashing shields and painted keels in such a place.
The men rowed day and night around long bends.
Varied trees cast shade upon the ships that wove
their way through living woods on silent waters.
When the blazing sun had scaled the heights of sky,
they saw a distant citadel and scattered homes.
(Rome's strength has since raised these to the heavens,
but at that time Evander's state was poor indeed.)   100
At once they steered their prows toward the town.

By chance, that day Arcadia's king was making
annual sacrifice in a forest near the city,
honoring the gods and Hercules. His son
Pallas, other princes, and the humble senate
offered incense with him. The altars steamed with gore.
When they saw the tall ships gliding from
the dusky trees, the crews pulling silent oars,
the sudden sight alarmed them. They sprang up to leave
the sacred feast. But brave Pallas would not let   110
the rite be interrupted. He grabbed his spear,
ran toward the ships, and shouted from a knoll:
"Men, why are you trying these uncharted paths?
What is your race? Your home? Where are you heading?
Do you bring peace or war?" From his high stern,
Aeneas proffered a sprig of peaceful olive.
"You see armed Trojans hostile to the Latins,
who rudely drove us off, though we're refugees.
We look for Evander. Take these words to him:
leading Dardan chiefs come asking for a treaty."   120
Pallas was struck dumb by Troy's famous name.
"Disembark, whoever you may be. Address
my father face to face, come to our home as guests!"
He took Aeneas' hand and clung to it
as they left the river, heading for the grove.

. . .

Aeneas hailed the king with friendly words:
"Best of the sons of Greece, Fortune saw fit
that I appeal to you with olive branches bound
by holy ribbons. The fact that you're Arcadian,
a Greek chief, kin to Atreus's sons—this   130
didn't alarm me. Divine oracles, my courage,
our fathers' shared blood, and your vast fame
have joined us. Fate leads with my consent.
That Dardanus who sailed to the Troad
was Troy's first father and her founder.* He was
son to Atlas' child, Electra (so the Greeks say),
that massive Atlas on whose back the earth
is balanced. Now, your father's Mercury.
Shining Maia had *him* on the snowy peak of
Mount Cyllene. But tradition tells us Atlas   140
who holds up the stars was also Maia's father.*
So our two peoples split off from one line.
Believing this, I refused to send you envoys
or make some crafty overture. I risk my life,
and approach your door as suppliant.
Those Daunians that hunt you down in war
hunt us as well,* believing if they drive us out
nothing will prevent their taking Italy.
Their rule will reach both seas that lap her shores.
Let's make a pact. We Trojans have hearts strong   150
in battle. We're brave and our men are tried in war."

Evander had been looking at his face
and eyes, scanning all his body. He said:
"How glad I am to welcome and acknowledge
the bravest of the Trojans! How gladly I recall
the words and voice and face of great Anchises!
Priam, Laomedon's son, visited
our cold Arcadia from Salamis,

the kingdom of Hesione, his sister.
At that time my first beard was mere fuzz   *160*
upon my cheeks. I admired the Trojan chiefs,
I admired Priam, but Anchises walked
the tallest of them all. I burned with boyish
longing to speak with the hero, to clasp his hand.
I happily escorted him to our city,
Pheneus. When he left he gave me gifts: a lovely
quiver, Lycian arrows, a cloak of golden weave,
a pair of golden bridles that my Pallas has.
We'll join our hands in treaty, as you ask.
You'll go home at dawn, glad to have my help—   *170*
I'll offer what I have. But now, since you've
come as allies, share our celebration
of these yearly rites (we can't postpone them)
and feel at home, feasting among friends."

Evander ordered that the cleared food and goblets
be reset. He himself seated the guests
on grassy benches. Aeneas had the place of honor
on a maple throne and shaggy lion-skin.
Men picked to help the altar-priest were quick
to carry out roast bulls. They heaped the baskets   *180*
high with bread, the gift of toil, and offered wine.
Aeneas and the Trojans shared the feast:
whole sides of beef, and organs vowed to gods.

Their hunger gone, their appetite now sated,
King Evander said: "No blind superstition,
no ignorance of early gods, imposed on us
the habit of this ritual feast, this altar to so
great a god. We were saved, Trojan guests,
from awful danger. For this we renew the rites
we owe. Once there was a rocky cliff above us;   *190*
now its mass is scattered far and wide. The home

it held is empty, its rocks a pile of ruin,
but then it was a vast receding cavern.
In it, out of reach of sunny rays, lurked
the horrible half-human Cacus. The cave's soil
steamed constantly with still-warm slaughter. Fixed to
the grim doors hung bloodless, rotting heads.
Vulcan sired the monster, it was Vulcan's black flames
that he spewed as he heaved himself around.
At last, time brought the help we'd hoped: a god   200
arrived. He was the greatest of avengers,
proud of butchering and looting Geryon's
triple bulk—Hercules, driving huge bulls.
These cattle crammed the glen and riverbanks.
But Cacus' mind, feral, frenzied, could leave
no crime or cunning undared or untried.
He stole from their stabling four perfect bulls,
four cows of startling grace. To ensure
their tracks did not face forward, the robber dragged them
by their tails to his cave, all signs of their   210
route reversed, and hid them in the sunless rock.
No one could find tracks that pointed to the cavern.
Meanwhile, the other cows had grazed their fill,
and Hercules was set to leave with all his cattle.
Then the herds began to low. They filled the glen
and hills with protest as they noisily departed.
From the giant cave, one cow mooed back, and
though imprisoned, shattered Cacus' hopes.
Hercules blazed up with anger and black bile.
He grabbed his weapons and his heavy knotted   220
club and ran for the hill's summit. Just this
once we saw Cacus afraid, terror in his
eyes. He fled back to his cave, faster than
the wind—it was fear that winged his feet—
and shut himself inside, breaking the iron chains
Vulcan had forged to hold a giant boulder

that hung at the entry. It fell and blocked the access.
Just then Hercules arrived in all his fury.
He scanned the cliff, looked here and there,
and gnashed his teeth. Three times he furiously   230
circled the Aventine Hill and stormed that rocky
entrance: it was no use. Three times he sank back.

A flinty tower, sheer on every side, rose up
from the rooftop of the cave, a fitting home
for stinking vultures' nests. It leaned to the left,
toward the river. Grabbing it, he jammed it
hard the other way, then tore it from its base
and hurled it down with force. It landed with a crash:
the heavens boomed, the water in the stream
leapt up and fell back on itself in fear.   240
Cacus' cavern, his huge home, appeared.
The dark grotto was laid open to its core
as if the earth had cracked under some force,
gaping to the heart of Hell, the pallid lands
loathed by the gods; as if the vast abyss below
were visible, and ghosts trembled at the light.
Cacus was caught by the sudden glare, and trapped
inside the hollow rock, howling now
in a new key! The hero's arrows rained on him,
and any weapons he could find, branches and huge   250
boulders. Cacus had to deal with the danger.
He belched a giant smoke-cloud from his jaws,
amazingly, and wrapped his home in inky fog,
stealing it from view. From inside his cave
he spewed out smoky fire mixed with darkness.
Hercules lost patience. He took a headlong leap
right through the flames, where the smoke seethed
densely, black clouds warping in the heat.
As Cacus spouted useless fire into the dark,
the hero grabbed him in a strangling chokehold.   260

His eyes bulged out and blood drained from his throat.
His pitch-black lair lay open, the doors ripped away.
At once the stolen cattle and his lies
were exposed for all to see. The monstrous corpse
was dragged out by the feet. Our men could not
get their fill of looking at its awful eyes
and face, the chest of matted hair, his jaws' dead flames.
Since then, grateful generations such as we
have marked this day. Potitius established it,
and now the Pinarii watch over it.   270
In a forest, they set up this altar we call
'greatest.' It will always be the greatest.
Come, men, wreathe your hair with leaves to praise him,
hold out goblets in your hands, call on
our shared god, offer him wine willingly."
He veiled his hair with braided fronds of poplar,
the dappled shady growth of Hercules' tree,
then took up a sacred goblet. All were glad to
pour wine on the altar and call upon the gods.

Meanwhile heaven circled and the sky grew dark.   280
The priests, led by Potitius and wearing pelts
(the custom), carried torches. They resumed the feast
and brought in welcome offerings for the second course,
heaping up the tables with the loaded plates.
The Salii chanted around the lighted altars,
their heads ringed with poplar—two choruses,
one young, one old, to chant Hercules' famous deeds:
how he grabbed and throttled with his hand
snakes sent by his stepmother, twin monsters;
how he overthrew outstanding cities, Troy and   290
Oechalia, and endured a thousand
tasks set by Eurystheus and hostile Juno.
"Unconquered one, you killed the cloud-born Centaurs,
Pholus and Hylaeus, with bare hands, you killed

the Cretan hybrid and the giant Nemean lion.
Stygian waters trembled, and so did Orcus' guard,
lying on half-eaten bones in his blood-stained
cave. No shape could scare you—not even Typhoeus,
towering and armed. You devised a way
to kill the Hydra as its heads bobbed all around you!   300
Hail, true son of Jupiter, the gods' own glory,
be present and support us and your rites."
So they celebrated him in song, with Cacus'
cave as climax, and the half-man breathing fire.
The forests rang with sound, the hills echoed it back.

When the rites were over, they turned back to town.
The king proceeded slowly, burdened by his age.
He kept Pallas and Aeneas close,
lightening the walk with varied tales.
Aeneas admired everything. Charmed by the site,   310
he gladly looked at what Evander noted, asking for,
and hearing of, the memories of men of old.
King Evander, founder of Rome's stronghold, said:
"Native fauns and nymphs once held these groves,
and a race of men from hardy oak-tree trunks.
They had no culture and no customs, no notion
of yoking bulls, amassing wealth, or storing food.
Acorns fed them, and hunting's harsh livelihood.
Saturn was first to come from high Olympus,
fleeing war with Jupiter, an exile with no   320
kingdom. He united the unruly race
that was scattered on the mountains, gave them laws,
and called it Latium—he'd safely hidden here.*
He was king during the age called Golden
and he ruled the people in unbroken peace
until a duller and degraded age came in,
mad for war, greedy for gain. Then came
Ausonian mobs and Sicanian tribes.

The land of Saturn often changed its name.
Next came many kings and the cruel giant Thybris—   *330*
we Italians named the river Tiber for him.
The ancient name of Albula was lost. And I:
I was an exile sailing to the ends of Ocean.
Ineluctable all-powerful Fate settled me
here. The dread warnings of my mother, the nymph
Carmentis, drove me, and the god Apollo's plans."

Evander pointed out the altar on their path,
and the Carmental Gate (so the Romans call it),
an ancient tribute to the nymph Carmentis, who sang
the fates and first foretold the future of Aeneas'   *340*
noble sons and the famed Pallanteum.
He showed the spacious grove used by stern Romulus
as a refuge, then, in a cliff's cool shade,
the Lupercal, named for Arcadia's Lycian Pan.
He marked out Argiletum's sacred pasture,
and swore that his guest Argus died right there.
Next, the Tarpeian Rock and then the Capitol,
golden now, rough then with thorny thickets.
Even then, the eerie godhead of the place
alarmed the nervous farmers, who trembled at the   *350*
woods and rock. "A god lives in this very grove
and leafy hill (we don't know who). Our men
believe they can see Jupiter himself, shaking
his black shield in his hand and bringing storms.
You see these two towns, their walls in ruins?
They're what's left of monuments to men of old.
Janus founded this stronghold, and Saturn that:
one's Janiculum, one Saturnia."
With such talk they neared Evander's humble home.
Herds were everywhere, lowing in the Forum   *360*
and the grand Carinae. When they reached
his house, he said, "Triumphant Hercules

came in this door, this king's lodging hosted him.
My guest, dare to despise wealth! Be like
a god yourself. Don't look down on my poverty."
He led massive Aeneas under this narrow roof
and set him down on bedding: the skinned pelt of
a Libyan bear on heaped-up stacks of leaves.
Night fell, wrapping Earth with dusky wings.

Venus, fearful for her son and rightly fretful   370
at the Latins' threats and angry clamor,
now spoke to Vulcan in their golden bedroom,
breathing divine love into her words:
"Dearest husband: when Greek kings destroyed
doomed Troy, and her citadel was falling
to the flames, I didn't seek help for the victims,
I didn't ask for weapons from your skill and strength.
I didn't want your labor to be wasted,
though I owed much to Priam's sons and often
wept over Aeneas' hardships. Now, as Jove   380
commands, he's landed on Rutulian shores.
So I've come to beg you after all—you whom
I adore—to ask for weapons for my son.
The mothers Thetis and Aurora moved you once
with tears. See how nations mass, how cities
sharpen swords behind locked gates to kill
my boy." As Vulcan wavered, Venus wrapped
her snowy arms around him in a soft embrace.
At once he felt the well-known flame. It sank
into his bones and ran along his weakened frame   390
just as forked lightning and its flash of light
tear through dark clouds with a thundering crash.
His wife knew her effect. Her cunning pleased her.
Vulcan, bound by his undying love, asked her:
"Why bring up the past? Goddess, where's your faith
in me? If you'd worried then, I'd have justly

armed the Trojans. Neither Fate nor mighty
Jupiter forbade Troy and king Priam
to survive for ten more years. Now too,
if you prepare to fight and your mind is set,   400
any care I can promise in my art,
whatever can be made with molten iron and
electrum, whatever flames and wind can do—
don't beg, don't doubt your power!"* He made love
to her as he desired. Then, lying draped
on his wife's breasts, he let slumber wind through him.

When a few hours of rest had banished sleep,
he rose. It was after midnight, when a woman
forced to use Minerva's loom to make her living
rises to add nighttime to her work, and pokes   410
the dormant embers. She calls the slaves to lamp-light
for the lengthy work of carding—all to keep
her widowed bed untouched and raise the little ones.
As industriously, the lord of fire
left his downy bed to labor at the forge.
An island rises near Lipare and the coast
of Sicily. It's steep, crusted in smoking rocks.
Beneath it lie the caves of Etna, eaten hollow
by the thunderous forges of the Cyclopes.
Strong blows strike the shrieking anvils in the din,   420
iron ingots hiss in furnaces with flames
dancing around them: it's Vulcan's home, Vulcania.
The lord of fire flew here from the sky.
Steropes, Brontes, and bare-armed Pyragmon
were wielding iron in the massive cave.
They held a roughly hammered thunderbolt,
part polished, part unformed. The father of the gods
hurls these endlessly from sky to earth.
They'd soldered on three strikes of twisting hail,
three each of storm, red fire, and winged south wind.   430

They added terrifying flashes, thunder,
fear, and the heat that follows rage.
Elsewhere they were busy with Mars' chariot
on flying wheels, the one he rides to enflame men
and cities, and polished eagerly a ghastly shield
for angered Pallas; it had golden serpent scales,
intertwining snakes, and at the center,
headless Gorgon, still too grim to look at.
"Cyclopes of Etna!" he yelled. "Drop your work,
set aside your projects, pay attention!   440
We must forge weapons for a fierce warrior.
Now's the time for strength, quick hands, and expert skill.
Hurry!" At this, they set to work at once,
splitting up the tasks. Bronze and gold ore
ran in rivulets, wounding chalyb* melted
in a massive furnace. They made a giant shield
to equal all the weapons of the Latins, welding
it with seven layers, circle upon circle.
Some drew in air and pumped it out with puffing bellows,
others tempered hissing bronze in water.   450
The cave groaned with the anvils' weight. Their arms
swung in a forceful rhythm, up and down,
as they twisted hot ore with their gripping tongs.

While the lord of Lemnos urged this work on them,
the gentle light and sunrise song of birds
called Evander from his humble home.
The old man rose, wrapped his body in a tunic,
and tied on Tuscan sandals. He attached a sword-belt
to his side and took up a Tegean shield.
A cloak of panther's hide hung at his left.   460
Two watchdogs went before him, crossing the high
threshold, and matched their master's steps. The hero
headed for the sheltered lodging of his guest
Aeneas, mindful of his promise to give aid.

Aeneas too was up this early. With Evander
had come Pallas; with Aeneas, Achates.
They met, clasped hands, and sat down in the courtyard.
At last they could have a frank exchange.
King Evander started: "Greatest leader
of the Trojans (while you live, I won't   470
admit Troy's kingdom has collapsed), despite
our fame, our resources for war are thin.
Tuscan Tiber hems us on one side, Rutulians
threaten on the other. Their weapons clang around
our town. But I have allies for you: large nations
and armed camps with many kingdoms. Fortune gives
this unexpected aid—your presence must be fated!
Not far from here, there's a city built of ancient
stone, Agylla, where the Lydians, famed
in battle, once settled the Tuscan hills.   480
But this town that flowered many years fell to
King Mezentius' cruel and brutal rule.
I won't dwell on this tyrant's godless murders
or barbarity. May the gods store it all up
for him and his! He used to yoke the living
to the dead, hand to hand and face to face,
a form of torture, so they died a lingering death,
dripping pus and gore within that grim embrace.
At last the citizens, sick of this horror, took up
arms and blocked the madman in his home.   490
They killed his allies and threw torches on his roof.
But in the carnage he escaped to the Rutulians.
Now he's defended by his ally Turnus' army.
All Etruria has risen up in rightful outrage.
They want the king for punishment, or else it's war.
Aeneas, I'll make you leader of these thousands,
whose ships are packed along the shore. They shout
for battle's start, but an ancient seer stops them
by singing of the fates: 'Lydia's chosen men,

finest flower of an ancient race: righteous   *500*
anger at Mezentius drives you to war.
But no Italian may guide your great people.
You must await a foreign leader.' Fearing
the gods' warning, they've pitched camp on this plain.
Now Tarchon sends me envoys with a crown
and scepter, hoping that I'll join the camp
and take the Tuscan throne. But my old age,
worn out by years, cold and sluggish, grudges me
such leadership. I'm too old for daring deeds.
I'd urge my son, but his mother, Sabella's   *510*
Italian, and his blood is mixed. Fate favors
your age, your race, and the gods ask for you:
march on, bravest chief of Trojans and Italians!
And I'll lend you Pallas, my hope and comfort:
he'll learn to be a soldier and do Mars' grim
labor, from your leadership. Let him
admire you from the start. From me he'll have
two hundred horsemen, the core of our strength,
and he'll bring as many on his own account."

Staunch Achates and Aeneas remained still,   *520*
eyes fixed on the ground, brooding over
all their hardships with sad hearts. But now
Venus sent a signal from the cloudless sky.
A sudden, booming lightning bolt came flashing
from above. The world seemed to reel,
the ring of Tuscan trumpets sounded through the air.
As they looked up, thunder cracked repeatedly.
Where the sky was clear they saw a single cloud:
in it, swords appeared to turn blood-red and clash.
The others were astonished, but the Trojan hero   *530*
knew the thunder of his divine mother's pledge.
"My host," he said, "there's no need to ask
what these signs mean. Olympus summons me.

My goddess mother said she'd send this omen
if war was imminent, and bring Vulcan's armor
from the sky to help. What carnage is in store
for the poor Laurentians! Turnus, how you'll
pay! Tiber, how many helmets, shields, and bodies
of the brave you'll tumble in your stream!
Let the Latins break the treaty and wage war!"   540

Aeneas spoke, and rose from where he sat.
He lit Hercules's smoking altars, gladly
honoring the humble house-gods, as he'd done
the day before. Evander offered chosen sheep
as due; the Trojans did the same. Afterward,
Aeneas went back to his crews still at the ships
and chose the bravest men to follow him to war.
The others glided downstream on the river's
helpful current, bringing news of these affairs
and of his father to Ascanius. Trojans   550
bound for Tuscan fields were given horses.
For Aeneas, they brought a special one; it wore
a tawny lion pelt that gleamed with gilded claws.

Rumor flew right through the little town at once:
horsemen were riding fast for Tuscan lands!
Frightened mothers renewed prayers, fear grew
with danger, and war's specter now loomed larger.
As Pallas left, Evander clasped his hand, clinging
to his son, sobbing inconsolably:
"If only Jupiter would give me back my youth,   560
the man I was when I subdued the front lines
at Praeneste and burned great piles of shields!
I sent King Erulus to Hell by this right hand.
Feronia, his mother, gave him three lives at birth
(dreadful to tell), and three sets of armor.
I had to strike him down three times, but still,

this hand took those triple lives and triple armor.
Then I'd never be wrenched from your sweet embrace,
my son. Mezentius would not have put so many
to the sword, insulting me, his neighbor;   570
our town would not be widowed all the time.
O powers above, and Jupiter, great ruler
of the gods, pity this Arcadian king, I beg;
hear a father's prayer. If fate and your strength
keep my Pallas safe, if I'll live to see him
and rejoin him, let me live. I can endure
anything. But Fortune, if you threaten
the unspeakable, let me cut off this cruel
life right now, while my worry is still vague,
while there's halting hope for what's to come,   580
while I hold you, dear son, my late and only
joy. May no painful news come to these ears."
As he poured this out at their last meeting,
he collapsed. The house-slaves carried him inside.

Now the cavalry left from the open gates,
Aeneas and loyal Achates in the lead,
then the other Trojan princes. Among his troops,
Pallas stood out in his cloak and ornamented
armor—like the Morning Star still wet with Ocean's
waves, his sacred face rising to dispel darkness,   590
Venus' favorite among the fiery stars.
The anxious mothers stood along the walls, watching
the dusty cloud and troops gleaming in bronze.
They rode with weapons through the brush, the shortest way.
A shout went up and all fell into line;
their horses' pounding hooves crumbled the soil.
There was a grove by cool Caere's stream,
held holy far and wide by age-old traditions.
It was ringed all round by hills of somber spruce.
The story's that the old Pelasgians, the first   600

to live in Italy, vowed it to Silvanus,
god of fields and flocks, and chose his holy day.
Tarchon and the Tuscans made camp nearby
in a safe place. From the heights, all the legions
could be seen, their tents pitched through the fields.
Aeneas joined them with his chosen warriors.
Tired, they tended to their horses and themselves.

Now Venus, shining goddess, came with gifts
through heaven's clouds. From afar she saw her son
in a secluded valley, alone by a cold stream.   610
She appeared to him and spoke these words:
"Look: your gifts, perfected by my husband's
art, as promised. So, my son, don't hesitate
to call to war fierce Turnus and the proud
Laurentians." She embraced her child and set
his gleaming weapons by an oak. Aeneas,
delighted by this honor, couldn't get his fill of
looking at the goddess' gifts. In awe, he scanned
each detail, turning over in his hands
the helmet pouring out its flamelike crest,   620
the deadly sword, the breastplate stiff with bronze
—massive, blood-red, like a dark cloud set afire
by the sun's bright rays and blazing in the sky—
the smooth greaves of electrum and forged gold, the spear
and the shield's engraving, complex beyond words.
The lord of fire, who knew of prophecies about
ages to come, had carved on it Italy's history:*
Roman triumphs, all the generations of
Ascanius's line, and their wars in sequence.
He'd carved a she-wolf sprawled in Mars' green grotto.   630
She'd whelped, and twin boys played around her teats,
hanging on them, suckling on their mother
without fear. She nuzzled them in turn, bending
her soft neck, licking their forms into shape.

Vulcan set Rome nearby, and the Sabines
lawlessly abducted from the theater
at the Circus Games, and a sudden war
with old Tatius and his severe Cures.
Next, the same two kings stood armed before Jove's
altar, their conflict laid aside, holding bowls.   640
They'd sacrificed a pig to sanctify their peace.
Close by, chariot teams had charged apart,
dismembering Mettus (he should have kept his word!).
Tullus dragged the traitor's entrails through the wood;
the thorns were drenched with bloody dew. Porsenna
ordered Rome to take back banished Tarquin
and ringed the city with a massive siege;
Aeneas' heirs died on the swords for liberty.
See his lifelike look—menacing and angry,
because Cocles dared to wreck the bridge,   650
Cloelia to break her chains and swim the river.
Manlius, guarding the Tarpeian fort,
the temple, and high Capitol, was at the top.
Romulus's roof was bristly with new thatch.
A silver goose flapped in a golden portico
warning that the Gauls were at the gates.
They lurked in the bush, about to take the fort,
covered by the dark, the gift of inky night.
Their flowing hair was gold, their clothes were gold,
their striped cloaks gleamed, twisted gold circled   660
their milky necks. In their hands were glinting
double Alpine spears; long shields hid their bodies.
He'd pounded out the leaping Salii and naked
priests of Pan, their caps tufted with wool, and shields
fallen from the sky. In cushioned carriages,
chaste mothers carried sacred vessels through the town.
Far off he placed Tartarus and Dis' high gates
(the wages of wickedness) and Catiline,
dangling from an overhang, fearful of the

Furies. The pious were set apart, receiving   670
Cato's laws. Between it all flowed Ocean's image,
a golden swell with dark blue white-capped waves.
Around the rim, silver dolphins swept the surface
with their tails, cutting through the surging sea.
In the center sailed bronze warships: they fought
the sea battle of Actium. Cape Leucas, its waves
bright with gold, frothed with the armada.

Here Augustus Caesar led all Italy
to war: the Senate, people, gods of sky and hearth.*
From high on the stern, his bright brow poured   680
twin flames; his father's comet rose above.
Tall Agrippa steered the fleet, with gods and winds
behind him. He wore a naval crown; on it gleamed
bright images of prows, a martial honor.
Antony was opposite, with Asian wealth
and hodgepodge troops,* victor over Eastern hordes
and the Red Sea. He brought Egypt, Eastern might,
distant Bactra—and (for shame!) a wife from Egypt.
The forces smashed together and the whole sea frothed,
torn by oars and three-spiked beaks of boats.   690
The crews made for the open. Massive ships rammed towering
sterns—you'd think the Cyclades, torn up, were free
to roam the waters, or that mountains smashed together.
Flaming flax and flying spears rained from their hands,
and just-spilled blood turned Neptune's fields red.
In the thick of it, the queen called to her fleet
with her native rattle—not seeing the pair of snakes
behind her. Monstrous mongrel gods and barking
Anubis turned weapons against Venus, Neptune,
and Minerva. Iron Mars was in their midst, mad   700
for battle. Awful Furies swooped in from the sky,
and Discord in her tattered cloak joined gladly.
Bellona followed with her bloody whip.

Apollo saw this* from his shrine, and aimed his bow.
At that, every Indian and Egyptian,
every Arab and Sabaean, cut and ran.
The queen herself was calling to the winds,
loosening the lanyards, in flight under full sail.
The lord of fire made her pale with future death,*
swept by waves and wind amid the sea of blood.   710
Opposite, he'd carved the mighty Nile in mourning,
opening his garment's folds, welcoming
the conquered to his blue-green bays and hidden streams.
But Caesar rode to Rome in triple triumph, and made
the gods of Italy an immortal vow:
three hundred spacious shrines across the city.
The roads rang with joy, applause, and revelry.
Bands of women were at every shrine and altar,
where slaughtered calves covered the ground. He himself,
seated by the snowy marble temple of bright   720
Apollo, reviewed the nations' gifts, to be fastened
on proud doorposts. A long row of conquered tribes
filed by, distinct in clothes, weapons, and languages.
Vulcan had forged Nomads, loose-robed Africans,
the Cares, Leleges, and Scythian archers,
the Euphrates, meeker now, the remote
Morini and the two-horned Rhine, the untamed
Dahae, and Araxes upset at his bridge.

Aeneas admires Vulcan's shield, his mother's gift,
pleased by images he does not understand.   730
He hoists the fame and fate of his descendants.

BOOK 9

NISUS AND EURYALUS

While these events unfolded far away, Juno,
Saturn's daughter, sent Iris from the sky to find
bold Turnus. By chance he was sitting in a sacred
valley, in his ancestor Pilumnus' woods.
Iris, Thaumas' daughter, spoke from rosy lips:
"Turnus, circling time has brought you freely
what no god would dare to promise. Aeneas leaves
his camp, his fleet and troops, making for
Evander's palace on the Palatine,
then farther still, all the way to distant towns   10
in Corythus, to arm a band of Lydian farmers.
Don't wait: now's the time to call for horse and
chariot. Surprise their camp and storm it."
With this, she rose into the sky on level wings,
drawing a huge arc beneath the clouds.
Turnus knew her. He stretched up his hands,
following her flight with words: "Iris, heaven's
glory, who sent you to me from the clouds?
There's a sudden glimmer in the air, the sky
divides to show the circling constellations.   20
I'll follow this great omen, no matter who
calls me to war." He approached the stream
and drank from its clear surface, then begged the gods
at length, his prayers piling in the sky.

. . .

All the army now marched on the open fields,
rich in horsemen, sumptuous garb, and gold.
Messapus rallied the front lines, Tyrrhus' sons
the rear. Turnus led the column's center.
They moved like the silent swell of the deep Ganges,   30
fed by seven gentle streams; like the Nile's
life-giving water when it overflows, then ebbs.
Suddenly, the Trojans saw a dusty black cloud
taking shape, darkness shadowing the plain.
From the ramparts, Caius was the first to shout:
"What's that swirling globe of dirt and dust?
Quick, bring swords and spears, man the walls:
the enemy's upon us!" Clattering, they
retreated through the gates and crammed into the camp.
This was the mighty warrior Aeneas' order   40
as he left: in case of crisis, they shouldn't dare
to draw up ranks or trust to open battle,
but guard the camp within the safety of the walls.
So, though shame and rage called them to fight,
they blocked the gates and followed orders, armed
inside the towers, waiting for the enemy.

Turnus rode on with twenty from the cavalry,
his horse a snowy dappled Thracian, his helmet
gold and crimson-crested. The army followed him.
He caught the camp unready. "Men," he cried,   50
"who comes with me, who's first to charge the enemy?"
He hurled his spear through the air, an overture
to war, and raced across the plain. His men
took up his shout and followed with a curdling cry.
They marveled at the Trojans' coward hearts—how they
shunned the battle on the field and sat snug
in their camp. Turnus, frantic for an entrance,
rode back and forth to scan the walls. Nothing.

As a wolf prowls around a crowded sheepfold,
howling by its gate, pelted in the dark   *60*
by wind and rain, while ewes keep safe the lambs
bleating beneath them; beside himself, the wolf
is mad for what he cannot have, exhausted
by long famine, his dry jaws parched for blood—
just so Turnus' anger flared up as he probed
the walls and camp. Rage burned in his bones.
How could he find an entrance? How shake out
the nesting Trojans and spill them on the plain?
Their fleet was anchored near the camp, guarded
on each side by earthworks and the river.   *70*
He called for fire from his cheering friends,
took up a flaming brand and stormed the ships.
His men leapt to work, spurred by Turnus' presence.
All took up lit torches looted from the fires.
The pitch-smeared pine produced a sooty light
and Vulcan wafted sparks and ashes to the stars.

What god, O Muses, repelled the hungry blaze?
Who kept the fire from the fleet? Tell me.
Ancient times trusted this tale; its fame lives on.
When Aeneas first built his fleet on Phrygian Ida   *80*
to sail the ocean's depths, Cybele (so they say),
mother of the gods, addressed great Jupiter:
"My son, since you've tamed Olympus, grant
this favor that your loving mother asks.
On a mountain summit was a grove I loved
for many years, where people brought me offerings.
Pitch-pine trees and maples lent it murky shade.
I gave it to Aeneas when he needed ships,
and gladly so, but fear makes me anxious now.
Comfort me and grant your mother's prayer: don't let   *90*
the boats be swamped at sea by waves or whirlwinds.
Let it help them that my mountain was their home."

Her son, who spins the constellations, said, "Mother,
how would you bend fate? What is this hope?
Should boats produced by mortal hands enjoy
immortal rights? Should Aeneas confront danger
without danger? What god has such power?
But when their task is done, when they've reached the ports
of Italy, I'll take away the earthly form
of the boats who brought Trojan Aeneas   100
to Laurentian fields, and make them ocean
goddesses, like Doto the Nereïd
or Galatea, fronting sea-foam as they swim."
He swore this by his Stygian brother's streams,
the banks that boil with pitch, the black abyss,
shaking all Olympus with his nod.

The promised day had come, and the Fates discharged
the debt of time. Turnus' onslaught cued the Mother
to keep the sacred fleet safe from the fire.
First a strange light blazed before their eyes.   110
From the east, a huge cloud carrying the goddess'
worshippers traversed the heavens. Then a dreadful
voice boomed down and deafened both the armies.
"Trojans, don't be anxious to defend my ships
or fight. Turnus can't burn down my sacred fleet
any more than burn the waves. Goddesses,
go freely: your Mother commands you." At once
the boats broke off their moorings from the bank
and dived down to the depths, plunging in beak-first
as dolphins do. Then, a miracle to tell: 120
nymphs in equal numbers rose to ride the waves.*

The Rutulians were stunned, the horses reared,
even Messapus felt fear. The Tiber slowed
its raucous course, then retreated from the sea.
Yet this barely touched bold Turnus' confidence.

Instead he raised their spirits—and added a rebuke:
"These omens target Trojans! Jove himself
held back his usual help from them—we didn't
need to torch the boats. Now these men can't cross   130
the sea, and there's nowhere to run! Half the world
is out of reach, we control this land, and countless
weapons arm the tribes of Italy. The gods' signs
that the Trojans boast of scare me not at all.
The fates and Venus have their due: Phrygians reached
the fertile soil of Italy. And here's *my* fate:
to extirpate this evil race who stole my wife.
That pain doesn't only touch the sons of
Atreus: just wars are fought by others too.
It's enough that Troy fell once? That they *stole* once   140
should be enough; you'd think they'd shun
all women now. Their barricades and ditches
give them heart—small delays before their death!
Didn't they see the walls of Troy collapse in flames?
Those were built by Neptune's hand! My chosen band,
who's prepared to follow me, to wreck the ramparts
with his sword and storm the quaking camp?
I don't need Vulcan's armor or a thousand ships
to fight the Teucrians. All Tuscany can join them!
No need for *them* to fear the night, cowards   150
stealing the Palladium, murdered sentries
on the heights, or a horse's hidden womb.
We'll ring their walls with fire in the light of day.
I'll make sure they realize they're not facing
the Greek soldiers Hector held off for ten years.
But now the better part of day is done.
Rest yourselves for what remains, be happy
with a job well done, and expect a fight!"
Messapus was told to block the gates with
sentries and set watch-fires round the walls.   160
Rutulians were picked to guard the camp,

fourteen of them. Each led a hundred men,
purple-plumed and bright with golden armor.
They dispersed, taking up the watch in turn,
or sprawling on the grass, enjoying wine,
tilting back bronze wine-bowls. The fires twinkled
as the sentries passed the sleepless night in games.

The Trojans watched this from the ramparts, on guard
with their weapons. Worrying, they checked
the gates, built high gangways linking towers,   170
and stockpiled spears. Fierce Serestus and Mnestheus
spurred them on. These two were Aeneas' choice
as the soldiers' leaders, their strategists in crisis.
The whole force on the walls shared in the risks
of night-watch, each man at a post assigned by lot.

Nisus, fearless in a fight, guarded the gate—
Hyrtacus' son, quick with lances and light arrows,
whom the huntress Ida sent to serve Aeneas.
His friend was Euryalus. Among the troops
there was no warrior more handsome—a boy   180
whose unshaved chin showed puberty's first fuzz.
They shared one mind, one heart; they rushed to battle
side by side. Now they shared watch at the gate.
Nisus asked: "Do gods enflame our hearts,
Euryalus, or do our fierce desires become
our gods? I'm not content with idleness.
I've long been keen to fight, to do something
heroic. You see how cocksure these Rutulians are.
Their fires are far apart, and they're sprawled around,
slack with wine and sleep. All's quiet. So hear   190
what I've been wondering, how my thoughts are taking shape.
The leaders and the army want to send news
to Aeneas and recall him to the camp.
If they give you my reward (the glory of

the exploit is enough for me), I think I see
a path along that hill to Pallanteum's walls."
Euryalus was stunned. A deep desire struck him
to win fame too, and he asked his fervent friend:
"Nisus, I'm not included in this crucial mission?
I'm supposed to send you into danger all   200
alone? That's not how my father taught me—war-steeled
Opheltes, who raised me during the Greek horror
and Troy's hardships. That's not how I've acted
at your side, risking death for great Aeneas.
I scorn the light of day! To me, this fame you want
is a bargain at the cost of losing life."
Nisus said: "I hardly feared you were a coward—
the thought! I swear it, by my hopes that Jove
(or any god who's just) brings me back a victor.
But if, as often happens in this sort of plan,   210
some god or chance puts me in jeopardy,
I want you to survive. You're young, you deserve
to live. If my body's rescued, or else ransomed,
I need you to bury me. If Fortune won't
allow that, gift my absence with a tomb
and funeral. I don't want to bring such grief
to your poor mother, the only one of all of them
who dared to follow you and leave Acestes' town."
Euryalus said: "You can grope for reasons:
there's no point. I won't change my mind.   220
Let's go." He roused some guards to take their place
and keep the watch in turn, then left his post,
heading off with Nisus to locate their king.

All the other living things throughout the land
were giving up their cares to sleep, their hearts
at rest from trouble. But a chosen set
of Trojan leaders were conferring on the crisis:
What to do? Who should take a message to

Aeneas? They stood in the middle of the camp,
leaning on long spears, gripping shields.   230
Both Nisus and Euryalus begged urgently
to be admitted at once on a crucial matter,
worth the time. Iülus let the eager pair
join in, and told Nisus to speak. Hyrtacus'
son began: "Aeneas' generals, hear us fairly.
Don't judge our offer by our age. The Rutulians
are silent, slack with wine and sleep. We've found
a place to bypass them, a spot to sneak through
by the gate that's closest to the sea.
Some sentry fires are out, others sputter
smokily. If you'll let us take this chance   240
to reach Aeneas in Pallanteum, we'll be
back here soon with spoils from many dead.
We won't get lost: we've often hunted in the
dark dells near the city and we know the river."
At this Aletes, bent with years but wise of mind
said: "Gods of Troy, whose power guards us always:
you don't intend to ruin the Trojans after all!
Such brave young men you've given us, such steadfast
hearts." Tears streaming down his face,   250
he clasped their shoulders and right hands. "What gifts,
you two, what presents could be worthy of your
bravery? The gods, and your own conduct
will grant the first and finest one. Pious Aeneas
will swiftly give the rest, as will Ascanius,
still so young, who'll recall this all his life."
Ascanius broke in: "In fact I beg you both
(since I'm only safe if Father's back)
by our great house-gods, Assaracus' Lar,
and white-haired Vesta's shrine: I place my life,   260
my trust, in you. Bring back my father, set him
in my sight. Once he's here, all will be well.
I'll give you double goblets chased in silver

that my father took after Arisba's fall,
two tripods, two large golden ingots, and an antique
bowl Sidonian Dido gave to me.
If we seize the soil and scepter of this land,
when I give out spoils by lot, I'll put aside
the horse that Turnus rode, and his golden armor
—you saw them, Nisus—to be yours, your prize,   270
that horse, the shield, and Turnus' crimson plumes.
Father will include twelve slave-girls chosen
for their beauty, and male captives with their weapons.
And more: all the land that King Latinus owns.
Euryalus, amazing boy, your age is nearer
to mine. I take you as my friend with all my heart,
to come with me no matter what I face.
I'll never look for glory in your absence.
In peace and war, in words and deeds, you're the one
I'll trust the most." Euryalus replied: 280
"No day will see me falling short of today's daring
—as long as Fortune smiles on us. But besides
these many gifts, I ask one thing. I have a mother
from Priam's ancient race. Poor thing, neither Troy
nor King Acestes' town kept her from coming
with me. I haven't told her of my mission,
which may be dangerous, nor have I said goodbye
because—I swear by night and your right hand—
I couldn't bear to see her tears. I beg you:
help her in her need and loneliness.   290
Let me take this hope with me, and I'll go
still more bravely into danger." This moved
the Dardans and they wept, handsome Iülus
above all. The image of this filial love
tore at his heart. He responded: "I'll do
everything your great feat earns for you.
She'll be a mother to me—only the name Creusa
will be lacking. No small thanks await her

for raising such a son. Whatever happens, I swear
by my own life, as my father used to do: 300
the gifts I promise if your mission turns out well,
those will still go to your mother's family."
In tears, he untied his gilded sword
and ivory scabbard. Lycaon of Knossos
forged it long ago with wondrous skill.
Mnestheus gave a lion-skin torn from
a shaggy beast, loyal Aletes traded helmets.
They armed and left at once; the group of leaders,
young and old, saw them to the gate.
Handsome Iülus, too, mature before his years   310
and with a grown man's cares, gave them many
mandates for his father. But the breezes
dispersed his words into the clouds, unheard.

They crossed the trenches to the fatal camp
in dark of night, bringing death to many
on the way. They saw bodies everywhere,
sprawled throughout the grass in drunken sleep,
chariots propped up on the shore, men lying
among the wheels and harnesses, wine goblets
and weapons. Hyrtacus' son spoke first:
"Euryalus, it's time to strike: the moment's here,
and so's our path. Keep watch against an ambush   320
from the rear. Be careful, look around you.
I'll make this camp a graveyard, and clear us a wide swath."
Then he fell silent. With his sword, he crept
toward proud Rhamnes, who by chance was sleeping
on a layered heap of rugs, and snoring loudly.
He was a king and augur loved by Turnus, but his
skill did not prevent his death. Near him, Nisus
killed three slaves who rashly slept among the weapons,
then Remus' armor-bearer and charioteer, slashing   330
their drooping necks as they slept under their horses.

Next he struck away their master's head, leaving
his body sobbing blood; warm gore soaked the earth
and bedding. He killed Lamyrus and Lamus,
then youthful Serranus, famous for his looks,
who'd played cards until the early hours, then
succumbed to wine—happier, if he'd only
played all night and carried on to dawn.
He was like a starving lion bringing chaos
to a sheepfold, when mindless hunger makes him tear   340
the soft sheep mute with fear; he roars with bloody jaws.
Euryalus matched Nisus' killing. On fire himself,
he mowed down the rank and file before him,
Abaris, Fadus, and Herbesus—all unaware.
But Rhoetus was awake and saw it all.
Terrified, he crouched behind a giant wine-jar.
As he tried to rise, Euryalus drove in
his sword and took it back dripping with death.
Rhoetus' crimson life pumped out, a mix of blood
and wine. The Trojan pressed on eagerly,   350
Messapus' allies his next target. He saw
the outer fires dead, and tethered horses cropping
grass. But Nisus sensed his friend was lost
to lust for slaughter. He said briefly, "Let's go. Dawn,
no friend of ours, is near. Enough revenge.
We've hacked a passage through the enemy."
They left behind many solid silver weapons,
also bowls and gorgeous rugs. Euryalus
took Rhamnes' breastplate and gold-studded sword-belt,
gifts that rich King Caedicus once sent to   360
Remulus of Tibur, his distant guest-friend.
In death, Remulus bequeathed them to his grandson.
With *his* death, the Rutulians took his war-spoils.
Euryalus put these on his sturdy shoulders
(they wouldn't save him) with Messapus' strong helmet
and fine crest. They left the camp, making for safety.

. . .

Just now horsemen chanced to come from Latium:
Volcens led three hundred armed with shields.
They were bringing Turnus a response
while the army waited, drawn up in the fields.   370
As they neared the camp's defenses, they saw
these two veering left, far off. In the predawn
gloom, Euryalus' helmet mirrored
the moon's rays and betrayed the thoughtless boy.
Taking note, Volcens shouted from the ranks:
"Halt! Why are you on the road? Why armed?
Where are you going?" The two made no reply,
but ran still faster to the woods, trusting to
the dark. The horsemen blocked the roads—they knew
them well—and set guards at the exits. The woods   380
bristled far and wide with thickets and black
holm-oaks; dense brambles clustered all around.
A narrow passage glimmered through the shrouded paths.
The forest's darkness and his heavy plunder slowed
Euryalus, and his fear misled him.
But Nisus had escaped the troops in a blind rush,
past a spot later called Alban (after Alba,
where Latinus had his stables). He stopped then,
looking for his missing friend in vain.
"Poor Euryalus, where did I lose you? Which way   390
should I go?" He traced back every winding trail
of that tricky forest, looking for his tracks,
wandering through the silent brush. He heard
horses and a hubbub, proof of the pursuers.
It wasn't long till shouting reached his ears
and he saw Euryalus, tricked by night
and forest and the sudden skirmish, struggling wildly
as the troop of horsemen dragged him off.
What should he do? How could he save the boy?
Should he throw himself at them, though doomed,   400

and die a noble death among their swords?
Quickly he drew back his arm to hurl his spear,
looking up at the high moon and praying,
"You, goddess, Latona's daughter, glory
of the stars and guardian of the woods, help me
in my trouble. If my father brought your altars
gifts from me, if I offered wild game from
my hunts and hung them from your dome and sacred roof,
guide my spear, let me break apart their band."
He hurled his weapon, using all his strength.   410
The flying shaft severed night's shadow.
It struck Sulmo's back and snapped, piercing
his heart with shattered wood. He slumped to earth.
Warm streams pumped from his chest and long convulsions
shook him; he grew cold. The group stared round.
Nisus, fiercer still, wielded a new spear
by his ear. He hurled the hissing weapon
at the panicked men. It went through Tagus' temples,
sticking there, warming in his punctured brain.
Savage Volcens raged, but couldn't see who threw   420
the spear, nor where to aim his furious attack.
Instead he turned his bare blade on Euryalus
and said, "You will pay me with hot blood
for both my men!" At this Nisus, insane
with terror, no longer hiding in the dark, unable
to endure such pain, called out, "It's me,
me, Rutulians, I did it, turn your swords
on me! I attacked you! He didn't, couldn't,
dare it: I swear by the sky and knowing stars.
He just loved his wretched friend too much."   430
But as he spoke, the sword plunged violently
through Euryalus' ribs, ripping open
his white chest. He crumpled, dying. Blood
ran down his lovely body; his neck slumped
like a purple flower cut down by a plow,

bending as it dies, like a poppy's drooping
neck when heavy rain drags down its head.
Nisus rushed at them. But among them all,
he aimed for Volcens only, took time for him alone.
The soldiers crowded him, jabbing with spears   440
to drive him off. He fought on still. His sword
swung round like lightning till he shoved it into
Volcens' shouting face. He killed him and died,
pierced through and through, flinging himself
on his friend's corpse, finding peace at last in death.

Lucky pair! If my song has any power,
no day will steal you from time's memory,* while
Aeneas' people settle by the Capitol's
unmoving stone, and a Roman father rules.

The Rutulian victors took up their spoils.   450
In tears, they carried Volcens' body back to camp.
Their grief was not reduced by bloodless Rhamnes
near the tents, by Serranus, Numa, and
so many leaders killed together. They rushed
as one to the dead and dying men. The ground
was warm with gore and streams of foaming blood.
The spoils were recognized: Messapus' gleaming helmet
and his breastplate's emblems, re-won with so much sweat.

Dawn was sprinkling new light on the lands,
rising early from Tithonus' saffron bed.   460
As sunlight soaked the world and laid it bare,
Turnus armed himself and roused his men to fight.
Each chief marshaled his bronze-armored ranks
for war, whetting their rage with varied rumors.
They stuck the heads of Nisus and Euryalus
on pikes held high, heart-rending to see,

and marched behind them with loud battle-cries.
Aeneas' hardened men stationed their front lines
to the ramparts' left (the right side touched the river),
guarding the deep ditches, or sadly manning   470
the high turrets—heartsick at the impaled heads,
oozing with black blood, of men they knew so well.

Winged Rumor flew across the anxious camp
and stole into the ears of the dead boy's mother.
At once warmth left her bones, poor thing. The shuttle
tumbled from her hands, its wool unwinding.
She leapt up in agony and tore her hair,
shrilling in a woman's grief, madly running
for the ramparts and front guard, forgetting soldiers,
spears, and danger, pouring pain into the sky.   480
"Is this you, Euryalus? Is this the comfort
kept for my old age? My cruel son, you left me?
Sent off to such danger, you didn't pause to say
goodbye to your unhappy mother? Now you're dead,
carrion for Latin dogs and birds
in a foreign land. I can't take your body
to the pyre, close your eyes, and wash your wounds,
or warm you with the robe I'd woven day and night,
racing time, the shuttle soothing my old years.
Where can I go? What place has your severed,   490
mangled corpse? This head is all you've left me,
son? *This* is what I followed over land and
sea? Rutulians, show your piety—
throw your weapons at me, kill me first.
Or you, great father of the gods, take pity,
use your bolt to plunge my hateful soul to Hades,
if that's the only way this bitter life can end."
They were stricken at her cries. A sad groan ran
through all of them; their strength for battle drained.

She was stirring too much grief. Ilioneus   500
and weeping Iülus ordered Actor and Idaeus
to carry her inside and lay her down.

The trumpet blared its terrible bronze notes
from far. A shout went up, the heavens bellowed back.
The Volscians raced up under overlapping shields,
keen to fill the ditches and tear down the walls.
Some tried to breach the camp, leaning ladders on the
walls where the ranks were thin, where the ring
of soldiers showed a gap. But long war had taught
the Trojans how to defend walls. They rained down   510
varied missiles, dislodging men with sturdy pikes,
rolling rocks of deadly weight, eager to break
through to the protected ranks. The Latins, huddling
under their locked shields, took pleasure in their safety.
But this was not enough, since the Trojans dropped
a giant boulder where the hostile throng
was thickest. It sent Rutulians flying far and wide,
breaking their roof of shields. The bold Rutulians
had no wish to keep on fighting blindly.
Instead they tried to clear the walls by hurling spears.   520
Elsewhere, grim to see, Mezentius brandished
torches made of Tuscan pine, hurling smoky fire,
while Neptune's son, Messapus the horse-tamer,
tore at the defenses and demanded ladders.

Calliope, I pray you and your sisters: inspire
me to sing of all the carnage there, the deaths
dispensed by Turnus, the killers and the victims.
Unroll with me the length and breadth of war.*

A turret with high gangways towered near
the camp, a vital spot which the Italians   530
tried with all their strength to storm and topple.

The Trojans fought to save it, crowding by
the open oylets to fling stones and spears.
Turnus was the first to hurl a burning torch.
The flame clung to the wall. Fanned by wind,
it consumed the planks and climbed the beams.
Inside, chaos and terror. Soldiers frantic to get
out were trapped. They retreated in a huddle
to the safer side. Suddenly, the tower   540
caved under their weight. The sky roared with the crash.
Half-dead men rained down, and the huge fort followed,
impaling them with weapons and hard timbers.
Only Helenor and Lycus made it out.
Helenor was in the prime of life, a bastard
son the Lydian king had sired on a slave,
Licymnia. Although it was forbidden,* he fought
in battle, with just a sword and unmarked shield.
When he found himself among Turnus's
thousands, the Latin legions all around,   550
he was like a wild beast close-ringed by hunters,
raging at their weapons, courting death
on purpose, leaping onto their tall spears;
just so, about to die, he flung himself
where he saw the hostile spear-tips thickest.
Swift Lycus sprinted through the swords and men
and reached the walls. He scrabbled for the top,
stretching up to grasp his comrades' hands.
But Turnus had kept up, armed and right behind him.
Catching him, he chided, "Fool, you thought   560
you could escape my grasp?" He seized him as he dangled,
and pulled a huge chunk of the wall away with him—
like Jove's lightning-carrier, the eagle, who grabs
a hare or snowy swan in his hooks, then soars;
or like a wolf, Mars' beast, stealing a lamb
out of the fold as its mother searches, bleating.
The Latins charged with war-cries; they filled the ditches

and flung flaming torches on the roofs.
With a giant rock, Ileoneus killed
Lucetius as he neared the gate with firebrands.   570
Liger, good with lances, killed Emathion.
Asilas' arrow, unseen, brought down Coryneus
from afar. Turnus slaughtered Caeneus (who'd killed
Ortygius), Itys, Dioxippus,
Clonius, Promolus, Sagaris,
and Idas on the turret. Capys killed Privernus,
whom Themillas' spear had grazed—the fool dropped his
shield to clutch his wound; the gliding arrow pierced him
on the left and tunneled deep, tearing
the pathways of his breath, a lethal wound.   580
Arcens' son was close in striking armor
and an embroidered cloak, bright with Spanish red:
a handsome boy sent by his father, who had
raised him in Mars' grove, near Symaethus' streams,
where Palicus has altars with rich offerings.
Mezentius threw down his spears, whirled a hissing
sling three times around his head, and threw.
He split open the boy's forehead with hot
lead and sprawled him on a sandbank, dead.

It's said this was the first time that Ascanius   590
let arrows fly in war. Before, he'd only scared
the skittish wild beasts. His strong hand killed
Numanus Remulus, now Turnus' kin—
he'd married Turnus' younger sister. This man strode
in front of the battle-line, shouting abuse,
not all fit to tell, swollen up with
his new kingdom, strutting his bulk around:
"Twice-beaten Phrygians! You're not ashamed to hide
behind ramparts *again,* delaying death with walls?
See these types who'd seize our wives in war!   600
What god, what lunacy drove you to Italy?

There are no sons of Atreus here, no lying
Ulysses. We're a flinty race. We take our newborns
to the streams and steel them in the icy water.
Our sons stay up to hunt, wearing out the woods.
Their play is breaking colts and shooting arrows.
Our men don't tire of work. They live off little;
they tame the earth with hoes, they humble towns in war.
Spears shape our lives—we use their butts
to drive our oxen! Slow old age can't sap   610
our bravery nor mute our vigor. We hide
our gray hair with a helmet, and never stop
collecting spoils to live on. But you! Your clothes
have violet and saffron stitching,* your hobby's
laziness, you love to dance, your tunics
have long sleeves and your hats are bonnets!
O Phrygian ladies (no men here), go prance over
Mount Dindyma's ridge, where the double flute plays
your sort of tunes. Your tambourines and Mother Ida's
boxwoods call you. Leave the weapons to real men."   620

Ascanius had had enough of this man's boasts
and threats. He pulled his horsehair bowstring
to its tautest point and stood, aiming his arrow,
beseeching Jupiter with many prayers.
"Almighty Jove, approve my daring act.
I'll bring offerings to your temple every year,
and I'll set a snowy calf before your altar.
He'll hold his gilded forehead as high as his mother's,
butting with his horns and pawing at the sand."
The Father heard. He thundered on the left   630
in the cloudless sky. The deadly bowstring twanged.
A taut arrow sprang out, hissing horribly,
and pierced Remulus's head, driving through
the hollow temples with its iron. Ascanius
said curtly: "Now use haughty words to mock our courage!

Here's how twice-beaten Phrygians answer you."
The Trojans shouted gladly; their spirits soared sky-high.

It happened that long-haired Apollo, seated on
a lofty cloud, was watching the Italian army
and the camp. He said to the victor Iülus: 640
"Bravo, my son. Your first brave deed, the pathway
to the stars. Born of gods, you'll father gods.
Under Assaracus' race, all wars will cease
—it's fated. Troy will be eclipsed." He sprang down
from the heights of heaven, parting airy winds,
and found Ascanius. First he took on aged
Butes' face, a man who'd been the armor-bearer
for Anchises long ago, a trusty guard;
Aeneas gave him as a tutor to his son.
Apollo mirrored the old man in every way,   650
his voice and color, white hair, jangling armor.
He said to Iülus, who was hot for battle:
"It's enough, Aeneas' son, that you shot
Numanus with impunity. Great Apollo
grants you this first glory. He's not jealous
that you too use a bow. But avoid the rest
of battle." He spoke and shed his human form,
slipping from their mortal eyes into thin air.
The Trojan leaders knew the god and his immortal
weapons; they heard his quiver clatter as he flew.   660
At Apollo's words and will, they restrained
Ascanius, who hungered for the fight. The rest
returned to battle and the open risk of death.
The clamor rang along the walls and towers
as they drew their bows and whirled their slings.
All the ground was strewn with spears; their shields
and hollow helmets clashed and clanged. The fighting
surged like rain out of the west, lashing earth
when watery Auriga rises; like a storm

that pelts thick hail into the waves, when south winds   *670*
freeze the rain and burst the hollow clouds.

Pandarus and Bitias, Alcanor's sons,
whom the nymph Iaera reared in Jove's groves,
men tall as pine-trees on their native hills,
threw open the gate they guarded, trusting
to their swords, inviting in the enemy.
They stood like towers to the right and left,
armed in iron, high plumes rippling on their heads:
like twin oaks soaring to the sky by clear waters
on Po's banks or near pleasant Athesis,   *680*
raising their unshorn heads to heaven; the tall
crowns bob up and down. The Rutulians
saw the open gates and charged at once.
But their men—led by Quercens and
Aquiculus, handsome in his armor, reckless
Tmarus, and Haemon, son of Mars—all died
at the very gates, or turned to run.
Now rage surged in both sides' hating hearts.
The Trojans massed together, daring combat
hand to hand and sallying beyond the gate.   *690*

As he rampaged elsewhere, causing chaos, Turnus
heard the news: a fever for fresh slaughter gripped
the enemy, they'd put their open gates on show!
He stopped what he'd begun. Wild rage drove him
to the gates where the proud brothers stood.
First he speared Antiphates, fighting at
the front, Sarpedon's bastard by a Theban
mother. The shaft of native cornel flew through
the thin air and speared him in the stomach,
just under his chest. The gaping hole spewed out   *700*
a bloody froth; the iron grew warm inside his lung.
Then Turnus slaughtered Erymas and Merops

and Aphidnus. Bitias died next, roaring,
his eyes blazing. But not by a spear (he'd never
die by spear). A shrieking Saguntine pike
sped his way like lightning. The shield of two bull's-hides,
the trusty breastplate with its double golden scales,
couldn't block it. His huge body crumpled, falling
to the groaning earth; the giant shield crashed
above him—like the shore at Baiae when   710
a pier of giant rocks collapses in the sea,
crashing in a pile of wreckage as it hits
the shallow bottom, making the sea churn. Black sand
swirls up and nearby islands tremble at the sound,
soaring Prochtya and Inarime, a hard bed
piled on Typhoeus by Jupiter's command.

Now Mars, lord of war, gave strength and courage
to the Latins, twisting his sharp spurs inside
their chests, dealing Flight and black Fear to the Trojans.
Latins swarmed from all around to seize   720
their chance. The god of battle goaded them.
Pandarus saw his brother's corpse, saw how
their fortune stood, how disaster drove the day.
He pushed against the gate with massive shoulders
and strained to turn it on its hinges, stranding many
of his men beyond the walls in bitter war.
The rest he shut in with him as they bolted through—
the fool, who didn't realize the Rutulian king
was in the crowd, and locked him in the city,
like a hulking tiger among helpless sheep.   730
Fresh fire flashed in Turnus' eyes, and his weapons
rang out horribly. His helmet's blood-red plumes shook;
lightning glimmered from his shield. Shocked,
Aeneas' men saw suddenly that hated face,
that massive frame. Huge Pandarus leapt in front,
boiling with rage at his brother's death. He shouted,

"This is not your promised dowry, queen Amata's
palace! These are not the coddling walls of your
town Ardea! It's a hostile camp—you're trapped!"
Turnus smiled at him and answered calmly, "Come, then,   740
if your heart has any courage, fight with me:
tell Priam you found Achilles here too."
Pandarus threw his spear, rough with whorls
and bark, with all his strength. But the breezes took it,
and Saturnian Juno bent away the wound
it brought. The shaft stuck in the gate, and Turnus cried:
"You won't escape *this* weapon, nor the power that's
behind it. The man who throws it gives no second chances."
Rearing high, he raised his sword and halved Pandarus'
head right down the center with the blade. The temples   750
and smooth cheeks were sliced in two, a monstrous wound.
With a thud, that massive weight crashed to the ground.
In death, he spilled onto the dirt his fallen body
and the armor dripping brains. His head,
split down the middle, hung over each shoulder.

Terrified, the Trojans turned and scattered;
and if the victor had thought then to smash
the locks and let his allies in, that would
have been the end of war—and of the Trojans.
But frenzy and an insane lust for slaughter drove him   760
blazing at his enemies. Phaleris
was killed, Gyges' hamstrings cut. He seized
spears and hurled them at the fleeing Trojans
(Juno gave him bravery and strength); then sent
Halys to the dead, then Phegeus, his shield
pierced; then Halius, Alcander, Noëmon
and Prytanis, caught off guard as they cheered
men from the walls. Lynceus attacked, calling
on his friends, but by the right-hand rampart Turnus
slashed him first, one strike of his flashing sword.   770

His severed head and helmet landed far away.
Next fell Amycus, slayer of beasts, best at
smearing arrow-tips and arming spears with poison,
and Clytius, Aeolus' son, and Cretheus,
the Muses' friend and follower, who always loved
the lyre and songs and setting verse to music;
he always sang of horses, war, battles, and men.*

At last the Trojan leaders heard news of the bloodbath.
Fierce Serestus and Mnestheus both ran up
to see the Trojans scattered, the enemy inside.   780
Mnestheus shouted: "Are you running? But where to?
What other walls or camps do you have? Citizens,
will a single man, fenced in by your ramparts,
deal death through our quarters unopposed,
and send the best of our young men to Orcus?
Cowards! Where's your shame and pity for your
suffering land, your ancient gods, and great Aeneas?"

These words fired them with courage. They joined up
to hold the line. Meanwhile Turnus edged back from
the fighting, aiming for a spot next to the river.   790
Now the Trojans fell on him more fiercely,
massing round him with loud yells—like a band
of hunters cornering a savage lion with spears.
He's afraid, hate in his eyes as he retreats.
Rage and nerve won't let him turn his back,
he longs to spring, but balks at men and weapons.
So Turnus fell back slowly, hesitating,
his mind seething with rage. Twice he charged
into their ranks, disrupting them, and pushed
the Trojans back against the walls, but they   800
quickly regrouped from the borders of the camp.
Juno, Saturn's daughter, didn't dare supply him
strength, since Jupiter had sent down Iris

from the sky to pass on his harsh threats
if Turnus didn't leave the Trojan camp.
The fighter couldn't hold his ground with shield
or sword. The spears heaped on him from every side
engulfed him, and his helmet rang around his head
with constant clangs. Flying stones had broken its hard
bronze and the crest had been knocked off. His shield   810
couldn't stop the blows. Now thundering Mnestheus
and the Trojan soldiers multiplied the rain
of spears. His whole body ran with grimy streams
of sweat. He couldn't breathe, and shook with gasps.
At last he leapt into the river, plunging in
headfirst with his armor. Its sandy currents welcomed
him and buoyed him with gentle waves. Rinsing
off the blood, it sent him, happy, to his friends.

BOOK 10

BLOODSHED,
AND PALLAS DOWN

Now great Olympus' palace was flung open.
The father of the gods and king of men convened
a council in that starry home, from whose heights
he saw all lands, the Trojan camps and Latin peoples.
When all were seated in the hall with double doors,
he began. "Great sky-gods, why this change
of heart, this bitter disagreement? My command
was that the Trojans and Italians should not fight.*
What's this conflict, then? What fear caused
each side to take to war and weapons? The time   10
for fighting will arrive (don't hasten it)
when fierce Carthage opens up the Alps*
to launch destruction on Rome's citadel.
Then they can compete in hate and pillage.
For now, stop. Be allies gladly, as agreed."

Jupiter spoke briefly, but golden Venus's
response was far from brief. "Father, eternal
king of mankind and the world entire,
who else could I appeal to now? Don't you see
how proudly the Rutulians strut, how boldly   20
Turnus gallops through the ranks, puffed up by
fresh victory? The Trojan camp no longer
offers safety. The fight's within the very walls

and ramparts, the trenches overflow with blood!
Aeneas is away and doesn't know. Will you
never let the siege be raised? Again
an army menaces the walls of a new Troy,
again Diomedes will attack the Trojans
from Greek Arpi. No doubt new wounds await me too
—your daughter, still harassed by human swords!*   *30*
If the Trojans came to Italy against
your will, let them expiate their error:
withhold your help. But if they followed many
oracles from gods and ghosts, how could anyone
overturn your orders now and alter fate?
Must I mention ships ablaze at Eryx,
the raging storms freed by the King of Winds,
or Iris on a mission from the clouds?
Now Juno even meddles with the dead,
the only realm she hadn't touched—suddenly   *40*
Allecto runs amok in the Italian towns.
I no longer care for empires; I just had hope
while my luck stood. Your favorites can win.
If there's no land your heartless wife will give
the Trojans, I beg you by Troy's smoking ruins:
let me take Ascanius away from war
unharmed. Allow my grandson to survive.
Aeneas can be tossed on unknown seas,
following whatever path Fate gives.
Just let me save the boy from battle's terrors.   *50*
I control Amathus, Cythera, high Paphus,
and a shrine in Cyprus: let him drop his sword
and lead an unheroic life there. Tell Carthage
to subdue Ausonia; Tyrian towns
can rise unhampered. What use was surviving
in a fatal war, surrounded by Greek flames,
and endless risks on land and sea, if they still lack
their Latium, their second Pergamum?

Better if they'd settled on the ashes
of their fatherland, the soil that was Troy.   60
Father, give back Simoïs and Xanthus,
let these wretched people live Troy's fate again."
Now deep rage stung Juno: "Why am I being forced
to shatter my long silence and lay bare old wounds?
Which god or man compelled Aeneas to choose war,
and make an enemy of King Latinus?
Fine, he came to Italy guided by fate
(or forced by mad Cassandra): did I urge
him to leave his camp and trust his life to winds?
To put his son in charge, rely on walls,   70
rile up Tuscan loyalties and peaceful clans?
Which god drove him to deceit? What harshness
of mine? Where's Juno here, or Iris from the sky?
If it's dreadful that Italians circled
a new Troy with flames, or that Turnus (divine
Venilia's son, Pilumnus' heir) has made a stand
on his own land, what about the Trojans torching
Latium, seizing foreign fields and plunder?
Or choosing in-laws, stealing fiancées, seeking
peace with words while fixing shields on prows?   80
It was fine for you to snatch Aeneas from the
Greeks, to hide him in a hollow puff of cloud,
to turn a whole fleet into just as many nymphs:
but it's an outrage if I've aided the Rutulians?
'Aeneas is away and doesn't know.' So what?
You own Paphus, Cyprus, lofty Cythera:
Why attack fierce hearts and burden towns with war?
Am I trying to topple Troy's unsteady rule?
Who threw the wretched Phrygians to the Greeks?
Europe and Asia rose in war and broke   90
their treaty—why? Who stole a woman? Was it
I who made the Trojan cheater storm and
capture Sparta, did I arm a lovers' war?

Your concern was due back then. It's too late now
for empty slander and unfair complaints."

So Juno pled her case. All the sky-gods murmured
in favor of one goddess or the other, like the
early rustling of winds caught in forests—a hidden
murmur warning sailors of the storms to come.
Then the almighty father, ruler of all things,   100
began to speak. The gods' high home fell silent,
the soil trembled underfoot. The heavens stilled,
the breezes died, the ocean waters settled.
"Listen, and take my words to heart. Since Troy
and Italy were not permitted to make peace,
and your quarrel knows no end, today
I won't distinguish Trojans from Rutulians,
no matter what their luck or what their hopes,
whether it's the fate of Italy that's caused
this siege, or Trojan error and vicious advice.   110
The Rutulians are not absolved. Each side
will bear the consequence of their acts.
Royal Jove is neutral;* the fates will find their way."
He swore this by his brother's Stygian streams,
the banks bubbling with pitch, and the dark abyss.
Olympus staggered with his nod: all talk was done.
The gods saw him from his gold throne to the door.

Meanwhile the Rutulians crowded all the gates,
keen to kill their enemies and ring the camp
with flames. Aeneas' troops were trapped inside the walls   120
with no hope of escape. Wretched, they stood
on the towers uselessly. Two Assarici,
Asius, Imbrasus' son, and Thymoetes,
son to Hicetaon, took the front positions
with Castor and old Thymbris: the ramparts' sparse defense.
Also Sarpedon's brothers from great Lycia,

Clarus and Thaemon. Acmon of Lyrnesus,
huge as his father Clytius or brother Menestheus,
hoisted a huge boulder, the good part of a hill,
with great effort. Some tried to save the camp   130
with spears, some with stones and fire and arrows.
Among them was the Trojan boy, Venus'
special care, his noble head uncovered.
He shone like a jewel set in yellow gold,
a gem for neck or brow, or like bright ivory
set skillfully in terebinth or boxwood.
His hair spilled down his milky neck, over
the circling choker of soft gold. You too,
Ismarus: your great-souled people saw you
aiming shots, arrows that you'd armed with poison,   140
noble son of Lydia, where farmers plow
rich fields watered with Pactolus's gold dust.
Mnestheus was there too, raised sky-high by glory
from the day before, when he'd beaten Turnus
from the walls; and Capys, who'd name Capua.

So they fought, in the bitter strife of war.
But in the dead of night, Aeneas left Evander,
sailing for the camp of the Etruscan king.
He explained his name and race, his needs and
assets, and pled with him, warning that   150
Mezentius was gaining allies, Turnus called for
violence, and his own plans might someday
fall apart. At once, Tarchon struck a pact
and gave him men, paying Lydia's debt
to gods and fate. They sailed with a foreigner
as leader. Aeneas was in front, his ship's beak
carved with Phrygian lions in Mount Ida's
shadow, a sweet sight for Trojan exiles.
He sat there thinking of the varied phases

of the war. Close at his left, Pallas asked   160
about the stars, their guides through the inky night,
then about his sufferings on land and sea.

Muses, open Helicon, inspire my song.
Tell me of the troops Aeneas took from Tuscan
shores to man the ships and sail the sea.

Massicus led. His bronze ship *Tiger* cut the waves,
a thousand of his men on board. They'd left
walled Clusium and Cosae, land of arrows,
lightweight quivers and bows dealing death.
With him was grim Abas, his men in striking   170
armor, a gold Apollo gleaming on his stern.
His native Populonia had given him
six hundred veterans. The island Ilva, dotted
with rich iron mines, sent three hundred more.
In third place was Asilas, seer of men and gods.
He read bulls' entrails and the stars above,
the speech of birds and lightning's fiery omens. He brought
a thousand men, thickset ranks of bristling spears.
Pisa, Tuscan offshoot of Alphean Pisa,
sent them to follow him. Then came handsome   180
Astyr, trusting in his horse and varicolored
armor. Three hundred more were sent, all keen
to join, from round the river Minio and Caere,
from ancient Pyrgi and Graviscae, land of fevers.

Cunarus, bravest leader of the Lydians,
I won't pass you by, nor you, Cupavo, followed
by a few. Your helmet's swan-plumes honored Cycnus—
your father, changed into a swan by Venus and
her son. They say he mourned his lover, Phaëthon,
under leafy poplars that were once his sisters,   190

finding comfort for grief in the Muse of song.
As he sang, he grew the downy plumes of white
old age, left the earth, and soared up to the stars.
His son drove forward the huge *Centaur,* leading
young men like himself. Its half-horse figurehead
loomed high above, threatening to throw a rock
into the waves. The long keel plowed deep ocean.

Ocnus mustered soldiers from his native banks,
son of the seer Manto and the Tuscan river.
He gave Mantua walls, and his mother's name—   200
Mantua, rich in different ancestors,
a city with three races and four clans in each.
Her strength came from Tuscan blood. Here, hatred
for Mezentius drove five hundred into war.
The river Mincius, Benacus' son, veiled
in gray-green reeds, was their warships' figurehead.
Next, Aulestes led the heavy *Triton,*
a hundred oars rising to thrash the waves
and roil the marble surface of the sea.
Triton's statue scared the blue sea with his conch,   210
to his waist a hairy man, a fish below.
Waves churned and roared under the hybrid's chest.
So many chosen princes came on thirty ships
to fight for Troy. Their bronze beaks cut the briny plains.

Now day had slipped from sky, and kindly Phoebe
trampled high Olympus with her nightly horses.
Aeneas (since his cares gave him no rest)
held the helm himself, tending to the sails.
Suddenly, far out to sea, a band of friends
appeared: the nymphs whom kind Cybele   220
had changed from ships into sea-goddesses.
A line of them cut through the waves, a number

equal to the prows that once were moored at shore.
They recognized the king from far, and circled him
in dance. Cymodocea, most skilled in speech,
held the stern with one hand, paddling softly under
water with the other, rising from the surface.
She asked confused Aeneas, "Are you keeping watch,
Aeneas, born of gods? Wake up, let out the sails.
We're the pines from Ida's sacred peak, once   230
your fleet—now ocean nymphs. When lying Turnus
rushed at us with flames and swords, we broke your ropes
unwillingly. Now we search for you at sea,
since Cybele pitied us and changed our form;
she made us goddesses that live under the waves.
Young Ascanius is trapped by walls and trenches,
besieged by spears and Latins barbed for war.
Arcadian horsemen hold their posts along with strong
Etruscans. But Turnus plans to send his central column
to stop their union with the Trojan camp.   240
Rise with the dawn, and quickly call your men
to arms. Take the deathless shield the Fire God
himself ringed with gold and gave to you.
If you trust my words, tomorrow's sun will see
huge heaps of dead Rutulians." As she left,
she pushed the high stern with her hand (she knew
the ways of boats). The ship flew across the waves,
quicker than a spear or wind-swift arrow.
The whole fleet sped up too. Anchises' Trojan son,
baffled, awestruck, took heart at the omen.   250
Gazing at the vault of sky, he briefly prayed:
"Kind Cybele, mother of the gods, to whom
Mount Dindyma and towered towns and harnessed
lions are dear, guide me now in battle, make this
omen good, and help your Trojans, goddess."
The full light of the wheeling day was rushing in

to rout the night already. Right away
Aeneas told his troops to rally round
the standards and to brace their hearts for war.

And now, as he stood on the high stern, he spied   260
the Trojans and their camp. He raised his blazing shield.
The soldiers on the wall raised a war-shout
to the stars; fresh hope spurred their rage.
Their spears flew—like cranes leaving the river Strymon
under storm-clouds, honking as they skim the air,
raucous with delight at fleeing the south wind.
The Italian chiefs and Turnus were surprised
until they turned to see a fleet nearing the shore,
a massive flood of ships converging on them.
Aeneas' helmet flashed; a flame poured from its crest   270
and his shield's golden boss shot fire,
like a glowing comet's blood-red tail, deathly
in the clear night; or scorching Sirius,
bringer of disease and drought to feeble mortals,
souring the night sky with unlucky light.

Yet bold Turnus was no less convinced
that he could hold the shore and block the ships.
He raised his men's spirits—and added a rebuke:*
"You have your wish—to break the Trojans' strength!
The god of battle's in your hands. Remember now   280
your wives and homes, the great deeds of the past,
and our fathers' glory. Let's catch them on the beach
while they're afraid, while their first steps totter
on the gangways. Fortune helps the brave."
He decided whom to take with him to fight,
and whom to trust with the blockaded camp.

Meanwhile, Aeneas' soldiers disembarked from
the high ships. Many waited for the surf

to ebb and weaken, then leapt into shallow water;
others rowed. Tarchon scouted out the shore,   290
avoiding shoals where breaking waves crashed loudly,
seeing where swells gently lapped the land.
He quickly pointed his prow there and asked the crew:
"Bend to oars, my chosen band; drive
your boats ahead, let the ships' beaks gouge
this hostile land, let your keels furrow it!
No matter if this mooring breaks our fleet apart,
as long as we make land." Tarchon spoke;
his crews surged to the oars. They drove the foam-flecked
ships onto the Latin shore until the beaks   300
were rammed into dry earth, and the keels
were beached and safe—Tarchon, all but yours,
which smashed into the shoals. For a while it tilted
back and forth, wedged on a jutting sandbar, battered
by the waves, then broke. The crew spilled out into
the sea—hampered by the splintered oars and floating
benches and an ebb-tow pulling at their feet.

No hesitation held back fierce Turnus. He threw
his front line at the Trojans. All clashed on the shore.
The bugles sang. Aeneas was the first to wade   310
into the throng of farmers (a good omen),
cutting Latins down, killing giant Theron
as he charged. His sword sliced Theron's gold-scaled
tunic and the chain mail made of bronze.
It gashed his flank and drank his blood. Lichas was next,
sacred to Apollo, cut from his dead mother.
The child escaped the blade—but to what end?
Soon he killed hard Cisseus and massive Gyas
as they clubbed the hordes. Hercules's weapon
didn't help, nor strong hands, nor their father,   320
Melampus, Alcides' friend while earth served him
hard tasks. As Pharus boasted uselessly,

a whirling spear wedged in his blabbing mouth.
You too, luckless Cydon: you'd have fallen
by that Trojan hand as you trailed Clytius,
your new passion. You'd be free of your eternal
love of boys as you lay there, pitiful.
But your brothers, Phorcus' sons, stopped Aeneas:
seven sons with seven hurtling spears.
Some glanced off his shield and helmet uselessly,   330
some kind Venus turned aside, so they only
grazed him. Aeneas called to loyal Achates:
"Bring the spears we pulled from Greeks I killed
at Troy. Not one I throw at the Rutulians
will miss its mark!" Grabbing a huge shaft,
he let it fly. It pierced Maeon's shield of bronze,
ripping open chest and breastplate in one go.
His brother Alcanor rushed up to catch him,
stretching out his hands, but a spear severed
his right arm and kept on flying, trailing blood;   340
the dead limb dangled from the shoulder by the sinews.
Another brother, Numitor, wrenched the spear
from Maeon's corpse, but failed to strike Aeneas
with it. He merely grazed mighty Achates' thigh.

Now Clausus of Cures, bold in his young strength,
hurled a spear that hit Dryops in mid-sentence.
It entered below the chin and tore his throat,
stripping him of voice and life together. He retched
thick blood and fell, his forehead thudding on the earth.
Next Clausus killed three Thracians of Boreas' noble   350
race, then three men from Ismara, sent by their
father Idas—different deaths for each. Halaesus
and a party of Auruncans charged with Neptune's
famous son Messapus, who excelled with horses.
One side, then the other, tried to rout
the enemy, right at Italy's doorstep. Like winds

fighting in the sky, as they clash with equal
force and spirit—not one yields, nor will the clouds
and sea; the battle's balanced in a violent lock:
so the Trojan ranks clashed with the Latin,   360
feet treading on feet, men crushing men.

Elsewhere, a stream in flood had strewn the ground
with tumbled rocks and trees torn from its banks.
The rugged, wet terrain forced Pallas' horsemen
to dismount, and they fled before a Latin
charge, unused to being on foot. When Pallas saw,
he summoned despair's last resort, and fired
their bravery with pleas and bitter words.
"You're retreating, friends? To where? By your brave acts,
by King Evander's name, by wars you've won,   370
by my hopes to match my father's fame, don't trust
this path. Our swords must slash a passage through
their ranks. Your noble country calls you
to the thick of battle, and me with you.
The gods are not against us; we're humans chased by
humans. We all have one soul, two hands. Look,
Ocean circles us, an endless obstacle.
Land's gone. Will you pick the Trojan camp, or sea?"
He spoke and charged at the packed enemy.

A cruel fate drew Lagus to confront him first.   380
As he tried to hoist a massive boulder, Pallas
pierced him with his whirling spear, where the ribs
meet spine. Pallas worked to free the shaft stuck in
the bone, and Hisbo hoped to catch him bending
and off guard. But Hisbo's fury at his friend's
cruel death distracted him. Pallas was quicker.
He plunged his sword in Hisbo's rageful lungs.
Next was Sthenius, then Anchemolus, Rhoeteus'
kin, who'd dared seduce his father's wife.

. . .

You too, twins Larides and Thymber, Daucus' sons,   390
each other's mirror, fell in the Rutulian fields,
once a source of sweet confusion to your parents.
But Pallas gave you now a cruel distinction.
Evander's sword-blade hacked off Thymber's head
while Laridus' lopped hand searched for its arm,
the dying fingers spasming on the hilt.
The sight of Pallas' dazzling acts, and angry shame
at his rebuke, armed the Arcadians anew.
Now Pallas pierced Rhoeteus as his chariot
sped past. This gave space and time to Ilus—   400
who'd been the distant target of that heavy spear.
Rhoeteus had been on the run from Teuthras and his
brother Tyres. As he died, he dangled from his
chariot, his heels hitting Rutulian soil.
Like fires that a shepherd lights in summer, at first
spaced through the woods; then, as hoped, the winds
arise and light the gaps, so a single jagged
burning line extends across broad fields; he sits
and gazes at the dancing flames in triumph—like this
his courageous comrades now united to help   410
Pallas. Then Halaesus, fierce fighter, charged them,
huddling in his shield's shelter. He killed Ladon,
Pheres, and Demodocus, and lopped off
Strymonius' right hand with his gleaming blade
as it grabbed his throat. Then he took a rock
and bashed in Thoas' face, spraying bone and blood
and brain. Halaesus' father, knowing fate, once hid him
in the woods, but when death closed his clouded eyes,
the Fates seized his son and sacrificed him
to Evander's spear. Pallas rushed him, praying: 420
"Father Tiber, give my spear good luck—
and a path through hard Halaesus' chest.
Your oak will get his armor and his spoils." The god

heard. While poor Halaesus shielded Imaon,
Pallas' spear found his unprotected chest.

But Lausus, no small part of battle,* wouldn't let
the scope of Pallas' slaughter terrify the troops.
First he butchered Abas, that bulwark of war.
Then Etruscans died, and Arcadia's prime,
and Trojan soldiers who'd survived the Greeks.   430
The front lines clashed, matched in strength and leaders.
The rear guard crowded them, and the crush
hampered their hands and swords. On one side
Pallas urged them on, on the other, Lausus.
These two were close in age, both handsome, both
robbed of homecoming by fate. But the king of
high Olympus didn't let them face each other.
A greater adversary would soon seal their fate.

Kind Juturna, Turnus' sister, urged him to help
Lausus. He cut through the lines with his swift chariot.   440
When he saw his men he shouted: "Stop the fighting!
It's for me to confront Pallas; Pallas is mine.
I just wish his father could be here to see."
The men cleared the field as told. When they left,
young Pallas, amazed by the proud command,
stared at Turnus from afar, and rolled his
fierce gaze across the man's great frame.
This was his retort to the king's words:
"I'll win glory either way: by taking your rich
spoils or by a splendid death. My father's   450
fine with both. Enough of threats." He walked into
the open. Blood froze in Arcadian hearts.
Turnus leapt down from his chariot, ready
for close combat. He came on like a lion
who spies a distant bull snorting for war
from his high overlook, and flies down for the kill.

When Pallas thought his spear could reach Turnus,
he ran forward, hoping bravery would help
this mismatched duel, praying to the great sky:
"I beg you, Hercules, by my father's welcome,   460
his feast for a stranger, help this great attempt.
Let Turnus see me ripping off his bloody armor
as he dies, let his dimming eyes fall on
his victor." Alcides heard, and stifled a great
groan within his heart, shedding futile tears.
Jove his father spoke kind words to him: "The day
of death awaits all men; their time is brief and comes
just once. But they can prolong their fame by action.
This is the task of valor. Many sons of gods
were killed by Troy's high walls; my son Sarpedon died   470
among them. Turnus too is called by fate.
The finish line of his allotted life is near."
Jove spoke, and turned his eyes from the Rutulian fields.

Pallas flung his spear forcefully, then pulled
his gleaming sword out of its sheath. The spear
flew and hit the shield's high rim, next to
Turnus' shoulder, forcing a path through.
Now even that huge body felt a graze. Turnus
aimed his spear, with its sharp iron tip, at Pallas,
brandished it at length, and shouted: "See if   480
my spear penetrates a little better!"
The quivering shaft ran through the center of the shield,
through so many bronze and iron layers,
so many folds of overlapping bull-hide. It pierced
Pallas' breastplate, boring into that great chest.
He tore the warm spear from the wound—it didn't help.
As his soul and lifeblood spurted from that hole
together, he collapsed in his own blood. His weapons
clattered and he hit his bloody mouth on the
hard earth. Turnus towered over him and said: 490

"Arcadians, remember this, and tell Evander:
I return the Pallas he deserves. I'll grant
whatever honor's in a grave, whatever solace
comes from burial. But being Aeneas' host
will not have proven cheap." Bracing his left foot
against the corpse, he ripped away the massive weight
of Pallas' sword-belt, carved to show a wicked crime:*
a band of husbands murdered in their bloody beds
on a single wedding night, worked by Clonus
with much gold. Turnus reveled in the spoils   500
he'd won. How blind the minds of men to fate
and future, to minding limits even in good luck!
There'd come a time when Turnus would wish
he'd left Pallas untouched. He'd hate this day, these spoils.
But a crowd of Pallas' friends, with many groans
and tears, set him on his shield and took him home.
Ah, Pallas, you'll bring grief and glory to your father!
You entered war and left it the same day, but still
you left behind huge heaps of the Rutulian dead.

A herald—no mere rumor of disaster—flew   510
to tell Aeneas his men were at the edge of death:
it was time to help the routed Trojans. Aeneas
mowed down those around him, slashing a wide pathway
through the fighters, on fire, hunting you, Turnus,
so proud of your fresh kill. In his mind
he saw young Pallas and Evander, their feast
for a stranger, and the pledge they'd made.
He took four of Sulmo's sons alive,
and four that Ufens raised, to offer to Hell's shades.
They'd splatter Pallas' pyre with captive blood.*   520
Then, from far, he hurled his deadly spear at Magus,
who had the wit to duck the shaft as it flew over.
He clasped Aeneas' knees in supplication:
"I beg you by your father's ghost, your hopes in Iülus

as he grows: spare me for *my* son and father.
Buried deeply in my noble home are bars
of engraved silver and gold ingots, some carved,
some natural. The Trojan victory doesn't turn
on this; a single soul won't matter much."
Aeneas countered with these words: "The many   530
bars of gold and silver that you speak of:
keep them for your sons. Turnus ended
barter in war when he murdered Pallas. So say
Iülus and the ghost of my father Anchises."
Gripping Magus' helmet in his hand, he bent
his neck back as he begged, and pushed in the sword.
Haemon's son was nearby, priest of Diana and
Apollo, his head bound with sacred ribbons,
gleaming in white emblems and white robes.
He fled across the field, but fell. Aeneas   540
killed him and Death's mighty darkness cloaked him.
Serestus carried back the armor as Mars' trophy.

Caeculus, of Vulcan's line, and Umbro,
from the Marsian hills, rallied the men.
The Trojan raged against them. He'd already
lopped off Anxur's left arm with his sword,
the shield falling with it. Anxur had made wild boasts
and thought his strength would back them. Perhaps he dreamed
of fame reaching the stars, and white old age.
Tarquitus, the son of sylvan Faunus and the   550
nymph Dryope, showing off his gleaming armor,
blocked Aeneas' blazing path. The Trojan pinned
Tarquitus' shield to his breastplate with a spear
and struck his head off as he begged in vain,
searching for more words. Rolling over
the warm trunk, Aeneas said with hatred:
"Lie there now and scare us. No dear mother
will bury you in earth or pile a tomb on you.

You'll be left to vultures, or the sea will take
your sodden corpse; hungry fish will suck your wounds."   560
Then he chased down Turnus' vanguard: Lucas and
Antaeus and brave Numa and blond Camers, son of
great-souled Volcens, richest landowner among
Ausonians, the king of quiet Amyclae.
As blood warmed his sword, Aeneas stormed
across the plain in triumph, like Aegaeon,*
said to have a hundred arms, a hundred hands,
and fifty fire-breathing mouths and chests;
when he clashed against Jove's lightning bolts
he had fifty shields and swords. Now he rushed   570
Niphaeus' four-horse chariot as it approached.
But the horses saw his giant strides and heard
his awful war-cry. They shied and bolted, spilling out
Niphaeus, and dragged the chariot to shore.

Lucagus, drawn by two white horses, charged Aeneas.
His brother Liger held the reins and steered
as Lucagus fiercely waved his unsheathed blade.
Aeneas could not tolerate this hot-headed
onrush. Huge, holding his spear, he ran to face them.
Liger shouted: "These are not the horses   580
of Diomedes! You don't see Achilles'
chariot, or the Phrygian plains. Your life
and the war end here." So the fool yapped loudly.
He received no answer. As Lucagus bent
to goad the horses with his sword, bracing
for the fight by planting forward his left leg,
Aeneas hurled his spear. It came tearing
through the bright shield's lowest rim and ripped
through his left thigh. He tumbled from the chariot,
writhing on the ground as death came over him.   590
Pious Aeneas spoke these bitter words:
"Lucagus, your chariot was not betrayed

by skittish horses shying at mere shadows:
you leapt from the wheels and abandoned it."
He seized the harness. Wretched Liger held out
helpless hands—he'd fallen from the chariot too:
"I beg you, by the parents who raised such a son,
Trojan hero, let me live, pity my prayers."
But Aeneas said to these frantic pleas: "That's not
how you spoke just now. Be loyal to your brother.   600
Die." He opened up his chest, the soul's dark home.
Such was the slaughter that Aeneas dealt across
the fields, raging like a torrent or black
whirlwind. At last his son Ascanius and
the men broke free of camp. The siege had failed.

Jupiter now came to talk to Juno. "Sister,
and most darling wife as well: as you thought
(and you were right), Venus is behind the Trojans'
strength—not just their hands so tireless in war,
not just their fierce souls inured to danger."   610
Juno meekly answered: "Best of husbands, why
torment a feeble wife who fears your rebukes?
If my love had the force it used to once,
and ought to still, you who are all-powerful
would let me carry Turnus from the battle
and keep him unscathed for his father, Daunus.
But fine, let him die and pay the Trojans
with his pious blood. And yet he's one of ours,
since Pilumnus was his ancestor. Turnus
has often heaped your shrine with lavish gifts."   620
The king of high Olympus answered briefly:
"If you seek some time for your doomed prince
by a stay of death, and you accept my terms,
then rescue Turnus, snatch him from Fate's tightening
noose: this much is allowed. But if some greater
favor lurks under your plea, if you want

the whole war changed, you feed on empty hopes."
At this, Juno wept: "Why can't you give me what
your words withhold, why can't Turnus have his life?
Unless I'm wrong, an awful death awaits   630
a blameless man. How I wish false fear toyed
with me, and you'd change your plans—you can!"

She spoke, and swooped down from the sky, through
the breezes, wrapped in mist, bringing storms.
She reached the Trojan army and Laurentian camp.
Then she formed a weak and wraithlike shadow
from filmy cloud to be Aeneas' look-alike
(a marvel!). She gave it Trojan armor, Aeneas' shield,
the plumes over that godly head, his gait,
and hollow words, sounds without a meaning: 640
like phantoms said to hover after death,
or visions that deceive our sleeping senses.
The image pranced before the front lines happily,
taunting Turnus with rude shouts, flaunting weapons.
Turnus attacked, throwing his hissing spear
from afar. The shadow turned and ran.
Turnus thought the real Aeneas had turned tail.
In confusion, he clung to that empty thought.
"Where do you run, Aeneas? Don't desert the wedding!
My blade will put you in the land for which you've sailed   650
the seas!" He chased him with such shouts, waving his sword,
blind to how the winds dispersed his triumph.

The ship of King Osinius from Clusium
happened to be moored at a tall and rocky
outcrop, its ladders and gangplank lowered. Into its depths
plunged the anxious phantom of Aeneas
on the run; but Turnus, just as quick, was at
its heels, not pausing once. He leapt over the ramp.
But he'd hardly reached the prow when Juno broke

the hawser and the current whisked the boat away.   660
The flimsy shade no longer tried to hide,
but flew up and merged with the dark clouds.
On land, Aeneas called Turnus out to fight. Looking
for the missing man, he sent many down to death
as a stormwind carried Turnus out to sea.
Confused and ungrateful to be safe,
he gazed back and raised his voice and hands
up to the stars: "Almighty Father, did I merit
such disgrace? Did you choose this punishment?
Where am I going? How can I return, who will   670
I be, if they think I ran? Will I see
my walls again? Or those who followed me to war?
Have I left them to a ghastly death (the horror!),
do I see them routed, do I hear their dying
groans? What should I do? What pit could open
deep enough for me? Show me pity, winds:
smash this boat against the rocky cliffs,
Turnus begs you. Drive me onto savage reefs
where no Rutulian can follow, nor my shame."
And now he wavered first this way, then that: 680
should he fall upon his sword, mad with
his disgrace, and drive the raw blade through his ribs,
or throw himself into the waves to strike out
for the curving shore and Trojans' spears again?
He tried both paths three times; three times great Juno
held him back, taking pity on him. Fair winds
and favoring tides carried the boat. It cut the waves
and reached his father Daunus' ancient city.

But now fiery Mezentius joined the fight
at Jove's command. As he charged the joyful Trojans,   690
Etruscan ranks surrounded him, raining
hatred and their weapons on a single man.
He was like a headland jutting out to sea,

facing the winds' fury, exposed to the waves,
bearing all the raging threats of sky and sea
unmoved. He hacked down Hebrus, Dolichaon's son,
and with him Latagus, and Palmus as he turned
to run. He smashed Latagus' face with a rock
torn from the cliff, then sliced through Palmus' hamstrings,
leaving him writhing weakly. He gave Lausus   700
Palmus' armor and his crest to wear. Next fell
Trojan Evanthes, then Paris' friend and age-mate
Mimas, son of Amycus and Theano,
born the night Queen Hecuba had Paris—
she was pregnant with Troy's future flames.
Paris lies in his paternal city, but Mimas
sprawls unknown on the Laurentian shore.
Like a boar protected many years
by Vesulus's pines or the Laurentian swamps'
reed forest—once chased from the heights by snapping dogs   710
and trapped in nets it takes a stand, snorting rage,
hackles raised, and no one dares to make the kill;
men attack with shouts and spears, safely distant,
while it slowly circles to attack, fearless,
gnashing teeth, shaking spears off its back;
just so, all the soldiers justly angry
at Mezentius didn't dare close combat.
They harried him from far with spears and shouting.

A Greek named Acron had arrived from ancient
Corythus, an exile, his marriage unfulfilled.   720
Far off, Mezentius saw him in the thick of battle,
wearing purple clothes, the gift of his betrothed.
Like an unfed lion prowling through high lairs,
driven mad by hunger, happy if he sees
a fleeing goat or young buck breaking in his horns;
then he crouches, huge jaws gaping, mane on end,
feeding on the entrails, letting stinking gore

rinse out his cruel mouth—this was swift
Mezentius, pouncing on the crowded ranks.
He hit unlucky Acron, whose heels beat on   730
black earth, the bloodied spear snapped by his fall.
But he didn't deign to kill fleeing Orodes
or inflict a spear wound from behind.
He ran to face him man to man: a better
victory without stealth. Bracing his foot
on the corpse, he pulled hard on his spear and cried:
"Men, here lies Orodes, a bastion of war!"
His friends took up his glad refrain. But the
victim gasped last words: "Vengeance will come,
stranger. You won't rejoice long. For you as well   740
an equal fate awaits. Soon these fields will hold you."
Mezentius smiled thinly through his rage: "Die now.
The father of the gods and king of men will see
to me." He yanked the spear from the body.
Bleak rest and iron sleep weighed down Orodes' eyes.
Their light was quenched for an eternal night.

Caedicus killed Alcathoüs, Sacrator
killed Hydaspes, Rapo killed Parthenius
and strong Orses. Messapus killed Clonius
and Erichaetes, one thrown from his bareback horse,   750
one on foot. Lycian Agis came up just to
fall to Valerus, brave as his ancestors.
Salius killed Thronius, but Nealces
got him. His stealthy long-range arrows were well-known.

Now grim Mars dealt death and sorrow equally.
They killed and died alike, victors and their
victims. Neither side would think to yield.
The gods in Jove's high halls felt pity for this rage,
so pointless awful suffering of men.

Here sat Venus and there Juno, looking on as 760
pale Tisiphone ran riot among thousands.

And now stormy Mezentius, shaking his great
spear, advanced across the field, towering like
Orion when he walks on foot along
the ocean's awesome depths, shoulder-high to waves,
or hauls an ancient ash tree down the mountain,
his feet on the ground, his head lost in the clouds.
So Mezentius rushed on with fearsome weapons.
Aeneas spied him in the enemy's front line
and closed in for the combat. Unperturbed and steadfast, 770
Mezentius waited for the great-souled fighter,
measuring how far his spear could fly. "Right hand,"
he said, "you're my only god. Help me now,
and you, the spear I throw! Lausus, I swear you'll wear
the spoils I rip from this pirate's corpse—you'll be
the token of my victory." He threw his hissing
spear. But it angled off Aeneas' shield
and struck noble Antores, Hercules's friend
from Argos, in the side. This man had joined Evander
and settled in a local town. Poor wretch, he died 780
from a wound not meant for him, as he looked up
at the sky and thought of lovely Argos.
Then pious Aeneas threw his spear. It pierced
the concave shield of three bronze layers, linen
folds, and three bull's-hides, lodging near
Mezentius' groin—but its flight stopped there.
The sight of Tuscan blood gladdened Aeneas.
He grabbed his sword and furiously charged
his shaken enemy. But Lausus saw, and groaned
with deep love for his father, shedding tears. 790
Lausus, I won't silence your memory,
your hard death, or your heroism, if indeed

history tells the truth about your exploits.
As his father turned to crawl away, helpless,
handicapped, dragging his shield and Aeneas'
spear, his son rushed in between them, parrying
Aeneas' sword just as his right hand rose to strike,
stopping him and fending off the blow.
His friends shouted loudly, throwing spears
and lances to repel Aeneas, so the father   800
could retreat while shielded by his son.
Aeneas, furious, kept under cover—as when
clouds fling down a fierce hailstorm; every farmer,
every plowman scatters from the fields,
the traveler finds shelter under riverbanks
or the arch of some high cliff while rain
batters the earth; but they resume their day when
the sun returns. So, lashed by spears all round,
Aeneas waited out the thunderhead of war,
shouting threats at Lausus and rebuking him: 810
"Why this hurry to meet death, to dare what's past
your strength? Your piety lures you to be rash."
But Lausus pressed on, the fool. Fury surged up
in the Trojan, and the Fates gathered the final
threads of Lausus' life. Aeneas drove his hard blade
through the young man's body. The pointed tip went through
his shield (too thin to match his threats) and the tunic
that his mother wove with soft gold mesh. It sank in
to the hilt. Blood filled his lungs; his mournful life
descended to the shades, abandoning his body.   820

But when Anchises' son looked at his dying face,
that ashen otherworldly face, he groaned deeply,
pitying the boy, and stretched his hand to him.
His own paternal piety came to his mind.
"Poor boy, what can pious Aeneas give you
worthy of your bravery and noble nature?

Keep the armor you so loved. I return you
to the ghosts and ashes of your ancestors,
if you can care. Your unhappy death has one sole
comfort: you fell to great Aeneas." Rebuking Lausus'   830
lagging friends, he lifted the corpse up from
the earth, as blood defiled his well-curled hair.

Meanwhile, by the Tiber's banks, Lausus' father
cleaned his wounds with water, propped against a trunk.
His bronze helmet dangled from a branch;
the heavy armor rested on the grass.
His chosen men stood round him as he gasped in pain,
neck bent, long beard spilling down his chest.
He kept asking about Lausus, he kept sending
men to call him at a sad father's request.   840
But Lausus' weeping friends were bringing the corpse
on his shield, a great man killed by a great wound.
His father heard the groaning from far off
with terrible foreboding. Defiling his white hair
with dust, he stretched both hands upward and embraced
his son. "Did such a lust for life possess me, child,
that I let you take my place before the killer's
sword? My son, did *these* gashes save your father,
who lives thanks to your death? Now at last I feel
the horror of my exile, the depth of my wound!   850
My son, I stained your name with my own crimes.
Hatred drove me from my father's throne and rule:
it was I who owed atonement to my people's
hate, the guilt was mine. I should have paid by any
death at all. I still haven't left this land,
this light. But leave I will." He got up on his injured
thigh, resolute, and though the deep wound sapped
his strength, he called for his horse. This was his pride
and comfort; on it he rode a victor out of every
combat. He spoke to the grieving animal: 860

"Rhaebus, we've lived long, if anything is long
in mortal terms. Today you'll bring back bloody spoils
and Aeneas' head, avenging Lausus' death
with me; or if our force finds no way forward,
we'll fall together. Brave beast, I don't think
you'd follow orders from a Trojan master."
Mounting his horse, he sat as he always did
and loaded both hands with sharp lances, his helmet
flashing with its horsehair-crest. Like this
he plunged into the fray, his heart seething   870
with great shame and madness mixed with grief.
And now he called Aeneas three times, loudly.*
Aeneas knew him and was glad. He prayed:
"May great Apollo and the father of the gods
bring this to be. Start the fight!" He ran
to face Mezentius, his spear poised.
But he replied: "Why try to terrify me now,
you savage who killed my son? That was the only
way to ruin me: I don't fear death or care
for gods. Hush. I come to die, but first I bring you gifts."   880
He hurled his long lance at the enemy,
then another and another as he circled.
They landed, but the gilded shield held them.
Three times he wheeled leftward round his watching
enemy, throwing lances; three times the Trojan
hauled around the massive iron forest fixed
in his bronze shield. Then, sick of long delay,
sick of plucking out so many lances, pressed by
the unequal fight, at last he broke away
and hurled his spear at the stallion's head.   890
The horse reared up and thrashed the air with hooves,
throwing his rider. Beast and man fell in a tangled
heap, the horse's shoulder broken. From both sides,
shouts set the sky on fire. Aeneas flew to him,
pulling out his sword, and said: "Where's fierce

Mezentius now, and that savagery of spirit?"
The Tuscan looked up at the sky, gulping air,
and answered as he came back to himself.
"Bitter enemy, why these taunts and threats?   900
Killing me's no crime; I didn't come to battle
on such terms. My Lausus made no pact with you
for me. I ask one thing, a kindness for a fallen
enemy: let my corpse be buried. I know
my people's bitter hate surrounds me: block their rage,
I beg you. Let me lie in Lausus' tomb." He spoke,
and took the sword into his throat, knowing death.
His life pumped out in bloody waves over his armor.

BOOK II

TRUCE AND CONFLICT

Meanwhile Dawn rose over Ocean's rim.
Aeneas' grief would have him turn to burying
his friends; he reeled with Pallas' death. Still,
he paid the gods a victor's vows at daybreak.
On a mound, he raised a huge oak stripped of branches
and dressed it in bright armor—spoils he took
from Lord Mezentius to be a gift for you,
great God of War: a helmet crest that oozed
with blood, the broken spears and battered breastplate
punctured in twelve places. He set the bronze shield   10
to the trunk's left side and hung the ivory-hilted
sword on top. Then he rallied the triumphant
soldiers as the leaders thronged around him:
"We've managed a great feat, my men. Let go any
fear that remains. Here stand a tyrant's spoils,
the first fruits of war; here's my Mezentius.
Now we march to King Latinus' walls.
Draw your swords, set your hearts and hopes on war!
Once the gods tell us to hoist the standards
and march our men from camp, don't be taken   20
by surprise—no second thoughts or fear!
For now, let's put the bodies of our friends
in earth, the only glory in deep Acheron.
Honor the great souls who won this country
with their blood; pay their final rites. But first

we must take Pallas to Evander's mourning city.
The day of darkness swept him off, for all
his courage, and plunged him into bitter death."

In tears, Aeneas went back to the threshold
where Pallas' lifeless body lay. Old Acoetes   30
was guarding it. He was once the armor-bearer
for Evander, then chosen as a ward for this
dear child, a pairing that would prove less happy.
The slaves stood round the body with the Trojan
troops and Trojan women, their hair loose in mourning.
And when Aeneas came through the high entrance,
the women beat their chests, and a great groan rose up
to the stars. The royal tent rang out with grief.
He saw Pallas with his head propped up, his face
pale as snow, the smooth chest gaping with its wound   40
from an Italian spear. His tears welled again.
"When Fortune smiled on me, poor boy, was your
life the cost, so you'd never see our kingdom,
or ride in triumph to your father's house?
This was not my promise to Evander when I
left, when he sent me off with an embrace
to win a mighty empire, warning me with fear
that we'd fight fierce men, a ruthless race.
Still now perhaps, beguiled by hollow hope,
he offers vows and heaps gifts on the altar   50
while we sadly escort back this lifeless boy—
an empty honor—who owes nothing to the gods.
Poor man, your child's bitter burial awaits.
Is this the glorious return we pledged?
Is this my solemn promise? But Evander, you won't
see him with shameful wounds, you wouldn't want to wish death
on a coward son. O Italy, you've lost
your great protector, and Iülus, so have you!"

. . .

Aeneas wept, and had them lift the wretched body.
He sent a thousand men selected from the troops   60
to escort the funeral and share the father's
tears, scant comfort for so great a grief, yet
an homage due a parent's sorrow. Others quickly
wove a bier of pliant wicker from arbutus
and oaken sprigs. On top they spread a canopy
of leaves. They laid the young man out, high on
his rustic litter. He was like a flower
plucked by a girl's hand, a fragile violet
or drooping hyacinth, whose bloom and beauty
had not started to fade, though Mother Earth   70
no longer offered nourishment or strength.
Aeneas fetched two garments stiff with gold and purple.
Sidonian Dido had made these for him with
her own hands, happy in her task, working
the fabric with fine threads of gold. He sadly
laid one over the young man, a final honor;
the one he put over the hair the pyre would burn.
He heaped up many war-prizes from the Laurentians
to be carried in the long procession, and added
spears and horses taken from the enemy.   80
Then he chose captives to be offerings to the dead
and bound their arms. They'd splash Pallas' pyre with blood.*
Now he told his captains to hoist tree trunks
named for the dead foes, armed with their weapons.
They fetched wretched Acoetes, weak with age.
He beat his chest with fists and clawed his face,
falling prostrate on the ground. Next came chariots
spattered with Rutulian blood, and Pallas' war-horse
Aëthon without regalia, weeping as
he walked, his muzzle wet with giant tears.   90
They brought his spear and helmet: the victor Turnus
had the rest. The grieving army followed: Trojans,

Etruscans, and Arcadians, their spears reversed.
When this line of comrades had gone a good way,
Aeneas stopped and said with a deep groan:
"The harsh fate of war calls me to other griefs.
Farewell forever, greatest Pallas; forever
goodbye." He said just this, then turned
his steps back to the high walls of his camp.

Meanwhile envoys turned up from the Latin city   100
wearing olive wreaths and asking for a favor.
Could the bodies cut down on the battlefield
be returned for burial? Surely there was
no quarrel with the lifeless victims? Let him
show mercy to those he once called hosts and in-laws.
Kind Aeneas granted them this favor,
not one to be rejected, but he added this:
"Latins, what bad luck unjustly tangled you
in such conflict? Why turn from your former friends?
You plead for grace for men killed in the lottery   110
of war. I'd gladly give it to the living too.
I've only come because my fated home is here.
It's not your people whom I fight, it's your king,
who broke our ties and put his trust in Turnus' army.
It would have been more fair for *Turnus* to face death.
If he plans to end the war by force and drive
the Trojans out, then he and I should have crossed swords.
The winner would have lived, through his own skill
or a god's help. Now go, and stoke the pyre
under your fallen citizens." Stunned to silence,   120
they looked at one another with a searching gaze.

Then the oldest, Drances, who detested Turnus
and kept hurling charges at the younger man,
replied: "Trojan hero, great in fame, greater
in war, how can I raise your praises to the sky?

Should I first admire your justice, or your prowess?
We're glad to take these words back to our native walls,
and if Fortune grants a way, we'll ally you
with King Latinus. Turnus can find his own treaties.
We'll even raise the great walls owed to you   130
by Fate, and load our backs with Trojan rocks."
He spoke; they all roared assent as one.
They fixed on twelve days' truce.* Now Trojans mingled
with the Latins, and safely roamed the forest ridges
in the short-lived peace. Tall trees rang with ax-blows.
Eagerly, they uprooted soaring pines,
cut down fragrant cedar, split oak trees with wedges,
and carried mountain rowans on their groaning carts.

Now winged Rumor, heartbreak's herald, filled
Evander's ears, home, and city—Rumor, who'd just   140
told of Pallas' victories in Latium.
Holding torches, their custom for funerals,
Arcadians streamed out to the gates. The road
became a line of flame lighting up the fields.
They fell in sadly with the crowd of Trojans.
When the mothers saw this group arriving at
their homes, they set the grieving town afire with cries.
Nothing could restrain Evander. He pushed
into the crowd. As Pallas' bier was lowered,
he collapsed and clung to it, groaning, sobbing.   150
At last his pain allowed a passage for his voice:
"Pallas, this wasn't what you pledged your father—
that you'd be careful on the killing fields of war.
I knew where pride in one's first arms could lead,
and the sweet honor of victory in first combat.
I mourn your too-young sacrifice, the harsh lessons
of a war too close, and my vows and prayers
heard by not one god! My blessed wife,

how fortunate you were to die before this grief.
I've outlived my very life: I'm my son's   160
survivor. I wish *I'd* joined the army of our Trojan
allies, that Rutulian spears had rained on me,
that this march brought my corpse home, not Pallas'!
I don't blame you, Trojans, nor our pact, nor
the hands we clasped as friends: this was the fate assigned
to my old age. But if an early death was destined
for my son, I'm glad he first killed thousands of the
Volscians, and led Trojans to Latium.
Pallas, I could want no nobler funeral
for you than one held by pious Aeneas, the great   170
Trojans, Tuscan chiefs and all their troops.
They bring great spoils from the victims of your sword.
You too would be a huge trunk decked with armor,
Turnus, if Pallas were your age or had your strength.
But my sorrow must not keep the Trojans
from the fight. Go, and tell this to your king:
with Pallas gone, I linger on in hateful life
only for your sword, which owes Turnus to me
and to my son. Only here is there room for
luck and glory; I find life's joys repellent.   180
I'll take the news to Pallas in the Underworld."

Now Dawn brought her kindly light to heartsick
humans—and with it, work and pain. Father
Aeneas and Tarchon set up pyres along the curving
shore. They fetched the corpses of their men.
As was the custom, sooty flames were lit below
the bodies; the sky was veiled by grimy smoke.
Three times the soldiers in their shining bronze
ran around the blazing fires, three times the horsemen
circled the sad pyres, calling out in grief.   190
Their weapons and the earth were wet with tears.

The shouts of men and blares of horns rose skyward.
Some threw spoils from slaughtered Latins in the flames
—helmets and fine swords, bridles, once-warm wheels
of chariots. Others added presents well known
to the dead, their own shields and luckless spears.
Many hulking bulls were sacrificed to Death.
Over flames, they slashed the throats of bristly boars
and sheep seized from the fields. Holding vigil
over half-burnt mounds, they watched their comrades blaze   200
along the shore. They could not tear themselves away
till damp night ferried in the bright star-studded sky.

Elsewhere, but no differently, the anguished Latins
raised up countless pyres. Of their many dead,
some they buried in the earth, some they hauled
to nearby fields or sent on to the towns. The rest
they set on fire—a massive heap of muddled corpses
without order, without honor. The ruined fields
and close-set biers blazed for both the armies.
When the third dawn drove chill dark away,   210
they raked and smoothed deep ash and nameless bones,
mourning, and heaped warm mounds of earth on top.
The greatest clamor, the greatest part of the long grieving,
was in rich Latinus' city and its homes.
Here sad wives and mothers, sons turned into orphans,
and the loving hearts of weeping sisters
all damned the deadly war and Turnus' marriage:
he and only he should end this by the sword,
he was the one who wanted to rule Italy!
Fierce Drances fed the flames: he swore that Turnus   220
had been challenged to a duel all alone.
But many dissenting views were heard as well
in Turnus' favor. He was shielded by the power
of the queen and his fame from many triumphs.

. . .

To crown this commotion, as the heated quarrel
raged, glum legates from Diomedes' great town
returned with his answer. All their efforts
had done nothing; the gifts and gold, their urgent
prayers had been useless. They had to look for
allies elsewhere, or ask the Trojan king for peace.   230
This dreadful blow prostrated even King Latinus.
The anger of the gods, the many fresh-dug graves,
showed him that Aeneas had been sent by gods
and Fate. He summoned a high council of the local
chiefs to meet within his home's tall gates.
They all gathered, pouring to the palace through
the crowded streets. As the oldest and most
powerful, Latinus, grim-faced, took the center.
He told the envoys who'd arrived from Diomedes
to report their news, everything in sequence.   240
There was a call for silence. Then, obeying
the king's order, Venulus began to speak:

"Citizens: we reached Diomedes' Argive
settlement, overcoming all the dangers
of the road. We clasped the hand by which Troy fell.
He'd built Argyripa, named for his father's folk,
after winning Iäpyx' fields near Garganus.
When we entered and were granted leave to speak,
we gave our gifts, told him our names and country,
named our attackers and the reason for our trip   250
to Arpi. He heard and answered calmly:
'Happy race of Saturn's realm, Italians
of old, what fortune rouses you from peace
and convinces you to rile up risky wars?
All of us whose swords defiled the fields of Troy
(forget what we endured in battle under those high

walls, all the men Simoïs drowned) paid dreadful
penance for our crimes, lashed across the earth.
Even Priam might have pitied us: witness
Minerva's cruel storm and the cliffs of vengeful   *260*
Caphereus. Homeless Menelaus, driven
from that war to other shores, reached Proteus'
Pillars; Ulysses saw the Cyclopes of Etna.
Think of Pyrrhus' realm, Idomeneus' ruined
home, Locrians left on the coast of Libya,
or Agamemnon of Mycene, who led the mighty
Greeks—his vile wife struck him down at his own door.
Her lover lurked in wait for Asia's conqueror.
The jealous gods denied me my ancestral altars,
my longed-for wife, and lovely Calydon.   *270*
Still the ghastly sight of portents harries me:
my vanished comrades seek the sky on wings
and flit among the streams as birds (this was their
punishment). They fill the cliffs with songs of sorrow.
I should have expected this, ever since
I madly struck a goddess' body with my sword,
defiling Venus' hand with blood. No:
don't impose this conflict on me. After the fall
of Pergamum, I've had no fight with Troy. I take
no pleasure in recalling these old sufferings.   *280*
The gifts you bring me from your homeland, give them
to Aeneas. I stood against his fierce sword
when we fought our duel. Trust me: I saw how high
he loomed above his shield, how forcefully
he hurled his spear.* If Ida's land had raised two more
like him, the Trojans would have reached the Argive towns
with ease, and defeated Greece would mourn her fate.
While we waited round the sturdy walls of Troy,
our victory was stalled by Hector and Aeneas,
rebuffed for ten years. Both men excelled   *290*
in bravery and skill in battle; Aeneas

in piety. If you can, clasp hands and make
a pact. Don't let your weapons clash in war.'
Best of kings, you've heard the king's response,
and the views he holds on this great conflict."

He'd hardly finished, when an anxious hubbub
of mixed voices rose up from the Latins—like
a rushing river slowed by boulders; its trapped waters
churn and roar, currents crash against the banks.
Once they were calm and the anxious cries died down,   *300*
the king invoked the gods and spoke from his high throne:

"Latins: I wish we'd made the better choice—
to solve this crisis earlier, and not to call
a council now, with enemies camped by our walls.
We were rash to battle with a race of divine
blood. They're unconquered; no fights tire them.
Even in defeat they can't lay down the sword.
If you hoped for Aetolian allies, cease to.
Anyone can hope, but you see the odds.
As for the rest of our affairs: everything   *310*
lies smashed in ruins before your eyes and hands.
I blame no one. What the greatest bravery
could do, we did. We fought with all our kingdom's strength.
I'll tell you the decision I've now reached
after much reflection; listen to my words.
I own an ancient tract along the Tuscan river.
It stretches west of the Sicanians.
The Arauncans and Rutulians plow the flinty
hills, and use the wildest parts for pasture.
All this land, with its pine-clad mountain   *320*
ridge, should be added to a Trojan pact.
Let's fix fair terms and summon them to share our rule.
If this is their desire, they can settle here
and build their walls. If they want other lands

and people, and can safely leave our soil,
let's build them twenty ships of native oak. If they
have the men for more, there's timber nearby.
They can say how many ships they need,
and of what sort. We'll give them workers, bronze,
and docks. Also: a hundred Latin nobles must go   330
to report my words and ratify the treaty.
Extend olive branches, offer gifts
and weights of gold and ivory, my throne
and robe of state, emblems of my rule.
Let's consult on how to help our ruined land."

Drances, hostile still, stood up. Turnus' glory
was a bitter goad to him, a source of secret
envy. He was free with wealth, and eloquent,
but froze in war; a wise guide in councils,
but good at rousing riots; noble on his   340
mother's side, but unknown on his father's.
With his words he stoked the common anger.
"Good king, you ask advice on issues that are
clear without debate. They all know how
our luck goes, but they won't say it aloud.
Turnus should stop his swaggering and let me speak.
His ill favor with the gods, his evil character
(I'll say it, let him threaten me with death)
have caused many of our greatest men to die,
have sunk our town in grief. Meanwhile he provokes   350
the Trojan camp and waves his weapons at the sky,
trusting in escape. Best of kings, add just
one thing to the many gifts and words you send
the Trojans: don't let anyone use violence
to stop a father from the marriage of his daughter
to a great man in a fitting union,
thus bringing peace. But if such fear grips your minds
and hearts, let's beg this favor from the man himself.

Turnus, grant our king and country their just rights.
Why keep throwing our poor people in harm's way?   *360*
You're the source of all our suffering.
War won't save us. We all ask for peace—
and the single sacred bond that brings it.
I'll be the first to beg, though you claim I hate you
(so be it): have pity on your people, set
your pride aside. You've lost, so leave. In our rout,
we've seen enough of death and ruined land.
If glory drives you and there's so much strength in you,
if a palace as your dowry is so precious,
dare *your* confidence against the enemy.   *370*
So Turnus can win a royal wife, should
our cheap lives be scattered through the battle-fields,
a crowd unburied and unwept? You—
if there's any spine in you, any of
your father's fight, go face your challenger!"

Turnus' temper blazed up at this speech.
He groaned and burst out with deep feeling: "Drances,
there's always floods of eloquence from you
when battle calls for action. You're the first to come
whenever council's called. But the senate doesn't   *380*
need the boasts that fly from you while you are safe,
while the enemy's outside the walls, and our
moats don't run with blood. So thunder eloquently,
as you do, but don't charge me with fear until
your hand has heaped up piles of Trojan dead
and decked the fields with trophies. Shall we see
what real courage can do? We don't have far to go
to find the enemy: they ring our walls.
Come, we're off to battle—why so slow?
Will your fighting always be your flapping tongue,   *390*
those feet so quick to flee? You say I've lost?
Who'd rightly say I'd lost, you filth? You saw

the swollen Tiber surge with Trojan blood,
Evander's house and family mowed down,
the Arcadians stripped of armor. 'Losing'
is not how Bitias and huge Pandarus
saw it, nor the thousand men I sent to Hades
in one day while trapped inside the Trojan walls.
'War won't save us'? Fool, prophesy this wisdom
to Aeneas and yourself. Go on, alarm   400
us all with panic, praise the power of a twice-
defeated race, deride Latinus' forces.
You'd claim the leaders of the Myrmidons tremble
at Trojan weapons—Achilles and Tydeus' son
as well! Indeed, and the Aufidus flows backward
from the Adriatic. The man says my threats
scare him (clever ploy!) and backs his lies by quaking.
Have no fear, you'll never lose your life
at *my* hands. Keep it in your coward chest.
King, I return to our important plans.   410
If you don't trust to weapons any more,
if we're on our own, and completely ruined
after one repulse, if Fortune cannot change,
let's beg for peace, holding out our wobbly hands.
But oh, if we had some of our usual courage!
I'd count the man who chose to die and bite the dust
instead of seeing such a day, lucky beyond
others in the fight, a paragon of courage.
But if we have supplies and unharmed men,
if Italian troops and towns are still our allies,   420
if the Trojans' glory cost them dear in blood
(they too had their funerals, the same storm battered
all of us), why this shameful hesitation
at the start? Why do we tremble at the bugle?
The passing days, the changes brought by shifting time
can improve much. Sly Fortune comes in different shapes.
She can set her victims back on solid ground.

If Arpi won't help, Messapus and good
Tolumnius will, and the chiefs so many sent.
No small glory will attend the chosen men   430
of Latium and the Laurentian fields,
and Camilla of the noble Volscian race,
with her mounted troops like blooms in bronze.
If the Trojans challenge me to single combat
with your blessing, if I impede our common good,
I'll take my chances, with so much at stake.
Victory hardly hates or shuns my hands.
I'll fight him bravely—no matter if he's stronger than
Achilles or wears Vulcan's armor like him. I pledge
my life to you and to father Latinus, I,   440
Turnus: a lesser warrior than none before.
Aeneas calls on me alone? I hope he does.
If the gods are angry, it should not be Drances
who pays the price of death, or wins glory and honor."

While they clashed over these doubtful matters,
Aeneas moved his camp and army. And now
a messenger ran through the palace, sowing
chaos, filling all the town with terror. His news:
the Trojans and their Tuscan troops were marching
from the Tiber. Their army swept the plains!   450
At once, the common folk were shaken and disturbed.
Their rage grew at this stinging provocation.
Eagerly, the young men roared for weapons;
sad fathers wept and murmured. Everywhere,
a clamor of dissent rose to the skies, noisy
as a flock that comes to roost in a high forest,
or raucous swans who honk along the fish-rich
Padusa and its chattering marshes. Turnus
grabbed his chance. "That's right, citizens, call
a council, sit here praising peace. Meanwhile,   460
they're armed and invading." He said no more,

but leapt up and sprinted from the palace,
commanding Volusus to arm the Volscian squadrons
and lead the Rutulians. "Messapus and Coras,
arm the cavalry with Coras' brother, and spread
them out. Some should back the gates, others man
the towers. The rest, attack where and when I say."

At once all the city scurried to the walls.
But Latinus left the council, dropping
his grand plans, dismayed at this dark turn,   470
blaming himself often for not welcoming
Aeneas to the city as his son-in-law.
Meanwhile men dug trenches at the gates or hauled up
stones and stakes. The harsh bugle blared war's bloody
signal. Then a mingled crowd of wives and children
ringed the wall: this last struggle called them all.
The queen rode in her chariot to Pallas' temple
and high citadel, many mothers with her,
bringing gifts. Lavinia sat beside her,
the cause of so much grief, her lovely eyes cast down.   480
The women entered and lit incense, scenting all
the shrine, pouring out sad pleas: "Virgin
Pallas, great in war, queen of battle,
break the spears of the Phrygian bandit, hurl him
prostrate on the ground before our city gates."
Turnus armed himself impatiently, raging
to fight. He put the bright breastplate on,
bristling with bronze mail. His calves were cased in gold,
his sword strapped to his side, his head still bare.
He gleamed with metal as he swept down from the   490
heights, exultant. In his mind, he'd already won.
He was like a horse who rips his tether and
escapes the stalls. Reaching open grassland,
free at last, he heads for pastures and for herds

of mares, or flashes out for streams he used to bathe in,
whinnying, holding high his head,
joyous as his mane plays on his back and neck.

Camilla and her Volscian army rushed to meet him.
At the gates, the queen leapt down from her horse.
All the cohort followed suit, dismounting   500
in a fluid move. She said, "Turnus,
if the brave are right to trust themselves,
I'll dare to charge Aeneas' troops and ride alone
against the Tuscan cavalry: this is my pledge.
Let me scout out war's first dangers while you
take a post along the walls and guard the city."
Turnus answered, eyes fixed on the dangerous girl:
"O glory of Italy, how can I thank you
or repay you? For now—since your courage
dwarfs reward—share the struggle with me.   510
Vile Aeneas (rumor says, and our scouts
confirm) has sent his light-armed horse ahead.
Their hooves shake the plains as he heads for town
over mountain peaks and lonely ridges. I'll set
an ambush at a byroad in the forest, and
guard the pass at both ends with armed men.
You'll confront the charging Tuscan cavalry
with fierce Messenus, Latin squadrons, and
Tiburtus' troops. Lead them and take charge."
He urged Messapus and the allied chiefs to combat   520
too. Then he left to meet the enemy.

There's a winding valley that's well suited
to treachery and tricks of war. On both sides,
dark slopes press it with dense growth. A faint pathway
leads there from a narrow, stinting pass.
Above, among the crags and near the peak,

there's a hidden clearing and safe shelter.
You can attack from either side, or roll down
giant rocks while standing on the ridge.
Turnus knew the way. He came to take   530
his post, lurking in the dangerous woods.

Now in her high home, Latona's daughter
summoned Opis, swift of foot, from her band
of sacred virgins. She said sadly: "Dear girl:
Camilla leaves for cruel combat with my armor,
which won't help. She's loved by me beyond all
others—not through some new passion; this is
no sudden sweetness that has moved my heart.
When Metabus, hated for his haughty rule,
left his land and ancient Privernum, fleeing   540
from the heart of war, he took his baby
with him. He called her Camilla, altering
her mother's name, Casmilla, by one letter.
Clutching her to his chest, he rode for long and
lonely forest crests. But when sharp spears menaced
on all sides, and Volscian soldiers circled him
as he fled, he spied the river Amasenus,
full and frothing at its banks—such a storm
had broken from the clouds. He could swim across,
but fear for his cherished burden held him back.   550
He thought it through and made a quick and painful choice.
He took the giant spear, hard with knots
and seasoned oak, that his strong hand carried
into war, wrapped his child in woodland cork-bark,
and tied this handy bundle to the spear's center.
He raised it in his massive fist and cried to heaven:
'Kind Diana of the woods, a father vows his
child to you. She's your supplicant, and holds
your weapon first, as she flies from enemies.

I beg you, goddess, take what's yours: I yield her now   *560*
to the chance winds.' He drew back and threw
the spinning spear. Poor Camilla flew across
the roaring river on the hissing shaft.
Metabus, the great crowd on his heels ever
closer, plunged into the river—and emerged.
The grassy bank gave back both spear and child,
Diana's gift. Since towns wouldn't let him in their
homes or walls (he was too fierce to be civil),
he fed his child among the brush and bristling lairs.
A humble shepherd in the lonely mountains,   *570*
he nursed her on a wild mare's fresh milk;
he'd squeeze the udder's drops onto her baby lips.
And when she first walked on her infant feet,
he armed her hands with a sharp lance and hung
a bow and arrows from her tiny shoulder.
Instead of gold clasps and long capes to wear,
a tiger's pelt draped from her head over her back.
Already then she scattered child-sized spears from tender
hands and whirled a smooth sling round her head,
bringing down a crane or snowy swan.   *580*
Many mothers in the Tuscan towns were keen
to wed her to their sons, in vain. She was happy
with Diana, and nursed an endless love of weapons
and virginity, untouched. I wish this war
had not encouraged her to challenge Trojans.
She's precious to me; she'd remain one of our band.
But since harsh fate is at her heels, glide down
from the sky and visit Latium, nymph,
where grim battle rages under gloomy omens.
Take this quiver, draw an arrow to avenge her: *590*
whoever wounds her sacred flesh, Trojan
or Italian, must pay an equal price
in blood. I'll carry her poor body and unlooted

armor in a hollow cloud for burial
in her own land." Jangling, veiled in a dark whirlwind,
Opis slipped down through the gentle breezes.

Meanwhile the Trojan army, Tuscan chiefs
and all the cavalry marshaled in ranks
approached the walls. The horses reared and whinnied
through the fields, fighting their tight reins, wheeling   600
this way and that. Everywhere, the land bristled
with spears, fields aflame with sunlit weapons.
Messapus and the fast-moving Latins faced them
on the plain; also Coras with his brother
and Camilla's wing. Spears jutted skyward
in hands pulled back to throw, and lances quivered.
The march of men and screams of horses grew hot.
Each side stopped short within a spear's throw,
then suddenly burst forward screaming, spurring
frothing horses. Weapons rained down on all sides   610
as thick as snow, shadowing the sky to darkness.
Tyrrhenus and fiery Aconteus smashed
head-on, wielding lances. They were the first to fall,
colliding loudly as their horses crashed together,
breastbone against breastbone. Aconteus
flew off like a thunderbolt or stone hurled from
a catapult. His life-breath scattered to the breezes.

Now the lines broke up. The Latins wheeled
their horses to the walls and slung their shields across
their backs. Acilas chased them with the Trojan troops.   620
But near the gates, the Latins raised the shout again
and pulled around their horses' supple necks.
Now it was Trojans who retreated with slack reins.
They were like the ocean's ebb and flow.
Sometimes it sweeps to shore and coats the rocks
with froth, its arc soaking the far sand,

sometimes it quickly ebbs, sucking back
the rolling scree as the shallows boil.
Twice, Tuscans pushed Rutulians to the walls;
twice, they were repelled, and had to guard their backs   630
with shields. But in the third clash, all the ranks were
tangled: each man marked his target. Then truly
you could hear the dying moans in that bloody
mess of bodies, weapons, half-dead horses
twitching in men's blood. The savage fighting surged.
Orsilochus, fearing to face Remulus,
flung his spear at his horse. It went in
by the ear and the stallion reared, pawing
at the air in agony; his rider, thrown,
writhed on the ground. Catillus killed Iöllas   640
and Herminius, a huge man with huge courage
and huge weapons, his blond head and torso bare,
not afraid of wounds, his giant frame exposed.
A spear pierced his broad shoulders and stuck there
quivering. It folded him in pain. Pools
of gore were everywhere. Fighting, they dealt
death with iron, seeking wounds to die with glory.

There in the carnage raged Camilla with her quiver,
one breast bared for battle like an Amazon.
She hurled a rain of pliant lances, or raised   650
her heavy battle-ax in her tireless hand.
Diana's gold bow jangled on her shoulder.
Even when she had to yield, she shot arrows
while escaping, her bow turned to face the fight.
Around her was her chosen band: young Larina,
Tulla, and Tarpeia swinging her bronze ax,
all daughters of Italy. Divine Camilla
chose them as her honor-guard to help in peace
or war—like Amazons riding across the river
Thermodon, or fighting by Hippolyte   660

in painted armor, or shrilling loudly when Mars' child
Penthesilea came back in her chariot
and her crescent-shielded women troops rejoiced.

Fierce girl, who were the first and last to fall
under your spear? How many dying bodies did you
spread on earth? First, Eunaeus, son of Clytius.
Her pine lance pierced his unguarded chest
and he fell, retching streams of blood. Dying,
he bit the bloody earth, coiling round his wound.
Next, Liris and Pagasus, one thrown from   670
his fallen horse and reaching for the reins,
one rushing to help, no weapon in his hand.
She dropped both there and added Amastrus,
Hippotas' son. Rising in her seat, she speared
Tereus, Demophoön, Harpalycus,
and Chromis. Every shaft whirled from her hand
found its Trojan. Far off, the hunter Ornytus
was riding an Iäpygian horse, in foreign armor.
A hide stripped from a bull sat on the fighter's
massive shoulders, and a white-fanged wolf-jaw   680
gaped over his head; in those rustic hands
he held a hunting knife. He rode in the middle
of the ranks but stood a full head higher.
Overtaking him (it was easy, in the rout),
she pierced him through and said with hate: "Tuscan,
did you think that you were flushing forest beasts?
The day has come that shows your boasts were lies,
and at a woman's hands! But you'll take great glory
to your fathers' shades: Camilla's spear killed you."

Next were Butes and Orsilochus, largest   690
of the Trojans. She speared Butes from behind,
between the helmet and the breastplate, where his neck
gleamed white, on the left, the shield-side.

Orsilochus chased her in a giant circle,
but she tricked him into tighter ones, hunting
the hunted, then reared up and smashed her heavy ax
into his bones and armor as he begged for mercy
frantically. Warm brains from the blows streamed down
his face. Aunus' fighting son, an Apennine,
chanced on her and froze in fear at the sight.   700
He was a good Ligurian liar, while fate allowed.*
When he saw he couldn't use his horse
to get away and dodge the queen's attack,
he tried a shrewd pretense and said with cunning:
"What's so great about a woman counting on
her brawny horse? Forget escape! Be brave enough
to meet me face to face on even ground, fight me
on foot. You'll soon know whose boasts of bravery
are meaningless." Enraged and hot with fury,
she handed her horse to a friend, facing him   710
on foot and unafraid. Their weapons were the same:
a bare sword and a light shield. The soldier
thought his trick had worked. Off he raced at once,
pulling round the bridle to escape,
using iron spurs to goad his horse. "Stupid
Ligurian," she cried, "puffed up with pride in vain!
You tried your slippery native skills for nothing.
Your ploy won't bring you back unharmed to lying
Aunus." On swift feet, just like a darting flame,
she overtook his horse, grabbed its reins,
and spilled his hated blood in vengeance—   720
easily, the way a sacred falcon soars from
some tall crag to chase a dove high in the clouds
and catches her, tearing out her guts with curling
claws. From the sky fall blood and tattered feathers.

The father of the gods and men, throned on high
Olympus, did not fail to see this. He spurred

Tuscan Tarchon into rage and bitter battle
with no gentle goad. Tarchon galloped out
to the slaughter and retreating ranks,
urging on the cavalry with varied shouts,   730
naming them, reviving beaten troops for war.
"What's your fear, Tuscans—always slow to fight
but never shamed by it? What's this great cowardice?
A woman scatters you and routs your ranks!
We carry swords and spears—for what? You're not
slack for love's nocturnal combat, or when
the curved flute calls for Bacchic dances! Yes,
wait for feasts and wine and groaning tables
(here's passion and dedication!), till the seer
says all's safe, till meaty sacrifices call you   740
to the groves!" With that he whipped his horse
into the fray, prepared for death, charging wildly
at Venulus. He tore him violently off his
horse and rode off with his enemy clutched to
his chest. Shouts rose to the sky; all the Latins
turned to watch. Tarchon flew like fire over
the plain with his armed prey. He snapped Venulus' spear
at its metal tip, groping for an open spot
to stab a death-blow. Venulus fought back,
keeping that hand from his throat, surviving force   750
by force. Like a tawny eagle who's snatched up
a snake and soared away, twining talons in
the wounded reptile; the snake forms slick coils,
raising its rough scales and hissing, trying
to rear up, but as the eagle beats the air
with wings, its hooked beak mauls its thrashing victim:
just so Tarchon took his prize from Tibur's ranks,
triumphant. The Tuscans followed on their chief's
example and success—they charged. Then Arruns,
doomed by Fate, deftly circled swift Camilla,   760

raising his spear, searching for an easy chance.
While the girl rode raging in the ranks,
Arruns stole up close and followed silently;
when she returned from killing enemies,
he yanked his quick reins furtively and trailed her.
Ruthless, he tried this approach and that, traced
her path on every side, and shook his well-aimed spear.

By chance Chloreus, once Cybele's priest,
was gleaming from afar in Phrygian armor.
He rode a foaming mount whose leather saddle-cloth   770
was plumed with bronze scales and golden links.
Standing out in his exotic reds and purples,
he shot Cretan arrows from a golden Lycian
bow. It hung from the seer's shoulders.
His helmet was gold too; a golden knot tied up
the rustling linen folds of saffron cloak.
His tunic and his Asian leggings were embroidered.
The huntress stalked this one man blindly in the strife
of war. She hoped to hang his Trojan weapons
in a temple, or flaunt herself in captive gold   780
—a girl on fire with a female's lust for spoils,
riding recklessly through all the ranks.
At last Arruns saw his chance from where he lurked.
He threw his spear, praying to the gods above:
"Greatest of the gods, you who guard sacred
Soracte, we worship you first, Apollo. When pine-trees
feed your flames, we, your followers,
trust our faith and plant our steps on your live coals.
Almighty Father, let my sword obliterate
this source of shame. I don't want spoils or trophies,   790
nothing that is hers. My other feats will bring
me fame. Just let me kill this pestilence,
and I'll return unhonored to my native town."

. . .

Apollo heard and granted one part of the plea.
The rest he scattered to swift breezes. Yes:
Arruns could kill the girl in her distraction
with a sudden blow, but he'd never see his
noble land again. The south wind took those words.
He threw his spear; it whistled through the breeze.
All the Volscians turned their sharp eyes, mindful,   800
to their queen. But she failed to note the rush
of air, the weapon flying through the sky,
until the spear found its mark. Wedged below
her naked breast, it drank deeply of her blood.
Her stricken band rushed up to catch their falling queen.
Arruns, the most terrified of all, fled
in mingled fear and joy. He didn't dare to trust
his spear further, or face Camilla's weapons.
He was like a wolf who's killed a shepherd
or a giant bull and runs to hide in trackless   810
heights before the vengeful spears can find him.
He knows he went too far, and tucks his trembling tail
below his belly, heading for the woods.
Anxiously, he hid himself from sight,
content to get away and mingle with the ranks.
Camilla, dying, tugged the spear, but its iron
tip was wedged too deeply in her ribs.
Her blood draining, she collapsed; her eyes fell,
chill with death. Her bright complexion faded.
As she died she called to her friend Acca.   820
She'd been loyal beyond others to Camilla,
the only one to share her cares. "I've fought
this far, sister Acca. Now a bitter wound
has finished me. The world grows dark with shadow.
Run and take these last commands to Turnus:
he must take up the fight and keep the Trojans

from the town. And now, goodbye." She released
her horse's reins and weakly slipped to earth, cold,
departing from her body bit by bit. Her head
and neck drooped down in death; her weapons fell. Her soul   830
fled with a groan of protest to the shades below.
Now a huge cry rose and struck the golden stars.
With Camilla down, the fight was crueler still.
The Trojan army, Tuscan chiefs, and Evander's
cavalry rushed at each other in dense ranks.

Diana's sentry, Opis, had been resting on
a high ridge for some time, calmly gazing at
the fight. As the raging men sent up a roar,
she saw from far away Camilla's killing.
She groaned and said these heartfelt words: "Oh no—   840
my child, you've paid too cruelly for your attempt
to wound the men of Troy in war! Your service
to Diana, your solitude in the wild woods,
shouldering her quiver, was no help to you.
Yet the queen won't let you be dishonored
in your final hour. Your death won't want for fame
among the nations, nor will you suffer shame,
dying unavenged. He whose wound defiled you
will die as he deserves." Below that peak there lay
a giant burial-mound, its soil shaded by oaks,   850
for the ancient king Dercennus Laurens.
Swooping down, the lovely goddess landed
here first and looked for Arruns down below.
There he was, gleaming in his armor, puffed up
with vain pride. "Leaving us?" she asked. "Turn
this way, come and die. Receive a fitting prize
for Camilla's death. Diana's shafts will kill
even the likes of you." The goddess took a speedy
arrow from her golden quiver and drew her bow,

hating him, pulling evenly until   860
the curved tips almost met. Her left hand touched
the iron tip, her right the bowstring by her breast.
Arruns heard the hissing arrow and the rush
of air, just as the iron point lodged in his flesh.
His friends, forgetful, left him there, gasping out
his life, groaning in the fields' ignoble dust.
But Opis soared on wings to high Olympus.

Their leader gone, Camilla's light-armed wing fled first.
In shambles, the Rutulians and fierce Atinas
ran as well. The scattered chiefs and headless legions   870
looked to safety; horses wheeled in retreat.
None could hold against the Trojan onslaught
bringing death, none could take a stand.
Their unstrung bows on crouching backs, they shook
the pockmarked plain with horses at full gallop.
A murky cloud of black dust rolled toward the city.
Mothers beat their breasts along the lookouts
and raised their women's shrieks to the high stars.
The first to burst in at a gallop through the gates
brought the enemy mixed in with them, and met   880
a wretched death right at the walls. They died impaled
on swords on their own soil, next to the very safety
of their homes. A group closed the gates,
scared to admit allies, or yield to their pleas.
Then came a wretched slaughter of the Latins, those
guarding the gates and those impaled on the guards' swords.
Before the faces of their weeping parents,
some were thrown into the trenches by the
desperate stampede, some let go their reins
and wildly rammed the gates and bolted doors.   890
On the walls, trembling mothers strained to rain down
weapons on the Trojans, mimicking Camilla,
spurred by love of country. They used oaken posts

and fire-charred stakes in place of iron; they burned
to be the first to perish for their city's sake.

The ghastly news hit Turnus in his forest.
Acca told the young man of the massive rout,
the Volscian ranks wiped out, Camilla dead,
the enemy's assault, how Trojans swept the field
with Mars' support, the panic at the walls. In rage   900
(as Jupiter's cruel will demanded), Turnus
quit his hilltop ambush and left the rugged forest.
He was hardly out of sight, heading for
the plains, when Aeneas crossed the mountain ridge
to open fields and put dark woods behind him.
Now both were riding fiercely for the town
with all their troops, not much space between them.
At the moment that Aeneas saw the plain
smoking with dust and the Laurentian army,
Turnus saw savage Aeneas in armor, and heard   910
the infantry's approach and panting horses.
Both would have tried their luck in war at once,
but rosy Sun had washed his tired team in Spanish
waters, bringing night as day glided away.
They camped before the town and built their ramparts.

BOOK 12

THE LAST DUEL

As soon as Turnus saw the tide had changed
and the defeated Latins looked to him to pay
his pledge, he blazed with new and ruthless courage.
Like a lion on the plains of Africa
who strikes at last after the poacher's spear*
has pierced his chest—fearless, full of joy,
he tosses his thick mane, breaks the shaft wedged
in the wound, and roars from bloodstained jaws—
just so Turnus' burning fury reached its peak.
Wildly he addressed the king. "There's no delay   10
in Turnus, no reason for Aeneas' coward band
to eat their words or break their pledge: I'll fight.
Bring the offerings, father, set the terms.
Either I'll dispatch this Trojan traitor* down to
Tartarus (let the Latins sit and watch!), refuting
by my sword the charge against us all, or else
we'll be his slaves, and Lavinia his wife."

Latinus answered calmly: "Peerless fighter,
your fierce courage outstrips other men's.
So much the more I must reflect with care   20
on all the outcomes that I fear. You rule
your father Daunus' land, plus many towns taken
by force. You have my gold, my goodwill too.
Laurentian lands and Latium have other
girls of noble birth. Let me speak these harsh words

honestly; take them to heart. I had no right
to give Lavinia to any former suitor.
All the gods and men prophesied this.
Conquered by my love for you, our common blood,
my wife's sad tears, I broke all bonds, stole his   *30*
right bride from my son-to-be, and waged an unjust
war. You can see the battles and bad luck
that dog me since; you've borne the brunt of them.
Beaten in two fights, we can barely nurse
Italy's hopes at home. Our spilled blood warms
the Tiber's waters, our broad fields gleam white with bones.
Why go back and forth? To change my mind is madness.
If I'm prepared to accept allies once you're dead,
why not end this conflict while you live? How would
your Rutulian kin and all of Italy   *40*
respond if I gave you up to death (may god
forbid!) as you fought to win my child?
Think of war's uncertainty. Pity your old
father, forlorn and far away in Ardea."
These words had no effect on Turnus' fury.
It flared up, still more savage for being soothed.
As soon as he could speak, these words burst out:
"That care you have for me—kindly discard it,
best of kings, and let me trade my life for glory.
Father, I too fling spears with force; the wounds   *50*
that I inflict draw blood as well. His mother
won't be lurking near in swirls of empty mist
to cover his retreat in an unmanly cloud."

But the queen, aghast at this new combat's risk,
ready to die, wept and clasped her fierce
son-in-law: "Turnus, by these tears, by my
honor (if it touches you at all)—you're my
only hope, my sole relief in grim old age.
Latinus' glory and his power, our whole reeling

house, all rests on you. I ask just this: don't fight   60
the Trojan. Your fate in that duel's mine as well;
I'll leave this hated light of day with you.
I'll never be enslaved and see Aeneas as
my son-in-law." Lavinia heard her mother's words.
Tears ran down her burning cheeks; a deep blush
warmed her skin and spread its fire through her face,
just like Indian ivory stained by crimson blood
or snowy lilies tinted red by a rose
bouquet.* Such colors stood out on the young girl's face.
His love churned in Turnus. He stared at her, hotter   70
still to fight, and spoke curtly to Amata:
"I beg you not to send me off with tears and evil
omens, mother, when I leave for battle's brutal
combat. Turnus cannot choose his hour of death.
Idmon, take my message to the Trojan king.
It won't please him. When Dawn's rosy chariot
reddens the sky, he should not lead out his men;
let Trojan and Rutulian weapons rest.
We'll stop this string of battles with our blood.
On that field, Lavinia will be won as wife."   80

He spoke and hurried to his home, calling for
his horses, happy as they neighed before him.
Orithyia gave them to Pilumnus as an honor—
a team whiter than snow, swifter than the wind.
The chariot-drivers stood around, thumping the horses'
chests, combing their flowing manes. Turnus seized
a breastplate stiff with gold and orichalcus.*
He strapped on his sword and shield and placed
the crimson-crested helmet on his head.
The god of fire had forged the sword for Turnus' father,   90
Daunus, and tempered the bright blade in Stygian waters.
Then he raised the sturdy spear that leaned against

a giant central column, spoils from Actor
the Auruncan, and shook its undulating length.
"Now's the time, my spear, now! I've never called
in vain. Great Actor carried you, now Turnus'
right hand carries you: let me strike dead
that Phrygian half-man, let me strip and smash
his armor! I'll foul with dirt those waves of hair
dripping with scented oil and crimped with a hot iron."   *100*
Such a rage drove Turnus. As he raved, sparks flew
from his face; his eyes flashed fire. He was like
a bull that bellows terribly as combat starts,
trying out its anger on a tree trunk
with its tusks, goring all the winds with wounds,
pawing sand as prelude for the battle.

Just as fierce in his mother's armor, Aeneas
roused himself to fight and stoked his rage.
He was glad this mutual pact would end the war.
Then he soothed his friends and fearful Iülus   *110*
with talk of fate, and ordered that a firm response
be sent to King Latinus with the terms for peace.

As fresh dawn flecked the mountain peaks with light
and the horses of the Sun soared over Ocean's
edge, streaming light out of their flaring nostrils,
Rutulians and Trojans checked the dueling ground
next to the walls of the great city. They put out
fire-pans and grassy altars for their common
gods. Priests in aprons, wearing sacred vervain
on their brows, fetched the fire and water.   *120*
The Ausonians marched up with their lances, spilling
out the crowded gates. From the other side,
the Tuscan-Trojan army rushed up with diverse armor—
and so much iron you'd think Mars' own cruel strife

had mustered them. In the center, captains
milled around, proud in gold and purple:
Mnestheus from the blood of Assaracus, brave
Asilas, and Neptune's son, Messapus
the horse-tamer. At the sign, each side pulled back,
staking spears in the soil, propping up   130
their shields. Women, unarmed crowds, and weak old men
came in an eager flood to fill the roofs
and towers; others stood by the high gates.

Juno gazed down from a hilltop (now called Alban;
in those days it had no name, no glory, and no
honor), looking at the plain and armies,
Trojan and Laurentian, and Latinus' city.
At once, as one goddess to another, she spoke
to Turnus' sister, queen of lakes and roaring rivers
(Jupiter, the high sky-king, had honored her   140
this way—after stealing her virginity):
"Nymph, beauty of the rivers, dearest to me:
you know I've loved you more than any other Latin
girl who's suffered great-souled Jove's unwelcome lust;
I freely let you have a share of sky.
Learn the grief—not caused by me—that waits for you.
While the Fates and Fortune seemed to favor
Latium, I shielded Turnus and your city.
Now I see him heading to an unfair death.
The day of death and devastation comes.   150
I cannot watch this combat they agreed on.
If you dare to help your brother, do it; you should.
Maybe better times will come for us who suffer."
She'd barely finished, but Juturna's tears were falling;
she beat her lovely breast three or four times.
"This is not the time for tears," Saturn's daughter
told her. "Hurry! If there's any way, rescue him
from death. Stir up war and wreck the treaty

they drew up: I'll take responsibility."
She left her wavering, a harsh wound in her heart.   160

The kings rode out: Latinus in his massive four-horse
chariot, twelve golden rays around his gleaming
brow—the emblem of his ancestor, the Sun.
A snow-white pair pulled Turnus. In his hand,
he brandished two broad-headed iron spears.
From the facing camp marched out Father Aeneas,
founder of the Roman race, his star-bright shield
and god-sent armor blazing, and Ascanius,
Rome's other great hope. A priest in pure robes
fetched a bristly boar's young and an unshorn sheep   170
and stood the beasts next to the flaming altars.
The men now faced the rising sun, sprinkled salt meal
from their hands, and cut tufts off the victims' brows.
Then they poured libations on the altars.

Pious Aeneas drew his sword and prayed.
"I call on you as witness, Sun, and this land
for which I've borne such suffering, and you,
almighty Father, and you, Juno his wife
(a kinder goddess now, I hope), and you, famed
father Mars, whose will inflicts all wars on us;   180
I call on springs and flowing rivers, all the powers
in high heaven and the blue-green sea: if chance
grants triumph to Italian Turnus, the losers
will retire to Evander's town, Iülus
will leave this land, and Aeneas' men will never
rise in war as rebels, or bare their blades against
this realm. If, however, victory favors us
(as I believe, and may the gods confirm it),
I won't make Italians bend to Trojans,
or seize power. Let both peoples strike   190
a timeless treaty: equal laws for two free nations.

I'll give you gods and rites. Latinus, father to
my wife, will keep his throne and army. Trojan
hands will build a town named for Lavinia."

Next Latinus spoke. He looked up at the sky,
his right hand lifted to the stars. "Aeneas,
I swear by the selfsame land, same sea, and stars,
by Latona's double brood and two-faced Janus,
by the Hell-gods' power, the shrines of ruthless Dis.
Hear me, Father, you who bind pacts by your thunder.   200
I grasp your altar and I swear amid these flames
and holy forces: Italy will never break
this pact of peace, whatever comes to pass.
No force will bend my will, not even if
it pours the flooded Earth into the sea, and Heaven
into Hell—just as this scepter" (in his hand)
"hacked off in the forest, orphaned from its mother,
its leaves and twigs lost to the knife, will never
pour out tender shoots or shade, though it was
a branch until the craftsman wrapped it in wrought bronze   210
and gave it to the Latin lords to carry."
With such words they sealed the pact as all the nobles
watched. Then they slaughtered sacrificial
animals over the flames, ripping out live
entrails, and piled the altars with the heavy plates.

But the Rutulians had long since thought the duel
unfair. They felt a tumult of emotions,
still more when they saw the unmatched fighters close,
still more when they saw Turnus step silently
up to the altar, eyes downcast as he prayed,   220
his face so young, his youthful body pale.
When Juturna saw more people muttering,
the crowd wavering and losing heart,

she rushed among the soldiers, taking on Camertus'
form—his ancestors were a great clan,
his father's name was linked with valor, he himself
was fiercest in the fight—knowing well
what she must do and planting different rumors:
"For shame, Rutulians! You'd risk one life for all
of us? Aren't we matched in strength and numbers?   230
See what the Trojans and Arcadians amount to—
plus the doomed Etrurians who dare to take on
Turnus! Our enemy's too few for half of us!
Turnus goes in glory to the gods, whose altars
he'll exalt in death. He'll live on the lips
of men. But we, our country lost, will have to
serve proud masters, we who idle on these fields."

More and more, her words inflamed the men.
A murmur started snaking through the ranks,
and the very Latins and Laurentians   240
who'd hoped for peace and rest from battle
now once more wanted war and wished the pact
would fail. They pitied Turnus' sorry fate.
Juturna added a still greater spur.
She showed an omen in the sky, perfect
to muddle and mislead Italian minds.
Jove's tawny eagle, flying in the ruddy light,
was bothering the shore-birds, a large and noisy
flock. Suddenly he plunged toward the water:
his vicious talons seized the noblest swan.   250
The Italians took note as all the birds
wheeled round in raucous flight (an amazing
sight), darkening the sky with wings, chasing
the eagle through the air until, done in
by pressure and his heavy prey, he dropped the swan
into the stream and vanished in the clouds.

. . .

The Rutulians hailed the omen with great shouts
and prepared to arm. Tolumnius the augur
was the first to speak: "I've prayed for this so often!
I accept the divine sign. Take up your swords   260
and follow me, poor countrymen, whom that foreign
pirate preys on like an eagle as he sacks
your shores. He too will soon fly off, sailing for
deep ocean. One resolve for all! Close up
your ranks and fight to save your deposed king!"
He hurled his spear and charged the enemy.
The well-aimed cornel shaft sang out, whistling as it
cut the air. At once, a mighty roar rose up.
Chaos in the ranks as all hearts boiled in tumult!
It happened that nine handsome brothers stood right   270
in the spear's path, the sons faithful Tyrrhena
had borne Gylippus of Arcadia. It struck
one at the waist, where the leather sword-belt
chafed his stomach and the ends were pinned.
This beautiful young man, so bright in his armor—
the weapon split his ribs and splayed him on the sand.
His brothers, a brave phalanx fired by grief,
drew their swords or grabbed their iron spears
and blindly rushed ahead. The Laurentians charged,
then in response rushed in a flood of Trojans,   280
Agyllines, Arcadians in painted armor.
All felt the same desire, to let the sword decide.

The altars were stripped of kindling. A thick storm
of spears filled the sky, a pelting iron rain.
Wine-bowls and fire-pans were raided. Latinus
fled with his failed gods and broken pact.
Men harnessed chariots or vaulted onto horses,
swords bared, ready to fight. Messapus, keen to
end the treaty, drove his horse at terrified

Aulestes, an Etruscan king decked in a king's   *290*
regalia. As he quickly backed away,
the poor man tripped over an altar, falling on
his head and back. Fierce Messapus flew in
on his great horse, his spear in hand; as the king
babbled in prayer, he struck him dead and said,
"He's done. Here's a better offering to the gods!"
Italians ran to loot the still-warm corpse, but
Corynaeus stormed them with a smoking altar-
branch. Then Ebysus charged in to stab him.
The flaming branch, thrust in his face, set fire to   *300*
his beard, which gave off a scorched smell. Corynaeus
grabbed his frantic victim's hair in his left hand,
kneed him to pin him down, and sank his vicious
blade into his side. Next Podalirius
chased the shepherd Alsus as he fled among
the front line's swords. But as he raised his naked blade,
Alsus heaved his ax at him and split his head
down to his chin. Spurting blood soaked all his armor.
Iron sleep and cruel silence pressed upon
his eyes, their brightness buried in eternal night.   *310*

Pious Aeneas, head bared for the ritual,
stretched out unarmed hands and shouted to his men:
"What's this attack? How can battle start again?
Control yourselves! The treaty has been struck, all
the terms are set. The right to fight is mine alone.
Let me do it, don't feel fear. I'll confirm
the pact by my own hand. Our rites owe me Turnus."
But as he spoke these words, a hissing arrow
sliced the air toward him. No one knows
whose bowstring whirled it home, who brought   *320*
the Rutulians this honor, a god or chance.
The great glory of the act was stifled;
no one boasted of Aeneas' wound.

When Turnus saw Aeneas yield, saw his captains
at a loss, he burned with sudden, eager hope.
Calling for his armor and his team, he proudly
leapt into his chariot and took the reins.
He raced along the ranks, sending many brave men
down to death, crushing others half-alive
under his wheels, grabbing spears to throw at those   330
who ran. He resembled blood-soaked Mars
in action, when he clangs his shield by icy Hebrus
to start a war, and drives his frothing horses through
the empty plain, faster than the winds from west
and south; Thrace groans under pounding hooves.
By Mars ride pitch-black Terror, Rage, and Treachery.
With such fervor, Turnus lashed his steaming,
sweaty team in the center of the skirmish, trampling
the defenseless dead. The racing hooves sprayed
crimson dew, throwing up the blood-soaked sand.   340
He killed Sthenelus, then Thamyrus and Pholus,
the last two hand-to-hand, the first speared through. He killed
Glaucus and his brother Lades, Imbrasus' sons,
raised by him in Lycia. They had the same weapons,
fit for combat or to race the winds on horseback.

In another part, Eumedes rode to battle,
old Dolon's son, renowned in war. His name was
from his grandfather, but his strength and courage
were his father's—who once dared to claim Achilles'
chariot as a prize for scouting the Greek camp,   350
but Diomedes paid him in a different coin:
he no longer hopes to win Achilles' team.
Turnus saw him far away across the open
plain, and transfixed him with a flying lance.
He flew up and leapt down from his chariot,
tall over the Trojan dying on the ground,
then planted his foot on his neck and wrenched away

the man's own sword. He dyed the bright blade ruddy in
Eumedes' throat. "See the fields of Italy
you fought to win—lie there now and measure them!   360
Such are the prized city walls for those who cross me."
He speared Asbytes to keep Eumedes company,
and Chloreus, Thersilochus, Sybaris,
Dares, Thymoetes just thrown from his horse.
As the Thracian north wind howls over
the deep Aegean, chasing waves to shore—
gusts buffet the sea, clouds scuttle from the sky—
so the ranks fell back where Turnus cut a path,
and columns turned and fled. His momentum
carried him; his crest shook in the airstream.   370
Phegeus would have none of this attack,
these roars. Flinging himself at the chariot,
he pulled aside the bolting horses' foaming bridles.
As he hung there, dragged alongside, Turnus stabbed
his bare flank with a broad-tipped lance that pierced
the two-ply chain mail. The lance stuck in the shallow wound.
Phegeus turned to block him with his shield,
pulling out his sword in self-defense, but
the wheel and spinning axle threw him to the ground.
With his sword, Turnus struck his head off   380
between the helmet and the breastplate's upper edge,
and left the headless body on the sand.

While Turnus dealt relentless death across the plain,
Mnestheus, staunch Achates, and Ascanius
brought Aeneas into camp. He was bleeding, leaning
on his lengthy spear with every other step,
and furious. He struggled to rip out
the broken arrow, shouting for the easiest
solution: to cut the wound wide open with a sword
and find the buried arrow-head, then go back   390
to battle. Now Iäpyx, Iäsus' son, arrived, Apollo's

favorite. Once, in passion's painful grip,
the god had offered Iäpyx his own skills and talent:
augury, the lyre, and flying archery.
But to stall his ailing father's death, Iäpyx
chose to learn the use of herbs and medicine,
to practice silent arts that brought no glory.
Aeneas leaned on his huge spear, grumbling
bitterly. A throng of soldiers crowded round him
as Iülus grieved. He ignored their tears. Old   400
Iäpyx hitched his cloak and tunic, as healers do.
Quickly, he applied Apollo's potent herbs
and potions. Nothing worked: not tugging at the arrow
with his hand, not clamping on the iron head
with a forceps' grip. Fortune and the god
offered no help, and meanwhile battle's horror crept
across the plain, so close they could see a wall
of dust. As the cavalry approached, arrows
rained into the camp. The awful screams of men
who fought and fell in the hard combat rose to sky.   410

Then Venus, distressed at her child's undeserved pain,
plucked sprigs of dittany from Cretan Ida,
a plant of purple blooms and downy leaves
not unknown to wild goats struck in the side
by flying arrows. She fetched it, her face shrouded
in thick mist, and made a secret potion, steeping
the stems in a gleaming bowl of water,
adding an elixir of healing ambrosia
and fragrant panacea. Aged Iäpyx soothed
the wound, using this brew without knowing.   420
At once all pain left Aeneas' body,
and the bleeding in the wound was stanched.
Now the arrow came out freely when he pulled.
New strength restored Aeneas to his former state.
The first to fire their hearts against the enemy,

Iäpyx shouted: "Hurry, bring the man his weapons!
Don't just stand there! Aeneas, no human art
or doctor's skill cured you, nor did my hand.
A great god did. He sends you to greater work."*
Eager to fight, angry at lost time, Aeneas   430
sheathed his calves, right and left, in golden
greaves, and took up spear, sword, and breastplate.
He clasped Ascanius with chain-mailed arms,
kissed him lightly through the visor, and said:
"Son, learn bravery and real work from me;
from others, luck. My right hand is your
defense: it will lead you to great prizes.
Make sure to be mindful, when you are a man,
of the models that your family left. Let me
and your mother's brother, Hector, spur you on."   440

With these words he left the gate, a great figure
wielding a great spear. Mnestheus and
Antheus and a dense throng marched with him.
The reserves all left the camp as well.
The plain trembled under tramping feet as blinding
dust rose up. From the rampart, Turnus saw them
as they came. The Ausonians saw too,
and felt an icy shiver. Juturna heard and knew
the sound before the Latins did. She fled,
afraid, as Aeneas raced across the open   450
field with his dark troops. Like a storm breaking
at sea, whose thunderheads approach the shore
as howling winds precede them; foreboding fills
the wretched farmers' hearts, for the storm will blast
their trees and crops, destroying everything—*
just so the Trojan leader drove his men against
the enemy, their columns close-packed round him.
Thymbraeus killed great Osiris with his sword,
Mnestheus killed Arcetius: Achates killed

Epulo, Gyas killed Ufens: Tolumnius   460
the augur fell, the first to throw his spear.
Shouts rose to the sky, and the Rutulians,
routed in turn, ran across the dusty fields.
Aeneas didn't stoop to killing fugitives,
nor those he met on foot nor horsemen holding lances.
Through clouds of dust he tracked only one man,
his challenge was for one alone: Turnus.

At this, Juturna, numb with fear, became
a warrior. She heaved Metiscus, Turnus' driver,
from the reins, and he fell, hitting the beam.   470
Leaving him behind, she took his post, his voice,
his form and armor, pulling on the reins to swerve,
like a dusky swallow flying round the halls
of some rich lord, circling the high rooms in flight,
gathering tidbits for her cheeping fledglings
as she flutters through the empty porticoes
or by the wet rain gutters: so Juturna
veered through the enemies and all the plain
in her rapid chariot. Now here, now there,
she granted glimpses of proud Turnus, but steered him   480
far away, avoiding conflict. Aeneas tracked
her twisting course, chasing Turnus, calling for him
loudly through the scattered ranks. But every time
he spotted him and ran toward the racing horses,
Juturna turned the chariot aside.
What could he do? He was carried on a sea
of thoughts, none useful; his cares pulled at him.
Messapus approached, stealthy on his feet,
two spears in his hand, each tipped with iron.
He threw one with unerring force. Aeneas stopped   490
and crouched behind his shield, dropping to one knee.
But the flying spear still sliced off his helmet's
crested peak. Then he saw Turnus' chariot

eluding him again, and fresh anger at
Italian treachery rose up in him. Calling
Jove to witness, and the altars of the broken
treaty, he plunged into the heart of battle
with Mars on his side. Now he killed at random,
terrifying as he let his rage run free.

What god can help me sing of so much horror,   500
the great slaughter and slain generals, the men
whom Turnus, then the Trojan hero, drove over
the plain? Jupiter, did you want nations fated
for eternal peace to clash so violently?
Rutulian Sucro didn't keep Aeneas long.
He stabbed Sucro in the side (the first fight
to slow the Trojan rush) and pushed the hard blade
through the ribs that hold the heart, an instant death.
Turnus unhorsed Amycus and his brother
Diores. He hit one with his lengthy lance   510
as he approached, then the other with his sword,
and hung both severed heads, dripping blood, from
his chariot. Aeneas sent Tanaïs, Talos,
and brave Cethegus to death, three at once,
and sad Onites, Peridia's Theban son.

Turnus killed the brothers from Apollo's Lycian
fields, then Menoetes of Arcadia,
whose aversion to war was no use. He'd fished
Lerna's fertile streams, his pauper home unknown
to patrons; his father farmed on rented fields.   520
Like fires set in arid woods from facing sides
racing through the crackling laurels, like foaming rivers
roaring as they crash down mighty mountains
in their rushing course, blasting open
their own channels as they run into the sea:
so Turnus and Aeneas tore through the lines.

Rage boiled in them both. Without restraint, hearts
bursting, they used all their strength for slaughter.

As Murranus bragged of ancestors and ancient
names, all his race back to the Latin kings,   530
Aeneas whirled a giant rock and smashed him
to the ground, under the yoke and reins. The wheels
rolled him forward, and his horses, careless of
their master, trampled him with thudding hooves.
Hyllus charged with a huge roar; Turnus threw
a spear at that gold-clad head. The weapon pierced
his helmet and lodged in his brain. Cretheus,
strongest of the Greeks, your strength didn't ward off
Turnus; Cupencus, your gods didn't save you
from Aeneas. As the spear hit your chest,   540
your bronze shield offered one poor second of delay.
Aeolus,* Laurentian fields saw you die too.
You sprawled across the soil on your back—
you whom Argive phalanxes had failed to kill,
and Achilles, though he toppled Priam's kingdom.
Here was death's finish line. Your noble home
was near Ida, in Lyrnesus, but your grave
was in Laurentian earth. Now all the lines wheeled round:
the Latins, Trojans, fierce Serestus and Mnestheus,
Messapus the horse-tamer and brave Asilas,   550
the Tuscan legion and Evander's Arcadians.
It was each man for himself with all he had.
There was no pause, no rest, in the ravages of war.

And now his lovely mother put a notion
in Aeneas' head: that he should hurl his army
at the city walls and stun the Latins
with this new calamity. Tracking Turnus,
he gazed around and saw the town untouched

by the huge war, immune. The thought of greater
stakes enflamed him. He called to him the chiefs   560
Mnestheus, brave Serestus, and Sergestus,
and stepped up on a mound. The Trojan legions
ringed it, not setting down their shields or spears.
From the center, he cried: "Jupiter stands with us.
Let my orders meet with no delay, even
if this strategy is new. No holding back!
Today I'll storm the town that's caused the war, Latinus'
capital, and raze its smoking rooftops to
the ground, unless they surrender and submit.
Should I wait till Turnus deigns to fight   570
with me—a man I've beaten once before?
Citizens, this is the source and sum of unjust war.
Bring torches, quickly. We'll reclaim the treaty
with our flames." All of them, with eager effort,
made a wedge formation; the dense mass stormed
the walls. Ladders, torches, suddenly appeared.
Some ran to kill the sentries at the gates,
others showered spears. The sky was dark with weapons.
Aeneas himself, in the front and by the walls,
raised his right hand and denounced Latinus loudly,   580
swearing by the gods that he was forced to war
again, Italians again had broken faith,
turned foe. Discord broke out in the trembling town.
Some wanted to fling the gates wide open to
the Trojans and drag the king up to the walls,
some rushed to guard the ramparts with their weapons:
just like bees, when a shepherd tracks them
to a porous rock and fills it with harsh smoke:
disturbed, they scurry round their waxy camp
sharpening their outrage with loud buzzes.   590
As the black stench fills their home, the rock
resounds with humming; smoke coils in the clear sky.

. . .

Now a new misfortune struck the weary Latins,
one that shook the city to its core with grief.
When the queen, at home, saw the enemy
approach, saw the walls attacked, torches flying
at the roofs, no Rutulians defending,
none of Turnus' troops, the unhappy woman
thought he'd died in combat. Pierced by sudden grief,
she cried she was the cause and culmination   600
of their pain. Speaking wildly, in despair
and set on death, she tore her purple robe
and hung a noose around a beam—an ugly end.
When the wretched Latin women heard this news,
first Lavinia tore her golden hair and gouged
her rosy cheeks, then the group around her,
insane with grief. The palace echoed their lament.
From here the tragic rumor spread across the city.
All hearts sank. Latinus tore his clothing,
stunned by his wife's death and his town's ruin,   610
fouling his white hair with filthy dirt.

Meanwhile fierce Turnus, at the edge of battle,
still followed some stragglers, but more slowly.
His horses' skill now pleased him less and less.
On the wind came shouts of unseen horror.
He listened to the ominous low rumbles,
sounds of a city in distress, and cried,
"What great grief disturbs our walls? What's this   620
uproar coming to us all the way from town?"
With these words, he seized the reins, frantic to stop.
But his sister, posing as the charioteer
Metiscus, still steering team and chariot,
countered: "This way, Turnus. Let's pursue
the Trojans—we've found victory on this path.
There are others to defend the walls by force.

Aeneas is attacking the Italians;
we can inflict brutal deaths on Trojans.
You won't leave the battle his inferior   630
in honor or men killed." Turnus answered:
"Sister, I knew you long ago, when you ruined
the treaty with your wiles and joined the fight.
You don't deceive me, goddess. But who wanted you
to leave Olympus and endure these efforts?
Was it to see your luckless brother's brutal death?
What should I do? How can Fortune save me?
Murranus died before my eyes, calling out
my name: a great fighter, he fell to a great wound.
No one I love equally still lives.   640
Unlucky Ufens perished so he wouldn't see
my shame; the Trojans have his armor and his corpse.
Should I let our homes be razed, all that's left,
and not silence Drances' insults by the sword?
Should I turn tail, and let this land see Turnus
run away? Is death so dreadful? Smile on me,
shades of the dead, since the gods are hostile. My soul
descends to you unmarred by cowardice. I've never
been unworthy of my noble ancestors!"

And now Saces galloped through the fighting,   650
his horse foaming, himself wounded by an arrow
to the face. He begged Turnus as he passed:
"You're our last hope, Turnus! Pity your people.
Aeneas thunders in his armor, threatening
to raze our citadel and ruin us all.
Already, burning torches land upon our roofs.
We look to you. King Latinus is still muttering
about whom to call his son-in-law, which pact
to pick. As for the queen, who loved you most,
she's killed herself in fear and left the light of day.   660
Messapus and brave Atinas stand alone

before the gates and hold the line. Legions press them
all around, a dense and spiky crop of swords.
Still you drive in circles on the empty grass!"
The image of these losses staggered Turnus.
Silent, he stood and stared. His heart seethed with
mixed emotions: shame and grief mingled with madness,
love driven by fury, and self-conscious courage.
When he shook the shadows from his mind
and could see clearly, he turned his burning eyes toward   670
the walls and city from his chariot, aghast.

A spiral flame was rolling up a tower's stories,
billowing to sky, eating the whole structure—
a tower he himself had built with jointed beams,
set on wheels, and fitted with high walkways.
"Sister, fate has won. Stop delaying me.
Let's go where Jove and heartless Fortune call.
I'm resolved to fight Aeneas, and ready
for death, even if it's bitter—no more disgrace.
Just let me rage this final bout of rage."   680
Leaping from his chariot, he bolted through
the hostile swords, deserting his sad sister,
and burst into the center of the fighting.
Just as a rock uprooted by the wind will tumble
down a mountainside after violent rain
or passing years have weakened its grip;
flying down the sheer slope, the ruthless boulder
bounds over the ground, bowling over trees
and herds and men; so Turnus flung apart the ranks,
racing to the city walls. There the earth   690
was soaked with blood; spears whistled through the air.
He raised his arm to signal, shouting loudly:
"Rutulians, now stop; Latins, hold your weapons.
The plans of Fate are meant for me. It's right

that I pay for the broken pact alone; my sword
will decide." All pulled back and left a space.

But when Father Aeneas heard Turnus' name,
he left the walls and towers, breaking off from
all war's work—not a moment of delay.
Exultant, he clanged his weapons grimly,   700
looming like Mount Athos or Mount Eryx,
or father Apennine as he soars skyward, joyous
when gusts rustle oak trees on his snowy peak.
Now they all turned eagerly to watch:
Rutulians, Trojans, and Italians, men on
the high ramparts, men with battering-rams below.
They all put down their shields. Even Latinus
was stunned to see great men from distant points on earth
meet and clash with swords: a contest to end war.
When a level space was clear on the field,   710
they hurled their spears and ran toward each other.
Bronze shield hit bronze shield, and the fight began.
The earth groaned as the two men rained down sword-strokes,
blow on blow, chance and courage in the mix—
like two bulls butting heads in mortal combat
on huge Sila or Taburnus' heights;
the cowhands retreat in fear, and the herd
waits silently. The heifers wonder who will
rule the forest, who will lead the herds;
the bulls trade wounds with brutal violence,   720
locking horns, goring flesh, splashing blood
across their shoulders as the woods echo their grunts:
just so Trojan Aeneas and the Daunian hero
clashed with shields. A huge din filled the air.
Jupiter himself balanced a scale
and put the two lives in the pans to see
whose acts were doomed, whose weight plunged down to death.

. . .

Turnus sprang forward, seeing a safe chance.
He surged to his full height, raised his sword,
and struck. The Trojans and the Latins cried out   730
anxiously, on edge. But the faithless blade
snapped off and failed him. His only recourse was
to run. Seeing the strange hilt in his defenseless
hand, he fled faster than the eastern wind.
They say that when he climbed into the chariot
for battle, in his haste he left his father's sword
and grabbed Metiscus's instead. It served
him all the while he chased the straggling Trojans.
But when it came to Vulcan's divine weapons,
the mortal blade shattered like brittle glass,   740
its fragments glinting on the yellow sand.
Desperate, Turnus looked for any way to get
away, tracing confused circles in the field.
But the mass of Trojans shut him in all round,
and here a huge marsh stopped him, there high walls.

Aeneas too, though troubled by his knees,
(the wound slowed them down; it was hard to run)
pressed his frantic enemy, step for step—
like a hunting dog whose barks threaten
a stag trapped by a stream or feathered cordon;   750
fearful of the bank and snares, the stag wheels round
a thousand times, but the nimble Umbrian
hound pursues him closely, mouth agape;
he thinks he has him any moment now
and bites, but his jaws snap shut on empty air.
Now shouts rose up in earnest. The banks and lakes
echoed the sound, the whole sky thundered with
the din. As he ran, Turnus chided all
his men by name, demanding his own sword,
while Aeneas vowed instant death to anyone   760

who helped, and terrified the trembling enemy
with threats to raze the city. He pressed on though wounded.
They raced five full circuits, and five in reverse,
this way and that: since they sought no small or paltry
prize, but vied for Turnus' life and blood.

An olive tree with bitter leaves once grew there,
holy to Faunus and revered in the old days
by sailors saved from sea-wrecks. On it they nailed
gifts to the Laurentian god, and hung their votive
clothing. But the Trojans had chopped down the tree   770
without a thought, so they could fight on open ground.
Here stood Aeneas' spear, wedged into
the stubborn roots by the force with which it flew.
The Trojan bent to wrench it free: he'd use
the spear to strike the prey he couldn't catch
on foot. Then Turnus cried out, wild with fear:
"Faunus, please, have pity! And you, kind Earth,
hold fast that spear, if I ever kept your rites—
which Aeneas' men have profaned in their war."
He didn't pray for the gods' help in vain.   780
Aeneas, though he struggled long and hard
over the stubborn stump, could not pry apart
its wooden grip despite his strength. While he strained,
Juturna, again appearing as the driver
Metiscus, dashed up to give Turnus his sword.
Venus, outraged at the nymph's audacity,
came and pulled Aeneas' spear from the roots.
Spirits soaring, both men rearmed: one trusting
to his sword, one tall and fierce with his spear.
They faced each other, panting in the toil of war.   790

Now the king of great Olympus said to Juno
as she watched the battle from a golden cloud,
"Wife, what will be the end of this? What's left?

You yourself admit Aeneas will reach
the stars and rise to heaven as the nation's god.
What's your plan, what hope keeps you in chill clouds?
A mortal man wounded a god: was that right?
Or that Turnus got his sword (I know you helped
Juturna) and the losers have new strength?
Stop, at last, and be persuaded by my prayers.   800
Don't let silent grief consume you; don't make me
hear again your sweet mouth utter sad concerns.
It's over. You harassed the Trojans across
land and sea, you ignited awful wars,
you ruined a home and mingled grief and marriage.
I forbid you to do more." So he spoke.
Juno answered with bowed head: "I knew
your will, great Jupiter; that's why I left
the earth and Turnus. I didn't want to. Otherwise
you wouldn't see me sitting in a cloud alone,   810
enduring everything. I'd be in the front lines,
ringed with flames; I'd drag the Trojans into battle.
It's true I told Juturna she could help
her distressed brother, and dare more for his life,
but not to use her bow and arrow. I swear it
by the river Styx's unforgiving source,
the only oath revered by the upper gods.
Now I'll yield and leave this loathsome war.
But I beg one thing,* not forbidden by fate's
laws, for Latium and the glory of your   820
Latin kin: when there's peace and wedding
celebrations, when they join in laws and pacts,
don't command the Latins on their native soil
to change their name to Teucrians, becoming
Trojans, or to change their clothes and speech.
Let Latium and Alban kings last through the ages.
Let Rome's children triumph with Italian courage.
Troy perished: let her name perish as well."

The maker of all men and matter smiled and said:
"Truly, you're Jove's sister and a child of Saturn: 830
such waves of anger surge inside your heart.
Come now, give up this rage you honed for nothing:
I grant your wish, and willingly. You've won.
The Ausonians will keep their fathers' speech,
customs, and name. The Trojans will subside into
mixed stock. I'll add Trojan rites to local ones;
they'll all be Latins with one language.
You'll see a race arise from their mixed blood
that will surpass both gods and men in piety.
No other race will pay you so much honor."   840
Agreeing to these terms, Juno turned her mind
to happiness. She quit her cloud and left the sky.

This done, the Father pondered a new problem:
how to drive Juturna from her brother's side.
Men say there are twin plagues called Furies, daughters of
the dead of Night, born with hellish Megaera.
Night wrapped them all in serpent coils and added
wind-swift wings. They serve before Jove's throne,
on the threshold of the savage king, and whet
the terror of weak humankind, any time   850
the king of gods devises vile death and disease
or terrifies a guilty town with war.
He told one to hurry from the sky
and cross Juturna's path, an evil omen.
A rapid whirlwind carried her to earth
like an arrow springing from a bow, Parthian
or Cydonian, that races through the clouds
carrying venom, a wound beyond curing,
crossing the swift shadows hissing and unseen.
So rushed the child of Night, heading for earth.   860
When she saw the Trojan lines and Turnus' troops,
she quickly took the shape of a small owl

that sits on tombs and lonely rooftops late at night
and hoots her eerie notes among the shadows.
The monster fluttered around Turnus' face,
screeching, her wings beating at his shield.
A strange numbness left him weak with dread.
His hair stood up in horror, his voice choked in his throat.

Turnus' unhappy sister knew the Fury's shrilling
wings from far. She tore her hair and gouged her face   870
with fingernails, pounded on her chest with fists.
"Turnus, how can your sister help you now?
Should I give up heartlessly? But what skill
of mine could stall your death? I can't fight a Fury.
I'll go, I'll leave the battle. Vile bird, don't scare me,
I'm afraid already. I know the deadly drumming
of your wings. Great Jove's proud commands
are clear. Is this my virginity's reward?
Why give me immortality? Why can't I die
as humans do? Then I could end this crushing grief   880
and follow my sad brother to the shades.
Immortal life is worthless: What will bring me pleasure
without you? What earth can gape open so deeply
as to send a goddess to the shades below?"
She said this groaning deeply, then draped her head
in gray-green robes and plunged deep in the river.

Aeneas was in pursuit. He shook his massive spear,
almost a tree, and spoke these savage words:
"What's the delay now? Turnus, why retreat?
This contest is a duel, not a race.   890
Go on, change yourself to any shape, gather
all your strength and skill (such as you have), chase
the stars on wings, hide yourself in Earth's deep
hollows." Turnus shook his head. "Fierce Aeneas,
your hot words don't scare me; it's the gods I fear,

and Jove's enmity." He looked around and saw
a giant rock, an ancient giant rock set in the plain,
a boundary mark for conflicts over land.
Hardly twelve men could lift it on their shoulders,
such men as Earth produces now. But the hero   900
grabbed it in his hands and rose, then ran
toward his enemy and heaved the rock at him.
But even as he ran, even as he raised and
threw the giant boulder, he didn't feel like Turnus
to himself: his knees couldn't hold him, fear chilled
his blood. His rock, tumbling through the empty air,
didn't bridge the gap, didn't reach its goal.
It was like a dream, when drowsy sleep lies on
our eyes: we feel we're trying to run, but somehow
it's no use; we collapse weakly as we try.   910
The strength we know is gone, we cannot speak,
no words or sounds come out. Just so the awful goddess*
kept Turnus from success despite his bravery.
Then mixed emotions churned inside his heart.
He hung back in dread and gazed at the Rutulians
and the city, trembling at his coming death.
There was no place to run, no strength to fight,
no chariot to see, no charioteer, no sister.

As Turnus faltered, Aeneas saw his chance.
Raising his fatal spear, he put all his body   920
in the throw. No stone hurled from a siege engine
ever roared so loudly, no clap of thunder ever
crashed like this. The spear flew, a black tornado
bringing dreadful death. Hissing, it tore through
the breastplate's border and the outer circle of
the seven-layered shield, and ran right through his thigh.
His legs folded, and huge Turnus crumpled
to the ground. The Rutulians leapt up groaning.
The hills and forests echoed their cry far and wide.

Humbly, Turnus raised his eyes, his hands,   930
and begged: "I deserve this. I don't ask for mercy:
use your chance. But if a parent's grief can touch you,
have pity for old Daunus (you had such a father
in Anchises) and return me to my people,
as a corpse if you prefer. You've won,
the Ausonians have seen me stretch my hands out
in defeat. Lavinia's yours; give up your hate."
Fierce Aeneas stood there, armed, his eyes
roaming restlessly, holding back the death-blow.
And now more and more, Turnus' words began   940
to move him and he hesitated—when high on Turnus'
shoulder, he saw the fatal sword-belt of young Pallas,*
the strap flashing with its well-known studs—Pallas,
whom Turnus killed when down, and took that emblem
of the enemy to wear upon his shoulder.
Aeneas drank in this reminder of his savage
grief. Ablaze with rage, awful in anger, he cried,
"Should I let *you* slip away, wearing what you
tore from one I loved? Pallas sacrifices
you, Pallas punishes your profane blood"—and,
seething, planted his sword in that hostile heart.   950
Turnus' knees buckled with chill.* His soul fled
with a groan of protest to the shades below.

NOTES

Notes correspond to lines starred in the text.

BOOK I: LANDFALL AT CARTHAGE

10: *a man famous for piety*: See introduction, page xx, and note to 1.220 for Aeneas' epithet, "pious." His piety, at least at the beginning, contrasts with Juno's anger, and provides an interesting play on the *Iliad*, in which it is Achilles, the mortal hero, whose anger drives the epic.

26–28: *Paris' scornful verdict . . . her hatred for that race*: Paris, son of Priam, King of Troy, was once asked to judge which goddess was the most beautiful, Aphrodite (Roman Venus), Hera (Roman Juno), or Athena. As a bribe, Aphrodite offered him Helen of Troy, so he selected her, offending Juno in the process. Ganymede was a beautiful young Trojan boy snatched up by Jupiter in the guise of an eagle to be his lover and a cup-bearer in Olympus. Juno hated the Trojans in general because their founder, Dardanus, was the son of Jupiter by Electra—that is, the product of Jupiter's infidelity.

41: *the mad crime of Ajax*: Ajax the Lesser raped Cassandra in her temple when Troy fell and was punished for this by Pallas Athena.

42: Jupiter was also known to the Romans as Jove; the two forms alternate in this poem.

84: The Roman winds had names. Eurus was the southeast wind, Notus the south, Zephyrus the west, Aquilo the north, Africus the southwest. In the original they are referred to by these names, but after their first appearance (Aquilo appears only once), the translation usually names them by their directionality instead, e.g. north, south, and so forth.

118–19: In the Latin, line 119 starts with *"arma virum,"* the first two words of the epic, but now in a situation less than heroic.

131: Jupiter calls in Zephyrus, even though Vergil has not mentioned his involvement in the storm.

148–53: The famous "statesman simile" confronts us immediately with the forces of rage (*furor*) versus piety (*pietas*), one of the major tensions in the epic—and in Aeneas. *Furor* is also used of Dido's love for Aeneas, Turnus' rage in battle, and Aeneas' fury as he kills Turnus. Disconcertingly, Juno's own *furor* (12.832) has driven much of the plot of the poem.

156: In the description of the storm and the statesman, and also elsewhere—Hercules' attack on Cacus in Book 8, the battle of Actium in the same book, and the war with the Italians in Books 9 through 12—Vergil contrasts civilization/order with barbarism/disorder, often employing images from the myth of Gigantomachy, as Philip Hardie has shown in *Virgil's Aeneid: Cosmos and Imperium*. But sometimes the imagery reverses, as when Aeneas is compared to the hundred-handed Aegaeon in 10.565–70.

205–206: *we make for Latium. There the fates / promise us rest:* Aeneas assures his men of rest to come, and Creusa echoes this positive prophecy by telling Aeneas that he will find a happy situation in Italy (2.783). These two prophecies are contrasted with ones predicting great war and strife, given by Jupiter (1.263–64) and the Sibyl (6.86–87). They also omit mention of the great war Aeneas will have to fight in Latium.

209: *he feigns hope on his face:* This is the only positive use of a verb of simulation (*simulo*) in the *Aeneid*. Aeneas here fulfills his role as a leader in encouraging his men. Later, verbs of *simul-* carry the negative connotation of deception and trickery, and it's possible that Aeneas' capacity to hide his real feelings may be troubling in retrospect.

220: *Pious Aeneas:* Aeneas' epithet, "pious," is impossible to fully translate into English, as noted in the translator's note. For this reason I have left it in the form "pious" or "piety" so that the reader will be aware each time this quality in Aeneas is evoked.

262–64: *Your son will . . . give them walls and customs:* Jupiter promises Venus that the Trojans will impose their customs on the Italians and rule in Latium. However, this promise is in direct contradiction to what he will say to Juno in Book 12, where he agrees to Juno's plea for Trojan ways to die out (12.823–28) and says Aeneas will build his own town. While such inconsistencies used to be explained by arguing that Vergil had not finished his final revisions, in *Inconsistency in Roman Epic* James O'Hara has argued that we are meant to interpret them, not dismiss them. Jupiter tells Venus one thing and Juno something else—who the recipient is affects the message. What does that imply for us as readers of Vergil's "message"?

271: Here it's Iülus, Aeneas' son with Creusa, who rules Alba Longa; at 6.763, it's Silvius, his son with Lavinia. The epic may be combining Julian and anti-Julian propaganda.

273–74: *the priestess Ilia:* the other name for Romulus and Remus' mother was

Rhea Silvia, and her descent was from Silvius, not Iülus, so Jupiter's prediction seems aimed at pleasing Venus rather than telling the future.

285: *Assaracus' house will conquer Argos and crush Phthia and famed Mycenae:* The three Greek locations were the homes of prominent Greek heroes in the Trojan War, Achilles, Agamemnon, and Diomedes; the general meaning is that Rome will conquer Greece, as it did by 146 BCE.

286: Trojan Caesar is Augustus, not Julius, Caesar.

318: *Huntress-like:* Why does Venus disguise herself as a huntress in particular? We may recall that she does have a prey: the wounded Dido-deer of 4.69ff. Iülus will precipitate a war by similarly wounding a deer at 7.475ff.

343–426: The story Aeneas tells Dido (Books 2 and 3) bears an uncanny resemblance to the story Venus tells Aeneas about Dido's past.

367: *Byrsa* is the Greek word for a bull's hide.

390–91: *I have some news: your friends are safe:* in fact, as so often, this prophecy is overly optimistic, for we know Orontes and his men are dead. As Servius comments of Venus' line, "through this she shows that auguries for the most part deceive." James J. O'Hara in *Death and the Optimistic Prophecy* studies the overly optimistic prophecies of the epic and suggests that the epic's projection of the Augustan future is itself such a vatic pronouncement.

407–9: *Why trick your son so often with disguises?:* Aeneas reproaches Venus for always deceiving him by using false appearances. But in his flashback story on the Trojan War, Aeneas speaks of how his mother appeared to him as she appeared to the other gods (2.589–92).

450–52: *to have more hope in troubled times:* Aeneas, looking at the scenes of Trojan defeat depicted on the Temple of Juno, feels relief and joy and believes they show that the Carthaginians are sympathetic to Trojan suffering (1.462). His comments foreground the question of misreading (and misinterpreting), as Juno hated the Trojans. This has implications not only for Aeneas, but also for the poem's readers.

473: *before they tasted Trojan grass:* Servius tells us there was an oracle foretelling that if the horses of Rhesus tasted the grass or water of Troy, Troy would not fall.

487: Hector is singled out as Aeneas' friend, as if to contradict the legend that they were hostile to each other.

488: *He saw himself as well:* Most obviously and literally, Aeneas "mixed in with the Greeks" is a depiction of Coroebus' plan (as told by Aeneas)—a comrade who suggested that they wear Greek armor (2.386–90). Beyond the surface level, it may point to the legend that suggests Aeneas is the one who betrays Troy by siding with the Greeks.

600: *bereft:* Aeneas tells Dido that they have nothing, but within less than fifty lines, he asks Ascanius to bring and present to Dido luxurious gifts, including a veil that Helen gave him, Priam's daughter's scepter, a necklace of pearls, and other jewelry and gold (1.648–55). This contradicts the image of Aeneas fleeing for his life, leaving Troy with only the Penates, Anchises, Iülus, and his wife Creusa. How did he get all this material, including, of all things, Helen's finery?

619: This Teucer is not to be confused with Teucer, the ancestor of the Trojan kings and the reason the Trojans are called Teucrians. Teucer here is Trojan on his mother's side—the nephew of King Priam of Troy and the cousin of Hector and Paris—but he fought on the Greek side in the Trojan War as the son of King Telamon of Salamis.

636: *The gods rejoiced at the gifts:* The line is corrupt in the original; I have provided a reasonable translation.

710: This line is considered spurious.

752: *Diomedes' horses:* Dido asks Aeneas to tell her about the horses of Diomedes when they originally used to belong to Aeneas (*Iliad* 5.263ff.). Is this a little jab about how Venus had to save Aeneas from Diomedes? Perhaps a little suggestion that Dido knows more about Aeneas than she lets on.

BOOK 2: AENEAS' STORY: THE FALL OF TROY

19–20: *the massive / womb was packed with warriors and weapons:* As Michael Putnam points out in *The Poetry of the Aeneid,* the theme of hollow spaces in which violence is contained, but only temporarily, is central to the poem, recurring with Aeolus' winds, the Trojan Horse, and Cacus' cave.

79–80: *if wicked Fortune's ruined / Sinon:* Sinon's "confession" contains a lot of conditional clauses, with the result that he often speaks truth. For example, wicked Fortune has not ruined Sinon, so the rest of the clause is irrelevant. Appropriately, his name translates as "If not" in Latin.

112–13: *this horse of maple / planks:* What kind of wood the Trojan Horse is made of is an unresolved matter. Four different types are offered: pitch pine (*abiete* 2.16), maple (*acer* 2.112–13), oak (*robur* 2.230), and pine (*pinus* 2.258). Ralph Hexter in "What Was the Trojan Horse Made Of? Interpreting Vergil's *Aeneid*" suggests that readers glide over such inconsistencies, filling gaps with explanations rather than acknowledging them. Is this how we ought to read the discrepancies in the epic as a whole?

116: Agamemnon sacrificed his daughter, Iphigenia, in return for good winds to Troy.

166: The fateful effigy of Pallas Athena was the Palladium, a wooden cult statue that supposedly guaranteed the safety of Troy as long as it was physically in Troy.

285: *But who so vilely mangled your kind face?*: Aeneas questions Hector about his wounds, despite the fact that he must have already known how and why Hector had been mangled behind Achilles' chariot. Servius suggests that Aeneas spoke of this dream to appeal to Dido, who also had a dead ghost (her husband, Sychaeus) appear before her with brutal wounds.

379: *a hidden snake*: An interesting simile. Aeneas seems to compare himself to a snake, amid many negative snake images in the poem—the snakes who kill Laocoön and his sons, the snakelike Pyrrhus, both in Book 2. In fact, serpent imagery winds all through Book 2, lending an ominous tone to the activities of the doomed Trojans, as Bernard Knox points out in "The Serpent and the Flame."

396: *mixed in with the Greeks*: The same phrase as Aeneas' description of himself on the Temple of Juno frieze in Book 1.

558: *he lies now on the shore*: It is unclear how Priam's corpse made it onto the shore, since he was killed at the altar (2.550). Vergil may have been thinking of the fate of the Roman general Pompey, or combining his version of Priam's death with another tradition in which Pyrrhus drags the body to Achilles' tomb on the shore.

565–67: *They'd all abandoned me*: Aeneas appears to be the sole survivor of the warriors mentioned in his narration. There is no one present who can either corroborate or denounce his story of Troy's fall.

568–88: The Helen episode: These verses were neither commented or quoted by any other ancient commentator apart from Servius, who said that Vergil's editors removed them. As they seem on the whole misplaced and discrepant with the narrative, many editors chose to disregard this episode entirely. Helen is described as crouching by the altar and hiding, but if, as Aeneas suggests and Deiphobus later corroborates (6.511ff), she was helping the Greeks, why would she be hiding and scared? In a story told by her husband, Menelaus, in *Odyssey* 4, Helen helps the Trojans by taking on the voices of the wives of the men in the horse and calling out to them, just in case the horse contains soldiers.

643: *the sacking of the city once already*: Anchises refers to Hercules' sack of the city after he was tricked by its founder, Laomedon, who destroyed Hercules' ships in port.

649: *his thunderbolt's hot breath*: According to some versions of the legend, Jupiter struck Anchises with lightning because he boasted about having slept with Venus.

721–23: This image of Aeneas leaving Troy with his son and father is as old as

Greek black figure vases, although the household gods (*penates*) are not shown till Roman times.

741: *I hadn't turned. . . . :* As R.O.A.M. Lyne remarks in *Further Voices in Vergil's Aeneid,* "Vergil seems curiously disinclined to show Aeneas responding or relating to others" (150).

781: *Lydian Tiber:* So named because the traditional origin of the Etruscans was in Lydia.

BOOK 3: AENEAS' STORY: MEDITERRANEAN WANDERINGS

64: *dark ribbons:* Throughout, I have used "ribbon" or "headband" to translate the Latin word *vitta,* a woolen fillet often associated with religious ritual. At Rome, it was worn by priests, prophets, statues of deities, and victims decked for sacrifice.

75: The pious Archer is Apollo, who fixed Delos in one place as a favor to the inhabitants, who had allowed his mother Leto to give birth there.

104: *Crete . . . the cradle of our race:* Anchises wrongly interprets Apollo's prophecy (3.94ff) to mean Crete instead of Italy, by tracing the Trojans' ancestry to Teucer (3.107–8) and noting the existence of a Mount Ida in Crete as well, instead of identifying Dardanus as their ancestor. But outside Vergil, Dardanus' place of origin is also ambiguous: tradition traces it to Arcadia, Crete, the Troad, or Italy. Oddly, Aeneas seems to forget that Creusa told him his destination was Italy (2.781). Like Cassandra, she seems to have gone unheard.

213: *Phineus' home was closed to them:* Phineus was a local Thracian king who had chosen blindness rather than death as punishment for a crime. Helios (the Sun), feeling scorned, sent the Harpies to plague him. They were eventually driven off with the help of the Argonauts.

255–57: The Trojans are cursed with the future eating of their own plates, although the Harpies' grim prophecy is lightened by Helenus' reassurance a hundred lines later. In Book 7, while the Trojans eat their "pizza" of fruits on bread, Aeneas accepts Iülus' exclamation (7.116) as a harmless fulfillment of the prophecy, which he wrongly credits to Anchises (7.123).

302: *a second Simois:* Andromache has tried to re-create Troy in Italy; see 349ff. This is precisely what Aeneas will not do; he looks forward rather than backward by the second half of the epic.

303–6: Andromache worships Hector, her dead (first) husband, and weeps piteously. Aeneas thus depicts Andromache as a *univira,* a woman wholesomely dedicated to one man, though in reality she is currently married to Helenus and was Pyrrhus' concubine before that. Aeneas may be indirectly praising the virtues of Dido, who was known for her chastity and devotion to Sychaeus. Of course, this is a touch ironic since Aeneas will be the one to lead Dido away from this devotion.

340: *The son that your Trojan wife*—: This is one of the half-lines in Vergil's poem, and here it works exceptionally well with the idea that Andromache is overcome by emotion.

496: Of course the fields of Italy are not literally receding; Aeneas feels that despite all his travel, he gets no closer to his destination.

712–13: Aeneas complains that the prophecies of Celaeno and Helenus left out his father's death and the pain it would bring him.

BOOK 4: DIDO'S SUICIDE

19: *this one fault:* See comments on 4.126, below.

65: *But what can prophets know?:* The Latin reads, "Alas for the ignorant minds of prophets," a striking line in its use of *vates,* poet-seer, for prophet. Vergil is a *vates* himself—and so are Calchas in Book 2 and Cassandra and Celaeno in Book 3. These are interesting models.

92–104: Juno, seeing Dido hopelessly in love, suggests to Venus that she should marry Aeneas and that the Trojan empire should be set up at Carthage. Juno likes the idea, because she opposes the foundation of a city in Italy by the Trojans. Venus agrees, wanting Aeneas to be safe with the Carthaginian queen and knowing that Jupiter will not condone this plan in the longer term.

126: *a stable marriage:* Juno sees their future union as a marriage, and uses the appropriate language; Venus sees it as an affair. Dido is not wrong, then, when she also thinks she is married; she's merely on the losing side of the struggle between Juno and Venus. But does the narrator take sides? Vergil says that Dido cloaks her "fault" (*culpa,* 4.172) with the word "marriage." When Dido anticipates marriage with Aeneas, she too uses *culpa,* but only to refer to remarrying and thus betraying the memory of her dead husband. So what does Vergil mean? Is her *culpa* referring to the union as marriage, or infidelity to the memory of her husband, Sychaeus, along with her indifference to rumor, or even the trust she shows in him? It may not be an answerable question; the text, as often, seems to offer us two versions of the same event.

160–72: Aeneas and Dido take refuge in the same cave, and their marriage is ratified by Juno. It appears that the true mastermind is Venus, who knows of Juno's plans but twists them for her own agenda (4.127–28).

215: *Paris, with his retinue of half-men:* Iärbas speaks of Aeneas as an effeminate easterner in his clothing and perfume. Juno later corroborates this description in her comparison of Aeneas and Turnus (7.321), speaking of Aeneas as both a wife-stealer and unmasculine. Turnus is particularly eloquent on this topic, insulting Aeneas in battle as a man who uses a curling iron for his hair (12.97–100). This ridicule applies to the Trojans in general, as seen through Remulus Numanus, who, scorning the Trojans, said they love to dance and wear luxurious garments (9.614–16).

261–64: Aeneas' clothing: The description Vergil gives us shows that Aeneas is comfortable with Carthaginian luxury. His wearing of jasper, purple cloth, and gold is a sign of how much he has become Dido's partner, and Mercury charges him with "acting the good husband." According to Jupiter's speech to Mercury, Aeneas has no intention of leaving Carthage, though he will claim otherwise to Dido after his warning from Mercury.

288–91: *to prepare the fleet without a word . . . and hide the change of plans:* Aeneas explicitly commands his men to hide the reason for rigging the ships (*dissimulent*). However, when Dido confronts him with this behavior, using the same verb (4.305, *dissimulare*), Aeneas claims that he hid nothing from her (4.337–38), a wholesale lie.

368: *Why should I pretend now?:* Is Dido asking: Why should I pretend not to care? Or is she referring to a more sinister alternative, the idea that she was pretending to think Aeneas was a great hero from the start, though she knew better? Again, the verb is *dissimulo*.

421–24: *Only you could catch him in an easy mood:* Anna here is described as the only person in the epic to know Aeneas' innermost thoughts. Vergil may be pointing to an earlier tradition in which Anna, not Dido, killed herself on a funeral pyre.

427: *I didn't exhume Anchises' ghost:* The ancient commentator Servius mentions a story told by Varro in which the Greek Diomedes disinterred Anchises' bones, which he afterward restored to Aeneas under duress.

496: *impious man:* This of course alludes to Aeneas' ordinary epithet *pius,* which Dido no longer believes.

515: *the warty love charm:* Ancient lore had it that foals were born with tubercles on their foreheads, which were bitten off by their mother, and that if this had been previously removed, the mother would refuse to rear the foal.

528: This line is considered spurious and is not translated here.

541–42: *don't you / know or feel the treachery of Trojans yet?:* This is the same sentiment Aeneas expressed about the Greeks in his narrative to Dido. In Dido's mouth it suggests she should have known of Trojan treachery (as a national characteristic) earlier, a possibility corroborated by her comment at line 596.

596: *Poor Dido, do his impious actions touch you now?:* There is debate over whether the impious actions are Dido's or Aeneas'. As John Conington remarks in his

Commentary on Vergil's Aeneid, the latter is supported by Dido's language at 4.496 above, and by Tibullus' *Carmina* 3.6.42 use of the same term for Theseus' desertion of Ariadne. Those who wish to apply the impious actions to Dido argue that she had no reason to think Aeneas treacherous when she offered to share her kingdom. But the narrative invites us to speculate that she had, in fact, heard the most common version of Aeneas' actions at Troy—the version that spoke of his treachery.

625–29: This curse originates the enmity between Carthage and Rome. The unknown avenger will be Hannibal. It also speaks of the war Aeneas will have to fight in Italy; the parting with Dido will not be the end of the Trojan's struggles.

632: Barca was the name of Hannibal's family, here a nod to the future Punic Wars between Carthage and Rome.

644: *ashen and splotchy at her coming death:* This is echoed almost directly in the description of Cleopatra on the shield of Aeneas (8.709).

668–71: *as if Carthage / or ancient Tyre were falling:* The military imagery reminds us that Carthage is, indeed, doomed to be sacked, and that Aeneas' departure ensures this.

BOOK 5: TROJAN GAMES

69: The feast and funeral games in honor of Anchises in Book 5 were a Roman custom. Vergil is also, as always, looking back to Homer; here, to the funeral games in honor of Patroclus.

412: *Your brother Eryx:* Aeneas and Eryx shared a mother in Venus.

487: It's unclear whether we should read Serestus or Sergestus here.

522–23: *a sudden miracle took place, important / in the future:* The meaning of this slightly obscure passage seems to be that what happened here would later be understood as an omen of future evil, but only after that evil had occurred. Aeneas, however, interprets it favorably (5.530–31). Scholars are not sure what event is referred to here; possibly Roman war with Sicily.

811–12: *the walls I built:* Neptune wanted to destroy Troy's original walls because Laodemon refused to pay the promised reward.

845ff: The account of Palinurus' death at the hands of Sleep is somewhat different from Palinurus' own description of his death in the Underworld (6.347–62). There, Palinurus also absolves Apollo of blame through a technicality. Apollo had promised that Palinurus would make it to Italy safely, and he did in fact reach the Ausonian shores, only to be killed by barbarians minutes later.

BOOK 6: A VISIT TO HADES

21: *the Athenians who paid an awful price:* The Athenians were required to sacrifice seven young men and seven maidens to the Minotaur every seven years in reparation for the murder in Athens of Minos' son Androgeos.

29: *a princess' love:* A reference to Ariadne, the daughter of Minos, king of Crete. One year, one of the seven young men sent from Athens to be given to the Minotaur was Theseus, with whom Ariadne fell in love. With Daedalus' help, Theseus killed the Minotaur and eloped with Ariadne, but according to most accounts, he later abandoned her on the island of Naxos.

69–70: *I'll raise a shrine of solid marble:* This suggests the Temple of Apollo on the Palatine Hill at Rome, built by Augustus and dedicated in 28 BCE.

211: *as it held on:* Oddly, the bough does not break off as easily as it should.

348: *No god drowned me at sea:* Vergil shows us here the limited perspective of human beings.

458: *did I cause your death?:* Aeneas expresses disbelief at both finding Dido in the Underworld and realizing that he is the primary cause. This astonishment is odd, as Dido herself tells him she will kill herself (4.321) and that her ghost will haunt him (4.386).

460: *I left your shores against my will:* Vergil has Aeneas repeat a somewhat comic line from Catullus' poem 66, in which a lock of hair bemoans its departure from Queen Berenice's head. This would have jolted ancient readers as incongruous with its new context.

476: *tears and pity:* As R.O.A.M. Lyne points out, Aeneas shows emotion *after* the death of both Creusa and Dido. In this case he shows the very reactions whose absence so much pained Dido during their confrontation in Book 4: tears, pity, consideration. But *too late.* Repeatedly, Aeneas loses his chances for affective interactions with others in his drive to follow his mission.

749: The shade of Anchises explains the doctrine of the transmigration of souls, which are first purged, then sent up to earth to live in new bodies. The doctrine is already present in Plato's *Phaedo* and *Republic;* here it clashes somewhat with the more traditional accounts of reward and punishment in the afterlife.

758: *who'll take our name:* A confusing claim, since as part of her compensation for her concession to Jupiter in Book 12, Juno wants the Trojan name to vanish.

763–66: Here the Roman's ancestry is traced to Aeneas' second son, Silvius, and not to Iülus/Ascanius. Ascanius is cited as the ancestor of the Roman line by Jupiter (1.286–88), in the description of Ascanius and his troop during Anchises' funeral rites (5.596–603), and by Tiberinus (8.48–49). This is significant because if indeed it is Silvius who carries on the lineage, Augustus cannot claim ancestry with Iülus, who is the source of the name Julius, as in Julius Caesar. The two accounts exist side by side in the poem.

792–93: *who'll bring / a golden age to Latium:* The Latin literally says "who will found golden centuries," using the verb *condere* that is so prominent at the beginning and end of the epic and that I have translated there as "plant." But to "found centuries" is an isolated occurrence in Latin; usually this verb plus a period of time means "end, lay to rest." Vergil continues to play with the ambiguity of the epic's foundational verb, which both creates and destroys.

836–38: *This one's . . . That one:* Probably Mummius, conqueror of Corinth in 146 BCE, and L. Aemilius Paullus in 168 BCE.

847: *Others . . . will beat out bronze:* Anchises dismisses artworks within a work of (literary) art, the *Aeneid,* suggesting that Vergil cannot share his view.

851: *You, Roman, remember your own arts:* These programmatic lines have suggested to many that Aeneas' murder of Turnus, who has already been defeated (marking the end of the war), is in violation of his father's exhortation.

893–98: *There are twin Gates of Sleep:* Aeneas' departure through the gate of false visions, right after he has seen the glorious future of Rome, has yet to be explained to anyone's satisfaction. One attempt to mitigate the shock value of this ending to Book 6 is to suggest that because Aeneas is not a shade (not dead), the gate's falsity does not reflect on him. But why did Vergil choose this gate in the first place? What does it mean that this gate is a work of art, like the poem itself?

BOOK 7: ITALY—AND WAR

1: *you died here too:* i.e. besides Misenus and Palinurus.

37–45: *Come, Erato!:* The invocation to the muse Erato, the muse of love poetry, begins the second part of the *Aeneid*—books full of war. Servius commented on this odd choice, perhaps due to the fact that the upcoming war must be fought over a woman, Lavinia (a precedent for summoning Erato may be Apollonius' choice of the same muse in *Argonautica* 3.1–5), perhaps due to the influence Venus wields in Aeneas' fate.

46–47: *ruled . . . in long peace:* Yet Tiberinus tells Aeneas that Evander and his men have been in a long war with the Latins (8.54).

99: *They'll raise our name up to the stars by blood:* There may be an underlying meaning here—they'll raise us by the mingling of our two bloodlines, or, perhaps, by bloodshed.

122–26: *My father / (I remember!) left me with this fateful secret:* Aeneas wrongly credits Anchises with this prophecy; the true speakers were the Harpies (3.255–57).

190–91: *to change him / to a bird:* Vergil's source for this story is not entirely clear. In Ovid's later *Metamorphoses* 14.321, Circe is in love with Picus, but not his lover. She turns him into a bird because he prefers the nymph Canens.

236–37: *many tribes and nations sought us for themselves:* Not precisely true. Ilioneus exaggerates the Trojans' desirability.

247: *a sacred scepter and a diadem:* Aeneas now has with him not only Priam's daughter's scepter, but Priam's own scepter, and his crown. There is no way of explaining how and when he received these according to his narrative in Books 2 and 3. The "traitor" legend, however, has it that the Greeks gave Aeneas many treasures for betraying Troy.

304–7: *undeserving victims both:* Athena had been permitted to destroy the Greek fleet for the sin of Ajax, son of Oïleus, as noted above on Book 1.41. Servius tells us that Peirithous invited all the gods but Mars to his marriage feast, and that Mars in revenge made the Centaurs and Lapiths fight, with many resultant Lapith deaths.

312: *then I'll move Acheron:* Freud used this bold sentiment, in Latin, as the epigraph to *The Interpretation of Dreams.*

394ff.: *They left home wearing fawn-skins . . . :* This description of Bacchic "orgies" was probably taken from a Greek source. The Bacchanalia were introduced into Rome from southern Italy, but they were eventually linked with excess and depravity by the Romans and suppressed throughout Italy in 186 BCE by a decree of the Senate.

606: *and claim our standards from the Parthians:* At the Battle of Carrhae in 53 BCE, the Parthian general Surena delivered a great defeat to the numerically superior Roman army led by M. Licinius Crassus. It was seen by the Romans as a crushing and humiliating defeat, and there was later much propaganda made of the fact that Augustus was able to get the captured Roman standards back in 20 BCE.

759–60: *Angitia's forest . . . will weep for you:* For Adam Parry in "The Two Voices of Virgil's *Aeneid,*" these lines encompass "the sense of emptiness is the very heart of the Virgilian mood," part of what he calls the "further voices" of the *Aeneid.*

BOOK 8: AN EMBASSY TO EVANDER

40–41: *the gods' swollen anger is all over:* Tiberinus' promise is misleading, given that Juno summons Allecto in Book 7—in sum, another overly optimistic prophecy.

46: Line 46, repeated from 3.393, is omitted here as spurious.

134–35: *That Dardanus . . . was Troy's first father:* Does Dardanus found Troy, as Servius says, or does he come to a city already founded by Teucer of Crete? This ambiguity explains the confusion at 3.107 about the Trojans' ancient mother. Servius calls the claim about Dardanus a mistake.

141: *Maia's father*: It seems most likely that Aeneas is simply fabricating this genealogy by melding different Atlas figures from mythology, all in order to claim kinship with Evander. Ironically, he engages in this fabrication at the very moment that he attributes it to "tradition"—a narrative sleight of hand perhaps not unlike that of Vergil himself.

146–48: *Those Daunians that hunt you down*: Aeneas misrepresents the situation.

322–23: The pun in the Latin cannot be rendered into English. "Latium" is linked with the verb *latuisset*, "he had hidden himself."

346: *and swore that his guest Argus died right here*: The Argiletum was a paved road leading from the Roman Forum to the busy quarter of Subura. Here, Vergil parses the name as *Argi letum*, "the death of Argus." Evander, king of Pallanteum, received Argus as a guest, but Evander then discovered that Argus was plotting to kill him and take over his empire. Evander accordingly killed Argus.

404: Vulcan is so excited that he doesn't finish his sentence before rushing on to the end. He seems mostly persuaded to make Aeneas' armor by the fact that Venus appeals to his lust.

445 *chalyb* (khal'-ib): A metal forged by people who resided on the southern coast of the Black Sea in the region of Pontus (10.175).

628ff: *Aeneas' shield*: The engravings on the shield show Rome's future (from Aeneas' point of view), starting with Romulus and Remus being suckled by a wolf, then moving on to the Battle of Actium, September 2, 31 BCE, in which Octavian and his general Agrippa (representing the forces of order) defeated Antony and Cleopatra (representing the immoral East, animal divinities included). The temporally last item shown is Augustus' triple triumph in 29 BCE, conquered peoples in his wake. The events alluded to are Rome's expulsion of its last king, Tarquinius Superbus, the kidnap of the Sabine women, Horatius Cocles' defense of a Roman bridge against the Etruscan king Lars Porsenna, the Gallic attack on Rome in 390 BCE, the punishment of Mettus Fufetius, a traitorous king of Alba Longa, and the Catilinarian conspiracy. The shield's Homeric counterpart is the shield of Achilles in *Iliad* 18, but that shield shows generic scenes while this one celebrates Rome's particular history and her glory. Nonetheless, it leaves room for multiple interpretations, and parts of its narrative (for example, the peoples mentioned bringing gifts to Augustus) would not have occurred in Vergil's lifetime.

679: *the Senate, people, gods of sky and hearth*: A variant of Aeneas' list of companions in 3.12 ("with my people, son, and gods of sky and hearth"). Likewise, at 680, Augustus is described as standing high on the stern, an echo of Aeneas at

10.260 (261 in the Latin). Augustus on the shield is presented as a latter-day incarnation of Aeneas—except that he is leading the *Italians* into battle. The slurs on Mark Antony (his barbarian wealth, Egyptian wife, and half-men followers) in Octavian's propaganda are picked up on the shield, though they coexist uneasily with the charges against Aeneas himself by Turnus and others.

686: *hodgepodge troops:* Actually, there were several hundred Roman senators on Antony's side.

704: *Apollo saw this:* This may be a compliment to Augustus, in whose propaganda Apollo featured. The Temple of Apollo on the Palatine Hill was vowed by Octavian in return for the victories over Sextus Pompeius at the Battle of Naulochus in 36 BCE and over Mark Antony and Cleopatra at the Battle of Actium in 31 BCE.

709: *pale with future death:* A close repetition of Vergil's description of the dying Dido at 4.644, reminding us of the connection between the two north African queens as threats to Roman power.

BOOK 9: NISUS AND EURYALUS

121: Line 121 is considered spurious and is not included here.

446–47: Vergil's words to Nisus and Euryalus are now part of the World Trade Center memorial.

528: This line is left out of the best manuscripts.

547: *Although it was forbidden:* It is not entirely clear why Helenor was not allowed to fight; perhaps due to his status, perhaps because he was too young.

613ff: Vergil rather boldly characterizes the Trojans (through Remulus' insults) as effeminate weaklings, as does Turnus.

777: *sang of horses, war, battles, and men:* Cretheus' songs include *"arma virum,"* the first two words of Vergil's own epic. But rather than sing of war, he is killed by it.

BOOK 10: BLOODSHED, AND PALLAS DOWN

8: *the Trojans and Italians should not fight:* Actually, Jupiter foretold this very war when speaking to Venus in Book 1. He also continues to intervene in the war even after swearing by the Styx that he will not. Is there any sound moral ground in this poem?

12: *when fierce Carthage opens up the Alps:* Hannibal famously crossed the Alps on his way to Rome in the Second Punic War, 218–202 BCE.

30: *your daughter, still harassed by human swords!*: Venus/Aphrodite was wounded in the wrist by Diomedes during the Trojan War (*Iliad* 5.336).

113: *Royal Jove is neutral*: Jupiter swears that he will no longer interfere in the fighting, but five hundred lines later, he seems to enflame Mezentius into entering the fray.

278: This line, identical with 9.127, is omitted in several manuscripts.

426: *Lausus, no small part of battle*: This wording (literally "a major part of battle") closely recalls Aeneas' self-description to Dido as "no minor part [of Troy's downfall]," 2.6. The difference is that Lausus is participating in the thing he is "a major part of," while we are supposed to read Aeneas' words as *not* implicating him in the fall of Troy.

497–99: *Pallas' sword-belt, carved to show a wicked crime*: The scene inscribed on the belt is the story of the Danaids, who murdered their husbands on their wedding night. This belt famously provokes Aeneas' murder of Turnus as the closing scene of the epic.

520: *They'd splatter Pallas' pyre with captive blood*: Aeneas takes victims for human sacrifice at Pallas' pyre. Here his piety is certainly in question.

565–68: *like Aegaeon*: One of the giants who warred with Jupiter and the Olympian gods. In this simile, Aeneas seems opposed to the forces of order.

872: This line is omitted as an interpolation from Book 12.

BOOK 11: TRUCE AND CONFLICT

82: *They'd splash Pallas' pyre*: As he promised he would do, Aeneas commits the *nefas* (unspeakable act) of human sacrifice. Human sacrifice was not customary and had been condemned since Homeric times (see *Iliad* 23.176). According to Suetonius, Octavian was rumored to have sacrificed one hundred senators and one hundred equestrians after the fall of Perusia in 40 BCE, but Suetonius is skeptical.

133: *They fixed on twelve days' truce*: In "Does Aeneas Violate the Truce in *Aeneid* 11?" Andrew Carstairs-McCarthy argues that Aeneas violates the truce at 11.446 and attacks the Latins on the eleventh day.

283–85: *how forcefully / he hurled his spear*: Diomedes is very complimentary to Aeneas here, which may surprise readers who remember their duel in the *Iliad*, when Aeneas' mother has to save him.

701: The Ligurians, though Italians, had a bad reputation for lying, fraud, and treachery.

BOOK 12: THE LAST DUEL

5: *the poacher's spear*: the word I have translated as "poacher" is *latro* (in 12.7), which usually means "brigand" or "robber" and is reminiscent of what Amata has to say about Aeneas in Book 7.

14–15: *I'll dispatch this Trojan traitor*: These words suggest that Turnus believes in the version of the tradition in which Aeneas betrays Troy; the Latin is "the deserter of Asia."

65–69: Why does Lavinia blush and weep at her mother's words? Does she love Turnus? The imagery of heat and flowers derives from an erotic context, and the blood (as well as the Latin *violare*, "violate," here rendered as "stained") points to what happens to virgins on their bridal night—perhaps another reason Turnus is driven mad.

87: Orichalcus was an ancient metal, second in value only to gold. It may have been a gold-copper alloy.

429: *He sends you to greater work*: This line echoes Vergil's invocation of the muse Erato at the beginning of Book 7, when he announces that he is turning to a greater work, i.e. warfare.

451–55: Vergil's sympathy for the farmers in this simile is an example of what R.O.A.M. Lyne dubbed "further voices," voices beyond the triumphant narrative of empire. The further voices are particularly striking in this simile, which in context brings to mind the Italian farmers and their destruction in war.

542: This Aeolus bears no relationship to the master of the winds in Book 1.

612–13: These two lines are omitted in the best manuscripts.

819ff: Juno makes her plea for the Trojans to "disappear," and Jupiter grants it. Thus the Romans could have their cake and eat it too: they came from legendary stock, but they had no Trojan customs or values.

912: *Just so the awful goddess*: Jupiter thus uses the same means to end the war as he did to begin it: a Fury. And yet Allecto was characterized as evil through and through.

942ff: An unsettling ending. Aeneas chooses violence over restraint, vengeance over mercy, rage over self-control. The fact that Vergil chose this ending instead of a resolution such as the return of Hector's body in the *Iliad* and Odysseus' homecoming and reconciliation with Penelope in the *Odyssey* has puzzled readers for centuries; some scholars use the abruptness of the ending as support for the idea that the *Aeneid* was never finished. Pallas' sword-belt, the trigger of Aeneas' murder of Turnus, ascribes a dangerous value to the power of art, which, as we've seen, can be misinterpreted and (here) used as justification for violence. In addition, the violence is personal, not on behalf of the public good; in this, Aeneas is like Hercules before him (when his cattle are stolen). This is noteworthy in the general Roman context of Hercules as a hero of civilization, and also in the context of Aeneas' learning to subordinate his own will to a larger plan. It is also noteworthy in relation to Augustus' citing *pietas* in the *Res Gestae* as the driving force behind his civil war: he had to avenge his father, as Aeneas here his ward.

Attention must be paid to the verb *condo* (here translated as "plant"), which frames the beginning (1.5) and end of this epic. It was a difficult task to plant the Trojans in Italy; but here, at the end, *condo* is the verb Vergil chooses for Aeneas' murder of Turnus as he plants his sword in his chest (12.950). The act of foundation is thus literally connected with violence, the two framing the epic. In another sense, the epic is doubly framed by Aeneas and Juno, who have switched positions by the poem's end: Juno gives up rage and agency, while Aeneas adopts them—though ascribing Turnus' murder, oddly enough, to Pallas.

951: *Turnus' knees buckled with chill:* As do Aeneas' knees the first time we meet him in the epic, 1.92. These are the only two times this phrase is used: Turnus is now the victim that Aeneas once was.

BIBLIOGRAPHY

WORKS CITED IN THE INTRODUCTION TO THE POEM

Ahl, Frederick. (1989) "Homer, Vergil, and Complex Narrative Structures in Latin Epic: An Essay," *Illinois Classical Studies* 14:1–31.

Barchiesi, Alessandro. (1997) *The Poet and the Prince: Ovid and Augustan Discourse.* Berkeley, CA.

Barthes, Roland. (1957) *Mythologies.* Paris.

Biow, Douglas. (1994) "Epic Performance on Trial: Virgil's *Aeneid* and the Power of Eros in Song." *Arethusa* 27:223–46.

Casali, Sergio. (1999) "Facta impia (Virgil, *Aeneid* 4.596–9)." *Classical Quarterly* 49:203–11.

———. (2014) "The Development of the Aeneas Legend," in *A Companion to Vergil and the Vergilian Tradition,* ed. J. Farrell and M.C.J. Putnam, 37–51. Hoboken, NJ.

Chiappinelli, F. (2007) *Impius Aeneas da Omero a Dante.* Tricase.

Conte, Gian Biagio. (1986) *The Rhetoric of Imitation: Genre and Poetic Memory in Virgil and Other Latin Poets.* Ithaca and New York.

———. (2007) *The Poetry of Pathos: Studies in Virgilian Epic.* Oxford, UK.

Eliot, T. S. (1957) "Virgil and the Christian World," in *T. S. Eliot on Poetry and Poets,* 134–48. London.

Hardie, Philip. (2014) *The Last Trojan Hero: A Cultural History of Virgil's Aeneid.* London and New York.

Harrison, Stephen J. (1990) "Some Views of the *Aeneid* in the Twentieth Century," in *Oxford Readings in Vergil's Aeneid,* ed. Stephen J. Harrison, 1–20. Oxford, UK.

Horsfall, Nicholas M. (1979) "Some Problems in the Aeneas Legend," *Classical Quarterly* 29:372–90.

———. (1986) "The Aeneas-Legend and the 'Aeneid.'" *Virgilius* 32:8–17.

Levitan, W. (1993) "Give Up the Beginning? Juno's Mindful Wrath (*Aeneid* 1.37)." *Liverpool Classical Monthly* 18:14.

O'Hara, James J. (1990) *Death and the Optimistic Prophecy in Vergil's* Aeneid. Princeton, NJ.

———. (2007) *Inconsistencies in Roman Epic.* Studies in Catullus, Lucretius, Vergil, Ovid and Lucan. Cambridge, UK.

Quint, David. (1993) *Epic and Empire: Politics and Generic Form from Virgil to Milton.* Princeton, NJ.

———. (2018) *Virgil's Double Cross.* Princeton, NJ.

Scafoglio, Giampiero. (2012) "The Betrayal of Aeneas." *Greek, Roman, and Byzantine Studies* 53:1–14.

Seider, Aaron M. (2013) *Memory in Vergil's Aeneid: Creating the Past.* Cambridge.

Shields, John C. (2001) *The American Aeneas: Classical Origins of the American Self.* Knoxville, TN.

Thomas, Richard. (1990) "Ideology, Influence, and Future Studies in the Georgics." *Vergilius* 36:64–70.

Ziolkowski, Jan, and Michael C. J. Putnam, eds. (2008) *The Virgilian Tradition: The First Fifteen Hundred Years.* New Haven, CT.

WORKS CITED IN NOTES

Carstairs-McCarthy, Adam. (2015) "Does Aeneas Violate the Truce in *Aeneid* 11?" *Classical Quarterly* 65:704–13.

Conington, John. *Commentary on Virgil's Aeneid.* Most easily accessible online through www.perseus.tufts.edu.

Hardie, Philip. (1986) *Virgil's Aeneid: Cosmos and Imperium.* Oxford, UK.

Hexter, Ralph. (1989–90) "What Was the Trojan Horse Made Of? Interpreting Vergil's *Aeneid*." *Yale Journal of Criticism* 3:109–31.

Johnson, Ralph. (1976) *Darkness Visible.* Berkeley, CA.

Knox, Bernard. (1950) "The Serpent and the Flame: The Imagery of the Second Book of the *Aeneid*." *American Journal of Philology* 71:379–400.

Lyne, R.O.A.M. (1992) *Further Voices in Vergil's Aeneid.* Oxford, UK.

O'Hara, James J. (1990) *Death and the Optimistic Prophecy in Vergil's* Aeneid. Princeton, NJ.

———. (2007) *Inconsistency in Roman Epic.* Cambridge, UK.

Parry, Adam. (1963) "The Two Voices of Virgil's *Aeneid*." *Arion* 2:66–80.

Putnam, Michael C. J. (1965) *The Poetry of the Aeneid.* Cambridge, MA.

GLOSSARY

This is a full glossary of all the proper nouns in the *Aeneid,* and it includes much contextual information. The line numbers are cued to the first appearance of the term in the text; entries without line numbers occur in the Latin, but not in the translation, where a more familiar term may have been used. I have reproduced Latin rather than English phonetics unless the name is already very familiar, e.g. Ceres is here rendered *see'-reez* although the Latin uses a hard C.

ABARIS (*a'-ba-ris*): A Rutulian in Turnus' forces who besieged the Trojan camp in Aeneas' absence; killed by Euryalus (9.344).

ABAS (*a'-bas*): (1) A captain in Aeneas' fleet whose ship suffers off the coast of Carthage (1.121); (2) A Greek warrior killed at Troy whose weapons Aeneas dedicates at Actium (3.286); (3) An Etruscan ally from Populona who aids Aeneas in the war against the Rutulians and the Latins (10.170).

ABELLA (*a-bel'-la*): A town in Campania known for its apple orchards (7.740).

ACAMAS (*a'-ka-mas*): A Greek, son of Theseus and brother of Demophoön; one of the soldiers who hides in the Trojan Horse (2.262).

ACARNIAN (*a-kar'-ni-an*): A Greek from Acarnania, a mountainous region in west central Greece (5.298).

ACCA (*ak'-ka*): An ally of the warrior queen Camilla (11.820).

ACESTA (*a-kes'-ta*): A city in western Sicily, originally named after Acestes, and later called Egesta, but now known as Segesta (5.718).

ACESTES (*a-kes'-teez*): A king of Sicily of Trojan lineage, who hosts Aeneas and his men after they depart from Carthage. During Anchises' funeral games, he wins the archery contest because his arrow bursts into a flaming omen (1.195).

ACHAEMENIDES (*a-kae-men'-i-deez*): A Greek crewman of Ulysses who is abandoned on the Cyclopes' island and later rescued by Aeneas and his men (3.614).

ACHATES (*a-kah'-teez*): A faithful companion of Aeneas (1.120).

ACHERON (*a'-ke-ron*): A river in the Underworld known as the "River of Grief." It can also be used as a referent for the Underworld generally (5.99).

ACHILLES (*a-kil'-eez*): The son of Peleus, king of Phthia, and Thetis, a goddess; the grandson of Aeacus and the father of Pyrrhus, killer of Priam. The commander of the Myrmidons, the greatest warrior in the Greek army at Troy, and the killer of many Trojans, including Hector. Killed by Paris after Apollo empowers him (1.31).

ACMON (*ak'-mon*): A Trojan crewman of Aeneas, son of Clytius, and brother of Menestheus (10.127).

ACOETES (*a-kee'-teez*): An Arcadian armor-bearer of King Evander and his son, Pallas, whom he treats as his own (11.30).

ACONTEUS (*a-kohn'-te-us*): A Latin who is thrown off his horse and killed by the Etruscan Tyrrhenus (11.612).

ACRAGAS (*a'-kra-gas*): The Greek name for a coastal city in southern Sicily, which Aeneas uses for direction as he sails around the island. Now known as Agrigento (3.703).

ACRISIUS (*ay-kree'-si-us*): A mythical king of Argos and father of Danaë (7.372).

ACRON (*a'-kron*): A Greek ally of Aeneas; killed by the Etruscan Mezentius (10.719).

ACTIUM (*ak'-ti-um*): A town and peninsula off the northwestern Greek coast; a place where Aeneas makes landfall on his way from Crete to Sicily, and the site where Octavian would defeat Antony and Cleopatra on September 2, 31 BCE (3.280).

ACTOR (*ak'-tor*): An ally of Aeneas who defends the Trojan camp in his absence (9.501).

ADAMASTUS (*a-da-mas'-tus*): An Ithacan; the father of Achaemenides, the soldier who is abandoned by Ulysses on the Cyclopes' island (3.614).

ADRASTUS (*a-dras'-tus*): A legendary king of Argos during the war of the Seven Against Thebes; father-in-law of Tydeus and Polynices (6.480).

ADRIATIC (*ay-dree-at'-ik*): The Adriatic Sea, bordering Italy's eastern coast (1.243).

AEACUS (*ay'-a-kus*): The father of Peleus, grandfather of Achilles.

AEAEA (*ay-ay'-a*): An island southeast of Rome; home of the goddess Circe (3.387).

AEGAEON (*ay-jee'-on*): The hundred-handed giant who warred against the gods as described in Hesiod's *Theogony*; referred to as Briareus by the gods (10.566).

AEGEAN (*ay-jee'-an*): The Aegean Sea, located between the Balkan peninsula and Asia Minor; also applied to the sea god, Neptune (3.74).

AENEAS (*ay-nee'-as*): The hero of the *Aeneid*. The son of Anchises and Venus, leader of the Dardanians, member of a royal house of Troy (1.92).

AEOLIA (*ay-oh'-li-a*): A group of islands off the northern coast of Sicily, named after their king, Aeolus (1.50).

AEOLUS (*ay'-o-lus*): (1) The king of the winds; father of Salmoneus and probably also of Misenus, a king of Elis (1.51); (2) The father of Clytius; a Trojan, killed by Turnus (9.774).

AEQUI FALISCI (*ay'-kwee fa-lees'-kee*): An Etrurian city, twenty-five miles due north of Rome, located on the western edge of the Tiber valley adjacent to modern Città Castellana (7.695).

AËTHON (*a-e'-thon*): The name of Pallas' warhorse; the name is also given to Hector's warhorse in the *Iliad* (11.89).

AETOLIAN (*ay-toh'-li-an*): A native of Aetolia, a region in northwestern Greece and the birthplace of Diomedes (11.308).

AFRICUS (*a'-free-kus*): The southwest wind (1.85).

AGAMEMNON (*a-ga-mem'-non*): The son of Atreus, brother of Menelaus, husband of Clytemnestra, and father of Orestes; the king of Mycenae and supreme commander of the Greek armies at Troy. Sacrificed his daughter, Iphigenia, to obtain favorable winds for the Greek fleet. Murdered by his wife and her lover, Aegisthus, on his return home. Avenged by his son at the order of Apollo (3.54).

AGATHYRSI (*a-ga-theer'-si*): People of Scythia who practiced the art of tattooing (4.146).

AGENOR (*a-ge'-nor*): The legendary ruler who founded Phoenicia, whose capital came to be Carthage. Progenitor of Dido (1.338).

AGIS (*a'-jis*): A Lycian ally of Aeneas; killed by the Etruscan Valerus (10.751).

AGRIPPA (*a-grip'-pa*): Marcus Vispanius Agrippa, a Roman statesman and military commander, close friend and son-in-law of Octavian; second in command at the battle of Actium (8.682).

AGYLLINES (*a-geel'-leyenz*): People of Agylla, an Etrurian city allied with Turnus (12.281).

AJAX (*ay'-jaks*): The son of Oïleus, or "Lesser Ajax." The commander of the Greek Locrians at Troy. Athena destroyed him and his entire fleet on their way home from Troy because he raped Cassandra in her temple (1.41).

ALBA (*al'-ba*): A city fifteen miles southeast of Rome, destined to be founded by Aeneas' son (1.271).

ALBAN (*al'-ban*): Of Alba (1.7).

ALBULA (*al'-bu-la*): The ancient name for the Tiber (8.332).

ALBUNEA (*al-bun'-e-a*): The site of a woodland and a fountain, or a sulfur spring, near Lavinium (7.83).

ALCANDER (*al-kan'-der*): A Trojan killed by Turnus while defending Aeneas' camp against the Rutulian attack (9.766).

ALCANOR (*al-ka'-nor*): (1) A Trojan, father of Pandarus and Bitias by the nymph Iaera (9.672); (2) The son of Phorcus and brother of Maeon; ally of Turnus; killed by Aeneas (10.338).

ALCATHOÜS (*al-ka'-tho-us*): A Trojan killed by the Etruscan Caedicus (10.747).

ALCIDES (*al-kee'-deez*): A patronymic meaning "descendant of Alcaeus," used especially when referring to Hercules. Name based on that of Alcaeus, son of Perseus, who was the father of Amphitryon and the grandfather of Hercules (10.321).

ALETES (*a-lee'-teez*): A Trojan who survives the shipwreck off the coast of Libya; ally and adviser to Aeneas (1.122).

ALLECTO (*al-lek'-to*): One of the three Furies, daughter of Pluto, with serpents growing from her head (7.324).

ALLIA (*al'-li-a*): A tributary of the Tiber River, on whose banks Rome suffered a disastrous defeat to the Gauls on July 19, 360 BCE; this defeat gave the river an ominous name from then onward (7.718).

ALMO (*al'-moh*): The first son of Tyrrhus, a Latin farmer; the first to be killed in battle between the Trojans and the Latins (7.532).

ALOEUS (*a-lee'-us*): A giant who fathered Otus and Ephiates, who are perhaps most infamously known for attempting to overthrow Jupiter. As punishment, they were confined in Tartarus (6.582).

ALPHEUS (*al-fe'-us*): A river and its personification, located in southern Greece (3.694).

ALSUS (*al'-sus*): A Rutulian shepherd who kills the Trojan Podalirius (12.304).

ALTARS: The name given to certain reefs in between Sicily and Africa that were a regular danger to mariners (1.109).

AMASENUS (*a-ma-se'-nus*): A Latian river located east of the Pontine marshes, which Vergil addresses as a god. Associated with allies of Turnus from Praeneste (7.685).

AMASTRUS (*a-mas'-trus*): A Trojan warrior killed by Camilla, the warrior queen (11.673).

AMATA (*a-mah'-ta*): The wife of King Latinus and mother of Lavinia; she kills herself, wrongly believing that Turnus has died in battle (7.343).

AMATHUS (*a'-ma-thus*): A city on the southern coast of the Isle of Cyprus, one of Venus' favorite places, and the location of a temple dedicated to her honor (10.51).

AMAZONS (*a'-ma-zons*): A storied nation of women, led by Penthesilea, who comes from somewhere in the north. Legend holds that they invaded Phrygia in Asia Minor (1.491).

AMITERNUM (*a-mi-ter'-num*): A Sabine city in central Italy whose contingent is allied with Turnus and led by Clausus (7.710).

AMPHITRYON (*am-fi'-tri-on*): The husband of Alcmena and a cuckold by Jupiter. The supposed father of Jupiter and Alcmena's son, Hercules.

AMSANCTUS (*am-sank'-tus*): A sulfurous lake and valley located east of Naples in the territory of the Samnites, known as a breathing vent for the God of Death and an entrance into the Underworld (7.565).

AMYCLAE (*a-mee'-klay*): A town in Latium, located between Caieta and Anxur and ruled by the Camers (10.564).

AMYCUS (*a'-mi-kus*): (1) A Trojan ally of Aeneas who is reported missing in the shipwreck off the Libyan coast (1.221); (2) A prominent Trojan during the Trojan War and later the king of Bebrycia in Bithynia, Asia Minor. A renowned boxer, he is ultimately defeated by Pollux (5.373); (3) A Trojan ally of Aeneas, expert hunter, and defender of the Trojan camp against the Rutulian attack; killed by Turnus (9.772); (4) A Trojan, father of Aeneas' ally Mimas, by the Trojan Theano; killed by Mezentius (10.703); (5) A Trojan, brother of Diores, killed by Turnus, perhaps the same person as Amycus (1) (12.509).

ANAGNIA (*a-nag'-ni-a*): A town in Latium, east of Rome, that provides troops allied with Turnus' forces (7.685).

ANCHEMOLUS (*an-ke'-mo-lus*): The son of Rhoteus, king of the Marsi; had incestuous relations with his stepmother and fled to Turnus' side; killed by Pallas (10.388).

ANCHISES (*an-kai'-seez*): A Trojan of royal blood, father of Aeneas by the goddess Venus, grandson of Assaracus, son of Capys, and second cousin of Priam. Dies on Sicily en route from Troy to Latium (1.618).

ANCUS (*an'-kus*): Ancus Martius, the fourth king of Rome, according to tradition (6.815).

ANDROGEOS (*an-dro'-ge-os*): (1) A Greek captain killed during the sack of Troy (2.371); (2) The son of Minos, King of Crete, who is murdered by the Athenians. As restitution, King Minos demanded the Athenians to offer seven boys and seven girls to the Minotaur annually, to be eaten (6.20).

ANDROMACHE (*an-dro'-ma-kee*): The wife of Hector, then of Pyrrhus, then of the prophet Helenus; daughter of Eetion and mother by Hector of Astyanax. After the fall of Troy she was given to Achilles' son Pyrrhus/Neoptolemus as a spoil of war. Once Pyrrhus was murdered by Agamemnon's son Orestes, she married Helenus, and together they ruled over the kingdom of Epirus (2.455).

ANGITIA (*an-gi'-ti-a*): A sorceress who is generally associated with snake charming; her name may in fact mean "snake." She is the sister of Medea and also possibly the same person. A revered goddess of the Marsi people (7.759).

ANIO (*a'-ni-o*): A tributary of the Tiber River that passes through the Sabine region of central Italy (7.683).

ANIUS (*a'-ni-us*): A priest of Apollo and the king of the island Delos, who shows a warm welcome to Aeneas and his crew upon their flight from Troy (3.80).

ANNA (*an'-na*): The sister and close companion of Dido. Sent by Dido to persuade Aeneas not to leave Carthage (4.9).

ANTAEUS (*an-tay'-us*): A Latin ally of Turnus; killed by Aeneas (10.562).

ANTANDROS (*an-tan'-dros*): A town in Asia Minor, near Troy, under the Phrygian Mount Ida, where Aeneas compiles his fleet (3.6).

ANTEMNAE (*an-tem'-nay*): A Sabine town in central Italy located at the junction of the Tiber and Anio rivers. Later conquered by Romulus (7.631).

ANTENOR (*an-te'-nor*): A nephew of Priam who escaped during the fall of Troy; reached Italy prior to Aeneas and founded Patavium, now known as Padua (1.242).

ANTHEUS (*an'-theus*): A Trojan, son of Sarpedon, and an ally of Aeneas. He captains one of the ships that is wrecked off the coast of Libya (1.182).

ANTIPHATES (*an-ti'-fa-teez*): A Trojan ally of Aeneas who is killed by Turnus (9.696).

ANTONY (*an'-toh-nee*): Marc Antony, historical figure (ca. 82–30 BCE). Assigned by the second Triumvir to rule the eastern Roman Empire. Fell in love with Cleopatra, the queen of Egypt, and staged a war against Octavian for mastery of Rome. Ultimately was defeated at Actium, where he and Cleopatra committed suicide (8.685).

ANTORES (*an-toh'-reez*): Hercules' aide, Evander's affiliate, and Aeneas' ally (10.778).

ANUBIS (*a-noo'-bis*): An Egyptian god who is typically portrayed as having a human's body and a dog's or a jackal's head. He is the protector of tombs and part of Cleopatra's retinue at Actium (8.699).

ANXUR (*anks'-oor*): (1) A coastal town of Volscians in southern Latium, also referred to as Terracina, and the site of a grove that Jupiter presided over; (2) A Rutulian ally of Turnus who is killed by Aeneas (10.546).

APENNINE (*ap'-e-nyne*): Of the mountain range in central Italy called the Apennines, referred to as Father by Italians (11.699).

APHIDNUS (*a-feed'-nus*): A Trojan who defended the Trojan camp in Aeneas' absence; killed by Turnus (9.703).

APOLLO (*a-pol'-loh*): One of the twelve Olympian gods, the god of light, the arts, and medicine. Son of Jupiter and Latona (Leto), twin brother of Diana, born at Delos. Allied with the Trojans during the Trojan War and, in Vergil's description, is said to have presided as Augustus' patron divinity over the battle at Actium. Also referred to as Phoebus (1.329).

AQUICULUS (*a-kwee'-cu-lus*): A Rutulian who attacks the Trojan camp in Aeneas' absence and is stopped at the gates (9.685).

ARAXES (*a-rak'-seez*): An Armenian river (8.728).

ARCADIANS (*ar-kay'-di-anz*): The occupants of Arcadia, a mountainous territory in the central Peloponnese and the birthplace of King Evander (5.299).

ARCENS (*ar'-kens*): A Sicilian whose unnamed son is killed fighting for Aeneas (9.581).

ARCETIUS (*ar-ket'-i-us*): A Rutulian who is killed by Mnestheus, one of Aeneas' captains (12.459).

ARCHIPPUS (*ar-kip'-pus*): A Marsian king whose troops were killed while aiding Turnus' forces (7.751).

ARCTURUS (*ark-too'-rus*): The brightest star in the constellation known as Bootes, or the Wagon. It rises in stormy weather, particularly during the spring rains (1.744).

ARDEA (*ar'-de-a*): The Rutulian capital. Located south of Rome, it is the birthplace and home of Turnus (7.412).

ARETHUSA (*a-re-thoo'-sa*): A fountain in Syracuse that is rumored to take its water from the Alpheus River in Greece. The legend holds that Alpheus, god of the river which is his namesake, fell in love with the nymph Arethusa when she was bathing in it one day, and chased her all the way to Italy (3.696).

ARGILETUM (*ar-gi-le'-tum*): A district of northern Rome that Vergil maintains was named after a certain Argus, one of Evander's guests, who was put to death here (*letum*) for treachery; regarding the name of the district, it is more likely that it was related to the word for clay, *argilla* (8.345).

ARGIVE (*ar'-give*): Greek, more specifically from Argos or favoring Argos (1.40).

ARGOS (*ar'-gos*): An area in the northern Peloponnese loved by Juno. Also used as a referent for the Greek people, in the form Argive (1.285).

ARGUS (*ar'-gus*): (1) The hundred-eyed monster commanded by Juno to guard the beautiful nymph Io after Juno turned her into a heifer (7.791); (2) Evander's guest who was killed at Argiletum for plotting treachery (8.346).

ARGYRIPA (*ar-gi'-ri-pa*): Also known as Arpi. City established by Diomedes in Apulia, the heel of the boot of Italy (11.246).

ARICIA (*a-ree'-ki-a*): Virbius' mother, a nymph (7.762).

ARISBA (*a-reez'-bah*): A city on the Troad peninsula north of Troy; in the *Iliad*, it is said to have sent additional forces to assist Troy (9.264).

ARPI (*ar'-pee*): A city in Apulia, also known as Argyripa (10.29).

ARRUNS (*ar'-runz*): An Etruscan, allied with Aeneas, who killed Camilla, the warrior virgin (11.759).

ASBYTES (*as-bye'-teez*): A Trojan who was killed by Turnus (12.362).

ASCANIUS (*as-kay'-ni-us*): Son of Aeneas and Creusa, grandson of Anchises. After the fall of Troy his name changed from Ilus to Iülus to establish him as a member of the house of Iulius and an ancestor of Julius Caesar and his adopted son Octavian/Augustus (1.267).

ASIA: In Latin, Asia Minor and its western coast. The name was originally that of a town in Lydia, a Bronze Age kingdom in western Asia Minor.

ASILAS (*a-see'-las*): (1) A Rutulian soldier who kills the Trojan Corynaeus (9.572); (2) An Etruscan general and oracle who comes to Aeneas' aid (10.175).

ASIUS (*a'-si-us*): A Trojan who defends Aeneas' camp (10.123).

ASSARACUS (*as-sa'-ra-kus*): An early king of Troy; brother of Ilus and Ganymede, son of Tros, father of Capys, grandfather of Anchises, and great-grandfather of Aeneas (1.284).

ASTYANAX (*as-tee'-a-naks*): The infant son of Hector by Andromache, his Greek name meaning "Lord of the City." Thrown to his death off the walls of Troy at Pyrrhus' command (2.457).

ASTYR (*a'-stir*): An Etruscan ally of Aeneas (10.181).

ATHENA (*a-thee'-na*): The warrior daughter of Jupiter, also known as Minerva, Pallas, and Tritonian (1.480).

ATHESIS (*a-thee'-sis*): The Adige, a river in northern Italy (9.680).

ATHOS (*a'-thohs*): A mountain in Macedonia located on a peninsula jutting into the northern Aegean Sea (12.701).

ATINA (*a-tee'-na*): An Italian town southeast of Rome whose people were Volscians; its name is unchanged today (7.630).

ATINAS (*a-tee'-nas*): A Rutulian leader, who was stopped with others of Turnus' allies at Aeneas' gates (11.869).

ATLAS (*at'-las*): Father of the Pleiades, the seven sisters who are Artemis' companions; the Titan condemned to support the world on his shoulders before being transformed into Mount Atlas in northern Africa, near Carthage (1.741).

ATREUS (*a'-trey-us*): Father of Agamemnon and Menelaus, and king of Mycenae; son of Pelops, grandson of Tantalus, and brother of Thyestes (1.457).

ATYS (*ah'-tis*): A young Trojan and close friend of Iülus. By making Atys the progenitor of the house of Atia, Vergil foretells the relationship between Augustus, whose mother was of the house of Atia, and Julius Caesar, who was of the house of Iulia (5.567).

AUFIDUS (*aw'-fi-dus*): A river in Apulia, on the heel of Italy's boot, that flows into the Adriatic (11.405).

AUGUSTUS (*aw-gus'-tus*): A title given to emperors of Rome. First awarded in 27 BCE to the first Roman emperor, Octavius Caesar, who was the grand-nephew of Julius Caesar and was adopted as his son (6.792).

AULESTES (*aw-les'-teez*): An Etruscan captain, ally of Aeneas; pilots the *Triton* (10.207).

AULIS (*aw'-lis*): A port in the strait between Euboea and the Greek mainland, where the Greek forces assembled before their departure to Troy.

Infamous for being the spot where Agamemnon sacrificed his daughter, Iphigenia, so as to receive favorable winds by which he and his fleet could sail to Troy (4.425).

AUNUS (*aw'-nus*): A Ligurian whose son is killed by Camilla (11.699).

AURORA (*aw-roh'-ra*): An alternative name for the goddess Dawn, mother of Memnon; she is also called Eoas.

AURUNCANS (*aw-run'-kanz*): Original inhabitants of the Italian peninsula, named after Aurunca, a town in Campania (7.207).

AUSONIAN (*aw-soh'-ni-an*): (1) Of southern Italy, which is also called Ausonia (7.328); (2) An inhabitant of Italy (not necessarily Ausonia) (9.639).

AUTOMEDON (*aw-tom'-e-don*): Achilles' armor-bearer and charioteer; in some versions, that of Pyrrhus as well (2.477).

AVENTINUS (*a-ven-tye'-nus*): (1) A son of Hercules by a priestess, Rhea, and the namesake of the hill (7.655); (2) The Aventine Hill, one of the seven hills in Rome (7.660).

AVERNUS (*a-ver'-nus*): A lake in a volcanic crater between Cumae and Naples; the name means "birdless" or "over which birds will not fly," because its fumes were thought fatal to birds. Located near a legendary entrance to the Underworld, it is often taken as a synonym for the Underworld (3.386).

BACCHANTS (*bak-kantz'*): The female worshippers of the god Bacchus (to the Greeks, Dionysus). They would roam the mountains and forests in rapturous devotion to their god's rites. Known in Greek as Maenads, literally "madwomen" (3.125).

BACCHUS (*bak'-kus*): The god of wine and pleasure, son of Jupiter and Semele. Also known as Lyaeus, Liber (both derivatives of the verb "liberate"), and in Greek, Dionysus (1.734).

BACTRA (*bak'-tra*): A remote region that existed in what is now northern Afghanistan. On the shield of Aeneas, it sends troops for Antony and Cleopatra (8.688).

BAIAE (*bay'-ay*): A resort town known for its hot springs, near modern-day Naples. It was the home to luxurious villas that were constructed on piers protruding over water (9.710).

BARCAN (*bar'-kan*): A member of the Libyan tribe that occupied the north African city of Barce (4.42).

BARCE (*bar'-ke*): Dido's attendant and the nurse of her deceased husband, Sychaeus (4.632).

BATULUM (*ba'-tu-lum*): A city in Campania, built by the Samnites, and allied with Turnus' forces (7.739).

BEARS: Ursa Major and Minor, also known as the Big and Little Dippers (1.744).

BEBRYCIAN (*be-bri'-ki-an*): A citizen of Bebrycia, a territory in northern Asia Minor (5.372).

BELLONA (*bel-lo'-na*): The Roman goddess of war and consort of Mars (7.319).

BELUS (*be'-lus*): (1) The father of Dido (1.621); (2) The father of the Tyrians (1.729); (3) The father of Palamedes and, Vergil claims, of Danaus and Aegyptus, and king of Egypt (2.82).

BENACUS (*be-na'-kus*): The personification of a lake in the region of Verona in northern Italy, where the Minicius River finds its source. Also called "Father Benacus" (10.205).

BERECYNTHIAN (*be-re-kin'-thi-an*): Of a rugged Phrygian territory, Asia Minor, known for being holy to the "Great Mother" of the gods, Cybele.

BEROË (*be'-roh-e*): The aged wife of Doryclus the Rutulian, who is impersonated by Iris during one of Juno's attempts to wipe out Aeneas' troops (5.620).

BITIAS (*bi'-tee-as*): (1) A nobleman and courtier of Dido (1.738); (2) A Trojan ally of Aeneas, brother of Pandarus, both killed by Turnus (9.672).

BOLA (*bo'-la*): A future town in Latium (6.775).

BOREAS (*bo-re´-as*): The god of the north wind. He is often imagined as coming out of Thrace (10.350).

BRIAREUS (*bri-ar´-yoos*): The name used by the gods for the hundred-handed giant who warred against them during the titanomachy. Known as Aegaeon by mortals. Known in Greek as Hecatonchires, literally "hundred-handed ones" (6.287).

BRONTES (*bron´-teez*): A Cyclops (8.424).

BRUTUS (*broo´-tus*): Here, Lucius Junius Brutus, the first consul of the Roman Republic. He expelled the Tarquins, Rome's former kings, and later killed his sons after they tried to lead an insurrection on behalf of the Tarquins (6.818).

BUTES (*boo´-teez*): (1) A boastful relative of Amycus who was once defeated in a boxing match by Dares (5.371); (2) Anchises' armor-bearer, whom Aeneas asks to protect his son, Ascanius (9.646); (3) A Trojan, killed by Camilla (11.691).

BUTHROTUM (*boo-throh´-tum*): A city on the coast of Epirus built by Andromache and Helenus (3.293).

BYRSA (*beer´-sa*): A walled citadel that stood above Carthage, on a hill of the same name. According to legend, Dido purchased the hill the citadel stood on from the Libyans by striking a deal to purchase as much land as could be covered by a single bull's hide. Dido cut the bull's hide into strips, narrow enough so that they could ring the hill. The hill's name, up until that point Borsa, became the Greek Byrsa, meaning "ox-hide" (1.367).

CACUS (*ka´-kus*): The fire-breathing, monster son of Vulcan, who terrorized the country around the Aventine Hill in Pallanteum until he was killed by Hercules. The anniversary of his death marks the occasion for annual celebrations among the inhabitants of Pallanteum. Name means "the Bad" in Greek (8.195).

CAECULUS (*kay´-ku-lus*): The son of Vulcan, founder of the city Praeneste, and an ally of Turnus. Legend holds that his mother conceived him from a spark that flew up from the hearth (7.678).

CAEDICUS (*kay'-di-kus*): (1) A Latin, a friend and guest of Remulus (9.360); (2) An Etruscan ally of Mezentius (10.747).

CAENEUS (*kay'-nyoos*): The male name of a Thessalian nymph transfigured by Neptune into a man, who was ultimately restored to being a woman (6.448); (2) An Etruscan soldier in Mezentius' unit who killed Ortygias and was killed by Turnus (9.573).

CAERE (*kay'-re*): An Etruscan city, known formerly as Agylla and now as Cervetri. Located on the northwest coast of Rome, its banks were a place of worship to Silvanus, god of forests, and the source of soldiers led by Lausus (7.652).

CAICUS (*ka-ee'-kus*): A Trojan ally of Aeneas whose ship is briefly missing in the storm off the Libyan coast (1.183).

CAIETA (*kay-ee'-ta*): Port on the western coast of Italy about halfway between Rome and Naples, named for Aeneas' nurse. It is now known as Gaeta (6.900).

CALCHAS (*kal'-kas*): A Greek prophet important in the Trojan War (2.100).

CALES (*ka'-leez*): The site of a temple of Juno; this town, now called Calvi, sent troops to serve Turnus (7.727).

CALLIOPE (*kal-eye'-o-pee*): The muse of epic poetry and the leader of the nine muses. Vergil invokes her for assistance in his craft, but only after invoking Erato in Book 7 (9.525).

CALYBE (*ka'-li-be*): An aged Rutulian priestess at Juno's Rutulian temple. The fury Allecto imitates her to rouse Turnus to engage in war (7.419).

CALYDON (*ka'-li-don*): An Aetolian city and the birthplace of the chieftain Diomedes (7.306).

CAMERINA (*ka-me-ree'-na*): A city and marsh on the southern coast of Sicily. The marshland was said to have been guarded by the Fates as protection against an attack on the city (3.700).

CAMERS (*ka'-mers*): The son of the Latin commander Volcens, and a comrade of Turnus; killed by Aeneas (10.562).

CAMILLA (*ka-mil'-la*): A Volscian female commander and ally of Turnus (7.803).

CAMILLUS (*ka-mil'-lus*): Marcus Furius Camillus; took back Rome from the Gauls in 390 BCE (6.825).

CAMPANIAN (*kam-pan'-yan*): A citizen of Campania, a region in western central Italy surrounding Naples. Its ancient capital was Capua, whose name, Vergil claims, was derived from that of Aeneas' ally Capys.

CAPENA (*ka-pen'-a*): A town in Etruria, about twenty miles north of Rome; it sends troops to Turnus' aid (7.697).

CAPHEREUS (*ka-fer'-yoos*): A cape on the eastern coast of Euboea where the Greeks were shipwrecked when heading home from Troy (11.261).

CAPITOL (*ka'-pee-tol*): A reference to the Capitoline Hill in Rome, on which stood the temple of Jupiter Optimus Maximus, the center of the Roman state religion and the destination of triumphal marches (6.837).

CAPREAE (*ka'-pre-ay*): An island off the coast of Italy, near Naples, that supplied troops to Turnus. Modern-day Capri (7.736).

CAPYS (*ka'-pis*): (1) A Trojan ally of Aeneas and killer of Privernus. Aeneas and he are reunited after the storm off the coast of Euboea. Also mentioned as the founder and namesake of Capua (1.182); (2) A Trojan who urges against admitting the Trojan Horse (2.35); (3) A king of Alba Longa of whom Anchises foretells to Aeneas when listing their descendants (6.768).

CARIANS (*ka'-ri-anz*): A people from western Asia Minor, inhabitants of Caria, a region down the coast from and allied with Troy.

CARINAE (*ka-reen'-ay*): An aristocratic district in future Rome, just north of the Forum (8.361).

CARMENTAL (*kar-men'-tal*) GATE: One of the gates into ancient Rome, named after the nymph Carmentis (8.338).

CARMENTIS (*kar-men'-tis*): A nymph, the mother of Evander by Mercury (8.336).

CARPATHIAN (*kar-pa'-thi-an*): A citizen of Carpathus, an Aegean island between Crete and Rhodes (5.594).

CARTHAGE (*kar'-thaj*): A city in northern Libya on the coast of the Mediterranean. It maintained a long-standing rivalry with Rome that developed into the three Punic Wars fought between 264 and 146 BCE. Vergil traces the genealogy of this conflict to Aeneas' betrayal of the city's founder, Dido (1.14).

CASMILLA (*kas-mil'-la*): The wife of Metabus and mother of Camilla (11.543).

CASPERIA (*ka-sper'-i-a*): A town in the Sabine region of Italy that supplies troops to Turnus (7.714).

CASPIAN (*kas'-pi-an*): The area surrounding the Caspian Sea; includes the modern-day countries of Russia, Kazakhstan, and Iran, among others (4.367).

CASSANDRA (*kas-san'-dra*): The daughter of Priam and sister of Hector; although she foretold events accurately, nothing she said would ever be believed because she rejected Apollo, who gave her the gift of prophecy (2.246).

CASTOR (*kas'-tor*): A Trojan ally of Aeneas who held the first line of defense at the camp when Aeneas was away (10.125).

CASTRUM INUÏ (*kas'-trum i'-nuï*): A town in the region of Latium; the word *castrum* means "military camp" (6.775).

CATILINE (*ka'-ti-line*): Lucius Sergius Catilina. A Roman senator who tried to overthrow the government in 63 BCE. His conspiracy was thwarted by Cicero, after which he fled Rome and died in battle in 62 (8.668).

CATILLUS (*ka-til'-us*): The brother of Tiburtus and twin brother of Coras. He and his brothers founded Tibur, a town in central Italy that supplied troops to Turnus (7.672).

CATO (*ka'-toh*): (1) Marcus Porcius Cato (the Elder) (234 BCE–149 BCE), a statesman of the Roman Republic, known for his strong moral conviction and for advocating the destruction of Carthage (6.841);

(2) Marcus Porcius Cato (the Younger) (95 BCE–46 BCE), great-grandson of Cato the Elder and opponent of Caesar. He committed suicide rather than be defeated by Caesar (8.671).

CAUCASUS (*kaw'-ka-sus*): A mountain range near the Caspian Sea, where Prometheus was famously chained while an eagle eternally devoured his liver (4.366).

CAULON (*kaw'-lon*): A city on the southwestern Italian coast (3.553).

CAYSTER (*kay'-ster*): A river in Lydia, the western region of Asia Minor, that flows into the Aegean Sea. Now known as the Küçükmenderes River in modern-day Turkey (7.701).

CELAENO (*se-lay'-noh*): The leader of the Harpies. She gives Aeneas prophecies of his upcoming journeys when he encounters her at Strophades (3.211).

CELEMNA (*se-lem'-na*): A town in Campania that supplies troops to Turnus (7.739).

CENTAUR (*sen'-tawr*): The name of the ship that Sergestus captains in the ship-race at Anchises' funeral games. It finishes in fourth place out of four (5.122).

CENTAURS (*sen'-tawrz*): A race of wild beings that are half man and half horse, who resided near Mount Pelion in central Greece. They are descendants of Ixion, who, in his lust for Juno, is tricked by Jupiter into copulating with a cloud (6.286).

CERAUNIA (*ke-raw'-ni-a*): A region on the northwestern coast of Epirus, which itself lies on the western coast of Greece near modern Albania. Greek for "thunder-headlands," it was a notoriously dangerous place for ships to sail, but also along the shortest route to Italy (3.505).

CERBERUS (*ker'-ber-us*): The three-headed dog that guards the gates of the Underworld. As his twelfth and final labor, Hercules brought Cerberus to the upper world and back down again (6.417).

CERES (*see'-reez*): Known to the Greeks as Demeter. Mother of Proserpina (Persephone). The goddess of agriculture, the grain lands, and their products (and the etymological root of the English word "cereal") (1.713).

CETHEGUS (*ke-the'-gus*): A Rutulian soldier killed by Aeneas (12.514).

CHALCIS (*khal'-kis*): A city on the island of Euboea, which is itself off the eastern coast of the Greek mainland. Cumae was a colony founded by citizens of this city (6.17).

CHAONIA (*kay-oh'-nia*): A region in Epirus where Jupiter's oracle, Dodona, was located (3.292).

CHAOS (*kay'-os*): According to Hesiod, the original state from which the Earth originated. For Vergil, Chaos is personified as the father of Erebus, "darkness," and Nox, "night" (4.510).

CHARON (*ka'-ron*): Son of Erebus and Nox, he is the god in Hades who ferries dead souls across the river Styx (6.298).

CHARYBDIS (*ka'-rib-dis*): A monstrous whirlpool on the Sicilian side of the Strait of Messina between Italy and Sicily (3.420).

CHIMAERA (*kye-may'-ra*): The name of the ship that Gyas captains at Anchises' funeral games. It finishes in third out of fourth place (5.118).

CHIMAERA: A fire-breathing monster that was part lion, part serpent, part goat; watches over the entrance to the Underworld. There is an awe-inspiring representation of it on Turnus' helmet (6.288).

CHLOREUS (*kloh'-ryoos*): A Trojan priest of Cybele. He was pursued by Camilla, until she was killed by Arruns. Chloreus was killed by Turnus (11.768).

CHROMIS (*kroh'-mis*): A Trojan killed by Camilla when she throws a spear at him from a distance (11.676).

CIMINUS (*ki'-mi-nus*): A region in Etruria in northwestern Italy containing a lake surrounded by hills. Now Lago di Ronciglione (7.696).

CIRCE (*sir'-see*): The goddess of the island Aeaea who turned Ulysses' men into pigs before he came and rescued them (3.387).

CISSEUS (*kis'-syoos*): (1) The king of Thrace, father of Hecuba, and father-in-law of Priam (5.536); (2) A Latin warrior, the son of Hercules' companion Melampus; killed by Aeneas (10.318).

CITHAERON (*ki-thay'-ron*): A mountain in central Greece, where wild festivals for Bacchus were held (4.303).

CLARUS (*kla'-rus*): A Lycian, brother of Sarpedon and ally of Aeneas (10.127).

CLAUDIAN (*klaw'-di-an*): A member of the Roman *gens* (family) that descended from Clausus (7.707).

CLAUSUS (*klaw'-sus*): A Sabine commander who fights for Turnus (7.706).

CLOANTHUS (*kloh-an'-thus*): A Trojan ally of Aeneas, who despite being lost in the storm off Carthage eventually reunites with his fellows and pilots the ship *Scylla* to victory at Anchises' funeral games (1.222).

CLOELIA (*klee'-li-a*): A Roman girl praised in Livy for bravely escaping her captor Porsenna by swimming all the way across the Tiber (8.651).

CLONIUS (*klo'-ni-us*): (1) A Trojan, killed by Turnus (9.575); (2) A different Trojan, killed by Messapus (10.749).

CLONUS (*klo'-nus*): The son of Eurytus, the skilled metalworker who decorated the belt that was stripped off Pallas' dead body by Turnus (10.499).

CLUENTIUS (*klu-en'-ti-us*): A Roman family, progeny of Cloanthus (5.123).

CLUSIUM (*kloo'-si-um*): One of the twelve main cities in Etruria, located on the banks of the river Clanis (10.168).

CLYTIUS (*kli'-ti-us*): (1) A Trojan, son of Aeolus; killed by Turnus (9.774); (2) The father of Menestheus and Acmon, two comrades of Aeneas (10.128); (3) A Rutulian comrade of Turnus, and a warrior who loves Cydon, who is protected by his brothers from Aeneas (10.325); (4) A Trojan, father of Euneus, who is killed by Camilla; perhaps identical with Clytius (2) (11.666).

CNOSSUS (*knos'-sus*): The capital city of Crete, the location of both the god Minos and the Labyrinth.

COCLES (*koh'-kleez*): Publius Horatius Cocles, a famous Roman who is most well known for containing, along with two others, Lars Porsenna's invasion of Rome (509 BCE) long enough for his comrades to cut down the bridge and prevent enemy access of Rome (8.650).

COCYTUS (*koh-kee'-tus*): One of the rivers of the Underworld; means "lamentation" in Greek (6.132).

COEUS (*kee'-us*): The son of Mother Earth, one of the Titans, brother of Enceladus and Rumor, father of Latona (4.179).

COLLATIA (*kol-la'-ti-a*): A Sabine town near Rome, built by the progeny of Silvius Aeneas, the grandson or great-grandson of the *Aeneid*'s hero (6.774).

CORA (*ko'-ra*): A town in Latium, in central Italy, built southeast of Rome in the Volscian mountain range by the progeny of Silvius Aeneas, the grandson or great-grandson of the *Aeneid*'s hero (6.776).

CORAS (*ko'-ras*): Brother of Tiburtus and twin of Catillus. A founder of Tibur along with his two brothers, he also fought for Turnus (7.672).

CORINTH (*ko'-rinth*): A city in central Greece that gives its name to the strip of land on which it is situated. Conquered and destroyed in 146 BCE by Lucius Mummius (6.836).

COROEBUS (*ko-ree'-bus*): The Phrygian fiancé of Priam's daughter Cassandra; he is killed while fighting alongside Aeneas during the sack of Troy (2.342).

CORYBANTS (*ko-ri-ban'-tez*): The eunuch priests who honored the "Great Mother," Cybele, at Mount Cybelus; they were famous for their euphoric rituals and dances (3.112).

CORYNAEUS (*ko-ri-nay'-us*): (1) A Trojan priest, killed by Asilas, a Rutulian (6.227); (2) Another Trojan, who kills the Rutulian Ebysus (12.298).

CORYTHUS (*ko'-ri-thus*): (1) An ancient town in Etruria and the reputed birthplace of the Trojan progenitor Dardanus (3.170); (2) The founder of that Etruscan town (9.11).

COSAE (*ko'-say*): An Etruscan coastal city that sends troops to fight for Aeneas (10.168).

COSSUS (*kos'-sus*): Aulus Cornelius Cossus, a Roman general who is most well known for being one of the three Roman generals to have ever won the "commander's spoils" by killing the enemy commander and stealing his armor; killed Tolumnius the Etruscan general in 437 BCE (the only others to hold this honor were Romulus and Marcellus) (6.841).

CRETAN (*kree'-tan*): Of Crete (3.117).

CRETE (*kreet*): The largest Aegean island, south of the Peloponnese, and the kingdom of Idomeneus (3.104).

CRETHEUS (*kre'-thyoos*): (1) A Trojan singer, soldier, and warrior-lord who defended Aeneas' camp against the Rutulians but was killed by Turnus (9.774); (2) A Greek soldier fighting for Troy, who was killed by Turnus (12.537).

CREUSA (*kre-oo'-sa*): The daughter of Priam, first wife of Aeneas, mother of Ascanius. Killed in the fall of Troy (2.562).

CRINISUS (*kri-nee'-sus*): A Sicilian river and the god that rules it. Sometimes referred to as Crimisus (5.38).

CRUSTUMERIUM (*kroos-too-mer'-i-um*): Ancient Sabine town near Rome that supplied weapons for the Latin troops (7.631).

CUMAE (*koo'-may*): An Italian town located close to Naples. Founded by Greeks who moved from the Euboean city of Chalcis. It was also the home of the Sibyl, Aeneas' guide to the Underworld, the entrance to which was close by (3.441).

CUNARUS (*ku'-na-rus*): The son of Cycnus, brother of Cupavo, a Ligurian ally of Aeneas (10.185).

CUPAVO (*ku-pa'-vo*): The son of Cycnus, brother of Cunarus; a Ligurian commander and ally of Aeneas. Stood at the helm of the *Centaur* on her quests (10.186).

CUPENCUS (*ku-pen'-kus*): A Rutulian priest killed by Aeneas during battle (12.539).

CUPID (*kyoo'-pid*): The son of Venus; god of love, here always called Amor (1.659).

CURES (*koo'-rez*): The capital of the Sabine region near Rome. Ruled by king Tatius. Also boasted the inhabitance of Numa Pompilius, the second king of Rome and its famous law giver (6.810).

CURETES (*koo-re'-teez*): A group who resided on Crete and would later become priests of Jupiter. They attained their status as priests by hiding the infant Jupiter from his raging father, Saturn, who wanted to eat him (3.131).

CYBELE (*ki-bee'-le*): Known in Greek legend as Rhea, she was considered the Great Mother (Magna Mater) of the gods (8.784).

CYCLADES (*si'-cla-deez*): A group of islands in the Aegean that circumscribe Delos (3.127).

CYCLOPES (*sye'-klop-eez*): One-eyed monsters who live on the island of Sicily and eat human beings; Aeneas' encounter with them acts as a sequel to Ulysses' in the *Odyssey*, when Ulysses tricks the Cyclops Polyphemus and blinds him. The Cyclopes also work in Vulcan's foundry, where they constructed Aeneas' shield (3.569).

CYCNUS (*keek'-nus*): Legendary king of Liguria, father of Cupavo, lover of Phaëthon (10.187).

CYDON (*see'-don*): A Latin who fights for Turnus (10.324).

CYLLENE (*keel-le'-ne*): Mountain in Arcadia; Mercury's birthplace, sacred to him (4.256).

CYMODOCEA (*kee-mo-do-ke'-a*): A sea-nymph, daughter of Nereus, in Neptune's entourage who is known for her gifted ability of speech (10.225).

CYMOTHOE (*kee-mo'-tho-e*): A sea-nymph who works with Triton to pull Trojan ships off the rocks (1.144).

CYNTHUS (*kin'-thus*): A mountain on the island of Delos, where both Apollo and Diana were born; a favorite stomping ground for both of them (1.498).

CYPRUS (*sye'-prus*): An island in the Mediterranean that Venus made her home and called sacred. It is the same island as the modern Cyprus (1.622).

CYTHERA (*ki-the'-ra*): An island off the southeastern coast of the Peloponnese that is said to be Aphrodite's birthplace (1.681).

CYTHEREA (*ki-the'-re-a*): Another name for Aphrodite.

DAEDALUS (*day'-da-lus*): The brilliant artifex who built the Labyrinth for Minos, the king of Crete. When imprisoned on Crete with his son Icarus, he made his escape by constructing wings made of feathers affixed to wooden beams with wax (6.14).

DAHAE (*da'-hay*): A nomadic Scythian people who roam east of the Caspian (8.728).

DANAÄNS (*da'-na-ans*): A name for the Greeks which comes from Danos, the ancient king of Argos (2.398).

DANAË (*da'-na-ee*): The daughter and only child of Acrisius, king of Argos; the mother, by Jupiter, of Perseus. Servius says that her father imprisoned her because of a prophecy that said he would die by the hand of his daughter's son. While she was imprisoned, Jupiter visited her and they had a child, Perseus. Her father put her and the baby into a wooden chest and tossed it into the sea. They washed ashore on the coast of Italy at Ardea, the city she founded (7.409).

DARDANIAN (*dar-day'-ni-an*): Of the kingdom of Dardanus (4.366).

DARDANUS (*dar'-da-nus*): The son of Zeus and Electra, Atlas' daughter. Ancestor of Priam and the kings of Troy, as well as of Aeneas. Because of him the Trojans are sometimes called Dardanians or Dardans (3.94).

DARES (*da'-rez*): A Trojan boxer who was bested by Entellus at Anchises' funeral games; killed by Turnus (5.368).

DAUCUS (*daw'-kus*): The father of the twins Thymber and Larides, who were both killed by Pallas (3) (10.390).

DAUNUS (*daw'-nus*): According to legend, the king of Daunia, an Apulian region; father of Turnus (10.616).

DECII (*de'-ki-ee*): Roman family of which two members, father and son, share the name Publius Decius Mus. The two were heroes of the Roman republic, the father sacrificing himself at the time of the Latin War in 340 BCE at the battle of Veseris, and the son at the battle of Sentinum in 295 BCE, fighting against the Samnites (6.824).

DEIOPEA (*de-i-o-pe'-a*): A sea-nymph of Juno's whom she offers as a bribe to Aeolus to wipe out Aeneas' fleet with a storm as they sail near the Libyan coast (1.72).

DEIPHOBE (*de-i'-fo-bee*): The Cumaean Sibyl, daughter of Glaucus, who directs Aeneas through the Underworld (6.35).

DEIPHOBUS (*de-i'-fo-bus*): A son of Priam, leader of the Trojans after the death of Hector. Married Helen after Hector's death. Killed by Menelaus during the fall of Troy; Aeneas encounters his spirit in the Underworld (2.310).

DELOS (*de'-los*): An island in the Aegean that drifted until Latona gave birth there to Diana and Apollo (3.124).

DEMODOCUS (*de-mo'-do-kus*): An ally of Aeneas, killed by Halaesus (10.413).

DEMOLEOS (*de-mo'-le-os*): A Greek whose armor Aeneas strips from his dead body and offers as a prize for second place in the ship-race at Anchises' funeral games (5.260).

DEMOPHOÖN (*de-mo'-fo-on*): A Trojan killed by Camilla from close proximity (11.675).

DERCENNUS (*der-ke'-nus*): An ancient king of Laurentum, whose tomb Opis, Diana's messenger, uses as a lookout point (11.851).

DIANA (*dye-an'-a*): Also known as Artemis, daughter of Latona and Jupiter, twin sister of Apollo, virgin goddess of hunting and the moon (1.498).

DICTE (*dik'-te*): A mountain in eastern Crete. Jupiter's birthplace; as a baby, he was hidden from his father, Saturn, in its caves.

DIDO (*dye´-doh*): An exile of Phoenicia, founder of Carthage, initially the wife of Sychaeus, then, after his death, the lover of Aeneas. She ultimately commits suicide upon his departure from Carthage (1.299).

DIDYMAÖN (*di-di-may´-on*): A metalsmith (5.359).

DINDYMA (*din´-di-ma*): A holy Phrygian mountain, home of the Great Mother, Cybele; a place of worship for her followers (9.618).

DIOMEDES (*deye-o-mee´-deez*): A Greek, son of Tydeus, king of Argos, founder of the Apulian city Argyripa (1.96).

DIONE (*di-oh´-ne*): A goddess, mother of Venus.

DIORES (*di-oh´-reez*): A Trojan, brother of Amycus; places third in the running race at the funeral games of Anchises; killed by Turnus (5.297).

DIOXIPPUS (*di-oks-ip´-us*): A Trojan, killed by Turnus (9.574).

DIS: The god of the Underworld and husband of Persephone (4.703).

DODONA (*doh-doh´-na*): The location of an oracle of Zeus in Epirus (3.465).

DOG STAR: Orion's Dog, whose appearance is interpreted as a "fatal sign" since it portends plague and kills crops (3.141).

DOLICHAON (*doh-li-kay´-on*): A Trojan, father of Hebrus, killed by Mezentius (10.696).

DOLON (*do´-lon*): A Trojan scout, son of Eumedes; killed by Diomedes while trying to spy on the Greek camp (12.347).

DOLOPIAN (*do-lo´-pi-an*): Of Phthia, the home of Achilles, and a region of southern Thessaly (2.7).

DONUSA (*do-noo´-sa*): One of the central Cyclades islands; on the southeastern side of Delos, in the Aegean (3.125).

DORIC (*do´-rik*) : Of the Dorians, a Greek people after whom a dialect of ancient Greek was named (2.28).

DORYCLUS (*do-ree´-klus*): A Rutulian, husband of Beroë (5.620).

DOTO (*do´-toh*): A sea-nymph, daughter of Nereus (9.102).

DRANCES (*dran'-seez*): A Rutulian who openly criticizes Turnus (11.122).

DREPANUM (*dre'-pa-num*): The town on the northwest coast of Sicily where Anchises died. Now called Trapani (3.707).

DRUSI (*droo'-zee*): A patrician family of Rome from which many great generals were born (6.824).

DRYOPE (*dri'-o-pe*): A wood-nymph, mother by Faunus of Tarquitus, a Rutulian who is killed by Aeneas (10.551).

DRYOPIANS (*dri-oh'-pi-anz*): A people who have long been said to reside in northern Greece on the flanks of Mount Parnassus (4.147).

DRYOPS (*dri'-ops*): A Trojan from Cures, killed by Clausus (10.346).

DULICHIUM (*doo-li'-ki-um*): An island in the Ionian Sea, near Ithaca (3.271).

DYMAS (*di'-mas*): A Trojan, Aeneas' aide. Killed unintentionally by other Trojans in the midst of Troy's destruction (2.340).

EARTH: The earth personified as a goddess (4.166).

EBYSUS (*e'-bi-sus*): A Rutulian killed by Corynaeus (12.299).

EDONIAN (*e-doh'-nee-an*): A member of the Edoni, a Thracian tribe who lived on the Strymon.

EGERIA (*e-ge'-ri-a*): Latin water-nymph, whose healing grove shielded Hippolytus (7.763).

EGYPT: The country in north Africa, a synonym for Cleopatra, the Egyptian queen. Sometimes reckoned by the ancients as belonging to Asia (8.687).

ELEAN (*e-lee'-an*): From Elis, a region in the northwest Peloponnese, home of the Epeans. Its chief city, Olympia, held the Olympic games.

ELECTRA (*e-lek'-tra*): One of the daughters of Atlas; the sister of Maia, mother by Jupiter of Dardanus, founder of Troy (8.135).

ELISSA (*e-lis'-sa*): Another name for Dido.

ELYSIUM (*e-li'-zi-um*): A region in the Underworld reserved for the righteous. The location where Aeneas reunites with his father's spirit (5.734).

EMATHION (*e-ma'-thi-on*): A Trojan killed by Liger (9.571).

ENCELADUS (*en-kel'-a-dus*): The Giant child of Gaia. One of those who rebelled against Jupiter's rule and was struck down by him with a lightning bolt and buried underneath Mount Etna as eternal punishment (3.578).

ENTELLUS (*en-tel'-lus*): A Sicilian boxing champion who bests Dares during Anchises' funeral games (5.387).

EOAS (*e'-os*): Dawn, goddess of the morning, daughter of Hyperion, wife of Tithonus, and mother by Tithonus of Memnon.

EPEUS (*e-pe'-us*): A Greek, builder of the Trojan Horse, and one of the troops concealed in it (2.265).

EPIRUS (*e-pye'-rus*): A mountainous region of northwestern Greece by the Adriatic coast (3.292).

EPULO (*e'-pu-lo*): A Rutulian killed by Achates (12.460).

EPYTIDES (*e-pi-tye'-deez*): A Trojan; guardian and companion of Ascanius (5.546). .

EPYTUS (*e'-pi-tus*): A Trojan who fights alongside Aeneas at the fall of Troy (2.339).

ERATO (*e'-ra-toh*): A muse associated with love poetry. It has been suggested that her name was invoked in Book 7 because the second half of the *Aeneid* deals with a war kindled by Lavinia's suitors (7.37).

EREBUS (*e'-re-bus*): A child of Chaos. Father, by his sister Night, of Day. God of primeval darkness; also a name for the lower world (4.510).

ERETUM (*e-re'-tum*): An ancient Sabine city on the east bank of the Tiber, north of Rome. Its troops are under the command of Clausus (7.711).

ERICHAETES (*e-ri-kay'-teez*): A Trojan son of Lycaon, killed by Messapus (10.750).

ERIDANUS (*e-ri'-da-nus*): A legendary river thought to flow from the Elysian fields to the living world. Commonly identified as the Po (6.658).

ERIPHYLE (*e-ri-fee'-lee*): The wife of the prophet Amphiaraus, king of Argos. In the war of the Seven Against Thebes, she accepted a bribe to plot to betray her husband, resulting in his death. She was killed by her son Alcmaeon (6.445).

ERULUS (*e'-ru-lus*): The king of Praeneste, son of Feronia, who gave him three lives, which forced Evander to slay him three times (8.563).

ERYMANTHUS (*e-ri-man'-thus*): A mountain range in Arcadia in southern Greece, and the home of a legendary boar that Hercules killed while he was performing his Twelve Labors (5.449).

ERYMAS (*e'-ri-mas*): A Trojan ally of Aeneas, killed by Turnus (9.702).

ERYX (*e'-riks*): (1) A mountain and city on the northwestern coast of Sicily, with a temple of Venus (1.570); (2) The king of Sicily, son of Venus and Butes, half brother of Aeneas. Although a prizewinning boxer, he was killed by Hercules in a famous match (5.392).

ETHIOPIA: A country south of Egypt in northeastern Africa, and one of Neptune's favorite stomping grounds (4.480).

ETNA (*et'-na*): A volcano in eastern Sicily; home of the Cyclopes (3.554).

ETRURIA (*e-troo'-ri-a*): An Italian region north of Rome, now Tuscany; home of the Etruscans (8.65).

ETRUSCAN (*e-trus'-kan*): Of the people of Tuscany who originally came from Lydia in Asia Minor; synonymous with Tuscan (7.43).

EUBOEAN (*yoo-bee'-an*): Of Euboea, a large Aegean island lying just east of Greece; *see* Cumae.

EUMEDES (*yoo-me'-deez*): A Trojan, son of Dolon (12.346).

EUMELUS (*yoo-me'-lus*): A Trojan companion who notifies the Trojans that their ships are ablaze (5.664).

EUNAEUS (*yoo-nay'-us*): A Trojan, son of Clytius, killed by Camilla (11.666).

EUPHRATES (*yoo-fray'-teez*): Along with the Tigris, one of the two rivers of the Fertile Crescent in Asia Minor, later fixed as the easternmost boundary of the Roman Empire (8.726).

EUROTAS (*yoo-roh'-tas*): A river running through Lacedaemon on which Sparta stood (1.498).

EURUS (*yoo'-rus*): The southeast wind (1.84).

EURYALUS (*yoo-ree'-a-lus*): A Trojan, close friend of Nisus, ally of Aeneas, winner of the footrace at the funeral games of Anchises; killed by the Volscians (5.294).

EURYPYLUS (*yoo-ri'-pi-lus*): A Greek delegate to Apollo's oracle (2.114).

EURYSTHEUS (*yoo-ris'-thyoos*): A king of Mycenae, grandson of Perseus. He ordered Hercules to perform his Twelve Labors (8.292).

EURYTION (*yoo-ri'-ti-on*): A Trojan, son or brother of the archer Pandarus, from Lycia. He comes runner-up in the archery contest because while he shot the target dove, the arrow of the victor, Acestes, burst into a flaming omen (5.495).

EURYTUS (*yoo'-ri-tus*): The father of the goldsmith Clonus.

EVADNE (*e-vad'-nee*): The wife of Capaneus, one of the Seven Against Thebes. When her husband was killed, she threw herself on his funeral pyre and burned to death (6.447).

EVANDER (*e-van'-der*): The mythical king of Arcadia, son of Mercury by the nymph Carmentis. Immigrated with his people to found the city of Pallanteum on the banks of the Tiber. He hosts Aeneas and his Trojans; his son, Pallas, becomes Aeneas' ally (8.52).

EVANTHES (*e-van'-theez*): A soldier in Aeneas' army (10.702).

FABARIS (*fa'-ba-ris*): A river of the Sabine region, branch of the Tiber. Now called Farfa (7.715).

FABII (*fa'-bi-ee*): A prominent family that included several Roman leaders throughout its lineage. Its most well-known member was Quintus Fabius Maximus (died in 203 BCE), known as the Delayer because he wore down Hannibal by slowly killing his troops instead of directly engaging with them in battle, where he would have lost (6.845).

FABRICIUS (*fa-bri'-ki-us*): Caius Fabricius Luscinus, Roman consul (282 BCE) and general; conqueror of Pyrrhus the Macedonian. Regarded by many as the epitome of the ancient Roman virtues (6.843).

FADUS (*fa'-dus*): A Rutulian who besieged Aeneas' troops in his absence, killed by Euryalus (9.344).

FATES: Often personified as three goddesses, they are also known as the Parcae; visualized as spinning thread that shaped the destinies of mortals, their names were Clotho, the "spinner," who spun the thread, Lachesis, the "allotter," who measured the length of the thread, and Atropos, the "eternal," who cut the thread (1.22).

FAUNS (*fawnz*): Mythical beings, half human, half horse, from the fields of the Roman countryside (8.314).

FAUNUS (*faw'-nus*): A Roman deity or deified king, often identified with Pan. In the *Aeneid* he is represented as the son of Picus by the Latin nymph Marica, grandson of Saturn, father of Latinus and of Tarquitus (7.47).

FERONIA (*fe-roh'-ni-a*): The mother of Erulus; ancient Italian nature divinity, worshipped in groves. She was a goddess of fertility to whom flowers and fruits were offered, as well as the goddess of emancipation; newly freed slaves would don the cap of liberty at her holy site (7.800).

FESCENNIA (*fe-sken'-ni-a*): A town in southern Etruria; its troops fought for Turnus (7.695).

FIDENA (*fi-de'-na*): A town in Latium, north of Rome, founded by Alban kings (6.773).

FIELD OF MARS: Known in Latin as the Campus Martius. Originally founded as an open space of ground at Rome lying north of its center and outside of the walls. Bounded on the east by the Quirinal, Capitoline, and Pincian hills and on the west by the Tiber (6.872).

FLAVINIA (*fla-vin'-ya*): A southern Etruscan city (7.696).

FORTUNE: The personification of luck, who had famous places of worship in Rome, and even more so in Praeneste.

FORULI (*fo'-ru-lee*): A town in the Sabine region, south of Amiternum, whose troops were allies of Turnus. Now called Civita Tomassa (7.714).

FUCINUS (*foo-kee'-nus*): A Latin lake in the Apennines east of Rome, near which stood the grove of Angitia and city of Marruvium, the capital of the Marsi. Also inhabited by Umbro (7.759).

FURIES: The Erinyes, Eumenides, or avenging goddesses. Their names are Megaera, Allecto, and Tisiphone. They are particularly concerned with crimes between family members (3.252).

GABIï (*ga'-bi-ee*): An ancient Latin town, due east of Rome, a site of Jupiter's worship (6.773).

GAETULIAN (*gay-tool'-yan*): Of a warlike tribe from north Africa that resided in Morocco (4.40).

GALAESUS (*ga-lay'-sus*): An old Latin, killed at the outbreak of the war between the Italians and the Trojans while trying to broker peace (7.535).

GALATEA (*ga-la-te'-a*): A sea-nymph daughter of Nereus (9.103).

GANGES (*gan'-jeez*): A river of India, which flows from the Himalayas into the Bay of Bengal (9.30).

GANYMEDE (*ga'-ni-meed*): One of the three sons of Tros, the first king of Troy. He was carried away by Jupiter's eagle for his beauty to Olympus to become the cupbearer of the gods, replacing Hebe, Juno's daughter (1.28).

GARAMANTS (*ga'-ra-mantz*): A tribe from inner Africa, located in the eastern Sahara and southeast of the Gaetulians. Conquered by Rome in 19 BCE (6.794).

GARGANUS (*gar-ga'-nus*): A rugged Apulian peninsula (11.247).

GATES OF SLEEP: The Gate of Ivory and the Gate of Horn. Aeneas exits the Underworld through the Gate of Ivory, which is said to send false shades to the world above (6.893).

GATES OF WAR: Meant to recall the temple of the god Janus at Rome. He was the god of doors and gates, and protector of the state during wartime. The temple was closed twice throughout the history of the Republic but thrice during the reign of Augustus, all in times of peace (1.294).

GAULS (*gawlz*): Celtic tribes in France and northern Italy; also used to refer to people from northern Europe. Around 390 BCE they laid siege to and captured Rome. Though they were soon expelled, the following centuries saw them a constant menace to Rome (6.858).

GELA (*ge'·la*): A coastal city of southern Sicily, situated on a river going by the same name (3.702).

GELONIAN (*ge·loh'·ni·an*): Of a Scythian tribe hailing from Russia, who were well known for their skill at archery.

GERYON (*ge'·ri·on*): A giant with three bodies, killed three times by Hercules, who drove his oxen from Spain to the Tiber as the tenth of his labors (6.290).

GETAE (*ge'·tay*): A Thracian tribe that lived along the Danube (7.604).

GLAUCUS (*glaw'·kus*): (1) A sea god, Deiphone's father, who accompanies Neptune (5.823); (2) A Trojan warrior, one of the three sons of Antenor. Aeneas sees his shade among the war heroes in the Underworld (6.483); (3) A Trojan, son of Imbrasus, killed by Turnus (12.343).

GNOSIAN (*gnoh'·zi·an*): Cretan.

GORGON (*gor'·gon*): A general term to refer to Medusa and her two sisters, Stheno and Euryale, who all had snakes for hair. Any mortal who looked directly at a Gorgon would turn to stone. Medusa had her head cut off by Perseus and it was given to Minerva, who fixed it to her shield, the aegis (2.616).

GORTYNIAN (*gor·tee'·ni·an*): Of Gortyna, a city in Crete, famous for its archers.

GRACCHI (*gra'·kee*): A prominent Roman family whose most famous members, Tiberius (died in 133 BCE) and Gaius Sempronius (died 121 BCE), died for their efforts to enact reform in the Roman constitution (6.842).

GRAVISCAE (*gra-vis´-kye*): An Etrurian port city, north of Rome. The name is related to *gravis,* "weighed down," because of the region's unhealthy climate (10.184).

GREAT MOTHER: Another term for Cybele (2.788).

GREATEST ALTAR: The Ara Maxima, an altar dedicated to the rites of Hercules Invictus. It was located in the Forum Boarium by the Tiber, and what remains of it lies beneath the modern Church of Santa Maria in Cosmedin (8.272).

GRYNEAN (*gree-ne´-an*): Of Grynia, a town in Aeolia in Asia Minor that had a temple and an oracle of Apollo.

GYAROS (*gee´-a-ros*): A small Aegean island, one of the anchors to which Apollo fastened his birthplace, the island of Delos, to stop it from drifting (3.76).

GYAS (*gee´-as*): (1) A Trojan ally of Aeneas, shipwrecked off the coast of Sicily, but later able to captain the *Chimaera* to third place in the ship-race at Anchises' funeral games (1.222); (2) A Latin, son of Melampus, ally of Turnus against Aeneas (10.318).

GYGES (*gye´-jeez*): A Trojan ally of Aeneas, who defended his camp in his absence, killed by Turnus (9.762).

GYLIPPUS (*gi-lip´-pus*): The Arcadian father whose nine sons ward off an attack by Tolumnius the Latin (12.272).

HAEMON (*hay´-mon*): (1) A Rutulian priest of Mars who participates in the attack on the Trojans' camp during the absence of Aeneas (9.686); (2) A Latin whose son, a priest of Diana and Apollo, was a soldier of Turnus and killed by Aeneas (10.537).

HALAESUS (*ha-lay´-sus*): An ally of Turnus, chief of the Aurunci. Once a companion of Agamemnon, his origin is Greek. Killed while defending Imaon (7.723).

HALIUS (*ha´-li-us*): Trojan ally of Aeneas, killed by Turnus while he defended the camp against Rutulian attack (9.766).

HALYS (*ha'-lis*): Trojan ally of Aeneas, killed by Turnus while he defended the camp against Rutulian attack (9.765).

HAMMON (*ham'-mon*): The god of the Libyans, who was Zeus to the Greeks and Jupiter to the Romans. Iärbas boasted of his descent from Hammon and introduced him as a deity to his countrymen (4.198).

HARPALYCE (*har-pa'-li-ke*): A legendary Thracian huntress and rider, a princess and warrior (1.316).

HARPALYCUS (*har-pa'-li-kus*): A Trojan ally of Aeneas, killed by Camilla (11.675).

HARPIES (*har'-peez*): Greek for "snatchers." Winged monsters with birds' bodies and women's faces (3.212).

HEBRUS (*he'-brus*): (1) A Thracian river that flows into the Macedonian Sea (1.318); (2) A Trojan, son of Dolichaön, ally of Aeneas, killed by Mezentius (10.696).

HECATE (*he'-ka-tee*): One of the three aspects of Diana, who makes up a triform deity. Diana on Earth, Hecate (also known as Trivia) in Hell, and Luna, the moon, in Heaven. Goddess of the Underworld and of witchcraft (4.511); *see* Diana.

HECTOR (*hek'-tor*): A Trojan, prince of Troy, commander of the Trojan army, son of Priam and Hecuba, husband of Andromache, father of Astyanax; killed by Achilles and dragged around the walls of Troy (1.98).

HECUBA (*he'-kyoo-ba*): Priam's queen and mother of Hector (2.501).

HELEN (*he'-len*): The daughter of Leda and Jupiter (who visited Leda disguised as a swan), wife of Menelaus, lover of Paris. The most beautiful woman in the world. When she married Menelaus, he made her suitors pledge that they would come to his aid if anyone kidnapped her. This pledge drives the Trojan War after Helen flees with Paris (1.649).

HELENOR (*he-le'-nor*): A Trojan, son of a Maeonian king and a slave, Licymnia; killed by the Rutulians when defending the Trojan camp in Aeneas' absence (9.544).

HELENUS (*he'-le-nus*): A Trojan, son of Priam. A prophet who was taken after the fall of Troy by Pyrrhus, son of Achilles, to his home in Epirus. After Pyrrhus' murder, he married Hector's widow, Andromache (3.294).

HELICON (*he'-li-kon*): A mountain in Boeotia, home of the Muses. Sacred to Apollo (7.641).

HELORUS (*he-loh'-rus*): A town and its river in southeastern Sicily with wide marshes and fertile land near its mouth (3.698).

HELYMUS (*he'-li-mus*): A Sicilian of Acestes' court, who places second in the running race at the funeral games of Anchises (5.73).

HERBESUS (*her-be'-sus*): A Rutulian who besieged Aeneas' troops in his absence; killed by Euryalus (9.344).

HERCULES (*her'-kyoo-leez*): The son of Jupiter and Almena, celebrated for his strength and completion of his Twelve Labors, twelve tasks imposed on him by Hera. Sometimes called by his patronymic, Alcides (10.321).

HERMINIUS (*her-mi'-ni-us*): A Trojan, killed by Catillus (11.641).

HERMIONE (*her-mye'-o-nee*): A Spartan, daughter of Menelaus and Helen and granddaughter of Leda; deserted her husband, Pyrrhus, to marry Orestes (3.328).

HERMUS (*her'-mus*): A river of Lydia in Asia Minor (7.721).

HERNICAN (*her'-ni-kan*): Of a warlike tribe of Latium whose home was a rocky territory in Latium, southeast of Rome. They sent troops to fight for Turnus (7.684).

HESIONE (*he-sye'-o-nee*): The daughter of Laomedon, wife of Telamon, sister of Priam, mother of Ajax and Teucer. When Laomedon initially withheld payment from Neptune and Jupiter for building the walls of Troy, the two gods sent a giant sea-monster to kill him. Hercules saved him, and Hesione and her husband went on to rule over Salamis (8.159).

HESPERIA (*he-sper'-i-a*): "Land of the Evening" or "Land of the West," another name for Italy (1.530).

HESPERIDES (*hes-per'-ee-deez*): Westerners or Italians in general, or the nymph daughters of Hesperus, the Evening Star, in particular, who are known to have dominion over a garden filled with golden apples (4.484).

HICETAON (*hi-ke-tay'-on*): A Trojan, father of Thyoetes, who is killed by Turnus (10.124).

HIMELLA (*hi-mel'-la*): A river that empties into the Tiber. The Sabine area surrounding it supplied troops to Turnus (7.714).

HIPPOCOÖN (*hip-po'-ko-on*): A Trojan ally of Aeneas. Places last in the archery contest at the funeral games of Anchises (5.492).

HIPPOLYTE (*hip-po'-li-te*): A renowned Thracian Amazon queen, wife of Theseus (11.660).

HIPPOLYTUS (*hip-po'-li-tus*): Son of Theseus and Hippolyte, father of Virbius, and faithful worshipper of Diana. When he rejected his step-mother's seduction, she accused him to his father. His father, Theseus, begged Neptune to kill his son and he did, by maddening the horses of Hippolytus so that they dragged him to his death. Vergil presents Asclepius, son of Apollo, as resurrecting him from the dead, so that he lives out the rest of his days under the name Virbius (like his son), protected by Diana (7.761).

HIPPOTAS (*hip'-po-tas*): A Trojan, father of Amastrus, who is killed by Camilla (11.674).

HISBO (*hiz'-boh*): A Rutulian in Turnus' army killed by Pallas (10.384).

HOMOLE (*ho'-mo-le*): A mountain in Thessaly inhabited by Centaurs (7.675).

HYADES (*hye'-a-deez*): A constellation which rises in the rainy season (1.744).

HYDASPES (*hi-das'-peez*): A Trojan killed by Sacrator (10.748).

HYDRA (*hye'-dra*): (1) A fifty-headed beast who guarded the entrance to the Underworld (6.576); (2) A seven-headed Lernean Hydra killed by Hercules as the second of his Twelve Labors; because the beast grew back its heads as quickly as they were cut off, Hercules had to cauterize the decapitations in order to defeat his foe (8.300).

HYLAEUS (*heel-lay'-us*): A Centaur killed by Hercules (8.294).

HYLLUS (*heel'-lus*): A Trojan killed by Turnus (12.535).

HYPANIS (*hee'-pa-nis*): A Trojan who fights beside Aeneas at the fall of Troy (2.341).

HYRCANIAN (*heer-kay'-ni-an*): Of Hyrcania, a region on the southern shores of the Caspian Sea (7.604).

HYRTACUS (*heer'-ta-kus*): (1) A Trojan, the father of Hippocoön, who places last in the archery contest at the funeral games of Anchises (5.492); (2) A Trojan, the father of Nisus (9.177).

IAERA (*i-ay'-ra*): A wood-nymph of Phrygian Mount Ida; mother by Alcanor of Pandarus and Bitias, to whom she gave birth in Jupiter's grove (9.673).

IÄPYX (*i-ah'-piks*): (1) An Apulian who resides in the fields surrounding Mount Garganus (11.247); (2) A Trojan, descendant of Iäsus; treats Aeneas' wound (12.391).

IÄRBAS (*i-ar'-bas*): An African warlord whose advances are rejected by Dido; son of Jupiter Hammon (4.36).

IÄSIUS (*i-a'-si-us*): A Trojan, son of Jupiter and Electra, brother of Dardanus, son-in-law of Teucer, Aeneas' forebear who had settled in Italy (3.168).

IÄSUS (*i'-asus*): Father of Palinurus, Aeneas' helmsman, and of Iäpyx (5.843).

ICARUS (*i'-ka-rus*): The son of Daedalus, imprisoned with him in the Cretan labyrinth. His father constructed wings for their escape and warned Icarus not to fly too close to the sun because its heat would melt the wax holding the feathers in place. Icarus disregarded the warning and soared too high; he fell into the Aegean Sea and drowned (6.31).

IDA (*eye'-da*): (1) A Phrygian mountain range south of Troy, frequented by Jupiter (2.697); (2) A huntress and nymph, possibly the mother of Nisus (9.178); (3) A mountain on Crete where Venus finds her herbaceous plants (12.412).

IDAEUS (*eye-day'-us*): (1) Priam's charioteer, who stays with his chariot even when Idaeus is in the Underworld (6.485); (2) A Trojan who defended Aeneas' camp in his absence (9.501).

IDALIA (*eye-da'-li-a*): A town, mountain, and forest on Cyprus; sacred to Venus, whose rites are performed there (5.760).

IDAS (*eye'das*): (1) A Trojan, killed by Turnus (9.576); (2) The father of three sons who were warriors and comrades of Aeneas, all killed by Clausus (10.352).

IDMON (*id'-mon*): A Rutulian and messenger of Turnus (12.75).

IDOMENEUS (*eye-doh'-men-yoos*): The son of Deucalion, king of Crete, one of the Cretan commanders against Troy. He was banished from Crete for killing his son by using him as an offering to the gods (3.121).

ILIA (*i'-li-a*): A priestess of Vesta and daughter of King Numitor; also known as Rhea Silvia. She was the mother of Romulus and Remus by the god Mars (1.273).

ILIAN (*i'-li-an*): Of Ilium/Troy.

ILIONE (*i-li'-o-ne*): A princess of Troy, the first of Priam's daughters born to Hecuba (1.654).

ILIONEUS (*i-li'-o-nyoos*): A Trojan comrade of Aeneas. Killed Lucetius, served as a representative of Aeneas when Aeneas himself could not be present, such as before Latinus and Dido (1.120).

ILIUM (*i'-li-um*) Troy (1.268).

ILLYRIA (*il-lee'-ri-a*): A region in northwestern Greece, on the coast of the Adriatic Sea. Navigating its shores was notoriously difficult for sailors.

ILUS (*i'-lus*): (1) The original name of Aeneas' son prior to the fall of Troy. Afterward, he has two names, Ascanius and Iülus (1.268); (2) The first son of Tros, father of Laomedon, grandfather of Priam, and founder of Troy, from whom it gets the name Ilium (6.649); (3) A Rutulian soldier of Turnus in Pallas' line of fire (10.400).

ILVA (*il'-va*): An island off the Etrurian coast; modern Elba (10.173).

IMAON (*i-may'-on*): A Rutulian soldier of Turnus, protected by Halaesus (10.424).

IMBRASUS (*im'-bra-sus*): (1) The father of Asius, a soldier of Aeneas (10.123); (2) A Lycian, father of Glaucus and Lades, both killed by Turnus (12.344).

INACHUS (*i'-na-kus*): The founding king of Argos, father of Io, and son of Oceanus. Vergil treats him as the god of the Argolid's chief river, and he is represented on the shield of Turnus as such (7.287).

INARIME (*ee-nar'-i-me*): A volcanic island in the Tyrrhenian, between the promontory of Misenum and Prochyta, or present-day Ischia. Jupiter buried Typhoeus here, if not under Etna (9.715).

INO (*eye'-noh*): Cadmus' daughter, previously a mortal, now a sea-nymph in Neptune's court (5.823).

IO (*eye'-oh*): The daughter of Inachus, the river god, and princess of Argos, a monster with a hundred eyes. Beloved by Jupiter and turned into a heifer by Juno, though Io eventually regained her human form (7.790).

IÖLLAS (*i-ol'-las*): A Trojan killed by Catillus (11.640).

IONIAN (*eye-ohn'-i-an*): Of Ionia, the maritime region of Asia Minor, below the Adriatic Sea and between southern Italy and Greece (3.211).

IÖPAS (*i-oh'-pas*): A bard of Carthage, at the court of Dido; he was taught by Atlas (1.740).

IPHITUS (*i'-fi-tus*): A Trojan who fought beside Aeneas at the fall of Troy (2.435).

IRIS (*eye'-ris*): A goddess who typically comes to earth in a rainbow as a messenger of the gods (4.694).

ISMARA (*iz'-ma-ra*): A mountain in Thrace, and city of the same name (10.351).

ISMARUS (*iz'-ma-rus*): A Lydian warrior who fights at the side of Iülus, one of the defenders of Aeneas' camp (10.139).

ITALUS (*i´-ta-lus*): One of the founders of Italy (7.179).

ITYS (*i´-tis*): A Trojan killed by Turnus (9.574).

IÜLUS (*i-u´-lus*): An alternative name for Ascanius (1.267).

IXION (*eek-see´-on*): The king of the Lapiths, father of Pirithoüs. He attempted to rape Juno and was punished by being stretched and bound to a wheel that revolved in the Underworld eternally (6.602).

JANICULUM (*ja-ni´-cu-lum*): A hill on the western side of the Tiber across from Rome, where Janus built a fortress, according to Evander (8.358).

JANUS (*ja´-nus*): A two-headed Italian god who presided over gateways, entrances, and beginnings, as of the day and the year. He was represented as facing both forward and backward, looking toward the past and future equally (7.181).

JOVE (*johv*): An alternative name for Jupiter (1.27).

JULIUS (*jool´-yus*): The family name passed down from Iülus; both Julius Caesar and Octavian, later Augustus, had this as their family name (1.288).

JUNO (*joo´-noh*): The queen of the gods, goddess of marriage, daughter of Saturn, sister and wife of Jupiter, patron deity of Carthage. She was hostile to Aeneas because of his Trojan origins. Known to the Greeks as Hera (1.4).

JUPITER (*joo´-pi-ter*): The king of the gods, alternatively called Jove, the son of Saturn, whom he dethroned, brother and husband of Juno, father of the Olympians as well as many mortals. Known to the Greeks as Zeus (1.79).

JUTURNA (*yoo-tur´-na*): Turnus' sister; she tries to protect him but has to yield to Jupiter's will (10.439).

KRAKEN (*kra´-ken*): The name of the ship that Mnestheus captains at Anchises' funeral games. It finishes in second place out of four (5.116).

LABICI (*la-bi´-kee*): The inhabitants of Labicum, a Latin town southeast of Rome, allied with Turnus (7.796).

LABYRINTH: A baffling and elaborate combination of pathways and passages. Designed by Daedalus for King Minos to house the Minotaur (5.588).

LADES (*la'-deez*): A Lycian, son of Imbrasus, brother of Glaucus; killed by Turnus (12.343).

LADON (*la'-don*): An Arcadian ally of Aeneas; killed by Halaesus (10.412).

LAERTES (*lye-er'-teez*): Father of Ulysses, son of Arcesius, husband of Anticleia (3.273).

LAGUS (*la'-gus*): A Rutulian soldier of Turnus; killed by Pallas (10.380).

LAMUS (*la'-mus*): A Rutulian with the troops besieging Aeneas' camp; killed by Nisus (9.334).

LAMYRUS (*la'-mi-rus*): A Rutulian with the troops besieging Aeneas' camp; killed by Nisus (9.334).

LAOCOÖN (*la-o'-ko-on*): A Trojan priest of Neptune; publicly spoke against accepting the Trojan Horse into the city, hurled a spear at the body of the horse, and was strangled by sea-serpents, convincing all around him that he was being punished by Minerva (2.40).

LAODAMIA (*la-o-da-mee'-a*): The wife of Protesilaus, the first Greek to land at Troy. He sacrificed himself for the expedition, and she committed suicide to join him in the world of the dead (6.447).

LAOMEDON (*la-o'-me-don*): The king of Troy, son of Ilus, father of Priam. He had a reputation for treachery because he refused to pay the agreed price after Neptune and Apollo built the walls of Troy for him (3.247).

LAPITHS (*la'-piths*): A tribe from Thessaly, condemned to hell; at the wedding of their ruler Pirithoüs, they fought a battle with the Centaurs but lost (6.601).

LARIDES (*la-ree'-deez*): A Rutulian ally of Turnus, twin brother of Thymber, son of Daucus; killed by Pallas (10.390).

LARINA (*la-ree'-na*): An Italian comrade of Camilla (11.655).

LARISA (*la-ree'-sa*): A Thessalian town; the native region of Achilles.

LATAGUS (*la'-ta-gus*): A soldier of Aeneas; killed by Mezentius (10.697).

LATINUS (*la-tye'-nus*): The king of Latium, son of Faunus, husband of Amata, father of Lavinia (6.891).

LATIUM (*la'-ti-um*): The land between the Tiber and Campania, named so because it was where Saturn had hidden when in exile from Jupiter (1.6).

LATONA (*la-toh'-na*): A goddess loved by Jupiter, mother of Diana and Apollo by Jupiter (1.502).

LAURENTIAN (*law-ren'-tian*): Of Laurentum (5.797).

LAURENTUM (*law-ren'-tum*): A coastal Latin city south of Rome (8.2).

LAUSUS (*law'-sus*): Mezentius' son and Turnus' comrade. He gives his own life to save that of his father, and is killed by Aeneas (7.648).

LAVINIA (*la-vin'-i-a*): The daughter and only surviving child of Latinus and Amata (7.71).

LAVINIUM (*la-vin'-i-um*): The capital city of Latium, which Aeneas was destined to found; named in honor of his queen, Lavinia (1.258).

LEDA (*lee'-da*): The wife of Tyndareus, king of Sparta, and the mother of Clytemnestra. She was also the mother of Helen and the twins Castor and Pollux, by Jupiter, who approached her in the form of a swan (1.652).

LELEGES (*le'-le-geez*): An ancient people of Asia Minor, conquered by Octavian, mentioned by Homer as Trojan allies (8.725).

LEMNOS (*lem'-nos*): An island in the northeastern Aegean where Vulcan fell when Jupiter flung him from Olympus. It is noted for its volcanic gases and became a site of worship for the cult of Vulcan (8.454).

LERNA (*ler'-na*): A marsh in Greece near the city of Argos, where the Hydra lived, and where Hercules killed it as the second of his Twelve Labors (6.287).

LETHE (*lee'-thee*): The river of forgetfulness and oblivion; one of the major rivers of the Underworld (5.855).

LEUCASPIS (*loo-kas'-pis*): A Trojan, lost at sea (6.333).

LEUCATA (*loo-ka′-ta*): A headland at the southern end of the island Leucas, in the Ionian Sea; holy to Apollo and the site of one of his temples (3.274).

LIBURNIA (*li-bur′-ni-a*): Land of the coastal people of Illyria, inhabiting the northeastern shores of the Adriatic (1.244).

LIBYA (*li′-bya*): A region of northern Africa bordering the Mediterranean, west of the Nile; its capital was the city of Carthage (1.22).

LICHAS (*li′-kas*): A Latin warrior born by Caesarian section from the womb of his dead mother; killed by Aeneas (10.315).

LICYMNIA (*li-kim′-ni-a*): A slave; the mother of Helenor (9.547).

LIGER (*li′-ger*): An Etruscan, brother of Lucagus, soldier of Turnus. Killed Emathion; killed by Aeneas (9.571).

LIGURIA (*li-goor′-i-a*): A region in Cisalpine Gaul, north of Etruria, around the Gulf of Genoa (11.701).

LILYBAEUM (*li-li-bay′-um*): A headland on the western tip of Sicily, notoriously a dangerous route for mariners (3.706).

LIPARE (*li′-pa-re*): One of the Aeolian islands off the coast of northern Sicily; associated with Aeolus, the king of the winds (8.416).

LIRIS (*lye′-ris*): A Trojan killed by Camilla (11.670).

LOCRIANS (*loh′-kri-ans*): People of Locris, a region of northern Greece, whose leader had been Ajax. When their party was shipwrecked, some settled in the toe of Italy to form a Greek colony called Naryx (11.265).

LUCAGUS (*loo′-ka-gus*): An Etruscan, soldier of Turnus, brother of Liger; killed by Aeneas (10.575).

LUCETIUS (*loo-ke′-ti-us*): A Latin warrior in the force that attacked Aeneas' camp; killed by Ilioneus (9.570).

LUPERCAL (*loo′-per-kal*): A cave on the Palatine Hill where Romulus and Remus were believed to have been found and nursed by a she-wolf; hallowed for its powers of fecundity (8.344).

LYCAEUS (*li-kay'-us*): A western Arcadian mountain sacred to Pan and Jupiter.

LYCAON (*li-kay'-un*): (1) A metalworker and artist in Crete (9.304); (2) The father of Erichaetes, a Trojan warrior (10.749).

LYCIA (*li'-sha*): A region in southern Asia Minor, between Caria and Pamphylia, famous for its fertile soil. Allied with Troy (1.114).

LYCTOS (*lik'-tos*): A Cretan city; its contingent was led by Idomeneus to Troy.

LYCURGUS (*li-kur'-gus*): The son of Dryas, king of Thrace; he attacked Dionysus and was punished by Jupiter with blindness (3.14).

LYCUS (*li'-kus*): A Trojan, soldier of Aeneas (1.221).

LYDIA (*li'-di-a*): A region in Asia Minor settled by the predecessors of the Etruscans (2.781).

LYNCEUS (*leen'-kyoos*): A Trojan defending Aeneas' camp against the Rutulian attack; killed by Turnus (9.768).

LYRNESUS (*leer-ne'-sus*): A town in the Troad, near Mount Ida (10.127).

MACHAON (*ma-kay'-on*): A Greek physician concealed inside the Trojan Horse; one of the commanders of the Thessalians at Troy (2.263).

MAENAD (*may'-nad*): Female follower of Bacchus who roams the hills in a state of euphoria, carrying the thyrsus (4.301).

MAEON (*may'-on*): A Rutulian, one of the seven brothers of Cydon, fights for Turnus; killed by Aeneas (10.336).

MAEONIA (*may-oh'-ni-a*): A synonym for both Lydia in Asia Minor and Etruria in Italy.

MAEOTIC (*may-o'-tik*): Of Lake Maeotis, which formed the northeastern boundary of the Roman Empire; a region settled by fierce Scythian warriors.

MAGUS (*ma'-gus*): A Rutulian in Turnus' army, killed by Aeneas (10.521).

MAIA (*may'-a*): The daughter of Atlas, mother of Mercury by Jupiter; one of the seven Pleiades (1.297).

MALEA (*ma'-le-a*): A stormy promontory at the southeastern tip of the Peloponnese, dangerous for sailors (5.193).

MANLIUS (*man'-li-us*): Marcus Manlius Torquatus Capitolinus, a Roman who saved the citadel from being destroyed by the Gauls (8.652).

MANTO (*man'-to*): The daughter of Tiresias, a prophetess, and the mother of Ocnus, who named his city of origin Mantua after his mother (10.199).

MANTUA (*man'-tu-a*): A city on the Mincius, north of the Po River; capital of the Etruscan alliance of twelve cities and (later) Vergil's birthplace (10.200).

MARCELLUS (*mar-kel'-lus*): (1) Marcus Claudius Marcellus, a Roman general who fought against the Gauls and in the Second Punic War (6.855); (2) The nephew and adopted son of Augustus; died young (6.883).

MARICA (*ma-ree'-ka*): A Latin water-nymph, wife of Faunus, mother of King Latinus (7.47).

MARS (*marz*): God of war, son of Jupiter and Juno, father of Romulus and Remus; known to the Greeks as Ares (1.273).

MARSIAN (*mar'-si-an*): Of the Marsians, a Sabellian tribe hostile to Aeneas that occupied land to the east of Rome (7.758).

MASSICAN (*mas'-sik-an*): Of Massica, a mountain slope between Campania and Latium, famous for its vines and wine; the source of soldiers under Turnus' command (7.726).

MASSICUS (*mas'-si-kus*): An Etruscan leader allied with Aeneas (10.166).

MASSYLIAN (*mas-si'-li-an*): Of Massylia, a region in eastern Numidia (4.132).

MAXIMUS (*mak'-si-mus*): Quintus Fabius Maximus, a Roman general who rescued the Roman army after they suffered a devastating loss to Hannibal in 216 BCE (6.845).

MEDON (*mee'-don*): A Trojan, son of Antenor; seen by Aeneas among the war heroes of the Underworld (6.483).

MEGAERA (*me-gae'-ra*): One of the Furies, the sister of Tisiphone and Allecto (12.846).

MEGARA (*me'-ga-ra*): A coastal city in eastern Sicily, named for the Greek city on the Saronic Gulf between Corinth and Athens (3.689).

MELAMPUS (*me-lam'-pus*): A companion of Hercules, father of the warriors Gyas and Cissaeus, both of whom were killed by Aeneas (10.321).

MELIBOEAN (*me-li-bee'-an*): Of Meliboea, a Thessalian city in the kingdom of Philoctetes (3.401).

MELITE (*me'-li-te*): A sea-nymph in Neptune's entourage, one of the Nereïds (5.825).

MEMNON (*mem'-non*): The king of the Ethiopians, son of Tithonus and Dawn. He fought for the Trojans at Troy in armor made by Vulcan and was killed by Achilles (1.489).

MENELAUS (*me-ne-la'-us*): The son of Atreus, brother of Agamemnon, king of Sparta, true husband of Helen (2.264).

MENESTHEUS (*me-nes'-thyoos*): A Trojan, grandson of Laomedon, son of Clytius, brother of Acmon (10.128).

MENOETES (*me-nee'-teez*): (1) A Trojan, the pilot of Gyas on the *Chimaera* in the boat race at the funeral games of Anchises (5.161); (2) A gifted Arcadian fisherman and soldier, killed by Turnus (12.517).

MERCURY (*mur'-kyu-ree*): The Greek god Hermes, son of Jupiter and Maia, messenger of the gods and guide of the dead to the Underworld (4.276).

MEROPS (*me'-rops*): A Trojan who defended Aeneas' camp, killed by Turnus (9.702).

MESSAPUS (*mes-sa'-pus*): The son of Neptune, leader of soldiers from southern Etruria, ruler in Italy, ally of Turnus (7.691).

METABUS (*me'-ta-bus*): The leader of the Volscians; the father of Camilla (11.539).

METISCUS (*me-tis'-kus*): A Rutulian, the charioteer of Turnus, impersonated by Juturna (12.469).

METTUS (*met'-tus*): Mettus Fufetius, Latin leader of Alba Longa; killed for treachery by Tullus Hostilius by being pulled apart by chariots (8.643).

MEZENTIUS (*me-zen'-ti-us*): An Etruscan king driven into exile by his people; father of Lausus and ally of Turnus (7.647).

MIMAS (*mi'-mas*): A Trojan ally of Aeneas; killed by Mezentius (10.703).

MINCIUS (*min'-ki-us*): Both the river and river god of Cisalpine Gaul in northern Italy, rising from Lake Benacus and flowing to the Po; a source of soldiers allied with Aeneas (10.205).

MINERVA (*mi-ner'-va*): Known to the Greeks as Athena, the goddess of wisdom, battle, and the arts of spinning and weaving; she was born fully armed from Jupiter's head and supports the Greeks (3.531).

MINIO (*mi'-ni-oh*): An Etrurian river, north of Rome; its people are supporters of Troy (10.183).

MINOS (*mee'-nos*): The son of Jupiter and Europa, king of Crete, father of Deucalion and Ariadne; asked Daedalus to build the labyrinth to confine the Minotaur; a judge in the Underworld (6.14).

MINOTAUR (*min'-o-tawr*): Half man and half bull, the offspring of King Minos' wife, Pasiphae, and a bull; confined in the Labyrinth; killed by Theseus (6.26).

MISENUS (*mye-see'-nus*): A Trojan, son of Aeolus, the trumpeter of Aeneas; punished by the gods for challenging them (3.239).

MNESTHEUS (*mnes'-thyoos*): A Trojan, one of Aeneas' captains; piloted the *Kraken* and finished second in the boat race at the funeral games of Anchises, and also finished third in the archery contest (4.288).

MONOECUS (*mon-ee'-kus*): A headland of Liguria; location of the temple for Hercules (6.831).

MOORS: Inhabitants of the northern African region of Mauritania (4.206).

MORINI (*mo-rí'-nee*): A tribe of Gauls who lived near the North Sea; conquered by Octavian (8.727).

MUMMIUS (*moom'-mi-us*): Lucius Mummius, a Roman general who conquered and destroyed Corinth in 146 BCE (6.836).

MURRANUS (*moo-ra'-nus*): A Rutulian killed by Aeneas (12.529).

MUSAEUS (*moo-zay'-us*): A legendary Greek singer and poet of Thrace who studied under Orpheus (6.667).

MUSE: A daughter of Jupiter, one of the nine goddesses of the arts, literature, and memory (1.8).

MUTUSCA (*mu-toos'-ka*): A Sabine city whose soldiers fight for Turnus (7.711).

MYCENAE (*mye-see'-nay*): A Greek city in the Argolid ruled by Agamemnon (1.285).

MYCONOS (*mee'-ko-nos*): A small Aegean island in the Cyclades (3.76).

MYGDON (*mig'-don*): The father of Coroebus, engaged to Cassandra, comrade of Aeneas; killed by Peneleus (2.342).

MYRMIDON (*mur'-mi-don*): A fighter from Phthia, in Thessaly; led by Achilles at Troy (2.7).

NAR: A Sabine river that flows from the foothills of the Apennines into the Tiber; known to be swiftly flowing and foaming, and its waters contain sulfur (7.517).

NAUTES (*naw'-teez*): A Trojan elder, seer, and adviser to Aeneas, taught by Minerva (5.704).

NAXOS (*nak'-sos*): An Aegean island, the largest of the Cyclades, south of Delos; a location frequented by the Maenads and noted for the worship of Bacchus (3.125).

NEALCES (*ne-al'-keez*): A Trojan; killed Salius (10.753).

NEMEAN (*ne-mee'-an*): Of Nemea, a city in Greece and sector of the Argolid; home to a massive lion, which Hercules killed as the first of his Twelve Labors (8.295).

NEOPTOLEMUS (*ne-op-to'-le-mus*): Another name for Pyrrhus, son of Achilles; too young to be a soldier in the early stages of the war, he arrived in Troy after the death of his father and, with Philoctetes, led the effort against the Trojans. He was married to Hermione (2.263).

NEPTUNE (*nep'-tyoon*): The god of the sea, son of Kronos and Rhea, younger brother of Jupiter, ally of Aeneas. Known as Poseidon to the Greeks (1.124).

NEREÏDS (*ne'-re-idz*): Sea-nymphs who form the sea-lord's entourage, daughters of Doris and Nereus (3.74).

NEREUS (*ne'-ryoos*): A god of the sea, father of Thetis, Achilles' mother, and all of the other Nereïds (2.418).

NERITOS (*ne'-ri-tos*): An island in the Ionian Sea near Ithaca (3.272).

NERSAE (*ner'-say*): An Aequian city east of Rome, friendly to Turnus (7.744).

NESAEA (*ni-zye'-a*): A sea-nymph, daughter of Doris and Nereus (5.826).

NIGHT: The mother of the Furies, sister of Earth, holds power over both men and gods such that even Jupiter is afraid of her (3.512).

NILE: An Egyptian river with a delta of seven mouths that empty into the Mediterranean Sea (6.800).

NIPHAEUS (*ni-fay'-us*): A Rutulian soldier, knocked from his horses by Aeneas (10.571).

NISUS (*nee'-sus*): A Trojan companion of Aeneas and older friend of Euryalus; killed by the Volscians (5.294).

NOËMON (*no-ee'-mon*): A Trojan defending Aeneas' camp against the Rutulians; killed by Turnus (9.766).

NOMENTUM (*noh-men'-tum*): An Italian town of the Sabines, northeast of Rome (6.773).

NUMA (*noo'-ma*): (1) Numa Pompilius, the second king of Rome (6.810); (2) A Rutulian killed during the foray of Nisus and Euryalus (9.454); (3) A Rutulian soldier under Turnus, trounced by Aeneas (10.562).

NUMANUS (*noo-ma'-nus*): A Rutulian, also called Remulus; husband of Turnus' younger sister; killed by Ascanius (9.593).

NUMICUS (*noo-mee'-kus*): A small, holy stream in Latium between Ardea and Lavinium; Aeneas was said to have died there (7.150).

NUMIDIANS (*noo-mi'-di-anz*): Wandering north African tribes whose people rode bareback (4.41).

NUMITOR (*noo'-mi-tor*): (1) The king of Alba Longa, father of Ilia, grandfather of Romulus and Remus (6.768); (2) A Rutulian fighting for Turnus who failed in his attempt to kill Aeneas (10.342).

NURSIA (*noor'-si-a*): A Sabine town in the Apennines, near Umbria (7.716).

NYMPHS: Female beings who are divine, but inferior to the Olympians. They made their homes in many environments of the natural world, such as woodlands, hills, fountains, and streams (1.71).

NYSA (*nee'-sa*): Indian city and mountain where, according to legend, Bacchus was born and raised; the central location of his cult and a favorite spot of the god himself (6.805).

OCNUS (*ok'-nus*): The son of Manto the seer and the Tuscan Tiber river, founder of Mantua, chieftain of troops who fought for Aeneas (10.198).

OEBALUS (*ee'-ba-lus*): The son of Telon, king of Capreae, and Sebethis, a water-nymph; he made extensive conquests of Capreae that extended his father's domain. Chieftain of troops who fought for Turnus (7.733).

OECHALIA (*ee-ka'-li-a*): A town of Greece on the island of Euboea which Hercules demolished when its king, Eurytus, rejected his request for the hand of his daughter, Iole, in marriage (8.291).

OENOTRI (*ee-noh'-tri*): The people of Oenotria, a territory in southern Italy (1.532).

OÏLEUS (*oh-ee'-lyoos*): The father of Lesser Ajax, the Locrian king (1.41).

OLEAROS (*oh-le'-a-ros*): An island in the Aegean, named for its olives; one of the Cyclades (3.126).

OLYMPUS (*o-lim'-pus*): The mountain in Thessaly whose summit the chief gods and goddesses call their home, hidden from mortal sight by clouds; also used as a general term for the sky and heavens (1.779).

ONITES (*o-nye'-teez*): A Rutulian, killed by Aeneas (12.515).

OPHELTES (*o-fel'-teez*): A Trojan, father of Euryalus (9.202).

OPIS (*oh'-pis*): A nymph; attendant and messenger of Diana (11.533).

ORCUS (*or'-kus*): A god of the underworld, punisher of broken oaths (6.273).

ORESTES (*o-res'-teez*): A grandson of Atreus, son of Agamemnon and Clytemnestra, brother of Iphigenia and Electra. He exacted vengeance for his father's murder at Apollo's command by slaying his mother and her lover, Aegisthus. For this he was haunted by his mother's Furies until he was saved by Athena (3.330).

ORICIA (*o-ri'-shya*): A coastal city of Epirus.

ORION (*o-rye'-on*): A legendary hunter, killed by Diana; after his death, he was put in the skies as a constellation, called the Hunter, whose rising and setting indicated stormy weather (1.534).

ORITHYIA (*oh-ree-thee'-a*): The daughter of Erectheus, the ancient king of Athens; wife of Boreas, the north wind. As gifts, she gives horses (12.83).

ORNYTUS (*ohr'-ni-tus*): An Etruscan, killed by Camilla (11.677).

ORODES (*o-roh'-deez*): A Trojan soldier of Aeneas; killed by Mezentius (10.732).

ORONTES (*o-rohn'-teez*): A Trojan comrade of Aeneas, leader of the Lycians. Dies in a storm at sea (1.114).

ORPHEUS (*orf'-yoos*): A mythical Thracian poet who could sing order and peace into the world and attempted to retrieve his wife, Eurydice, from the Underworld (6.119).

ORSES (*ohr'-seez*): A Trojan, killed by Rapo (10.749).

ORSILOCHUS (*or-si'-lo-kus*): A Trojan, killed by Camilla (11.636).

ORTINE (*or'-tyne*): Of Ortina, an Etrurian town near where the Tiber and the Nar rivers meet; the source of soldiers who fight on behalf of Turnus (7.716).

ORTYGIA (*or-ti'-ji-a*): (1) Another name for Delos; (2) An island in the harbor of Syracuse, Sicily (3.692).

ORTYGIUS (*or-ti'-ji-us*): A Rutulian in the force attacking Aeneas' camp; killed by Caeneus (9.574).

OSCANS (*os'-kanz*): A Campanian tribe friendly to Turnus (7.730).

OSINIUS (*o-sye'-ni-us*): The king of Clusium in Etruria; his troops fight for Aeneas (10.653).

OSIRIS (*o-sye'-rus*): A Rutulian, killed by Thymbraeus (12.458).

OTHRYS (*o'-thris*): (1) The father of Panthus (2.317); (2) A snowcapped Thessalian mountain, home of the Centaurs (7.676).

PACHYNUS (*pa-kee'-nus*): A headland at the southeasternmost tip of Sicily (3.429).

PACTOLUS (*pak-toh'-lus*): A Lydian river that looks golden and was said to carry gold dust after King Midas used its waters to wash off his golden touch (10.142).

PADUA (*pa'-dyoo-a*): Ancient Patavium, a city in the north of Italy near Venice, in Cisalpine Gaul, founded by Antenor (1.247).

PADUSA (*pa-doo'-sa*): One of the seven mouths of the Po River (11.458).

PAGASUS (*pa'-ga-sus*): An Etruscan comrade of Aeneas, killed by Camilla (11.670).

PALAEMON (*pa-lay'-mon*): The son of Ino and Athamas, a sea-deity, part of Neptune's entourage (5.823).

PALAMEDES (*pa-la-mee'-deez*): A legendary Greek hero; after he discovered how Ulysses hoped to evade service in the Trojan War, Ulysses falsely accused him of treason, and Palamedes was put to death (2.81).

PALATINE (*pa'-la-tine*): One of the seven hills of Rome, where Augustus resides in the city (9.9).

PALICUS (*pa-li'-kus*): One of the twin sons of Jupiter and Thalia (9.585).

PALINURUS (*pa-li-noo'-rus*): The Trojan pilot of Aeneas' fleet, swept overboard (3.201).

PALLADIUM (*pal-la'-di-um*): A miniature statue of Minerva, believed to have descended from heaven, with which the fate of Troy, and then Rome, was linked; Ulysses and Diomedes stole it from the temple of Pallas (2.184).

PALLANTEUM (*pal-lan'-te-um*): First an Arcadian city and Evander's home; later, the name of the Etruscan city Evander founded on the Palatine Hill where Rome was later built (8.53).

PALLAS (*pal'-las*): (1) A Greek name for Minerva, the Greek goddess Athena (1.39); (2) A legendary Arcadian king, the grandfather of Evander (8.51); (3) The son of Evander, who fights by Aeneas; killed by Turnus (8.105).

PALMUS (*pal'-mus*): A soldier of Aeneas; killed by Mezentius (10.697).

PAN: The guardian god of woods and shepherds, he is half man and half goat, goat-footed and satyr-faced (8.344).

PANDARUS (*pan'-da-rus*): (1) A Trojan, son of Lycaon, brother of Eurytion; a famous archer, he broke the truce between the Trojans and the Greeks when he shot an arrow at Menelaus (5.495); (2) A Trojan, son of Alcanor and Iaera, brother of Bitias; killed by Turnus (9.672).

PANOPEA (*pa-no-pe'-a*): A Nereïd, in Portunus' retinue (5.240).

PANOPES (*pa'-no-peez*): A Sicilian who contended in the running race at the funeral games of Anchises (5.301).

PANTAGIAS (*pan-ta'-gi-as*): A river in eastern Sicily (3.688).

PANTHUS (*pan'-thus*): The son of Othrys, a Trojan priest of Apollo (2.318).

PAPHOS (*pa'-fos*): A city on the island of Cyprus, sacred to the goddess Venus and a famous center of her worship (1.415).

PARIS (*pa'-ris*): A Trojan, son of King Priam of Troy and his queen, Hecuba; his abduction of Helen from Menelaus in Lacedaemon started the Trojan War (1.26).

PAROS (*pa'-ros*): An Aegean island famous for its white marble; one of the Cyclades (3.126).

PARTHENIUS (*par-then'-i-us*): A Trojan, killed by Rapo (10.748).

PARTHENOPAEUS (*par-then-o-pay'-us*): The son of Meleager and Atalanta, king of Argos, one of the Seven Against Thebes; Aeneas meets his ghost in the Underworld (6.479).

PARTHIANS (*par'-thi-anz*): A people living in a part of modern Iraq southwest of the Caspian Sea, famous for their archery (7.606).

PASIPHAE (*pa-si'-fee*): The queen of Crete and wife of King Minos, mother of the Minotaur by a bull (6.24).

PATRON (*pa'-tron*): An Arcadian companion of Aeneas, contender in the footrace at the funeral games of Anchises (5.298).

PELASGIANS (*pe-laz'-gi-anz*): Extremely early inhabitants of Greece whom Vergil considers to have inhabited the region north of Rome prior to the Etruscans (8.600).

PELIAS (*pe'-li-as*): A Trojan who fights beside Aeneas shortly before Troy falls (2.435).

PELOPS (*pee'-lops*): An early king of Argos, son of Tantalus, father of Atreus, grandfather of Agamemnon and Menelaus (2.193).

PELORUS (*pe-loh'-rus*): A headland on the northeastern tip of Sicily marking the western side of the Strait of Messina, separating the island from mainland Italy (3.411).

PENELEUS (*pe-ne'-le-us*): A Greek warrior who kills Coroebus during the fall of Troy (2.425).

PENTHESILEA (*pen-the-si-le'-a*): The queen of the Amazon women warriors, and a Trojan ally; killed by Achilles at Troy (1.490).

PENTHEUS (*pen'-thyoos*): The king of Thebes who opposed the rites of Bacchus and, as a punishment, was driven mad by the god and then dismembered by his mother, Agave, while she was in a state of Bacchic frenzy (4.469).

PERGAMUM (*per'-ga-mum*): (1) The Trojan citadel, as well as a general name for the city (1.466); (2) The name given by Aeneas to the city he founds in Crete (3.133).

PERIDIA (*pe-ri-dee'-a*): The mother of Onites (12.515).

PERIPHAS (*pe'-ri-fas*): A Greek comrade of Pyrrhus at the fall of Troy (2.476).

PERSEUS (*per'-syoos*): A Macedonian king who claimed to be descended from Achilles (6.839).

PETELIA (*pe-te'-li-a*): A small town of Lucania in southern Italy, founded by Philoctetes after fleeing his Thessalian home (3.402).

PHAEACIA (*fay-ay'-sha*): An island and kingdom off the western coast of Greece, ruled by Alcinous and Arete; the people were famous for the hospitality they offered travelers, including Ulysses (3.291).

PHAEDRA (*fee'-dra*): The daughter of Minos, second wife of Theseus; she fell in love with his son, Hippolytus, and committed suicide after he was killed as a result of her false accusation of rape, which she made when he rejected her. Aeneas sees her among the lovesick in the Underworld (6.445).

PHAËTHON (*fa'-e-thon*): The son of Clymene and Helios, the god of the sun. Killed by Jupiter's thunderbolt when he tried to guide his father's chariot across the sky but lost control of the horses (5.104).

PHARUS (*fa'-rus*): A Rutulian, killed by Aeneas (10.322).

PHEGEUS (*fe'-gyoos*): (1) A Trojan, servant of Aeneas (5.263); (2) A Trojan defending Aeneas' camp, killed by Turnus (9.765); (3) A Trojan, beheaded by Turnus (12.371).

PHENEUS (*fe'-ne-us*): A city in Arcadia, shown to Anchises by Evander (8.166).

PHERES (*fe'-reez*): A Trojan soldier of Aeneas, killed by Halaesus (10.413).

PHILOCTETES (*fi-lok-tee'-teez*): The son of Poias, a Greek chief who fought against Troy; after the Trojan War, he founded Petelia (3.401).

PHINEUS (*fee'-nyoos*): The son of Agenor, king of Thrace; blinded by the gods for unjustly blinding his sons. Jupiter also sent the Harpies to torment him by stealing or contaminating his food (3.213).

PHLEGETHON (*fle'-guh-thon*): One of the main rivers of the Underworld, whose name translates to "flaming fire" (6.265).

PHLEGYAS (*fle'-gi-as*): The father of Ixion, ruler of Lapithae, tormented in the Underworld, in Tartarus, for setting fire to Apollo's temple at Delphi (6.618).

PHOEBUS (*fee'-bus*): A title for Apollo; a Greek word meaning "luminous" or "radiant" and suggesting purity (2.318).

PHOENICIAN (*fee-ni'-shan*): Of Phoenicia, a coastal strip of land between Syria and the Mediterranean Sea, containing the towns of Tyre and Sidon; the original home of Dido (1.670).

PHOENIX (*fee'-niks*): A Greek, son of Amyntor, tutor of Achilles (2.763).

PHOLOË (*foh'-lo-e*): A Cretan slave girl, the prize given by Aeneas to Sergestus after the boat race at the funeral games of Anchises (5.285).

PHOLUS (*foh'-lus*): (1) A Centaur, killed by Hercules (8.294); (2) A Trojan, killed by Turnus (12.341).

PHORBAS (*for'-bas*): A Trojan, shipmate of Palinurus, whom the god of sleep tries to lure to his doom by taking Phorbas' shape (5.841).

PHORCUS (*for'-kus*): (1) An older sea-deity, leader of the Nereïds, son of Pontus and Gaia (5.239); (2) A Latin, father of Cydon and his brothers, seven warriors who fight against Aeneas (10.328).

PHRYGIAN (*frí-jan*): Of the inhabitants and place of Phrygia, a region east of the Troad, in Asia Minor, referred to derogatorily because it was held to be effeminate (1.381).

PICUS (*pee'-kus*): The Italian god of agriculture, son of Saturn, father of Faunus; he was transformed into a woodpecker by Circe after he rejected her advances (7.48).

PILUMNUS (*pee-loom'-nus*): Son of Daunus, ancestor of Turnus, a god of the household (9.5).

PINARII (*pee-na'-ri-ee*): A clan that performed the rites for Hercules, along with the Potitii clan (8.270).

PIRITHOÜS (*pee-rí'-tho-us*): Son of Zeus, friend of Theseus, with whom he attempted to abduct Proserpina from the Underworld; when he was caught, Pirithoüs was chained forever as a punishment (6.393).

PISA (*pee'-za*): An Etrurian city believed to have been founded by colonists from Pisa in Elis, Greece (10.179).

PLEMYRIUM (*ple-mí'-ri-um*): A Sicilian headland south of Syracuse (3.693).

PLUTO (*ploo'-toh*): The king of the Underworld, also called Orcus, Hades, and Dis (7.327).

PO (*poh*): The modern name of the ancient river Padus (9.680).

PODALIRIUS (*po-da-lee'-ri-us*): A Trojan, killed by Alsus (12.304).

POLITES (*po-lee'-teez*): A Trojan, the young son of Priam; killed by Pyrrhus (2.526).

POLLUX (*pol'-luks*): Son of Leda and Jupiter, brother of Helen and twin of Castor; together the twins are called the Dioscuri. The brothers alternate their days between the world above and the Underworld (6.121).

POLYBOETES (*po-li-bee'-teez*): A Trojan priest; Aeneas meets his shade among the war heroes in the Underworld (6.484).

POLYDORUS (*po-li-doh'-rus*): A Trojan, son of Priam; treacherously murdered by the king of Thrace, Polymestor (3.45).

POLYPHEMUS (*po-li-fee'-mus*): Son of Neptune, a Cyclops who trapped Ulysses and his crewmen and devoured their shipmates until they blinded him and made their escape (3.641).

POMETIÏ (*po-me'-ti-i*): A Latin town inhabited by the Volscians, near the Pomptine Marshes (6.775).

POMPEY (*pom'-pee*): The Great, a Roman general; ally of Julius Caesar and wed to Caesar's daughter, Julia. After her death, he became an opponent of Caesar and was defeated by Caesar, then murdered (alluded to in 6.829).

POPULONIA (*po-pu-loh'-ni-a*): A city on the coast of Etruria and source of both Etruscan arms and allies to Turnus (10.172).

PORSENNA (*por-sen'-na*): A king of Etruria; declared war on Rome to re-establish the rule of Tarquin (8.645).

PORTUNUS (*por-too'-nus*): The god of harbors; assists the *Scylla* so that it takes first place in the boat races at the funeral games of Anchises (5.241).

POTITIUS (*po-tee'-ti-us*): An ancestor of the Potitian clan that conducted the rites of Hercules in Evander's realm and later in Rome (8.269).

PRAENESTE (*pray-nes'-te*): An ancient city in Latium, near the Apennines east of Rome; modern-day Palestrina (7.678).

PRIAM (*pree'-am*): (1) The king of Troy, son of Laomedon, father of Hector, Paris, and others (1.458); (2) The son of Polites and grandson of Priam (5.563).

PRIVERNUM (*pree-ver'-num*): A Latin city inhabited by the Volscians, southeast of Rome; Camilla's birthplace (11.540).

PRIVERNUS (*pree-ver'-nus*): A Rutulian, killed by Capys (9.576).

PROCAS (*pro'-kas*): A king of Alba Longa, presented to Aeneas by Anchises in Elysium in the Underworld (6.767).

PROCHYTA (*pro'-ki-ta*): A small island off the Campanian coast, southwest of Cape Misenum.

PROCRIS (*proh'-kris*): The daughter of Erectheus, wife of Cephalus, who unintentionally killed her when he mistook her rustling in the bushes for an animal after she followed him into the forest to reassure herself of his fidelity (6.445).

PROMOLUS (*pro'-mo-lus*): A Trojan, killed by Turnus (9.575).

PROSERPINA (*pro-ser'-pi-na*): Also known as Persephone. Goddess of Spring, daughter of Ceres, wife of Pluto, who kidnapped her from Earth and took her to be his queen in the Underworld (4.698).

PROTEUS (*pro'-tyoos*): A sea-deity and prophet able to change himself into different shapes; a servant of Neptune (11.262).

PRYTANIS (*pri'-ta-nis*): A Trojan who defended Aeneas' camp against the Rutulian attack; killed by Turnus (9.767).

PUNIC (*pyoo'-nik*): Synonymous with Phoenician and Carthaginian (1.338).

PYGMALION (*pig-may'-li-on*): The brother of Dido; he killed her husband, Sychaeus, and drove her from Tyre into exile (1.346).

PYRAGMON (*pee-rag'-mon*): One of the Cyclopes in Vulcan's forge (8.424).

PYRGI (*peer'-gee*): An Etrurian coastal city; sent troops to Aeneas (10.184).

PYRGO (*peer'-goh*): A nurse in Priam's house (5.646).

PYRRHUS (*peer'-us*): The son of Achilles, also called Neoptolemus; killed Priam, married Hermione and, for this, was killed by Orestes (2.470).

QUERCENS (*kwer'-kens*): A Rutulian, member of the force who storms the Trojans' fort by the Tiber (9.682).

QUIRINUS (*kwi-ree'-nus*): An ancient Italian deity later identified with the deified Romulus; the words "Quirinal" or "Quirine" are used for that which relates to Quirinus or Romulus (1.292).

QUIRITES (*kwi-ree'-teez*): The inhabitants of Cures, a Sabine town north of Rome, and the birthplace of Numa (7.712).

RAPO (*ra'-po*): A Rutulian who kills the Trojans Parthenius and Orses in battle (10.749).

REMULUS (*rem'-yoo-lus*): (1) A warrior from Tibur, guest of Caedicus, who offers him extravagant gifts (9.358); (2) The family name of Numanus, a Rutulian killed by Ascanius (9.590); (3) A Rutulian killed by Orsilochus (11.640).

REMUS (*ree'-mus*): (1) The son of Mars and Ilia; brother of Romulus, who killed Remus for jumping over the wall of the city that would later become Rome (1.292); (2) A Rutulian in the force surrounding Aeneas' camp (9.327).

RHADAMANTHUS (*ra-da-man'-thus*): The son of Jupiter and Europa, brother of Minos, ruler and lawgiver famed for his justice in Crete. Later became a judge in the Underworld (6.566).

RHAEBUS (*ray'-bus*): Mezentius' horse, his name meaning "bandy-legs" in Greek (10.862).

RHAMNES (*rahm'-neez*): A Rutulian chief and augur, worker for Turnus, one of the forces besieging Aeneas' camp; killed by Nisus (9.322).

RHEA (*re'-a*): A priestess, the mother of Aventinus by Hercules; she gave birth to the boy in secret (7.659).

RHESUS (*ree'-sus*): The Thracian king; his horses were seized by Ulysses and Diomedes (1.470).

RHINE: The European river rising in the Swiss Alps and emptying into the North Sea. Identical with the modern river (8.727).

RHIPEUS (*ree'-pyoos*): A Trojan ally of Aeneas during the fall of Troy; fights at Aeneas' side (2.394).

RHOETEUM (*ree'-te-um*): A headland of the Troad slightly north of Troy (3.105).

RHOETEUS (*ree'-tyoos*): A Marsian, father of Anchemolus; soldier of Turnus; killed by Pallas (10.388).

RHOETUS (*ree'-tus*): A Rutulian, killed by Euryalus (9.345).

ROME: The capital city of Latium and the Roman Empire (1.7).

ROMULUS (*rom'-yu-lus*): The son of Mars and Ilia, twin brother of Remus, whom he kills; legendary founder of Rome. According to myth, Romulus and Remus were nursed and raised by a she-wolf (1.274).

ROSEAN (*roh'-se-an*): Of Rosea, a district in the Sabine territory, the fields near Lake Velinus known in Italy for their fertility; the region supports Turnus.

RUFRAE (*roo'-fray*): A city in northern Campania, supporting Turnus (7.739).

RUMOR: The personification of public talk and circulating gossip (4.173).

RUTULIAN (*ru-tul'-yan*): Of a powerful tribe ruled by Turnus; its capital city was Ardea (7.318).

SABAEAN (*sa-be'-an*): Of a people of the Arabian region, Saba or Sheba, famous for its perfumes; allied with Mark Antony and Cleopatra in the battle of Actium (8.706).

SABINES (*say'-byne*): A people of ancient central Italy, who lived in the Apennines (7.706).

SABINUS (*sa-bee'-nus*): The founder of the Sabine people of ancient central Italy, whose women were stolen by Romulus' men (7.179).

SACES (*sa'-keez*): A Rutulian ally of Turnus (12.650).

SACRANIAN (*sa-kray'-ni-an*): Of an early Latin people who fought under Turnus (7.796).

SACRATOR (*sa-kra'-tor*): An Etruscan ally of Turnus (10.747).

SAGARIS (*sa'-gar-is*): One of Aeneas' slaves. Possibly later killed by Turnus (5.263).

SALAMIS (*sa'-la-mis*): An island in the Saronic Gulf, its kingdom ruled by Telamon; also home to his son, Great Ajax (8.158).

SALIÏ (*sa'-li-ee*): Leaping priests of Mars who took part in the rites of Hercules (8.285).

SALIUS (*sa'-li-us*): (1) An Acarnanian friend of Aeneas who enters the footrace at the funeral games of Anchises (5.298); (2) A Rutulian, killed by Nealces (10.752).

SALLENTINE (*sal-len'-teen*): Of the Italian Sallentini, a people near coastal Calabria.

SALMONEUS (*sal-mohn'-yoos*): The son of Aeolus, king of Elis, punished in Tartarus forever by Jupiter because he imitated lightning with burning torches (6.585).

SAMÊ (*sam'-e*): An island off the west coast of Greece in the Ionian Sea (3.271).

SAMOS (*sam'-os*): An Aegean island off the central coast of Asia Minor; site of a temple to Juno (1.15).

SAMOTHRACE (*sam'-o-thrace*): An island off the southern Thracian coast; originally called Samos (7.208).

SARNUS (*sar'-nus*): A Campanian river, east of Pompeii; soldiers from there are allied with Turnus (7.738).

SARPEDON (*sahr-pee'-don*): The son of Jupiter and Laodamia, captained the Lycians, ally of Troy, killed by Patroclus in the Trojan War (1.99).

SARRASTIAN (*sar-ras'-ti-an*): Of the Sarastes, a Campanian people who lived near the river Sarnus. Their soldiers were friendly to Turnus (7.738).

SATICULA (*sa-tee'-kew-la*): A Campanian town northeast of Capua; their soldiers were friendly to Turnus (7.729).

SATURA (*sa'-too-ra*): A Latin swamp; its exact location was unknown, but it was believed to be a part of the Pontine marshes. Its people were friendly to Turnus (7.801).

SATURN (*sa'-turn*): Known to the Greeks as Kronos, god of agriculture and civilization, father of Jupiter, Juno, Pluto, and Neptune; reigned over Saturnian land in what was called its Age of Gold (1.569).

SATURNIA (*sa-tur'-ni-a*): (1) A legendary city built by Saturn, located on the Capitoline Hill (8.358); (2) Another title for Juno, Saturn's daughter (9.745).

SCAEAN (*skay'-an*) GATES: The strongest and most well-known gates of Troy; they faced the Greek camp and the sea (2.613).

SCIPIOS (*ski'-pi-ohs*): A Roman family of which two members became famous generals, Publius Cornelius Scipio Africanus Major and Publius Cornelius Scipio Africanus Minor, both of whom participated in the destruction of Carthage during the Punic Wars (6.842).

SCYLACEUM (*ski-la'-ke-um*): A city in western Italy whose coast was known to be treacherous for sailing (3.553).

SCYLLA (*skil'-la*): A sea-monster living opposite Charybdis in the Straits of Messina that attacked passing ships and ate sailors (1.200).

SCYLLA: The vessel that won the boat races at the funeral games of Anchises (5.122).

SCYRIANS (*skee'-ree-anz*): People from the Aegean island of Scyros off the Euboean coast; birthplace of Pyrrhus (2.478).

SEBETHIS (*se-be'-this*): A water-nymph, daughter of the river-god Sebethus, mother of Oebalus by Telon, friendly to Turnus (7.734).

SELINUS (*se-lee'-nus*): A coastal city of southwestern Sicily (3.705).

SERESTUS (*se-res'-tus*): A Trojan, shipwrecked but recovered, friend of Aeneas (1.611).

SERGESTUS (*ser-ges'-tus*): Trojan captain of the *Centaur* in the boat races at the funeral games of Anchises (4.121).

SERGIAN (*ser'-gyan*): A Roman family named after Sergestus (5.121).

SERRANUS (*ser-ra'-nus*): (1) A name for Marcus Atilius Regulus, consul in 267 BCE and hero of the First Punic War (6.844); (2) A Rutulian, killed by Nisus (9.335).

SEVERUS (*se-ver'-us*): A mountain in Sabine territory near the Apennines; its inhabitants fought for Turnus (7.713).

SIBYL (*si'-bil*): A prophetic priestess in Cumae who led Aeneas through the Underworld (3.443).

SICANIAN (*si-kay'-ni-an*): Of a group of ancient people who emigrated to Sicily from Italy; their soldiers fought for Turnus (7.795).

SICILY (*si'-si-lee*): A large island just south of the tip of Italy in the Mediterranean Sea (1.34).

SIDICINUM (*si-di-kee'-num*): A Campanian town whose citizens fought for Turnus (7.728).

SIDON (*sye'-don*): A major Phoenician city near the town of Tyre, which was an offshoot of Sidon; its inhabitants were called Sidonians (1.619).

SIGEUM (*si-ge'-um*): A headland north of Troy (2.312).

SILA (*see'-la*): A forested mountain range in Bruttium, modern-day Calabria, in southern Italy (12.716).

SILVANUS (*sil-va'-nus*): A Roman god of the woodlands (8.601).

SILVIA (*sil'-vi-a*): The daughter of Tyrrhus, whose calls for help, after Ascanius killed her pet deer, set off the battle between the nearby Latins and Trojans (7.487).

SILVIUS (*sil'-vi-us*): The youngest son of Aeneas and Lavinia; his birth was prophesied by Anchises from the Underworld (6.763).

SILVIUS AENEAS: An Alban king and Aeneas' namesake (6.769).

SIMOÏS (*sim'-oh-is*): One of the rivers of Troy, tributary of the Xanthus (1.100).

SINON (*sye'-non*): According to Aeneas, a Greek infiltrator and master of fraud who persuaded the Trojans to allow the Trojan Horse through the gates, resulting in the fall of Troy (2.80).

SIRENS: Beautiful creatures with women's faces and birds' bodies whose song lured sailors to their deaths on the rocks where the Sirens lived (5.864).

SLEEP: The god of sleep, son of the Underworld and Night, twin brother of Death (5.838).

SORACTE (*soh-rak'-te*): An Etrurian mountain west of the Tiber, which Apollo holds sacred to him (7.696).

SPARTAN (*spar'-tan*): Of Sparta, a city-state of Greece, first city of Laconia, home to its ruler, Menelaus, and his wife, Helen (1.315).

STEROPES (*ster-o'-pees*): One of the Cyclopes in Vulcan's forge (8.424).

STHENELUS (*sthe'-ne-lus*): (1) A Greek warrior concealed in the wooden horse; Diomedes' charioteer (2.260); (2) A Trojan, killed by Turnus (12.341).

STHENIUS (*sthe'-ni-us*): A Rutulian, attacked by Pallas (10.388).

STROPHADES (*stroh'-fa-deez*): Ionian islands, supposedly the home of the Harpies (3.209).

STRYMON (*stree'-mon*): A river in Thrace, loved by water-birds, home of the cranes (10.264).

STRYMONIUS (*stree-mon'-i-us*): A Trojan soldier of Aeneas; his hand is severed by Halaesus (10.414).

STYX (*stiks*): The main river of the Underworld, by which the gods swore binding oaths (3.215).

SUCRO (*soo'-kroh*): A Rutulian, killed by Aeneas (12.505).

SULMO (*sool'-moh*): (1) A Rutulian in Volscens' troop, killed by Nisus (9.412); (2) A Rutulian, the father of four sons who fought for Turnus and were captured by Aeneas to be killed at the funeral of Pallas (10.518).

SYBARIS (*si'-bar-is*): A Trojan, killed by Turnus (12.363).

SYCHAEUS (*si-kay'-us*): Dido's husband from Phoenicia, killed by her brother, Pygmalion (1.343).

SYMAETHUS (*si-may'-thus*): A river in eastern Sicily on the outskirts of Mount Etna (9.584).

SYRACUSE (*si'-ra-kyooz*): The main Sicilian city in classical history (3.693).

SYRTES (*seer'-teez*): The treacherous sandbanks of the Mediterranean, off the shores of northern Africa (6.60).

TABURNUS (*ta-boor'-nus*): Monte Taburno, a mountain range in Campania (12.716).

TAGUS (*ta'-gus*): A Rutulian, one of the men under Volcens' command; killed by Nisus (9.418).

TALOS (*ta'-los*): A Rutulian, killed by Aeneas (12.513).

TANAÏS (*ta'-na-is*): A Rutulian, killed by Aeneas (12.513).

TARCHON (*tar'-kon*): An Etruscan chief allied with Aeneas (8.505).

TARENTUM (*ta-ren'-tum*): A famous coastal city and bay in southern Italy on the Gulf of Tarentum, modern name Taranto (3.551).

TARPEIA (*tar-pay'-a*): A female warrior and ally of Camilla (11.656).

TARPEIAN (*tar-pay'-an*): A cliff on the Capitoline Hill from which criminals were thrown to their death; it is named after Tarpeia, the daughter of one of Romulus' generals, who betrayed Rome to the Sabines out of her love for the Sabine king (8.347).

TARQUIN (*tar'-kwin*): The name of both Tarquinius Priscus, the fifth king of Rome, and Tarquinius Superbus (Tarquin the Proud), the seventh and final king of Rome, son or grandson of Priscus (6.817).

TARQUITUS (*tar'-kwi-tus*): The son of Faunus and the wood-nymph Dryope; warrior of Turnus, killed by Aeneas (10.550).

TARTARUS (*tar'-ta-rus*): The darkest region of the Underworld, where Jupiter keeps enemies he has defeated, particularly the Titans (4.243).

TATIUS (*ta'-ti-us*): The king of the Sabines. After the abduction of the Sabine women, he led an expedition against the Romans in revenge, but after the intervention of the women themselves, reconciled with Rome and shared joint kingship of both peoples with Romulus (8.638).

TEGEAN (*te-gee'-an*): Of Tegea, an Arcadian town (5.299).

TELEBOEAN (*te-le-bee'-an*): Of an Acarnanian tribe descended from Teleboas, whom Homer describes as pirates among the Ionian islands; they later settle on Capri (7.735).

TELON (*te'-lon*): The king of the Teleboeans on Capri, father of Oebalus by the nymph Sebethis (7.734).

TENEDOS (*ten'-e-dos*): A small island in the northeastern Aegean Sea, where the Greek fleet gathered before its final assault on Troy (2.21).

TEREUS (*te'-ryoos*): A Trojan, killed by Camilla (11.675).

TETRICA (*te'-tri-ka*): An Apennine ridge in Sabine territory; supplied troops friendly to Turnus (7.713).

TEUCER (*too'-sur*): (1) An ancient king of Troy, father of Bateia, the wife of Dardanus, ancestor of Aeneas (1.236); (2) An Achaean, bastard son of Telamon, half brother of Great Ajax, founder of the city of Salamis in Cyprus (1.619).

TEUTHRAS (*too'-thras*): An Arcadian ally of Pallas and Aeneas (10.402).

TEUTONIC (*too-ton'-ik*): Of a savage northern tribe in Germany, the Teutons, some of whom invaded Italy in 102 and 101 BCE.

THAEMON (*thay'-mon*): A Lycian, brother of Sarpedon and Clarus, comrade of Aeneas (10.127).

THAMYRUS (*tham'-i-rus*): A Trojan, killed by Turnus (12.341).

THAPSUS (*thap'-sus*): A city on eastern Sicily's coast (3.689).

THEANO (*the-an'-oh*): A Trojan woman, mother of Mimas by Amycus (10.703).

THEBES (*theebz*): The seven-gated capital city of Boeotia, attacked by Polynices and the Seven (4.470).

THEMILLAS (*the-mil'-las*): A Trojan; his spear grazes Privernus (9.577).

THERMODON (*ther'-moh-don*): A river in Pontus flowing into the Black Sea. Frequented by the Amazons (11.660).

THERON (*the'-rohn*): A Latin, killed by Aeneas (10.312).

THERSILOCHUS (*ther-si'-lo-kus*): (1) The son of Antenor, a Trojan warrior whom Aeneas sees in the Underworld (6.483); (2) A Trojan, killed by Turnus (12.363).

THESEUS (*thees'-yoos*): The son of the king of Athens, Aegeus; he killed the Minotaur and abducted Ariadne to Naxos, where he then deserted her. Later he tried to help his comrade, Pirithoüs, abduct Persephone from the Underworld, but was caught; his punishment was to sit in one place for eternity (6.30).

THESSANDRUS (*thes-san'-drus*): A Greek soldier hidden in the Trojan Horse (2.260).

THETIS (*the'-tis*): A sea-goddess, daughter of Nereus, wife of Peleus, and mother of Achilles (5.824).

THOAS (*thoh'-as*): (1) A Greek soldier hidden in the Trojan Horse (2.262); (2) A Trojan soldier of Aeneas, killed by Halaesus (10.416).

THRACE: A region in northwestern Greece, north of the Aegean Sea, west of the Black Sea, favored spot of Mars (1.316).

THRONIUS (*thro'-ni-us*): A Trojan, killed by Salius (10.753).

THYBRIS (*thee'-bris*): A legendary Etruscan king, after whom the river Tiber is supposed to be named, for he died in battle on its banks (8.330).

THYMBER (*theem'-ber*): A Rutulian, son of Daunus, twin brother of Larides, killed by Pallas while fighting in the army with Turnus (10.390).

THYMBRA (*theem'-bra*): A city in the Troad on the Xanthus River, a site of worship to Apollo.

THYMBRAEUS (*theem-bray'-us*): A Trojan who killed the Latin Osiris (12.458).

THYMBRIS (*theem'-bris*): A veteran soldier of Aeneas. He is in the front line of defense at the Trojans' camp (10.125).

THYMOETES (*thi-mee'-teez*): (1) A Trojan who advocates the acceptance of the Trojan Horse (2.32); (2) A Trojan, son of Hicetaon, who defends Aeneas' camp and is killed by Turnus (10.123).

TIBER (*tye'-bur*): The main river in central Italy, which begins in the Apennines, runs south, and has its mouth at Ostia; Rome was established along its left bank (1.13).

TIBERINUS (*tee-bur-ee'-nus*): God of the Tiber River (8.31).

TIBUR (*tee'-bur*): Ancient Latin town, northeast of Rome on the Anio River, founded by emigrants from Greece (7.630).

TIBURTUS (*tee-boor'-tus*): One of the three Greek brothers (the other two being Catillus and Coras) who founded Tibur, the town named after Tiburtus; all three are comrades of Turnus (7.671).

TIGER: The ship captained by Massicus, an Etruscan allied with Aeneas (10.166).

TIMAVUS (*ti-ma'-vus*): A northern Italian river that flows with a swift current into the Adriatic Sea (1.244).

TISIPHONE (*ti-si'-foh-nee*): One of the three Furies; doles out punishments in Hades and guards the gates that confine the damned (6.555).

TITAN (*tye'-tan*): (1) The sun, Hyperion, one of the pre-Olympian gods (4.18); (2) One of the other pre-Olympian gods, the children of Uranus, locked in Tartarus by Jupiter for attempting to revolt against the Olympians (6.580).

TITHONUS (*ti-thoh'-nus*): Lover of Aurora, son of Laomedon, brother of Priam, father of Memnon. Aurora won him the gift of eternal life but neglected to grant him eternal youth as well (4.584).

TITYUS (*ti'-ti-us*): A giant killed by Apollo and Diana and then doomed to eternal torment in the Underworld for his attempt to violate their mother, Latona (6.595).

TMARIAN (*tma'-ri-an*): Of the mountainous region Tmaria in Epirus.

TMARUS (*tma'-rus*): A Rutulian participant in the attack on Aeneas' camp; killed by Aeneas' soldiers (9.686).

TOLUMNIUS (*to-loom'-ni-us*): A Rutulian augur, ally of Turnus (11.429).

TORQUATUS (*tohr-kwah'-tus*): Titus Manlius, an early Roman consul who put his own son to death for disobeying orders. Named for the torque (collar) he wore around his neck, a spoil from a Gaul he killed in battle (6.825).

TRITON (*try'-ton*): (1) A sea-god, son of Neptune, famous for blowing his conch horn (1.144); (2) (*italicized*) The name of a ship transporting Tuscan troops friendly to Aeneas, under Aulestes' command (10.210).

TRITONIAN (*trye-tohn'-yan*): An epithet of Minerva (Athena) because she was supposed to have been born near Lake Tritonis in north Africa (2.615).

TRIVIA (*trí'-vi-a*): An epithet of Hecate (Diana), because the crossroad (*trivium*) was sacred to Hecate.

TROAD (*tro'-ad*): The ancient name of the Biga peninsula in the northwestern part of Anatolia, Turkey. Its capital was Troy.

TROILUS (*troy'-lus*): A Trojan, son of Priam; killed by Achilles (1.474).

TROY: The capital city of the Troad, on the northwest coast of Asia Minor at the southern entrance to the Hellespont (the Dardanelles). Also called Ilium (1.2).

TULLA (*tool'-la*): A comrade of Camilla (11.656).

TULLUS (*tool'-lus*): Tullus Hostilius, the third king of Rome and the conqueror and destroyer of Alba Longa (6.812).

TURNUS (*tur'-nus*): The king of the Rutulians, son of Daunus and the water-nymph Venilia, rival of Aeneas for the hand of Lavinia; killed by Aeneas in battle (7.55).

TUSCAN (*tus'-kan*): Of the people who settled in the region of Etruria, north of Latium, modern-day Tuscany; synonymous with Etruscan (1.67).

TUSCAN SEA: An extension of the Mediterranean Sea, bordered by the Italian peninsula in the east. Also called the Tyrrhenian Sea (1.67).

TYDEUS (*tee'-dyoos*): A Greek, son of Oeneus, father of Diomedes, one of the Seven Against Thebes, killed in the futile assault on that city (6.479).

TYPHOEUS (*ti-fee'-us*): A rebellious monster with a hundred fire-breathing heads. Jupiter killed him with a lightning bolt and buried him either under Mount Etna or on the island Vergil calls Inarime (modern-day Ischia) (8.298).

TYRE (*tyer*): A maritime city of Phoenicia, known for its deep-blue dye (1.346).

TYRES (*ti´-reez*): An Arcadian ally of Aeneas; pursued Rhoetus with Teuthras, his brother, until Pallas killed him (10.403).

TYRRHENA (*teer-re´-na*): A Tuscan woman with an Arcadian husband, Gylippus (12.271).

TYRRHENUS (*teer-re´-nus*): An Etruscan, who killed Aconteus (11.612).

TYRRHUS (*teer´-rus*): A Latin who was the chief shepherd for King Latinus, with the help of his sons; father of Silvia (7.484).

UCALEGON (*oo-ka´-le-gon*): A Trojan whose house is burned by the Greeks at the fall of Troy (2.312).

UFENS (*oo´-fens*): (1) A Rutulian leader and chief of the Aequi, who led a party composed of hunters and farmers (7.744); (2) A Latin river; natives of that region supported Turnus (7.802).

ULYSSES (*yoo-lis´-eez*): The son of Laertes, grandson of Arcesius and Autolycus, husband of Penelope, father of Telemachus, king of Ithaca and its surrounding islands. Sometimes called "the Ithacan" for his home in Ithaca; renowned for his wisdom, he helped plot the Trojan Horse. Known as Odysseus to the Greeks, he is the central figure of Homer's *Odyssey* (2.6).

UMBRIAN (*oom´-bri-an*): Of the north-central Italian region of Umbria, inhabited by the Umbri, famous for the abilities of their hunting dogs (12.752).

UMBRO (*oom´-bro*): A Marsian warrior, ally of Turnus, priest, magician, snake charmer, and healer; killed by a Trojan lance (7.750).

VALERUS (*val´-er-us*): An Etruscan, who conquers Agis (10.752).

VELIA (*ve´-li-a*): A city on the western Lucanian coast, south of Salerno (6.366).

VELINUS (*ve-lee´-nus*): A lake and river in the Sabines' region, with sulfurous waters. It supplies soldiers to Turnus (7.517).

VENILIA (*ve-nee'-li-a*): A sea-nymph, mother of Turnus by Daunus (10.76).

VENULUS (*ven'-u-lus*): A Latin; Turnus sends him as a messenger to Diomedes to appeal for help (8.9).

VENUS (*vee'-nus*): Known to the Greeks as Aphrodite, goddess of love and beauty, daughter of Jupiter and Dione, wife of Vulcan, mother of Aeneas by Anchises, and of Amor. Devoted to the Trojans (1.227).

VESTA (*ves'-ta*): The goddess of the hearth, the home, and the family; her hearth fire was always burning (1.292).

VESULUS (*ves'-u-lus*): A mountain of the Italian Alps in Liguria, source of the Po River (10.709).

VIRBIUS (*veer'-bi-us*): (1) The son of Hippolytus and Aricia, ally of Turnus (7.761); (2) The name given to Hippolytus after he is resurrected (7.777).

VOLCENS (*vohl'-kens*): A Latin commander of a cavalry unit sent as reinforcement to Turnus; father of Camers (9.368).

VOLSCIAN (*vohl'-ski-an*): Of the Latin tribe the Volscians, who inhabited Latium, south of Rome, and supported Turnus (11.800).

VOLTURNUS (*vohl-toorn'-us*): A Campanian river emptying into the Tuscan Sea (7.729).

VOLUSUS (*voh-loo'-sus*): A Rutulian, commander of the Volscians, ally of Turnus (11.463).

VULCAN (*vul'-kan*): The god of fire and metalwork, son of Juno, husband of Venus. With the help of his Cyclops assistants, he forged the shield of Aeneas upon Venus' request. Known to the Greeks as Hephaestus (7.79).

VULCANIA (*vul-ka'-ni-a*): A volcanic island off the northeastern coast of Sicily where Vulcan's home is located, along with his forge, staffed by the Cyclopes (8.422).

XANTHUS (*ksan'-thus*): (1) A river of the Troad, tributary of the river Simoïs (1.473); (2) A brook in Epirus (3.350); (3) A Lycian river, near the town of the same name (4.144).

ZACYNTHUS (*za-kin'-thus*): An island off the western Greek coast, in the Ionian Sea and in Ulysses' kingdom (3.270).

ZEPHYR (*ze'-fir*): (1) In general, the collective name for the West Winds, both those disruptive and those advantageous to mariners (3.120); (2) The particular personification of the mild and warm Italian wind that brought about the melting of the snows and thus the beginning of spring (1.131).

SHADI BARTSCH is the Helen A. Regenstein Distinguished Service Professor at the University of Chicago. Her research focus is on Roman imperial literature, the history of rhetoric and philosophy, and the reception of the Western classical tradition in contemporary China. She is the author of five books on the ancient novel, Neronian literature, political theatricality, and Stoic philosophy, the most recent of which is *Persius: A Study in Food, Philosophy, and the Figural* (winner of the 2016 Goodwin Award of Merit). She has also edited or co-edited seven wide-ranging essay collections (two of them Cambridge Companions) and the Seneca in Translation series from the University of Chicago, for which she translated three Senecan plays. Bartsch is now writing a book on the contemporary Chinese reception of ancient Greek political philosophy. She has been a Guggenheim fellow, edits the journal *KNOW*, and has held visiting scholar positions in St. Andrews, Taipei, and Rome. Starting in academic year 2015, she has directed the Stevanovich Institute on the Formation of Knowledge, whose purpose is to explore the historical and social contexts in which knowledge is created, legitimized, and circulated.

ShadiBartsch.com
Twitter: @ShadiBartsch